"Starr Ayers' first novel is a masterful romance. She's created a haunting love story that is etched in my memory."

DiAnn Mills, *Best-selling Author of over 40 books, and two-time Christy Award Winner*

"Starr Ayers tipped the pot of "touching" over and filled my cup to overflowing. *For the Love of Emma* twists and turns at the heart leaving an impression you cannot forget. I've watched this author grow over the years and to say that this is her opus is probably an understatement. Unforgettable. Loveable. Sweet. Lasting. A must read."

Cindy K. Sproles, *best-selling author*

"*For the Love of Emma* is a captivating love story in which debut author Starr Ayers masterfully weaves elements of drama, humor, and faith. I look forward to spending more time with Emma, Tucker, and the rest of her wonderful characters in the sequel, *Emma's Quest!*"

Deborah Sprinkle, *Award-winning author of Deadly Guardian*

"What makes a love story irresistible? Is it the sweetness of new love, the conflicts, the drama of missing pieces needing to be solved? In *For the Love of Emma* by Starr Ayers, the discovery of a box of love letters unlocks these for two daughters. Caroline Myers and her sister Kate, experience the excitement of young love between their mother, a waitress at the Rainbow Restaurant, and a soldier at Fort Bragg prior to World War. This is a page-turner."

Leslie Stobbe, *Author, Writing Coach, Ghost Writer, and Long-standing Literary Agent*

"A packet of love letters discovered among the possessions of the author's deceased mother sparked this fascinating time slip story. Contemporary glimpses enhance the mystery of the unfolding historical romance. Realistic characters living in World War II's brink snagged my interest from the first chapter and held on. I enthusiastically recommend this gentle story to readers of historical romance, time slip, and nostalgia."

Sandra Merville Hart, *Author of Civil War romances, A Musket in My Hands, A Rebel in My House,* and *A Stranger on My Land.*

For the Love of Emma

For the Love of Emma

By
Starr Ayers

The Team: Miralee Ferrell, Alyssa Roat, Nikki Wright, Cindy Jackson
Cover Design: Indie Cover Design, Lynnette Bonner Designer
Front cover photo by Starr Ayers

Mountain Brook Ink is an inspirational publisher offering fiction you can believe in.
Printed in the United States of America

Dedication

To my loving husband, Michael

THANK YOU

for noticing me that day on the breezeway in high school

for hitchhiking from college with a huge red and
white stuffed Valentine's turtle under your arm

for being my soul mate, selfless provider,
and a wonderful daddy to our girls

for not getting upset with me the day
I wrecked your beloved Charger

for always making me feel safe in the throes of a storm

for never making me feel silly when I ask you
to accompany me on one of my crazy ventures

for doing the heavy lifting at more art shows than
we can count

for giving me space to be me

for always seeing the glass as running
over when I see it as empty

for believing in me on days I can't believe in myself

for always being willing to chase rainbows with me—
God has given us more than we deserve

I'm forever grateful to our heavenly Father
for allowing us to do life together for fifty-plus years

I pray for fifty more

In the words of Winnie the Pooh,
"If you live to be a hundred, I want to live to be a hundred
minus one day, so I never have to live without you."

May our heavenly Father richly reward you for loving me well

I love you!
Starr

DREAM OF ME

Acknowledgments

A book birthed in one's heart needs a community of selfless individuals to bring it to fruition.

Erica Wiggenhorn – The evening you called and invited me to a writer's retreat in the mountains outside of Phoenix was an invitation that changed the trajectory of my life. I was intrigued by the idea of exploring a side of my creativity I'd given little thought to, but the truth is—I accepted your offer to spend time with you, my precious friend. Little did I know that God would use my days there to align my plans with His purpose for me. Thank you for being the vessel God used to open my eyes to His gift within me. I'm blessed to share this path with you.

Kathe Wunnenberg and **Judith Couchman** – Thank you for pouring your lives into women for the glory of God and for hosting the retreat that changed my life. Falling two weeks after my mother's death, it not only served as a time of discovery but offered me a place of respite and healing. Thank you, Kathe, for the invitation to submit to your book, *Hopelifter: Creative Ways to Spread Hope When Life Hurts.* The inclusion allowed me to acquire my first traditional publishing credit.

Les Stobbe – How can I ever thank you for looking past my bumbling out-of-the-blue email and for seeing something in me I didn't know was there? If I'd known who I'd connected with that evening, I would have been too intimidated to pitch my not-so-good idea. You are a gentle giant, and I appreciate you signing me on as your client and introducing me to writers' conferences. Because of you, I have been able to grow into God's purpose for me.

Rachel Starr Thomson – Thank you for being my first editor and for hanging with me for three years. I learned so much from your insightful critiques. You knew which questions to ask and all the right comments to make so I could learn to navigate the world of writing.

Alycia Morales – Thank you for editing the first draft of my manuscript and for encouraging me when I needed it most.

Cyle Young – My fantastic agent. Thank you for falling in love with my story and for believing in my ability to tell it. Even though I was only three chapters in and knew very little about writing fiction, you signed me as your client and waited—and waited—and waited. Thank you for talking me down off the ledge more than once and for finding my heart's work a forever home.

Miralee Ferrell – I'm eternally indebted to you for taking a chance on this debut novelist. I knew from our first conference call that God had handpicked you as my publisher. Thank you for your insightful coaching and for the wisdom you willingly share. I'm blessed to have you in my corner, even if we are a continent apart.

Eva Marie Everson – I've learned so much from you. My assignment to your brainstorming group at my first novelist retreat was a God Stop in my journey. The ideas that came from those few short hours took root in my heart and today enrich my story. Thank you for believing in me.

Cindy Sproles and **Eddie Jones** – Thank you for giving me so many opportunities to grow as a writer. With your help, I learned to scratch out my first five hundred words and my first published devotion. Writing a novel wasn't even in my mind's eye then. But God…

DiAnn Mills and **Edie Melson** – What a team! Thank you for offering aspiring writers a multitude of avenues for growth. Your selfless natures and words of encouragement throughout the years enabled me to believe one day I, too, could write words that would inspire and encourage others.

Yvonne Lehman and **Lori Marett** – Your words of encouragement have meant more than you know. They picked me up when I was down and inspired me to press on. May God richly bless your dedication to helping writers realize their dreams.

Debbie Sprinkle, Sandra Hart, Denise Holmberg, Bonnie Beardsley, Linda Dindzans – Oh, my Word Weaver online friends, because of you, I have grown. When assigned to WW Page 3, I never imagined the special bond that would develop from our monthly critique sessions. Thanks for pouring into me and for rooting me on. I'm in your corner too.

Steve and **Shirley Bell** – I'm so grateful I found you. Thank you for opening your door to my sister and me the day we showed up on your doorstep and for opening your hearts to my dream. Reading between the lines of Steve's uncle's letters to our mother and crafting this work of fiction has brought me such joy. When we pulled into your long drive on that gorgeous spring day and saw the home from which Noah penned his letters to our mother, I was overwhelmed with gratitude to God for this amazing adventure.

April Riley – God could not have created a more perfect sister. I'm so glad He made you mine. No one can relate to this story, know its fictional characters, and feel their heartbeat quite like you. Thank you for accompanying me on my trip to Jonesville, for reading my work, and for helping me remember events that would enhance the story. Most of all, thank you for your love and for being my best friend.

Mother – Thank you for the letters. They were life-changing—but my stars, what were you thinking? Although you knew your daughters would find them, I'm sure the thought they would become the springboard for a novel never crossed your mind. I can't believe it crossed mine either, but I'm happy it did. I can only imagine what you'd say, but it's probably better this way. I choose to believe because of your love for writing, you'd be pleased I picked up the pen and ran with it. I'm grateful for this added glimpse into your young life and for the opportunity to "meet" Noah. I pray I've served his memory well—and yours. I only wish you were here to add this title to your list of books read in 2021.

To my launch and prayer team – What an amazing gift you are to me. I've felt your prayers. When I was overwhelmed or discouraged, I knew I could count on you to lift me up to the One who would provide my every need. Your words of love and encouragement continue to mean more to me than you'll ever know. May God bless you for loving and supporting me on this journey.

And thanks be to God, the Creator and Author of my life—the Giver of all good and perfect gifts. Thank you for the gift of story and the opportunities you've given me to fan into flame the words that burned within my heart. I'm humbled you'd use this frail and imperfect vessel to bring honor and glory to your name. I lift these pages to you and pray you'll reveal your heart to all who read them.

Chapter One

Friday, June 24, 1938
Fayetteville, North Carolina
Noah

Reaching for the brass door latch, Noah Anderson caught a glimpse of his reflection in the window of the Rainbow Restaurant. "Not bad," he assured himself. Perhaps there was truth to the notion the uniform makes the man.

As he swung open the door, two giddy young girls immersed in conversation all but tripped over his spit-shined shoes as they exited the room packed with GIs. The close-knit harmonies of the Andrews Sisters spilled from the jukebox and drifted into the street while waitresses scrambled to get food to the tables. Shouts of "Order up!" along with the clatter of dishes and frequent outbursts of laughter muffled the pitch of occasional catcalls. Lunch hour was in full swing.

He'd observed one waitress in particular—Rainbow Girl #9—yet had never sat in her section. With each visit, he'd hoped to muster enough courage to sit in one of the booths along the wall plastered with photos of GIs, but so far, he'd always taken his customary seat by the window. From there, it was easy to appear preoccupied as he stole glances at the one who captured his thoughts night and day.

This afternoon, he'd eat alone. It was the perfect opportunity to sit in her section and strike up a conversation without the incessant teasing of the fellas who'd detected the stars in his eyes for the slender, dark-haired girl.

But again, he took his seat by the window.

Next time, he promised himself.

He scanned the menu as the waitress slid a glass of water in front of him. "May I help you, soldier?"

"Yes, I'll have today's special—a grilled ham and cheese with a cup of white bean soup. Oh, and add a side of—" He looked up, then fumbled for the words to complete his order. The eyes of the fair-skinned beauty he'd been too afraid to approach seized his attention, and his order morphed into something incoherent and unimpressive.

"Is something wrong?"

"Uh, no, ma'am. I've just changed my mind. Soup and sandwich will be fine. And a Coca-Cola, please."

"Sure. I hope you're not in a hurry. We're short on help and running a little behind today."

"Hurry? Oh, no hurry. None at all."

"Great. My name is Emma. I'll be right back with your order."

He nodded. *Take your time, sweet pea. I'll enjoy the view from my window seat.*

His eyes followed her every move as she turned toward the kitchen and stepped around a table of soldiers to avert their insincere calls for service. He recognized a couple of fellas from his platoon at Fort Bragg and was caught off guard as jealousy flooded his heart. She wasn't even his girl.

Not yet, anyway.

As Emma exited the kitchen with his order, one of the soldiers jockeyed for her attention. "Hey, Emma. Tank here wants to know if you'll go out with him this weekend." The red-faced GI beside him lowered his head and poked at the ice cubes in his soda with a straw.

Unruffled, she balanced the tray above her head and made her way to Noah's table. "Here you go, sir," she said as she placed the meal in front of him. "Sorry you had to wait so long. I hope you enjoy it." She topped off his water glass. "Is there anything else I can help you with?"

"I think I'm good for now." His eyes became slits, and his

jaw tightened as the soldiers behind her laughed and slapped each other on the back. "But there is something I want to help *you* with." Smacking his napkin on the table, he edged past her, almost knocking over his glass. "Excuse me a minute."

Emma's large hazel eyes widened as he made his way toward the rowdy GIs. Anchoring his tall frame on the table with his hands, he leaned in only inches from the face of the smart-mouthed soldier. "Hey, Private McCormick. If I ever hear of you messing with my girl again, you'll wish you'd never stepped foot on Bragg."

McCormick paled and tilted backward in his chair. "Your girl, Sergeant Anderson? Didn't know, sir. More than sorry."

Noah nodded. "That you are, private. That you are—more than sorry." Turning his gaze to the soldier sitting next to McCormick, he snapped, "And as for you, Tank. Don't you even think about it."

The young man cowered. "No, sir, Sergeant Anderson. I won't."

Pushing away from the table, Noah straightened his shoulders, ran his fingers through his tousled hair, and turned to take his seat.

Emma was gone.

Chapter Two

Saturday, September 10, 2011
Hope Mills, North Carolina
Caroline

Ninety-seven years have a way of paring down a woman's contemporaries, leaving but a few to mourn her passing. Appropriate. Mother never liked crowds. A solitary person, she would've been happy in this quaint, out-of-the-way resting place. It was a seamless fit. Emma Rose Walsh was home again—beneath the towering longleaf pines she'd spoken of so often. Her life began in the Sandhills of North Carolina. It only fits it should end here.

The doors of the limousine slammed shut, their sounds magnified by the oppressive stillness of the historic Hope Mills cemetery. I could hear the muffled voices of a few remaining friends saying their goodbyes. The black sedan wound its way over the sandy soil, past weather-beaten markers bleached by the sun. Many bore names of loved ones Mother had mentioned as she reminisced with her sister on her occasional trips home. For a moment, I could've sworn I heard their sweet laughter.

The limousine looped toward the cemetery exit flanked by two brick pillars crumbling with age. Reaching for Stephen's hand, I glanced back. Gravediggers laid a blanket of red roses over the mound of freshly turned earth. Mother always had an affinity for red roses.

Red roses?

I looked toward Stephen and searched the pools of dark brown, which invariably revealed his heart. "Did you request a blanket of roses for Mother's grave?"

With a puzzled look, he shook his head. "No, Caroline. I didn't."

Squeezing his hand, I leaned forward and tapped the limousine driver on his shoulder. "Sir, will you please take us back to the grave?"

"Be more than happy to."

When the limo pulled in front of the tent, the attendants were laying the last of the flowers, transforming the parched sandy soil into an array of vibrant colors. One of the men turned to me as I stepped from the car.

"Excuse me," I said. "Do either of you happen to know who requested the roses for the grave?"

"No, ma'am. I'm sorry." He pulled a soiled handkerchief from his pocket and wiped large beads of sweat from his brow. "We're only in charge of placing them here. You'll need to call the funeral home and ask someone in the office. They've saved all of the cards for you."

"Sure. I'll do that." Inhaling the mingled scents of flowers, I glanced at the grave. "You've made everything look beautiful. Thank you for your hard work."

"No problem, ma'am. We're sorry for your loss."

I nodded. The blanket of roses would have pleased Mother. Noticing a wide red ribbon stretched across the top right corner, I walked over and read its glittery sentiment aloud. "Dream of Me."

Dream of me? How odd.

Walking to the car, I struggled to process the cryptic message and decipher its meaning. Who would have ordered such an elaborate, yet fitting, gift?

Monday, May 7, 2012

Eight months had passed since we'd buried our mother. Kate

and I agreed it was time to face the daunting task of sorting through her things. After unloading several empty boxes from my car, I unlocked Mother's house and stepped inside.

"Hey, Mom, it's me." Saying those words seemed ridiculous, but they'd always been my greeting when I came to visit. Speaking them now comforted me as I walked through the hall to her vacant room.

After stacking the boxes beside the bed, I opened the window next to her chair—the upholstered rocker that had been her mother's. A light breeze caused the sheer curtains to billow in and out as if breathing new life into the room. The house had been shut up far too long.

My grandmother's wooden steamer trunk sat to the right of the door. I'd walked past it hundreds of times before. Covered with an embroidered dresser scarf stitched by my mother as a young woman, it served as a catchall. Mother's purse, the mail, her car keys, and just about anything that needed a place to belong found its home there, while the trunk's interior safeguarded possessions dear to her heart and shielded memories she refused to abandon.

After unlatching and lifting the trunk's lid, I found my baby shoes and those of my sister, early letters from Dad, his shaving kit, Mom's Elgin watch, vacation mementos, family photos, and a worn hand-tooled leather box—its hinged lid cracked and split. The box's nostalgic charm summoned me.

I removed it from the trunk, seated myself on the floral coverlet folded at the foot of the bed, and opened the fragile lid. A hint of lavender drifted upward, carrying me to days long gone. Five bundles of letters, each tied with a black grosgrain ribbon, were tucked inside. The unmistakable care with which they were bundled and the sequential order of the letters hinted at the affection my mother had held for the sender.

Careful not to disturb the bow, I picked up the bundle with the earliest postmarks and slipped a yellowed envelope from beneath the ribbon. Penned in a script other than my dad's, it bore no stamp or return address. It simply read—Miss Emma Rose Walsh, c/o The Rainbow. Obviously, it had been hand-delivered to my mother, a nineteen-year-old waitress at the iconic restaurant in Fayetteville. As I unfolded the two pages, my chest tightened.

Station Hospital
Fort Bragg, North Carolina
Wednesday, July 27, 1938

I took a long, deep breath and exhaled slowly. Instinctively, I knew the words I was about to read would reveal a side of my mother I'd never been privileged to know.

Hello Sweetheart,

I received your card and letter a few minutes ago. You'll never know how glad I was to hear from you. I miss you so much. Tucker said he's going into town this evening and will pass by the Rainbow, so I decided I'd write you before he leaves.

I'm lonesome. I laid here today and looked out the window so long I imagined you getting out of the car and coming up to visit me. The sad part was, I awakened to find it all a dream. I realize your work schedule only gives you a chance to come once a week, but I do miss you. Why? Because I love you.

The doctors say my back is healing, but it's very painful. Because of the six hypodermics given to me after surgery, my legs are still numb. My recovery will take longer than I expected, and as I feared, I'll be forced to take early leave from the army. That wouldn't be too bad, except I know it will take me miles away from my darling Emma Rose. But I can't think about that right now. I must focus on the days I have left with you.

Well, Tucker stuck his head in the door and said

he's leaving in five minutes, so I'd better wrap this up. Try your best to visit me on Sunday. I can't wait to lay my eyes on your beautiful face.

Tell Mama T hello and thank her for the chocolate pie and cookies she sent. You're blessed to have such a wonderful landlady, not to mention someone who cooks like she does.

Take care, my love, and don't get distracted by all the soldiers eating at the Rainbow. Be sure to shoo them away from my seat. Let me know if any of them make eyes at you, and when I'm well, I'll reckon with them.

Will write again tomorrow.

I'll always love you,

Noah

My heart pounded as I lowered the letter to my lap and rolled the name over in my head. *Noah.* I couldn't remember Mother ever mentioning another love besides Dad.

My sister and I had been daddy's girls and couldn't have loved our father more. Yet, I now felt a deep sadness for this young man who had expressed great love for my mother. Who was he, and what had happened to him? Certainly, Mother knew her daughters would find these letters. Was there something specific she wanted us to know? If only she'd seen fit to share her memories. But doing so would have invoked questions that might have obliged her to expose the interior of her heart.

And that could never be.

I slipped the letter back in the envelope and returned it to the stack in the box. After closing the lid, I brushed my fingers over its tooled surface and tried to picture the young man who'd written the letters within. Pressing the box to my chest, I walked to the window. The gentle breeze carried with it the fragrance of roses. I peered out. The red rose bush Mother had volunteered Stephen to move from my childhood home after Daddy's death was in full bloom. Through her tender care, it had survived the shock of being uprooted, as she had been over forty years ago. I brushed away a tear, latched the window, and pulled the blinds.

Still holding tightly to the box and its sacred contents, I picked up my sweater and keys from the bed and walked down the hall flanked with family photos. I shut the front door behind me and jiggled the doorknob, making sure it was secure. After sliding behind the wheel of my car, I placed the key in the ignition and looked up at Mother's door. For a moment, I thought I saw her standing there. Smiling. Waving.

I blew a kiss, then dropped my head on the steering wheel and sobbed.

Chapter Three

Wednesday, August 24, 1938
Fayetteville, North Carolina
Emma

Emma burst through the door of Fayetteville's Rainbow Restaurant and skirted past Penny.

"Hi, Em."

"Hey." She pushed open the swinging doors to the kitchen and stormed by the cooks before they had a chance to acknowledge her. After opening the file drawer in the back room, she tossed her purse inside and slammed it shut. She then snatched a starched white apron from the shelf, shook it out, and cinched it around the waist of her neatly pressed uniform.

Penny cracked open the door. "Knock, knock. Is it safe to come in?"

Emma ignored her as she scanned the daily specials on the chalkboard.

Penny moved closer. "What's with you? You barely gave your best friend a nod."

She grimaced. "I'm sorry. I'm not mad at you, but I'm not at all happy with Mr. Cee Wellons."

Penny took a seat on the crates of canned tomatoes stacked in the corner. "What's going on with you two?"

"Cee called last night to say I needed to come into work this evening because Fran phoned in sick. I explained this was Noah's last night in Fayetteville and we had plans, but he said to be here, he couldn't get along without me." She placed her hands on her hips, tipped her nose in the air, and batted her eyelashes. "I suppose I should feel honored that I'm so indispensable."

"Well, Fran's absence does make it difficult for the rest of us."

"I know, and I certainly don't want to make things tough on anyone, but I find it hard to believe he can't get along without me for *one* evening—and tonight, of all nights."

"You'll see Noah after we close, won't you?"

"Sure, but he's got to be back at the base early. The bus to Jonesville leaves at two in the morning, which doesn't give us much time together."

Frowning, Penny stood and brushed off the back of her skirt. "I'm sorry. That is a tough break."

Emma glanced at her reflection in the steel freezer and smoothed out her large, white collar. "Where's Cee, anyway?"

"He left to deliver an order. He should be here shortly."

She threw back her shoulders, grabbed an order pad and pen and slipped them into her pocket. "From the sound of it, we've got a full house out there. I guess we'd better hustle."

Penny hugged her. "I do appreciate you coming in. It helps a lot."

"I know. I'm sorry I was rude."

"You're forgiven." Penny slipped her arm through her friend's. "Now, let's go."

Emma picked up an order in the kitchen, carried it out to Fran's section, and placed the entrees on the table in front of an elderly couple. After refilling their water glasses, she made sure they were taken care of before clearing the dishes from the adjacent booth.

The brass bell above the door jingled.

Turning to see who'd entered, Emma gasped. Noah stood at the door in his army-green dress uniform, holding a single red rose. When his crystal blue eyes met hers, he tipped his cap and winked.

"Noah." As she ran to meet him, her tray clattered to the

green and white checkerboard linoleum, then wobbled from side to side before circling to a stop. She wrapped her arms around his large frame, and he kissed her like no one was watching. Pulling away breathlessly, she blinked back tears, then pressed her lips to his once more. "I thought you weren't coming till we closed."

"I have a right to change my mind, don't I?"

"Sure, but it's only six-thirty. You know I don't get off till nine."

"That's okay. A man's gotta eat. After all, it would be ill-mannered to leave town without one last meal at the Rainbow."

Taking hold of his arm, she turned to show him to a table. One by one, customers rose to their feet and applauded. Blushing, she looked up at Noah. "What is this?"

"Like I said, I don't want to leave town without enjoying one last meal at the place where I met my darling Emma Rose." He motioned toward the booth by the window where he'd sat the day they met. "Care to join me?"

Her hand flew to her mouth. To her delight, the table was covered with a white linen cloth and black napkins. As Noah guided her, Penny and Fran topped it off with two silver candlesticks and a crystal bud vase.

Emma surveyed the restaurant. "But—I'm working."

Fran interrupted. "No, you're not. This is my shift." She untied Emma's apron, then slipped it over her own head and laughed. "It's amazing how much better I feel now."

Penny winked and grinned. "Yes. Rather miraculous, wouldn't you say?"

Giving them a knowing look, Emma dropped her rose in the vase.

Cee burst through the kitchen doors carrying a large tray above his head. "Take a seat, Em." He placed two specially prepared steaks, baked potatoes, and salads on the table, then pulled a pack of matches from his pocket and lit the candles. "Do you think you can find it in your heart to forgive your old boss, Miss Walsh?"

She nodded and laughed. "Oh, Cee, I'm sorry I gave you such a hard time on the phone. You are indeed forgiven." She reached over and hugged him. "This is such a wonderful surprise. Thank you."

Bending at the waist, he nodded at both of them. "I hope you enjoy your meals. Penny will take your drink orders, and if you need anything else, let her know."

Noah reached to shake his hand. "What more could we possibly need? Thank you, sir. I'm grateful for your help in arranging this for us."

Cee patted him on the back. "You're a good man, son. We're going to miss you around here. Take care of yourself and don't stay away too long."

"I'll try not to." He looked across the table at Emma.

Moisture pooled in her eyes. Noah would leave in the morning, but she was grateful God had joined their hearts. Tonight would *not* be the final chapter of their lives together.

Emma hugged Penny and Fran and thanked them for the special evening before stepping onto the sidewalk with Noah. "Hay Street is lovely at night. Could we window shop before you walk me home?"

"Of course. We have time." He took her hand in his, then leaned over and kissed her on the nose. "I'm going to squeeze out every minute I can with you this evening."

"Will the added walking bother your back?"

"No. The exercise will be good for me. I'm just not to lift anything heavy for a while."

They strolled the block in silence. Emma was afraid if she opened her mouth, she'd burst into tears. The enticing autumn displays in the well-lit shop windows were a welcome distraction.

Noah spoke up. "I'm glad I got to see the girls and Cee before I left."

"Me too." She led him over to the window of The Capitol and admired their new barrel-style sweaters. As she thought of how the full waistband would accentuate her slim waist, they walked on. "He's such a good liar. He certainly had me fooled."

Noah chuckled. "I'm glad you didn't catch on. The look on your face when I walked in was priceless."

She stopped to face him. His blue eyes sparkled in the light of the street lamps. "Thanks for all you did to make our last night together so special. I'll never forget it." She wrapped her arms around his waist.

"I think the customers enjoyed it, too, don't you?"

She laughed. "I know they did." She laid her head on his chest. "Noah, when do you think I'll see you again?"

He kissed her hair and softly stroked her cheek. "I don't know, hon, but you can bet whenever I get a job and save enough money, I'll head this way."

"You'd better." She nestled up to his side and slipped her arm through his.

They walked to the corner and crossed the street to Mae's Boutique Shoppe, where Mrs. Martin dressed the window with her latest purchases from Atlanta. She smiled and waved from behind the glass.

Emma nodded her approval of the new arrivals, clasped her hands over her heart, and mouthed, "Love them." Moving along the glass storefront, she noticed a display of perfume bottles on a small table and bent over to read their labels. "Oh ... lavender cologne. My favorite."

Noah moved toward the entrance. "Let's go in and get it."

Following close on his heels, she grabbed his arm. "They're closed."

"The clerk's in there." He rapped on the window.

"Noah, stop," she said, tugging on his arm.

"Quit being a worrywart. I'm sure she won't mind if we

come in and make a purchase." When Mrs. Martin looked up, he pointed to the display table.

Emma yanked him. "Come on. I don't have the money for that."

He stiffened and anchored his feet to the ground. "Well, perhaps I do."

Mrs. Martin, fashionably dressed as always, opened the door and smiled. "Hi, Emma. It's good to see you. Is this your handsome beau?"

"Yes, ma'am. This is Noah Anderson."

She held out her hand. "Nice to meet you, young man."

"This is Noah's last night as a soldier at Fort Bragg. He's going home in the morning."

"How wonderful." She tucked strands of graying hair back into her bun. "Where's home?"

"Jonesville."

"Pretty area. Traveled there years ago. You'll find it cooler, I'm sure. Will beat this stifling humidity." She motioned them in. "Now, what can I do for the two of you?"

"I'd like to buy a bottle of the cologne you have in the window. Lavender is Emma's favorite."

Emma elbowed him and huffed.

"Certainly." She stepped behind the counter and pulled a bottle from the shelf. "Looks like you're getting the next-to-last bottle in the store." After unscrewing the cap, she held it under his nose, then Emma's. "Nice, huh? It's my top seller this year."

Emma inhaled deeply. "Heavenly."

Noah counted out the money while Mrs. Martin placed the cologne in a box and put it in a sack for Emma. "I hope you enjoy it, dear."

"Thank you. I know I will." She eyed Noah and tossed her hair over her shoulder. "Who's going to spoil me when you're gone, Sergeant Anderson?" She rose on her tiptoes and kissed him on the cheek.

"No one, I hope. Not if you give thank-yous like that." He

winked and then turned to Mrs. Martin. "We certainly appreciate you opening the shop for us."

"My pleasure. It warms my heart to see a young couple in love." As she walked them to the door, she leaned in close to Emma. "That's some man you've got there. Nice looking too. I'd say you'd better hang on to him."

"Oh, don't worry. I intend to."

Mrs. Martin followed them out onto the sidewalk and looked up. "Thought I heard thunder a few minutes ago. Hope you kids don't get rained on." She stepped inside, then turned and waved before locking the door.

Emma couldn't wait to give Noah his gift. "Let's head to my house, handsome. I have something for you too."

His eyes widened. "Sounds swell. Will it warrant a kiss afterward?"

She laughed and linked her arm through his. "It better."

While they walked the short distance to Maiden Lane, the wind strengthened. Noah put his arm around Emma's shoulders and pulled her close. Sliding her arm around his waist, she thought of how safe she felt next to him and couldn't envision her days without him.

"Whoops. Here comes the rain." He grabbed her hand and ran as the first cool drops pelted their skin.

"Stop. Don't run, Noah. You'll hurt your back."

"I'll be fine, Em." He winced. "We're almost there."

The clouds burst the moment they stepped onto the porch. Emma brushed raindrops from her hair, then motioned toward the swing. "Have a seat. I'll only be a minute." She placed her cologne on the hall table inside the door and grabbed Noah's gift. Returning to the porch, she held it out as she approached the swing. She hoped he would like it as much as she did hers. Nothing was too good for him. If she could have purchased a star and hung it in his honor, she would have.

His eyes met hers. "What's this?"

"I'm not telling you, silly." She scooted in beside him. "Open it."

He untied the green bow and ripped off the brown kraft paper. Pushing aside the tissue, he pulled out a green suede box and brushed his fingers across its velvety surface. "Nice." Lifting the lid, he uncovered cream-colored writing paper with envelopes and a tortoise-shell fountain pen.

"Oh, sweetheart. This is too much." He picked up the pen and rotated it between his fingers. "It's beautiful."

She reached into the box. "And look. That's not all. I've included a dozen three-cent stamps." She flapped them in front of his face. "Now you have no excuses for not writing me, Mr. Anderson. You may be over 150 miles away, but I still expect to hear from you."

He set the box beside him and pulled her close. "You know I'll write to you." Lifting her chin, he lowered his face to hers as if to peer into the depths of her soul. "Do you promise you'll write me?"

A lump rose in her throat. "I promise." She placed her lips on his. His warm touch and the spicy scent of his skin summoned her to a realm where she wished to remain forever. As the sound of the rain intensified on the tin roof, so did their passion. In his embrace, she melted along with her fears.

"Please don't leave me, Noah. Please."

He placed his index finger on her lips. "Shh. I'm here now" As he covered her face with kisses, she tried not to think beyond then.

That moment.

Now.

Resting her head on Noah's shoulder, Emma listened to the rain pepper the tin roof. The sound that usually soothed her now failed to lift her spirits.

Noah slipped his hand into his pocket and pulled out his watch. "I need to make a run for it, Em. It doesn't look like this rain is going to let up anytime soon, and I can't afford to miss the eleven-thirty bus to Bragg."

She tightened her grasp on his arm. "I can't let you go."

"Leaving you is the hardest thing I've ever had to do." He

kissed her forehead. "But the sooner I leave, the closer we'll be to my return." Lifting her chin, he brushed a tear from her cheek. "Please be brave, Emma Rose. I want to remember you smiling."

She looked into his face. As she imagined their future together, her lips slowly gave way to a smile.

He kissed them lightly. "There you go. That's what I'll carry with me." He slipped his arm from hers, clasped her hand, and picked up the box. "Come on, sweetheart. We can do this." He led her to the edge of the porch and leaned in to kiss her. Then, tucking the box beneath his coat, he stepped out into the rain, opened the gate, and latched it behind him.

"Noah, wait." She ran toward him, reached over the fence, and kissed him one last time.

Without speaking, he broke from her embrace and walked down Maiden Lane.

Tears mingling with raindrops clouded her sight as every step carried him farther away. When he reached the corner, she saw him look back. His body, shrouded by fog, stood silhouetted against the light of the street lamp. Although she was sure he couldn't see her, he waved, turned onto Hay Street, and walked from view.

She returned to the porch and stepped inside the house. As the screen clapped shut behind her, she closed the door and flipped off the porch light. Pulling back the sheer curtain, Emma stared out into the darkness. She felt locked inside the moment—in a now she feared would last forever.

Chapter Four

Noah climbed the steps of the half-empty bus, pitched his worn duffel bag on the overhead rack, and dropped his lanky frame in the second row by the window. After slipping his garrison cap into the seat pocket in front of him, he pressed his head against the cracked vinyl cushion and pushed back. Buses were never able to comfortably accommodate his six-foot-two-inch frame.

He watched as large raindrops pelted the window and distorted the glaring fluorescent lights of Fayetteville's Greyhound station. The neon outline of the running greyhound above the red *Bus Depot* letters was the only spot of gaiety in this otherwise dreary morning. Noah sat mesmerized by the flashing movement of the dog's legs. It was as if the creature raced to keep up with his thoughts.

More than three years had passed since he'd swapped the familiar comforts and rural roads of his home for the uncertainty of a soldier's life at Fort Bragg. Letting go of this part of his journey was bittersweet. Though happy to trade the hot, sandy soil of eastern North Carolina for the cool, rolling foothills of the north-western Piedmont, leaving Emma was nothing short of heart-wrenching. He'd never dreamed he could fall head over heels in love so quickly. But then, he'd never met a girl quite like Emma Rose

As the bus pulled away from the station, he slipped a gold-plated watch from his pocket. *Two-ten. Right on time.* Slowly snapping it shut, he brushed his thumb over the worn initials etched in its shiny patina and recalled his departure that brisk October morning. His father's tight-lipped attempt to hold back his sadness, and the gentle pressure of his hand as he passed the treasured timepiece on to him, exposed a depth of emotion too close to the surface to voice. The tenderness of his father's steel-gray eyes, the work-weary slump of his once-broad shoulders, and the deep crevices of his weather-beaten skin revealed a dedication not uncommon to families in this depressed economy.

Noah recounted his father's steadfast routine. Up before dawn, he'd shuffle to the kitchen for a cup of strong black coffee, then spend time in the Scriptures and prayer at the table. Afterward, he'd help himself to a breakfast of scrambled eggs, bacon, grits, and cheese served with homemade biscuits and jelly prepared by his bride of forty-one years. He'd need plenty of fuel for his dawn-to-dusk workday on their Jonesville tobacco farm.

Noah was no stranger to hard labor. He'd considered his days working in tobacco some of the best and most important of his life. Earning less than sixty cents a day, he'd learned the value of money—how long it took to earn it, and how quickly he could spend it.

It was tobacco-harvesting time and his father's third season without him. Noah was the second of three children, but the only living son. Even though his cousins were around to help, he worried about his father toiling in the stifling summer heat. During the curing stages, temperatures in the barns climbed as high as 180 degrees. Their only reprieve was the shade of a 150-year-old oak tree. He remembered how he'd kick back for a quick break beneath its sprawling branches with an RC Cola and a Moon Pie or inhale a sack lunch packed by his mother's loving hands.

Harvesting was always a family affair. The camaraderie was good training for getting along in the workplace as well as an excellent opportunity to chase his little sister around the tobacco sled with a big green juicy tobacco worm. *"It's just a little ol' worm, Sadie Mae. Don't ya wanna hold it?"*

His own laughter jolted him from his thoughts. He looked around at the sleeping passengers and rechecked his watch before returning it to his pocket. His thoughts were too jumbled to sleep. He stood to stretch his legs, then reached for his duffle bag on the overhead rack. He pulled out the stationery set Emma had given him and dropped back in his seat. Writing her while separated wouldn't be a problem. It would be his lifeline. He flipped on the light above him, pulled out a sheet of vellum paper, and uncapped the tortoiseshell fountain pen.

My Darling Emma Rose,

I made it to the station on time. I was the only soldier on the shuttle out of Bragg this morning. I guess everyone else had enough sense to leave in the daylight hours. At least that's what Private Pope, the driver, thought. He said I must've lost my mind. He's probably right. Not even a dog should be out on a night like this. But then, Pope doesn't know my sweetie. You've always had a way of causing me to not think straight.

The trip shouldn't be too bad. I've got two seats to myself, so hopefully, I'll sleep part of the way home. Uncle Guy should be at the station in Winston-Salem when I arrive and will take me on to Jonesville.

Darling, it seems awful going away from you. Instead, I want to be going toward you. If there's anything I hate, its goodbyes—especially to the one I love. I'll carry with me the memories of our last evening together. Last for now, but not for always. As soon as I find a job and save enough money, I'll come for you. You'll see. Then, there will be no more lasts for us— only forevers.

You may be Rainbow Girl #9, but in my book, you are and always will be #1. I'm sorry I didn't have the

> nerve to talk to you sooner. Evidently, God got somewhat frustrated with me and stepped in to bring us together. For that, I'm ever grateful.

He looked up and yawned. As the bus's headlights cut a tunnel through the darkness, the hypnotic rhythm of the wipers and the hum of the tires on the wet pavement caused his eyelids to grow heavy. Shaking away his drowsiness, he scanned the dimly lit bus. Everyone was asleep except for a young boy playing with an army figure. The child locked eyes with him and displayed a sheepish grin as though he knew he'd been caught. Noah winked and smiled broadly.

The bus driver bellowed, "Next stop, Sanford." While groggy passengers prepared to exit the bus, Noah straightened in his seat and resumed his words to Emma.

> I guess by this time, you're asleep. I hate I kept you out so late, but I wanted to make the most of our time together. Dream of me, my love, and write soon. I'll be waiting for your reply.

> I'll always love you,
> Noah

After slipping his letter into the envelope, he tucked it inside the box with his pen and laid his head against the seat cushion. On the long road home, he could only hope to dream of his sweet Emma Rose and their life beyond tomorrow.

Chapter Five

Emma woke to the smell of bacon and the clatter of dishes. She wasn't much of a breakfast eater. Still, her landlady, Florence Turner, who preferred to be called Mama T, insisted she start her day with something in her stomach. Jellied toast, two strips of crisp bacon, and a cup of coffee with cream would serve a dual purpose—satisfy her hunger and fulfill Mama T's need to nurture someone. It had been two years since Mr. Turner's death, and after sixty-three years of marriage and no children, the loneliness seemed almost more than her landlady could bear.

Her room in the two-story clapboard farmhouse was a brisk five-minute walk from work. Her first few months as a waitress at the Rainbow Restaurant on Hay Street had been a bigger challenge than she'd imagined. Still, the owner was kind, and her newfound independence made it all worthwhile. On her first day off in over a week, she looked forward to cozying down with a good book. Books had always been her world and escape to places far beyond her small hometown of Hope Mills, North Carolina.

From the minute she'd stepped foot inside the house on Maiden Lane, she knew she'd call it home. Books of every genre filled the floor-to-ceiling shelves lining the walls of the front sitting room. Although she preferred poetry and biographies, she'd spotted the debut novel, *Look Homeward, Angel,* by Asheville author Thomas Wolfe and vowed to crack it open.

"Good morning, Mama T," she said as she bounded down the stairs and into the kitchen. "Did you sleep well?"

"I certainly did, but apparently not as good as you." The portly lady stood on her toes and reached into the cabinet for Emma's favorite blue salt-glazed mug. "You're risin' late this mornin', child."

"A bit." She leaned over and gave her a quick squeeze. "Noah didn't leave till after eleven last night, so it felt good to sleep in." She stretched her arms above her head. "Besides, I think my body's in rebellion after working so many hours this week. Cee underestimated the reception the restaurant would bring. But don't get me wrong. I'm thankful. I can use the extra money."

"Always a silver lining, baby doll." She placed two strips of bacon on a plate.

Emma pushed back the sheer lace curtains to let in the cool morning breeze. "I sure hope Noah got home okay. That was some rain."

"I hope so too. I'm gonna miss that young man around here. He's a fine fella."

Trying to maintain her composure, Emma leaned against the pie safe and brushed a tear from her cheek. "Well, today, Thomas Wolfe and I have a date on the porch swing. Chummy won't be happy about giving up his perch, but I think it's only fair. Besides, I've noticed that cat has gotten a little paunchy around the middle. Moving around a bit will do him good."

Mama T laughed and handed her a warm mug. "Here, missy. Have a seat and sip on this a minute while I pop some bread in the toaster." She wiped her hands on her faded floral apron and pulled the preserves from the icebox. "They're sayin' it's gonna be a scorcher today. May even get another afternoon thunder boomer. Sure hope we do. My tomatoes are dyin' on the vine. Can't seem to give 'em enough water to satisfy 'em."

Emma took a seat at the white pedestal table in the center of the room. She never tired of watching Mama T in the kitchen. Her short, rotund body moved with graceful command as she executed every detail of her morning routine.

"Just readin' this mornin' where families in the Midwest are abandoning their farms and headin' to California where the economy's stronger." She handed Emma the paper. "I sure hope the Good Lord sends some rain their way. Between the depression and the drought, the Dust Bowl states are really sufferin'. We may be strugglin' here in the South, but you can always look around and find someone havin' it worse than you."

"You're right about that." Emma's thoughts drifted to her friend Penny. She couldn't imagine the weight she carried on her nineteen-year-old shoulders day in and day out. Early last year, her mother had died in childbirth, leaving her and her dad responsible for the care of the baby and her younger siblings.

Mama T slathered some homemade fig preserves across the toast, then handed the plate to Emma. "There ya go, dear. Now, hurry on off to the porch and enjoy this beautiful morning before it gets hot. I've got work to do around here."

Laughing, she brushed back a stray wisp of Mama T's gray hair and gave her a peck on the cheek. "Sounds like a good option to me." After tucking the morning paper under her arm, she stopped by the sitting room, slid her book from the shelf, then pushed open the screen door.

"Aha. There you are, Chummy Choo. Just as I expected."

Chummy, the resident tomcat, rolled over on his back, yawned, and stretched himself across the porch swing. He wasn't about to relinquish his position without making his wishes known.

She laughed. "I understand how you feel, Chum, but remember what I told you yesterday? Today that swing is mine. As soon as I finish my breakfast, you'll need to find another place to hunker down. You should check out the back yard. If I'm not mistaken, I saw a field mouse scuttle across it a few moments ago. Looks like you've been asleep at the switch far too long."

After situating herself at the wrought iron table on the opposite end of the porch, she scanned *The Observer* over breakfast. The morning headlines read "German Military Mobilizes." Her stomach sank. Tension mounted worldwide. Although the warring countries seemed far away, another world war would have a tremendous impact on the people of their community. The neighboring army base of Fort Bragg had been a training center for World War I troops and continued to be a key testing facility for air and field artillery. She pictured the faces of the military families she served at the Rainbow each week and lifted up a quick prayer for their safety. At least Noah was out of harm's way.

She noticed Chummy had taken her advice and given up his position on the swing. Sipping the last of her coffee, she kicked off her sandals, then stretched out with her book for a leisurely read. Although she tried to stay focused, she found herself reading the same line over and over. She couldn't help but remember she'd been in this very spot the day Noah pulled up at the gate.

Two months earlier

"Good morning, Sunshine. Wanna go for a ride?"

Emma turned to see a soldier step out of a burgundy Ford convertible—the man who'd unexpectedly come to her defense the day before. She'd been instantly attracted to his gentle, yet strong demeanor. Not to mention his crystal-blue eyes, square jaw, and dimpled chin. Even in street clothes, he was enough to make a girl's heart flutter.

"That's some car you've got there, soldier. What's your fare?"

"No fare. I figure I owe you—an apology, that is." He

looked nervous. "I reckon I embarrassed you yesterday at the restaurant. I didn't mean to. I'm hoping a drive on this beautiful morning will more than make up for it."

Laughing, she stepped off the porch and walked toward him. "I'm not in the habit of taking up with strangers, Sergeant."

He reached for her hand. "Anderson. Noah Anderson, ma'am. I've been a customer at the restaurant since it opened. I always sit in Penny's section. I'm sure she'll vouch for me."

She smiled. "You think?"

He fumbled for words. "Uh, I was sorry to hear about her baby sister. I've missed Penny at the restaurant, but her absence has given me the chance to meet you. Clumsy as it was." Remembering the moment, he swallowed hard. "Penny knows I only have eyes for you. She told me you lived in a boarding house on Maiden Lane. Thought maybe I'd take my chances and see if I could find you. Looks like God's smiling down on me this morning—so far, anyway."

Emma strolled over to the car and slid her hand across its satiny coat of paint. "You're doing mighty well for yourself, aren't you, soldier boy?"

He grinned. "Well, I hate to admit it, but this beauty doesn't belong to me. It belongs to my friend Tucker. He's out of town for a few days and asked me to look after it for him. Said I could paint the town red while he's away. Wanna see how she rolls?"

The handsome soldier's offer was tempting, but she didn't know him. "I appreciate you asking, but I've already made plans for the day. After lunch, I'm going to visit Penny at the hospital and check on the baby."

"Perfect. I'd like to visit them too. What if I take you? It's too hot to walk, and you won't have to catch the bus. Just tell me what time, and I'll be here."

She looked him over again. *A man who wants to visit a sixteen-month-old toddler in the hospital can't be all bad. Besides, Penny knows him.*

"How about it?"

"Well, I've never ridden in such a snazzy car. It would be a shame to pass up the opportunity." She looked at her watch. "How does two o'clock sound?"

"Sounds swell to me."

"Perfect. Tom and I will be waiting on the swing."

"Tom?"

"Yes, Tom—Thomas Wolfe. He's quite a writer." She held up her book and waved it in the air. "Read much, soldier?"

Smiling, she spun on her heel and reclaimed her place on the swing.

Chapter Six

Startled by the sudden sound of the door chime, Emma glanced at her clock on the nightstand—a few minutes before two. Noah certainly was a man of his word.

"I'm coming," said Mama T over the dwindling whir of the electric sweeper.

She could hear Noah introduce himself, and the squeak of the rusty hinges on the screen door as Mama T welcomed him in. Staring at the array of clothes scattered across her bed, she waffled between the cotton day dress and the A-line skirt with the pleated blouse. Why had it been so hard for her to decide what to wear? Was this near stranger's opinion that important to her?

"Emma, Noah's here."

She poked her head around the doorframe. "Be down in a minute." Settling on the sleeveless pink floral day dress with the scalloped neckline, she threw on her white peep-toe flats and took one last look in the mirror. She fastened her mama's silver locket around her neck, pinched her cheeks for color, and grabbed a silk headscarf from the drawer. Lingering at the top of the stairs, she took a deep breath and exhaled slowly. Though she'd had several male suitors, this sudden influx of emotions was strange and unsettling. She interrupted Mama T's excited chatter as she entered the parlor. "Sorry to keep you waiting."

Noah sprang to his feet. "Well, aren't you a sight for sore eyes. When I didn't see you on the porch swing, I was afraid you'd taken off with Tom."

"Tom?"

He threw back his head and laughed.

"Oh, yes . . . Tom." She blushed.

Mama T chuckled and walked ahead of them into the foyer. "I was just tellin' Noah not to worry, if you stood him up, he could take me for a ride in that fine automobile." She pushed open the screen door then snapped her fingers. "Whoops." Emma jumped back as the screen slammed shut, and Mama T bolted toward the kitchen. "Wouldn't ya know it. 'Bout forgot."

Emma giggled and watched as Chummy shot from his place on the swing, dived off the porch, and crouched beneath the bushes.

Within moments, Mama T returned, clutching a small glass vase of black-eyed Susans. Struggling to catch her breath, she handed it to Emma. "I picked these early this mornin'. Thought maybe Penny could use a spot o' sunshine in her life. Please give her my love and tell her I'm prayin' for her and little Anna."

"Thanks. I sure will." She gave her landlady a big squeeze.

Noah followed Emma through the gate and opened the car door. Then, with a playful grin and a broad sweep of his arm, he bent at the waist. "Your carriage awaits, my lady."

Wide-eyed, she took hold of his hand and sank into the convertible's plush leather seat. "Why thank you, kind sir." She took in his every move as he sprinted around the car and dropped behind the wheel. After giving the key a quick turn, he drank in the sweet purr of the engine and cast his gaze toward her.

"Ready to roll?"

"Can't wait." She tied her scarf under her chin, tilted her face toward the sun, and inhaled the warmth and beauty of the day.

The receptionist in Highsmith Hospital's foyer directed Emma and Noah to the Critical Care Unit in the east wing. As they walked on polished checkerboard floors through sterile white corridors, a strong antiseptic smell permeated the air and stuck to the back of Emma's throat. Doctors and nurses systematically made their rounds speaking in hushed tones, while families huddled in waiting areas. They read, napped, laughed—did anything they could to make the long, arduous hours more bearable.

Emma took hold of Noah's arm and glanced up at him as they entered the unit. "I'm glad you're here with me."

"Me too," he said, covering her hand with his.

The door to Anna's ward at the end of the hall was shut. Taped to the wall, a yellow sign with large black letters affirmed Emma's worst fear and made her heart skip beats—Quarantine: Whooping Cough. Peering through the door's window into the dimly lit room, she noted twelve white iron beds occupied by children, some beneath transparent bed tents. At the end of the room, an open window helped ventilate the area. As her chest tightened and her legs grew weak, she leaned heavily on Noah's arm, then looked around the waiting room. On a couch in the corner, Penny sat motionless, her eyes glued to a small stuffed bear in her lap.

Emma passed the vase of black-eyed Susans to Noah, crossed the room, and took a seat beside her friend. Her breath caught in her throat as Penny lifted her head. Her once-sparkling green eyes were now dark and hollow. She collapsed into Emma's arms and sobbed. Emma wept too.

Collecting her emotions, Penny wiped her swollen red eyes with the sleeve of her sweater and spoke with the soft Tennessee drawl Emma loved. "I've never been so happy to see y'all. The doctors say Anna's not doin' good, and the next twenty-four hours will be telling." She clung to her friend and blurted, "How could Mama leave me like this, Em? She'd know what to do. She always did."

Noah motioned to Emma and pointed to a chapel sign at the

end of the hall. She nodded, then ushered her friend away from the congested waiting area. A sense of calm washed over her as they stepped inside the small room. It was cozy and welcoming—its peacefulness, a stark contrast to the pain and heartache that lay just outside the door. Three short pews with dark-blue velvet seat cushions lined either side of the aisle. The curved walls behind the altar wrapped around as if to scoop them forward.

Penny walked to the front of the room and studied the painting above the altar—Jesus beckoned with outstretched arms. Engraved on a bronze plaque attached to its frame was a Scripture. *Come unto me, all ye that labour and are heavy laden, and I will give you rest. Matthew 11:28.* She buried her face in her hands and fell to her knees.

Emma knelt, wrapped her arms around Penny, and held her securely. She prayed God would give her the strength and wisdom she needed. "Also, Lord, please have mercy on little Anna. We know you love her and are the Great Physician. Touch her tiny body and relieve her suffering. In Jesus' name, Amen."

Seating themselves on the steps of the altar, Emma listened and allowed Penny to release the in-most questions of her heart. There were no sufficient answers—only more questions.

Later, Noah helped them to their feet and ushered them back to the waiting room. Emma hugged her weary friend and handed her the vase of flowers from Mama T. Her heart broke as Penny returned to the corner and dropped onto the couch. She blew her a kiss, then looped her arm through Noah's and sighed. Glancing toward Anna's ward, she whispered a prayer for the tiny lives beyond its doors.

As Emma and Noah walked toward the entrance, neither spoke a word. Emma was unable to grasp the thought of moving on with her day while Penny kept vigil another night. It wasn't fair.

"Well, Mama T was right," Noah said as they entered the

lobby. "She thought we might get a late-afternoon thunder boomer. This one looks to be a gully washer."

They stood at the windows and watched the rain pour down in sheets, spill over the gutters, and etch a ditch in the sandy soil beside the entrance. To Emma, it was as if the heavens wept for sweet Anna.

Noah whistled and shook his head. "I'm glad I put the top up on Tucker's car. He said to paint the town red, but he didn't mention a thing about washing the upholstery."

Emma laughed. She loved his sense of humor. He could make her smile in the bleakest of circumstances. Life could get heavy in a hurry, and the ability to find laughter in the middle of a storm was an admirable quality for a life partner. Not that she was in a hurry to get married or anything. She simply didn't believe in wasting time with someone unless she could imagine spending the rest of her life with them. So far, Sergeant Anderson was shaping up to be a mighty fine candidate.

"Looks like it's slacking off," he said. "Wait here while I make a dash for the car and pull it around for you."

Nodding, she walked out with him and stood beneath the awning. As Noah darted in and out of the cars, she took note of his fine physique. Besides being the perfect gentleman, he was certainly easy on the eyes.

Yes. Noah might be one worth keeping.

Chapter Seven

Tuesday, May 8, 2012
Asheboro, North Carolina
Caroline

Revealed only by the stark light of my computer screen, Stephen stood at the door of the kitchen shaking his head. "Are you still up?"

Never averting my eyes from the screen, I glanced at the time on my laptop—1:44 a.m. "I'm looking for Noah's obituary."

He chuckled. "If Noah Anderson's obit is online after all these years, I think it'll be there later today. You need to get some rest, Caroline."

"I know. I know. I'll be there in a few." You'd think after forty-six years of marriage, Stephen would be accustomed to my nocturnal ways. Still, he always seems surprised to find me awake in the wee hours of the morning.

After cracking open the fridge, he unscrewed the cap on a water bottle and took a gulp before returning it to the door. "Well, it's back to bed for me. I've got to be at work early. Big sales meeting right out of the gate today." Shuffling his bare feet across the hardwood floor, he shook his head and mumbled. "Somebody's got to keep you up in the manner to which you're accustomed, my dear."

Stephen tells me I'm truly my mother's daughter. An incurable night owl, filled with gritty determination, and the possessor of a full-throttle approach to life. My nocturnal gene is part of the Walsh DNA and one I've passed on to our oldest daughter, Jenna. Each generation seems to suffer from the malady a notch worse than the preceding one.

Fighting sleep, I resolved to discover more about the young man Mother had held in high regard. I pounded out different combinations of his name, hometown, and other pertinent information I'd found in the letters. Then for the umpteenth time, I hit Enter. As a list of links popped onto the screen, my bleary eyes scanned them.

"Bingo." Was victory finally mine? I blinked and leaned in closer. "Is that really you, Noah Anderson?" After opening the obituary link for Sarah "Sadie" Anderson Montgomery, I read the details aloud.

Mrs. Sarah Mae Montgomery, ninety-five, formerly of Watson Mill Road in Jonesville, passed away at her home on Monday, March 7, 2010. She was preceded in death by her husband, Vincent B. Montgomery; her parents Jesse L. and Edith Gentry Anderson; and her two brothers, Harold Thomas and Noah Franklin Anderson. She is survived by her son Franklin Montgomery of Jonesville; a daughter, Mary Ann Miller, and husband, Greg, of Hickory; and three grandchildren.

"Aha. So that's where you've been hiding." I smiled and hit Print. With an air of smugness, I swayed to the hum of the printhead, which bled the leads I needed across the crisp white page.

Lifting the sheet from the tray, I reread the names of Noah's living relatives—a niece and nephew. Perhaps they would provide answers to the host of questions that had incessantly gnawed at my thoughts. With a starting line before me, I was happy to call it a night—or morning, whatever. I shut down my laptop, slid my chair under the tiger-oak pedestal table, and walked to the sink. Staring out the window at the waning moon overhead, I poured my cold coffee down the drain and whispered. "What have you done to me, Mother? You knew I'd never let this one rest."

Mid-morning and still in my pajamas and furry slippers, I dialed Mary Ann's number. The pounding of my heart increased with each ring. On the fourth, I attempted to shake the remaining sleep from my voice to leave a message.

"Hello. This is Caroline Myers. My mother was a friend of your family. I found some old letters in her things that I think you'll be interested in. Please call me. I'd love to talk with you."

After leaving my number, I placed the phone back in its dock and stared at the box filled with letters. Slipping one from underneath the black ribbon, I settled back on the couch with my second cup of coffee to read.

Hello Sweetheart,

HOME!

I arrived in Winston-Salem later than expected yesterday morning, but at least I'm home. After the bus broke down somewhere between Sanford and Siler City, they had to send in a backup. I'm all propped up on my bed now writing to you. Writing always makes you seem near. Almost as if you're here with me.

Mama is rustling around fixing breakfast. She loves to spoil me when I'm home and put a few pounds on me. She always thinks I'm too thin.

Since few were riding the bus yesterday, I had room to stretch out and managed to get a few winks of sleep. Uncle Guy was at the station when I got there and brought me home to Jonesville. I slept most of the day yesterday. My bed sure did feel good. Mom is happy to have me here. Pop too. He's looking forward to having another helping hand around. Of course, I'll have to go easy for a while with my back, but I should be good enough to help some in another week or two. Pop wants me to go with him to the market in Winston-Salem in a few days. He's hoping his tobacco will bring a better price than last year. This drought continues to be rough on our crops, so I can't complain about yesterday's rain. We really needed it.

I imagine you're at—

Startled by the ring of the telephone, I leaped from the couch, stubbed my toe on the coffee table, and spilled coffee on my pajama top. Wincing, I snatched the handset from the desk. "Hello."

"Good morning. Is this Caroline Myers?"

"It is." Craning my neck to anchor the receiver on my shoulder, I hobbled over to the sink, grabbed the dishtowel, and blotted the warm liquid from my shirt.

"This is Mary Ann Miller from Hickory."

Silently I mouthed "yes" while pumping my fist. "Thank you, Mary Ann, for returning my call. You'll probably think this is crazy, but I recently learned your Uncle Noah was my mother's first love. They met in Fayetteville while he was stationed at Fort Bragg."

"Are you serious? *My* uncle?" she said with an unmistakable southern drawl.

I tossed the towel in the sink, picked up the box of letters from the couch, and took a seat at the desk. "Yes. I found his letters postmarked 1938 and 1939 in my mother's trunk. She was a nineteen-year-old waitress working at the Rainbow Restaurant while he was a sergeant in the army."

"Oh, my. That's amazing. But how did you find me?"

"I went online to see if I could locate Noah's obituary and

ran across your mother's. It listed Noah as her predeceased brother. I'm sorry for your loss, by the way."

"Thank you."

"I know how difficult losing a mother can be. Mine died last September." I nervously traced the tooling on the leather box lid with my finger. "I don't mean to pry into your family affairs, but I wondered if there was anything you could tell me about your uncle."

"I wish I could, but I only know that he was my mama's older brother. He died long before I was born. I do remember her saying he was the family favorite—very polite, intelligent, and quite handsome."

"You wouldn't happen to have a picture of him, would you?"

"Not that I know of. Of course, I guess there may be one among Mama's things. I haven't had the time or the courage to go through them all yet." Her voice cracked. "I still can't seem to keep my emotions in check. You should connect with my brother, Franklin. He's Noah's namesake and still lives beside the homeplace in Jonesville. Perhaps he'll have one."

I took down the information and asked her to let me know if she ever found anything of interest, especially pictures—or Mother's letters to Noah. That would be the ultimate discovery in this whole incredible scenario.

I thanked her again for returning my call and hung up. Then lifting the towel from the sink, I blotted the remaining coffee from my shirt. After hanging the towel over the oven door handle, I hobbled to the couch and plopped down to examine my toe and read more of Noah's letters.

I imagine you're at work about now. I sure will miss seeing my sweetie at lunch tomorrow. Don't go letting any other fella turn your pretty head. As soon as I can find a job and get enough money, I'll show up down there. I can't stay away from my sweet Emma Rose for long. When I come, I want to take you back to our place by the river. Even though it didn't end well last time, that place will never lose its magic as far as I'm concerned. I hope it won't for you either.

How is Penny doing? I hope life is settling down for her by now. Give her my love and tell her I pray for her and her family often.

I'd better close. The smell of bacon calls me from the kitchen. Write me soon, sweetheart. I'll be waiting to hear from you. I miss you so much. I feel worlds away from you. Dream of me, please.

I'll always love you,

Noah

I dropped my head back on the couch. *Dream of me—a* coincidence? Had to be. Noah was long gone, and I was determined to find out exactly how long. I couldn't wait to know more about this "family favorite." Lifting the stacks of letters from the box, I counted them—seventy-nine in something over a year. "I think he was smitten with you, Mother. What on earth happened between the two of you?"

I looked at the clock above the sink and returned the box to the coffee table drawer. I'd read more later. Kate would be waiting to have lunch with me, and my PJs and furry house shoes had to go.

Chapter Eight

"Caroline! Over here."

Kate stood and waved from the far corner of the restaurant courtyard. Although three-and-a-half years my senior, she looked remarkable. Tall, blonde, and a stylish dresser, she never tired of trying to pass herself off as the younger of us. Because I opted not to color my white hair but preferred to call myself an "arctic blonde," she often pulled it off.

The Magnolia's midtown courtyard in Asheboro, sheltered by a large canopy of trees, was an ideal setting for us to reconnect on this gorgeous spring day. For me, losing our mother last fall had reinforced the fact that time is fleeting, and the moments we spend together are important. I knew Kate felt the same.

This afternoon we'd mix business with pleasure. Lunch first and then time sorting through Mother's things. Cleaning out her house was a difficult task, but one made easier in the company of a sister who'd always been my best friend.

"You were easy to spot." I gave her a big hug. "Love your yellow blouse. Is it new?"

"My latest consignment find." She twirled around. "Pretty good, huh?"

"I'll say. It's flattering. Makes your blue eyes pop. You always manage to find the best bargains. It's way past time for a joint shopping spree." I draped my sweater over the back of the chair, sat down, and opened the menu. "You hungry?"

"Famished." She pushed a long strand of hair from her eyes. "I didn't have a chance to eat this morning. Laura called. The boys are on spring break, and she's about to go stir-crazy with Emalie plus the two boys at home. She was starved for adult conversation. I didn't have the heart to cut her short."

I suppressed a laugh. "Oh, how I remember those days, but they slip away all too quickly." I scanned the menu. "I'm starved too. Let's order. What looks good to you?"

"Hmm. What doesn't?"

We both settled on the chicken pasta salad with fresh fruit and large glasses of sweet tea. After the waitress took our orders, I could contain my excitement no longer.

"Kate, since you're the oldest," I winked, "do you remember if Mother ever mentioned a boyfriend named Noah?"

"A boyfriend? No. Can't say that I do." She shook out her napkin and placed it in her lap. "Why do you ask?"

"I went over to her house yesterday to drop off some packing boxes, and while I was there, I spent time looking through her trunk. I came across a box filled with letters— seventy-nine, actually—from a young man named Noah Anderson."

"What?" Her eyes widened as she slid her stylish readers up into her hair and leaned in. "You're joking, right?"

"No. I'm serious. And you know me, I couldn't shut it off last night. Most of his letters were mailed from Jonesville, so I was online till two this morning searching for his obituary."

"And . . .?"

I paused as the waitress placed a basket of crackers and two Mason jars filled with tea in front of us.

"I didn't find his, but I found his sister's. She died in 2010. Noah was listed as a predeceased brother." Folding my arms on the table, I leaned in. "You're not going to believe this—I spoke with his niece on the phone this morning. She lives in Hickory."

Kate sipped her tea and slid back in her chair. "You're right. I don't believe it. And why on earth would Mother leave letters for us to find?" She swirled the straw in her tea. "I don't even want to think about her loving anyone besides Daddy."

"Kate, we always knew that only death would part those

two. They were married thirty years for heaven's sake. Aren't you the least bit curious as to what her life was like before Daddy?"

She straightened her back and plunked her tea jar onto the table. "No."

I sighed and reached for the crackers.

Over lunch, she softened as I filled her in on the details of my conversation with Noah's niece, Mary Ann. With little to go on, our imaginations ran wild, and by the time we'd finished eating, she was eager to explore Mother's things. Perhaps today, we'd find another clue to her life beyond the Rainbow Restaurant and her mysterious young suitor, Sergeant Noah Anderson.

Penned in by boxes, I cleaned out Mother's mahogany secretary, the desk she'd willed to my youngest daughter, Ashley. Kate sat in the middle of the floor, surrounded by reminders of Daddy. Among the precious keepsakes were his worn leather wallet—a Father's Day gift from me when I was twelve, the gold cufflinks he'd worn on Kate's wedding day, and his wire-rimmed glasses.

"Kate. Come look at this."

She glanced up from fingering through a box of trinkets. "What?"

"Just come here."

She groaned as she lifted her sixty-something body from the floor. "This better be good."

I held up a faded brown photograph of several soldiers standing on the sidewalk in front of the Rainbow Restaurant. "Do you think one of these men could be Noah?"

"Maybe. Is anything written on the back?"

"Only a date . . . 1938." I passed it over the mountain of boxes for her to see.

Taking it from my hand, she studied it. "Hmm, the year certainly fits. Mother was always good about documenting things. I'm surprised she didn't write names on the back." She held out her hands. "Pass me the box. Maybe I'll find another that will give us a clue."

While she thumbed through photos, I pulled a manila envelope from the bottom drawer. Discovering a floral, cloth-covered journal inside, I leafed through pages of random notes, original verses, newspaper clippings, and cards. A black-and-white postcard of the Rainbow was taped inside the back cover. The image of the restaurant's sleek art deco décor, with its highly polished floor and shiny Formica lunch counter, reflected a simpler time. I could envision Mother waiting tables there as a young woman.

After hours of sorting through boxes and sharing poignant moments sprinkled with laughter, Kate looked at her watch. "I've got to go soon. I thought perhaps we could go through some of Mother's jewelry before I leave. I'd love to have something of hers to wear. How about you?"

"You read my mind."

I returned the journal and photos to the drawer, then dropped my tired body onto the soft bed. Kate pulled a round box from Mother's dresser drawer, took a seat beside me, and dumped the contents onto the coverlet. "I know there's nothing of real value here—Mother liked to keep it simple—but a few of these pieces are sentimental to me."

"Me too." I ran my fingers through the shiny treasures and remembered specific occasions and certain items we'd given her. "Do you have something in mind you want?"

"I do." She selected a bangle bracelet with a small silver heart. "Would you mind if I keep this? Daddy gave it to her on their twenty-ninth wedding anniversary, their last before he died."

"Not at all. If you want it, take it." I picked up a silver necklace. "I can't think of anything I'd rather have than this tiny cross."

"Good choice. Where did Mother get it, anyway? I never thought to ask."

"I haven't a clue, but she wore it for as long as I can remember." My eyes widened as I flipped it over. "I didn't know it had a Scripture reference inscribed in it, did you?"

"No." She took it from my hand, scrunched her eyes, and read, "Proverbs 17:17. What does that verse say? Do you know?"

"I don't." After she passed it back, I fastened it around my neck. "I'll look it up later."

Kate glanced at her watch again. "It's almost four. I need to run a couple of errands before going to Laura's for dinner tonight. If it's all right with you, I'll put Daddy's things back in the chest-of-drawers next time we come." She held out her arm to admire the bangle now paired with her watch.

"No problem. I'll finish here and call you later to arrange another workday."

"Sounds good." She gave me a parting hug, then walked down the hall to the door.

I examined each bauble and bangle with new eyes as I dropped them one by one into the box and then returned it to the dresser. Afterward, I scooped Daddy's things into my arms and arranged them neatly in the top drawer of his chest. As I stepped away, a shiny object protruding from underneath it caught my eye. I reached down and picked up a key. Attached to it was a round tag with two words written in Mother's hand—*deposit box.*

Chapter Nine

Sunday, June 26, 1938

Emma shifted in the wooden church pew as beads of sweat rolled from under the loosely tied bun at the nape of her neck and trickled down her back. Amid sporadic bouts of fanning herself with a cardboard fan, she studied Jesus' face printed on its surface. She wondered if He looked anything like His picture. Was He as kind as the painting made Him out to be? His almond-colored eyes emitted warmth and compassion, but she wasn't sure the artist had gotten it right. The memory of Penny's little sister struggling to breathe replayed in her head. What type of God would allow little Anna to suffer? With flicks of her wrist, she flapped the fan, sending stray strands of hair fluttering in the breeze. She questioned if God even heard her prayers. He certainly seemed in no hurry to do anything about Anna's situation.

Amid trying to keep cool, worrying about Penny and the baby, and anticipating the afternoon with Noah, she heard little of Pastor Gardner's sermon. It was a good thing she wouldn't be eating lunch with her older sister, Lily. She would quiz her about the morning's message to see if she'd paid attention. Today the only thing she knew was the sermon text was from John—First, Second, Third, or the Gospel, she wasn't sure.

Emma liked First Baptist. It was Penny's home church and was only a couple of blocks from Mama T's. The large, red-brick, Romanesque Revival-style structure was a far cry from the modest white clapboard church she'd walked to as a child with her mother and sister. For a city church, people were friendlier than she thought they'd be—except for Mrs. Priddy.

The plump white-haired lady always sat two rows in front of her. Emma couldn't help but notice her stoic and somewhat distracted demeanor. The fact that she carried a large, black Bible that she never opened—not even to follow along with the morning's reading—always puzzled her. Emma had made it a game to see how many Sundays would pass before she could make Mrs. Priddy smile. Today was the seventh, and she hadn't seen her pearly whites yet, assuming she had some.

"Let's bow our heads in prayer as we close." The wooden steps creaked beneath Pastor Gardner's feet as he stepped into the aisle and prayed while walking toward the door.

Anxiously fanning herself, Emma glanced at her Elgin wristwatch, a graduation gift from her deceased mama, and prayed his prayer would be short. Noah would be at the house in less than an hour. Today was his last opportunity to drive Tucker's car, and he'd vowed to make the most of it. He'd found a spot near the Cape Fear River, the perfect place for a picnic, and was itching to take her there.

"In the name of Jesus, Amen . . . and have a wonderful Lord's Day."

Exiting the pew, Emma cast her eyes downward to avoid eye contact with anyone, but several women from the prayer circle made a beeline for her.

"How's Anna getting along, Em?"

She wished she could say the precious child was improving, but she didn't believe it herself.

"Please tell Penny we're praying for them."

At least it was nice to know so many ladies were talking to God about Anna. Surely if He didn't listen to her prayers, He'd hear theirs.

Anxious to get home, she attempted to skirt through the line of parishioners waiting to greet the pastor but was forced to succumb to its gradual flow. At the door, she shook his hand. "Thank you for your fine message today, Pastor Gardner." She didn't consider her compliment lying. She knew his sermon must have been a fine one, even if she hadn't heard it.

Once outside, she darted down the steps, lost her footing, and collided with—of all people—Mrs. Priddy. As the elderly lady grabbed the handrail, her Bible soared through the air and landed face-open on the steps below. Its contents scattered along the sidewalk. Whirling around, Mrs. Priddy peered over her glasses, which now sat cockeyed on her nose, and gave Emma a stern look—more stern than usual even.

"Oh, I'm terribly sorry. Don't worry. I'll get it for you." She scrambled to gather the papers, bookmarks, and photographs and stuffed them back into the large Bible. "Please forgive me, ma'am," she said as she held it out in disarray. "I think it's all here."

Mrs. Priddy repositioned her hat, straightened her glasses on her long, slender nose, and snatched the disheveled black book from her hand.

Emma swallowed hard and grappled for words. "Uh, that's certainly a lovely hat you're wearing today."

Mrs. Priddy shuddered and mumbled a terse reply.

Conjuring a smile, Emma wished her well, then broke into a run toward Maiden Lane.

"Hey, Chum! You'll be happy to know the swing is all yours today." Emma brushed her hand over the cat's fur as she breezed by. "I'm going on a picnic." As the screen door clapped shut behind her, she bounded up the stairs two at a time. "Mama T, I'm headed up to change. Noah will be here shortly."

"I hear you, child," she hollered from the kitchen. "I'll pull out the picnic basket and pack your things."

Emma kicked off her heels and shed her clothes as she darted through the bedroom door. After grabbing her aqua-striped clam-digger britches and white sleeveless blouse from the wardrobe, she threw on her new canvas Keds. Spending the day by the river with Noah and dipping her feet in the cool waters of the Cape Fear would be lovely.

"Please let me help you, Mrs. Turner." Noah took the large basket from Mama T's hand and grinned at Emma. "My goodness, this is heavy. What on earth did you put in here, Em? More than a few sandwiches, I'd say."

She laughed and shifted her eyes toward her landlady. "Only a couple of slices of pound cake."

Mama T rolled her eyes. "Clever, missy, real clever." She handed her a quilt and shooed them toward the door. "Run along, you two, and have a good time. You couldn't ask for a prettier day." She wagged her finger. "And Emma, promise me you won't get too close to the water."

"Yes, ma'am. I'll be careful." She looked at Noah and grinned.

"A young boy drowned in that river last year—such a sad thing. They've never located his body."

"I remember Lily saying something about that. It was a horrible tragedy. But on a lighter note, what are *your* plans for the afternoon?"

"I think I'll visit Polly. She's feelin' much better since her surgery. I may even celebrate Sis's recovery by makin' some blueberry ice cream." She pursed her lips and peered over her wire-rimmed glasses. "It'll sit good with the pound cake 'round my middle, won't it, child?"

Emma laughed as they followed Noah to the car. He placed the basket on the backseat and opened the passenger door for her. After giving Mama T a peck on the cheek, she threw the quilt beside the basket and slid in. A day by the river with Noah was the perfect prescription for the summer heat and a welcome reprieve for her weary body. Yes, Pastor Gardner, today was shaping up to be a mighty fine Lord's Day.

It was a short drive to the northern edge of town where the Cape Fear River cut through the heart of the state on its way to the Atlantic. Its lush green banks, home to wood ferns, creeping phlox, and sweet shrubs, were a sharp contrast to the river's deep black waters. The area was a popular hangout for local residents—a place to retreat and forget the rumbling threat of America being pulled into a full-scale war with Germany and her allies. The thought of Noah leaving for war right when she was getting to know him was a worry that lurked beneath the surface of her heart. One she dared not voice for fear it would become a reality.

Noah looked at home behind the steering column of the large sedan. She admired his strong profile beneath his yellow cabbie hat. His thick, dark eyebrows, long lashes, and angular features all complimented his boyish good looks and southern charm.

"Noah, you say you're a history buff. Answer this." She brushed her windswept hair from her eyes and pulled a few strands from her mouth. "Do you know how the Cape Fear River got its name? I've lived in Cumberland County all of my life and have never heard anyone say."

"I wondered too when I came to Bragg." He braked for the stop sign. "A fella in my platoon said explorers called it the Cape Fair because of its beauty. Later, when Sir Richard Grenville's ship almost wrecked on the shoals near Wilmington, he renamed it the Cape of Fear. Over time, it was shortened to Cape Fear."

She gave his shoulder a playful push. "Looks like you pass with flying colors. I've always heard the river's beauty is deceptive. Divers say anyone who jumps or falls in is at God's mercy. After four or five feet down, it's total blackness. That's the reason rescuers never found the body of the boy Mama T mentioned." She shuddered, trying to evict her unpleasant thoughts. "I hope we can find a safe place to dip our feet today."

"The only thing I want to dip right now is my hands in that basket behind me. Aren't you hungry?"

"As a bear. I'm surprised you haven't heard my stomach growl."

He laughed and pulled the car off the road. "We're here."

She looked over at a thick grove of longleaf pines and scrubby bushes. "We are? Where's the river?"

He pointed. "Right beyond those trees over there. This place is the best-kept secret along the Cape Fear. I happened on it one day while hiking. I remember thinking it would be a great spot to bring the perfect girl. The problem was, I didn't have a girl to bring, much less the perfect one." He winked. "But now, I have both."

Feeling heat rise in her cheeks, she lowered her head to avert his gaze.

"Grab the quilt. I'll get the basket and put the top up. This day's a-wastin'."

Chapter Ten

Hugging Mama T's hand-stitched quilt close to her chest, Emma placed her hand in Noah's outstretched palm. The sweet smell of honeysuckle enveloped them as he led her toward a grove of towering longleaf pines. Hiking through thick underbrush rooted in a floor of pine needles, they stepped over fallen tree trunks and skirted around large rocks. At the sound of rushing water, the coolness of the air settled over her warm skin.

After Noah crawled through an arched opening in the shrubs, he held back the branches for her to pass through. Once inside the clearing, she straightened her back, placed her hands on her hips, and gasped. "Oh, my goodness. How beautiful."

Tall banks of rocks lined both sides of the narrow riverbed. Across it, water cascaded down a two-story rock face, then spilled into a clear pool, snaking its way into a broad part of the Cape Fear.

"Quite a sight, isn't it?"

"I'm speechless."

He held out his hand and helped her across the rocks to level ground. "I figured this would be a good place for us to eat. What do you think?"

"It's perfect. I feel as if I'm a thousand miles away from Fayetteville and its cares. Who would've ever known this was here?"

"No one, I hope." He swiped his index finger down her nose. "And don't you go a-tellin'. I've waited a long time to bring the right girl here, and I'm happy it's you." He leaned over and kissed her forehead.

Blushing, she lifted her eyes to his and smiled. "I'm glad it's me too. I wouldn't have missed this for the world."

"All right, then. Since the place and the company meet your approval, let's eat." He set the basket in front of a large rock. "I'm dying to know what you've stashed in there besides pound cake."

She spread the quilt over the moss-covered ground, then pulled out a smorgasbord from Mama T's garden—tomato sandwiches, cucumber pickles, potato salad, baked beans, and a Thermos of freshly squeezed lemonade.

"Yum! I knew you were the perfect girl."

She shot him a glance, trying to suppress a grin. "Oh, it's about the food, huh? You should watch your mouth, Sergeant Anderson. One more infraction and I'll report you to your commanding officer." She reached into the basket, yanked out a large slice of cake wrapped in waxed paper, and slid it behind her back. "Better yet, I'll hold your cake hostage."

He let out a belly laugh, dished a large scoop of potato salad onto his plate, and helped himself to the meal. "I'm not worried. Those puny arms are no match for me." He turned to face the falls, braced his back against the rock, and took a bite of his sandwich.

Twenty minutes later, with a satisfied grin, he said, "This was quite a feast. Thank you. And be sure to thank Mama T for me." He polished off his second piece of pound cake and washed it down with a cup of ice-cold lemonade. "Let's take a look around. We should forge a path to the creek and dangle our feet in the water."

"Sounds good to me. Lead on."

Noah folded the quilt while Emma placed the remnants of their lunch in the basket. Taking her hand, he edged her down the steep bank to a large, flat rock jutting into the water. With Noah steadying her, Emma kicked off her shoes and dipped her toes in the strong current. "Yikes." Gasping, she yanked her foot from the water. "It's freezing."

He laughed and pulled off his shoes. After rolling up his pant legs, he sat and slipped both feet into the water. "Aw, come on. It's not cold." He patted the rock at his side. She tentatively followed his lead and allowed the swiftly moving current to wash over her feet.

As they sat in silence, taking in the beauty around them, Emma didn't sense the need to fill the empty space with idle chatter. She wondered if Noah felt the same. She'd never experienced a relationship that seemed so right. It scared her—and yet it was as refreshing as the water that spilled over her feet. "What a beautiful place. I think I could sit here forever. How about you?"

"With you by my side . . . you bet." He reached for her and pulled her closer.

Scooting next to him, she looped her arm through his. Usually, she'd be too shy to make such an overt move this early in courtship, but with Noah, she felt safe. It was easy to be herself with him. "Do you think we'll get to come back here? We'll have to ride the bus, you know."

"It's been nice having Tuck's car, hasn't it? But we'll come back. I promise."

"The river must remind you of home. Do you miss it much?"

"A lot. That's why this place is so special to me. Certainly uncharacteristic of the Sandhills. Have you ever been to the mountains?"

She shook her head. "Nope. Nor the ocean. I've only read about them."

"You should come home with me one weekend. You'd like it . . . and my family. I know they'd love you, especially Sadie. You two could swap books. I'm sure she's had a few dates with old Tom herself."

She laughed. "Yeah. Tom gets around. I'd love to compare notes with her." Noah's words made her heart beat faster. The thought of stepping outside of her small hometown, meeting his family, and seeing places she'd only read about thrilled her. "What do you miss most about home?"

"My family, of course, and the people. The residents of Jonesville are good God-fearing folks—sincere, hardworking, give-you-the-shirt-off-their-backs kind of people. And I miss the quiet. Lying on my bed at night and seeing the mountain behind our house silhouetted against the moonlit sky. It's quite a sight. A bit different from a barracks filled with twenty bunks and forty snoring troops."

She laughed.

His voice grew sober. "Nothing at home quite prepared me for the reality of life in the army as a medic—wheeling patients around, setting up IVs, drawing blood, changing bedpans. Don't get me wrong, I like my job. It's rewarding, but there's nothing like home."

"Are you afraid of going to war?" She rested her head on his shoulder and tightened her grip on his arm as if it would somehow hold her fears at bay.

"I don't know. Maybe. And then, maybe I'm not smart enough to be scared. I've not had to face the reality of it, and until I do, I guess I won't really know." He picked up a handful of smooth stones and tossed them one by one into the water. "They say there can be no bravery without fear. Our training teaches us to put mind over matter, to move past any fear or doubt, and do the jobs we're trained to do. All I know is I'd hate to leave my family—and you, now that we're getting to know one another."

"Hmm. I agree." She splashed her feet, trying to lighten the weight of his words.

"If needed, I'd be proud to fight for those I love and represent my country, but I hope we don't have to get involved in this horrible war. War always brings heartache."

Looking above at the river birch tree that had taken root between the rocks and towered over their heads, he reached into his pocket and pulled out his army knife.

Emma peered around him. "What are you doing?"

He nudged her away and chuckled. "Hold on. You'll see."

She watched as he carefully carved NFA and ERW into the trunk's softwood and followed the letters with 6-26-1938. After leaning back to admire his handiwork, he turned to face her. "Whatever comes, Emma Rose Walsh, as our initials remain carved in this tree, so will today remain etched in my heart forever."

As she opened her mouth to reply, thunder clapped overhead. Jumping, she looked up at the sunny blue sky. "Wow. Where did that come from?"

Noah turned and pointed to dark clouds moving in behind them. "A storm's coming. We should get back to the car."

As the wind swept through the trees and rustled the leaves overhead, she stared at the rushing water and frowned.

"Come on, Em. We'll come back. Mama T will skin me alive if anything happens to you." He grabbed their shoes, then scaled the bank and pulled her after him. As they gathered their things, the bottom dropped out of the clouds. "Run," Noah said, shaking open the quilt and throwing it over their heads

Scrambling barefooted through bushes and across pine needles with the quilt flapping above them, Emma couldn't contain her laughter. Even a stormy day with Noah was a good one.

After reaching the car, Noah threw open the passenger door for Emma, dropped the basket in the trunk, and hopped behind the steering wheel. "Whew," he said, shaking the rainwater from his arms. "So much for the drought."

Trying to catch her breath, she wiped the water from her face with the quilt. "Yes. We've needed a good earth-soaking rain, and I'm thankful for every drop."

He slipped on his shoes and cranked the engine, then turned south onto State Road 401. As the slow, steady shower intensified into a violent downpour, the car's wipers failed to clear the transparent sheet of water from the windshield. With every mile, Noah pressed his chest closer to the steering column. Then, as quickly as the showers had come, the rain slowed to a sprinkle, and the sun broke through.

Emma straightened in her seat and pointed. "Look. Maybe we'll see a rainbow. Wouldn't that be the perfect ending to a perfect day?"

He glanced over and smiled. "Yes. The perfect ending to a perfect day with the —"

As the car's tires lost contact with the pavement, Emma clamped her eyes shut, pressed her hands against the dashboard, and screamed.

Noah wrestled with the wheel, but his efforts weren't enough to counter the car's backward motion. Skimming across the road's wet surface, it spun around, slammed into the trees, and sent the sounds of crunching metal and breaking glass echoing through the towering longleaf pines.

Lying on her back with rain-drenched pine needles piercing her skin, Emma opened her eyes to a deafening silence. Struggling to focus, she peered through a thick pillar of smoke. She blinked, then blinked again as the faint colors of a rainbow appeared overhead.

Chapter Eleven

Still in grass-stained clothes, Emma sat barefooted in the chair beside Noah's bed. Pulling her legs tightly against her torso, she propped her chin on her knees and watched the rise and fall of his chest. His 6'2" frame lay helpless. His face was bruised and swollen. A large bandage above his right eye covered a gash that had required fourteen stitches.

The horrible accident replayed in her head. They'd come very close to meeting their Maker. Though thankful God had spared them, she wondered why He'd permit a delightful afternoon to end in such a horrific way.

"Psst! Emma." Penny peeped around the door. "May I come in?"

"Of course." Jumping to her feet, she ran and hugged her friend. "Thanks for coming."

Penny tiptoed over to Noah's bed. "How's he doing?"

She wanted to say okay, but her fears transcended her faith. Now, stuck in a quagmire of doubt, she harbored a thousand unanswered questions. "The doctors say it's too early to know. He's suffered a severe blow to his head. It'll be days before they can determine the extent of his injuries. In the meantime, they'll keep him sedated to reduce brain swelling." She wrapped her arm around Penny's waist. "It's hard to conceive that only yesterday we visited Anna, and now . . . now, this."

Penny tenderly rubbed her back. "Life has a way of throwing us unexpected curves, doesn't it?"

Emma nodded and thought of Penny's mother's death and

of her current bedside vigil with Anna. "I'm sure you know better than anyone. How's Anna today?"

"No change—but she *is* holding her own."

"Holding her own is good." She wished she could give her friend the hope her eyes pleaded for. "Have you been home at all since they admitted her?"

Shaking her head, she walked to the door and looked down the hall through the glass. "No. I've been too afraid to leave the waiting area. Dad's there now, so I stepped out to check on you and Noah." She tucked her long, auburn hair behind her ears and returned to the bedside. "When Dad overheard a nurse at the desk mention your name, he asked about you. She was kind enough to give him Noah's room number." Dropping into a chair, she let out a bewildered sigh. "I came the minute I heard. What on earth happened?"

Emma settled back in her seat across from Penny. "Noah and I had the most wonderful day." As memories scrolled across the silent screen of her mind, she shared every detail. It felt good to laugh about how she and Noah must have looked while running to the car with the quilt flapping over their heads, and of how they kept bumping into one another as she tried to match his long strides. Then, as the remembrance of their heartfelt talk by the river rushed in, she covered her face with her hands.

Penny scooted to the edge of her chair and patted her friend's knee.

"We were on our way home when the car skidded and spun out of control, throwing us headlong into ..." Her words caught in her throat as she stared at the floor and relived the tragic event. "Thankfully, an older couple in a car behind us saw our car run off the road and hit the tree. The lady was so kind. She never left my side while her husband drove to a nearby house to call for help. If it hadn't been for them ... I'm not sure when anyone would've found us. Except for a few scrapes and bruises, I checked out fine. But Noah, he—"

Penny pulled a handful of tissues from the box on the nightstand and passed a few to Emma.

Dropping her head, Emma silently struggled with why Noah had been injured, and she'd walked away. "He's been unconscious ever since and hasn't shown any signs of response. I'm so worried about him. I can't explain the connection we have. Noah's unlike anyone I've ever met." She sniffed. "The thoughts of losing him ..."

Penny grasped her hand. "Oh, honey, don't even think about it. He'll pull through this. You'll see."

Emma leaned back in her chair and looked at Noah.

"He's strong, Em. Very strong."

"I want to believe you're right, but—" She shook her head to dismiss her thoughts. "The doctors also suspect a back injury. They'd hoped to move him to Station Hospital at Bragg, but he wasn't stable enough. We should know more from the X-rays by the end of the week. All we can do is wait and pray." She paused, then wide-eyed stared into Penny's face. "You should see the car. It's a miracle we survived."

Penny shook her head in disbelief. "Is there anything I can do for you? Something I can get? Someone I can call? Does Mama T know you're here?"

"I called her from the desk, but evidently she's not home from her sister's. I'll keep trying. The hospital called the base. They'll get in touch with Noah's family."

Penny rose from her chair. "I hate to go, but I've got to get back to Anna. I'm sorry this happened. If you need me, you know where I am—around the corner on the left. Please come and get me if anything changes or you need to talk. In the meantime, I'll pray and expect a miracle for Noah."

"Thanks. Your prayers mean the world to me." She gripped Penny's hand as they walked to the door.

Penny turned, desperation filling her eyes. "Please continue to pray for Anna. Her little body's so frail. I'm not sure how much longer she can hold on."

Emma's throat tightened. "You know I'll pray, and the ladies in the prayer circle told me to tell you they're rattling the gates of heaven on her behalf."

She smiled. "And they will too." She hugged Emma. "Dad said he'd be happy to give you a lift home tonight. He'll come and get you as soon as visiting hours are over."

"Wonderful. Tell him I appreciate it." She opened the door. "You hurry on now and get back to Anna. I'll be okay, and I'm trusting Noah will too."

Penny nodded and turned to leave. "I believe that."

Emma left the door ajar, switched off the lights, and returned to Noah's bedside. Brushing his hair aside, she kissed his forehead and collapsed in her chair. Tilting back her head, she closed her eyes and hoped when she opened them again, she'd find this all was a horrible nightmare.

The next day

Emma stepped inside the Rainbow and lifted the shade on the door. Cee was on the phone at the register. He nodded and smiled broadly.

"Perfect, Fran. I appreciate your willingness to help out. Come in around three, and we'll talk about the rest of the week when you get here. And thanks again." He placed the receiver on the hook, skirted around the counter, and gave Emma a warm hug. "Am I happy to see you. You gave us all a real scare yesterday. How are you feeling?"

"A little stiff and sore, but I'm good. It's a miracle we're even alive. I guess you've heard Noah didn't fare as well."

"We did. One of his friends from the base called to fill us in." He shook his head. "I'm terribly sorry. He's such a great fellow. Any news this morning?"

"I haven't checked. The doctors said it will be a few days before we see much improvement."

"Well, I appreciate you showing up for work. I know it's not easy."

"I'm grateful I'm able to. With Penny out, I know you're stretched. Besides, I need the diversion. Staying busy is better than sitting around wringing my hands all day." She slipped off her sweater and put it along with her purse in a drawer behind the counter. "Did I hear you say Fran's coming in later?"

"Yes. She'll help as long as we need her."

"What a doll." She put on her apron and readied her tables for opening. Mondays were slow, but hopefully, today would be different. Three o'clock couldn't get here fast enough.

The brakes of the 3:40 Hay Street bus hissed as it came to a halt. Emma stepped closer to the curb as the doors flew open.

"Hiya, sunshine."

"Good afternoon, Sam." Climbing the steps of the empty bus, she smiled at the short, stocky driver and dropped her token into the meter.

"Y'all busy today?"

"Packed. Unusual for a Monday." She collapsed on a seat several rows back and slid toward the window. It felt good to sit down and not be bombarded with questions. She wanted to put yesterday behind her.

"Glad to hear it. My riders are giving it stellar reviews." He released the air brakes and inched the bus into the traffic. "One day, I'm gonna bring the wife and give it a try."

"You should do that." She took a silver compact and tube of lipstick from her purse. "Ask to sit in my section. I'll take good care of you."

"Sure will. The Wellonses are fine people, hard workers. I hope business holds. They deserve the best." He lifted his cap and wiped the sweat from his brow with his sleeve. "Have you met their boys?"

"Oh, yes. They're a couple of stem-winders."

"Yep. They keep things a-poppin', that's for sure. Their boy Benjie is in kindergarten with our youngest. Why, the other day ..."

Sam's words melted into the distance as her thoughts drifted to Noah. As much as she wanted to know how he was today, she'd resisted the urge to call the hospital. She believed no news was good news. Sometimes it was easier, not knowing.

"Em. You okay?"

She jumped at Sam's voice, straightened in her seat, and met his troubled eyes in his rearview mirror. "Yeah. Sure, Sam. I'm sorry. I'm somewhat distracted today." She applied her new raspberry-red lipstick, patted her nose with powder, and dropped the makeup into her purse.

"Where ya headed?"

"Highsmith. I have a couple of friends there, and it's hard not to worry about them. I hope I find them better this afternoon."

"I hope so too, sunshine. A visit from you should do the trick."

She smiled and shook her head. "I wish it were that easy."

After exiting the bus at the corner of Hay and Bradford, she walked up the hill to the hospital. Once in critical care, she peered through the door of Anna's ward. Except for labored breathing, she lay still. In the adjacent waiting area, Penny dozed. Emma was glad to see her resting. Four nights in the hospital had taken their toll.

After turning the corner at the nurses' station, she walked down a few doors to Noah's room. The blinds on the door were shut. She held her breath and peeked into the dimly lit room. She was surprised to see someone sitting in the shadows beside the bed.

Chapter Twelve

A young man dressed in a neatly pressed khaki uniform leaned forward in the chair. With elbows resting on his knees and strands of sandy-blond hair falling across his forehead, he fidgeted with his cap.

Emma walked toward him and extended her hand. "Good afternoon. I'm Emma—Emma Walsh."

Startled, he jumped to his feet and shook her hand. "Emma. It's good to finally meet you. I'm Tucker Baldwin. Noah's told me a lot about you."

"It's nice to meet you, Tucker." As she spoke his name, her thoughts returned to the crumpled burgundy convertible at the base of the large pine tree. "It was . . . *your* car we were in yesterday."

He nodded. "Yes, ma'am."

"I don't know what to say. I'm so sorry." She dropped her chin to avoid his gaze and shook her head. "It was a swell car, and you were so nice to loan it. You must be very upset with us."

"It was an accident. It could've happened to anyone. Cars can be replaced." He shifted his eyes and motioned toward Noah. "There's only one of that fellow right there. Maybe if I hadn't loaned him the car . . ."

She placed her hand on his arm. "No. Don't say that."

"I'm thankful you both survived. After seeing my car today, I'd say it's nothing short of a miracle."

"I agree. A huge one." She gestured toward the chair. "Please. Please, be seated." She sat across from him and was impressed that a man with his rugged good looks would possess such a compassionate and soft-spoken demeanor.

"What's the latest on my friend?"

She crossed her legs and shook her foot. "I haven't heard yet today, but yesterday I was told it would be a week or so before we'd see significant change. Once the brain swelling subsides, they'll know more. As for his back injury, we're waiting on the X-rays. Hopefully, the results will be in soon."

"I hope so too. Waiting is a hard thing."

Shifting in her chair, she slid her mama's silver locket back and forth along the chain around her neck. She looked at Noah. "He'll be devastated when he wakes up and finds out about your car. You mean the world to him."

Tucker smiled. "We've been through a lot together since we came to Bragg. As medics, we've pulled some mighty long night shifts."

"Where are you from?"

"Kentucky—Louisville. Lived there all my life. Flew back to the base late last night. I took full advantage of my ten-day pass. Had to see my girl, you know." He chuckled. "And my family, of course." His words drifted. "It was great to be home."

"I can imagine." She smiled. Tucker's "my girl" comment reminded her of how Noah had reacted on her behalf at the Rainbow the afternoon they met. She choked back tears. The idea of being *his girl* sat well with her.

"How long had it been since you'd been home?"

"Last Christmas. It looks like it will be Christmas again this year. Being so far away is tough." He checked his watch and slid to the edge of his chair. "I hate to cut this short, but I'd like to drop by and see Penny before I have to catch the five o'clock bus back to the base."

"You know her?"

"Best waitress around. She waits on me and several of the guys from our platoon every Friday night at the Rainbow. We were all crushed to hear about Anna."

"Of course. I should've known. Your visit will mean a lot to her."

He stood, picked up his cap from the arm of the chair, and patted Noah's shoulder. "You hurry and get well, soldier boy. We've got places to go, things to do, and officers to aggravate."

Tucker walked toward the door. "It's gonna be tough pulling duty tonight without him." His large brown eyes reflected his pain. "I'll call and check on him tomorrow. Please let me know if anything changes or you need something. My number is at the nurse's station."

She nodded. "Thanks. Maybe by the time you call, there will be good news to share."

"I pray so."

As he turned to leave, she took hold of his arm. "Oh . . . and Tucker. Thank you. Thanks for coming and for understanding. Noah's mighty fortunate to have a friend like you."

"Don't mention it. Wouldn't have it any other way, ma'am. He's like a brother to me." His voice cracked. "You try and get some rest, okay?"

"I'll try." She watched as he walked down the hall, his tall, lean frame held straight as an arrow, his stride smooth and steady. Noah would be relieved to know his friend wasn't upset about the car. His biggest challenge would be to forgive himself.

She glanced at his motionless body. He hadn't changed positions since she'd walked into the room. Turning out the light, she stepped into the hallway.

Emma pushed open the heavy oak door with the leaded-glass window shaped like a cross. After taking a deep breath, she exhaled slowly and collapsed onto the front pew. It was hard to believe it had only been two days since she'd been in this place of solitude with Noah and Penny. A lot had happened since then. It seemed like a lifetime ago, and yet, she felt trapped in a horrible nightmare in which time refused to move forward and morning never came.

She raised her eyes to the picture of Jesus with outstretched arms and missed her mother's sound advice more than ever. *God will never leave you or forsake you, Emma Rose. Remember that child.* She knew those words were true, but today she was conflicted. On the one hand, she felt as if God had somehow lost sight of her world, and on the other, He'd never felt closer. Reflecting on the accident, she remembered opening her eyes to the rainbow overhead. It wasn't the first time God had used a rainbow in her life to remind her of His presence. If only she could roll back the events of yesterday and relive her time at the falls with Noah. Maybe her older sister Lily had been right all along. *Get your head out of them clouds, Em. Don't you know happy endings are only found in fairy tales?*

She approached the altar and knelt at the railing. After praying for Anna and Noah for what seemed like the trillionth time, she sat on the kneeling bench and allowed the room's peacefulness to wash over her.

"Attention! Emergency in critical care. Emergency."

The somber alert spilled throughout the hallway and penetrated the chapel's heavy oak door. Respecting no boundaries, it invaded the furthest corners of Emma's mind and struck fear in her heart. Frozen, she lifted her eyes to the picture of Jesus and retched a silent scream—*No.* Her stomach flew to her chest. Scarcely able to breathe, she gripped the altar railing and pulled herself to her feet. Her legs were like rubber, and her feet like lead. Willing one foot in front of the other, she reached for the brass knob and cracked open the door. The alarm's deafening sound, now unleashed, flooded the chapel's tranquil air. She wanted to run to Noah's side but was unsure her legs would carry her and feared what she might find.

Sliding her hand along the rail, she inched her way to the end of the hall and turned the corner. Nurses moved through the corridor with the rote precision of a drill team. Noah's door was shut. Slowly pushing it open, she peered into the darkness. He hadn't moved. For the first time since the accident, his stillness comforted her. The room was a quiet oasis. She lifted a prayer of gratitude for his well-being, sank into the chair, and closed her eyes.

Anna! Oh—Anna! She leaped from her chair, darted into the hallway, and bolted past the nurses' station. From the corner, she could see Penny standing in the hall with her back and head pressed against the wall. She ran to her. "Penny, what's happening with Anna?"

Penny turned, her eyes, large and frantic. "Oh, Em. Anna started coughing and couldn't get her breath. Then she started convulsing." Her hand flew to her chest. "Nurses are working with her now." She slid down the wall and locked her arms around her knees. "I'm afraid. She's so weak."

Emma joined her on the floor and pulled her close. While ordered chaos unfolded as if in slow motion, the voices of the doctors and nurses faded into the background. The only sound Emma could hear was the pounding of her heart—its steady rhythm reminding her of the uncertainty of life.

Jesus! Where are you?

Chapter Thirteen

Thursday, June 30, 1938

The afternoon was warm and humid. Emma was grateful for the overcast skies as she walked the few blocks to First Baptist. Wanting extra time to process the events of the past few days, she'd left the house early. She couldn't imagine Penny's pain. It had been over a year since her mother's death, and now Anna. Emma's only consolation was to picture the sweet child cradled again in her mother's arms, surrounded by heavenly angel choirs.

There was so much she didn't understand. The Scriptures said God causes all things to work for good on behalf of those who love Him, but she couldn't see how even God could bring anything good out of this heartache. She'd need to trust Him to do what He said He would, but the problem was, she hadn't learned to master that.

As she turned onto Anderson Street, cars lined both sides. At the end of the block, men in dark suits directed traffic into the church parking lot. The sanctuary would be full, perhaps standing room only. Penny and her family were well-loved and long-time members of First Baptist. According to Mama T, after the Watsons moved from Tennessee, Penny's father made sure their family was in church every time the doors opened. For years, he'd served as chairman of the deacons and currently served as Sunday school superintendent. Her mother had taught in the children's department and had helped on the food committee with Mama T.

As Emma walked past the black hearse, organ strains of

"Jesus Loves Me" drifted over the sidewalk and stuck in the warm, moist air. Inhaling deeply, she climbed the stairs of the impressive red-brick structure, where an usher greeted her at the door and offered his arm. She was grateful for the support. Without it, she feared her knees would buckle. After scanning the packed pews, he seated her on the left of the center aisle toward the front. Although a young family inched down to make room for her, she felt alone. *If only Noah could be with me.*

Pulling a handkerchief from her purse, she lifted her eyes to Anna's tiny white casket. A tuft of the child's curly blonde hair and a portion of her angelic face were visible. Dressed in white and surrounded by the casket's satiny pink lining, she resembled a baby doll. It was all Emma could do to maintain her composure.

She checked her watch. Soon, the family would be led down the aisle and seated on the wooden pews across from her. She turned to view the somber faces throughout the congregation. Men sat stoically as if it took every ounce of their strength to not weep. Women of all ages dabbed their eyes with cotton handkerchiefs, while others anxiously swatted the moist air with cardboard funeral-home fans.

Emma spotted Mama T on the back pew. She looked spent. For the past two days, she'd cooked meals for the family and earlier had helped serve them lunch in the church basement.

A couple of rows in front of her, Mrs. Priddy sat in her usual seat. She was dressed in a dark navy-blue dress with a small white-collar buttoned high at the neck. A white rose was pinned to its pleated bodice. Her typical harsh countenance was softened as she sat with her head bowed, brushing an occasional tear from her cheek.

As the chords of "Jesus Loves the Little Children" flooded the sanctuary, the eyes of those in the congregation followed two men who approached the casket. After carefully tucking the satin lining around Anna, they lowered the lid and moved the spray of pink rosebuds and baby's breath to the center of the casket. Composed, yet visibly shaken, they turned and walked down the aisle.

Pastor Gardner's raspy voice broke the suffocating silence. "Please rise for the family."

Wooden floors creaked beneath the feet of the crowd as they stood. Emma wept at the sight of Penny leaning heavily on her father's arm, her younger brothers close on her heels. Penny's aunt walked behind them, guiding the boys with her hands on their backs, while relatives from Tennessee followed. With eyes fixed straight ahead, Penny seemed oblivious to the people who filled the room. Emma heard her muffled sobs as she passed.

Once the family was seated, Pastor Gardner motioned for the congregation to take their seats. As he placed his large, worn Bible on the pulpit and looked over his flock, the crescendo of creaking floors and wooden pews came to an abrupt halt. "We're gathered here today to celebrate the life of one of God's precious children, Anna Patricia Watson. Her short life serves as a reminder of the brevity and uncertainty of our days here on earth."

His words struck Emma with surprising force, then receded into the background as her thoughts raced to the accident. Only by God's grace were she and Noah alive. After losing her parents, she'd hadn't given death a passing thought. It was an older person's malady. But this week, death had crossed the line. It had tramped into the soil of her mind. Ravaged the lives of those she loved and uprooted a tender shoot. It was a merciless thief with defiant disregard for person or age, and she resented its audacity. *It had better stay away from Noah's door.*

Tender voices of the children's choir lassoed her thoughts and pulled her back into the beautiful, historic sanctuary. For a moment, her heaviness lifted as the sun's rays filtering through stained-glass windows showered the room with delicate hues of multicolored light. She observed Penny. A slight smile briefly erased her grief-stricken lines. Emma wanted to pull her friend close and to somehow erase her pain and make her load lighter.

After the service, Emma stepped onto the church portico and scanned the crowd gathering below. Bittersweet memories paired with quiet laughter filled the air as family and friends offered words of consolation to the Watsons. Penny stood beside the black limousine, dressed in the stylish black suit Emma had helped her pick out the day before. She looked tired, yet at peace, as she talked with a visibly shaken Mrs. Priddy. The stalwart lady nodded and gave her a lingering hug before taking the white rose from her chest and pinning it to Penny's lapel. She then kissed her forehead and walked away, blotting her cheeks. As Penny moved to seat herself in the shiny black vehicle, Emma ran down the steep brick steps and embraced her.

"The service was lovely. Such a sweet tribute to Anna and her brief time with us here on earth." She brushed a stray curl from her friend's cheek. "I wanted you to know I won't be at the cemetery. Cee needs me to come in as soon as I can get there."

"Sure, Em. I understand. You and Mama T have already done so much. Please give the girls at work my love and thank them for filling in for me."

"Of course."

"I'll call Cee tomorrow. I plan to be at work Monday. The sooner I can return to my routine, the better."

"It'll be great to have you back. We've all missed you. And please, know we'll continue to pray for you." Emma gave her a parting hug. "I'll call you tonight."

Stepping away from the curb, Emma waited as Penny seated herself in the car. After her brothers darted for places by her side, the doors clicked shut, and the sedan inched its way into the street. A continuous stream of cars fell in behind. When the solemn procession turned right onto Old Street, Penny waved. Emma blew her a kiss, then walked down Anderson toward Maiden Lane.

A young couple in front of her strolled hand in hand. Their laughter and unmistakable affection for one another made her miss Noah all the more. Not being able to share the events of the last few days with him had been difficult. She longed for the remarkable way he made her laugh, even in the most trying times.

"Hey, Emma! Wait up."

Turning, she saw Tucker cutting his way through the crowd.

Chapter Fourteen

"Mind if I walk with you? I'm on my way to the Hay Street bus stop."

Emma smiled. "Not at all. I could use the company." Tucker looked handsome in his gray double-breasted suit, white shirt, and striped tie. "I didn't see you inside. Where did you sit?"

"We were on opposite sides. I saw you when you walked in." He took off his fedora and loosened his tie as a breeze sliced through the afternoon mugginess.

"For a moment, I didn't think I'd have a place to sit." She pressed her navy straw hat securely on her head and pulled her long, brown hair to one side. "The service was sweet, wasn't it?"

"It was. The children's choir got to me, though. Not a dry eye around."

"That's for sure. Their sweet faces and angelic voices lifted my spirits, and after everything that's happened this week, they needed lifting." She wondered if her life would ever return to normal—or worse yet, perhaps this *was* normal. It certainly wasn't how she'd envisioned her newfound freedom to unfold. For the first time since moving away from Hope Mills, she was homesick.

"We all needed it. How about that little boy with dark curly hair?"

"Oh, my goodness, yes." Chuckling, she placed her hand over her mouth. "When he jumped off the platform and yelled, 'I'm flying!' I thought he'd dive headfirst into the flowers. Too precious."

They walked in silence. Emma tilted the brim of her hat to shield her eyes from the sun and searched for something to say, but Tucker spoke first.

"Any news about Noah?"

"Afraid not." Her answer to that question was always the same, and the longer his condition remained unchanged, the more fearful she became. "But the doctors have high hopes there will be signs of improvement soon."

"That's good to hear."

The silence returned.

She blurted, "I've got more good news."

"Swell. Let's hear it."

"Noah's mother arrives from Jonesville today."

His eyes widened. "That *is* good news. I wondered if she'd make it. I'd heard she was under the weather and might not be up to the long bus ride." He took off his tie and stuffed it in his coat pocket, giving up on fashion altogether in the muggy air. "She's such a great lady."

"You've met her?"

"I have. I went home with Noah a couple of times. Both of his parents are mighty fine people."

She felt a twinge of jealousy at the history he shared with Noah. "I look forward to meeting her. Hopefully, he'll respond to the sound of his mama's voice. Mamas have a way of getting their children's attention, you know."

He chuckled. "I sure do." They arrived at the corner of Maiden Lane. "Which way are you headed?"

She pointed to the left. Feeling the light pressure of Tucker's hand on her back as he ushered her across the street reminded her of Noah, and of how he'd pulled her close that day by the river. She motioned ahead. "I live in the two-story yellow boarding house a couple of blocks down on the right. Just past that huge oak tree up there."

"I've always loved this street. Living here must be nice. It's such a quiet oasis against the busy backdrop of Hay."

She couldn't have said it better. "I know. I'm grateful for this place. It's close enough for me to walk to town, and yet it feels like country living. And Mrs. Turner, the owner—she's more like a second mother to me than a landlady."

"How long have you lived here?"

"Since . . ." Emma grabbed for her hat, then watched as it sailed away. "Oh, no!"

Tucker darted into the street. "Don't worry, Em. I'll get it." As soon as he reached for her hat, the wind swept it inches from his fingertips. As he zigzagged through the street, dodging an occasional car, Emma laughed at his repeated near conquests. Finally, not about to be outdone, he stomped on the hat's brim. Savoring his victory, he glanced back at her, then with a long sweep of his arm, snatched it from the pavement.

"Hurrah!" She bounced on her toes and clapped at his victory, then covered her mouth to muffle her laughter. "I'm sorry. I shouldn't laugh."

Tucker took a bow, brushed off her hat, and slapped it on his head before ambling back across the street.

She held her stomach and broke into hysterical laughter, all the strain of the week releasing at that moment. "You're too much. But you do look smashing. And if I do say so myself, the navy is perfect with your gray suit."

Smirking, he took off her hat and tamped it down on her head. "There you go, my dear."

"Thank you." She struggled to compose herself. "And thanks for being such a good sport."

He bent at the waist. "The pleasure is all mine. Anything for the lady."

She felt a twinge of guilt for enjoying this time with him. She hadn't laughed like this since that day on the river. She took off her hat. "I believe I'll hold it the rest of the way. Unless, of course, you need the exercise."

"That's okay. I've had enough for one day." He wiped the sweat from his brow. "Now, where were we?"

"You asked how long I've lived on Maiden Lane."

"Oh, yes."

"Since early spring. My sister, Lily, wanted me to stay at home with her, but it's been too hard since Mother passed last fall. I needed a change . . . and independence. I love my sister, but it's best if we live apart. When I found Mrs. Turner's boarding house, Sis finally agreed to my move to the *big* city. A country girl, I wasn't quite sure I'd like it here. But I do." She glanced up at Tucker. "How long have you been at Fort Bragg?"

"Almost three years. Noah came six months before me, so when I arrived at the base, he showed me the ropes. We've been fast friends ever since. I'm an only child, so he's more like a brother."

She stopped in front of Mama T's. "This is home. I'd better run in and change for work. Thanks for the walk." She extended her hand. "The company's been nice. And, oh, how I needed the laugh." She looked into his eyes. "Sorry, it was at your expense."

He grinned. "Think nothing of it. Will you drop in on Noah later today?"

"No. I work late tonight. I won't check in on him again until tomorrow."

"Same for me. I plan to head that way before work in the morning. I look forward to seeing Mrs. Anderson. Maybe we'll run into one another there."

She unlatched the gate. "Possibly." She liked the idea of seeing Tucker again. The thought surprised her.

Tucker glanced at his watch. "I'd better run if I plan to catch the bus to Bragg. You have a good night."

"Thanks. You too." She shut the gate and watched as he jogged down the block and turned the corner. Noah was fortunate to have such a wonderful friend.

As usual, Chummy lay stretched across the swing. Emma reached down and rubbed the docile cat's belly. Yawning, he gave her a feeble meow. She envied him. After the week she'd had, she wished she could join him there, but settling into her regular routine would be best. She hoped for a better day tomorrow.

Emma stepped off the Hay Street bus. "Bye, Sam. You have a great day. I'll look for you and Liz at the Rainbow tomorrow."

As the bus pulled away from the curb, she walked up the hill toward the hospital. Between worrying about Noah and meeting his mother for the first time, it was hard for her to curb her emotions. Noah was close to his mother and had always spoken highly of her. Would Mrs. Anderson approve of her?

She chided herself for thinking of such trivia at a time like this. Enough. How would Noah be this morning? Would she find him the same? Better—or possibly worse? She shuddered.

Entering the lobby, she waved at the switchboard operator. "Hi, Lillian. It looks like it's going to be another warm day." The tall, matronly lady who wore her long hair in a rolled bun nodded and waved before picking up another call.

As Emma neared the ward where Anna had spent the last week of her life, a surge of loneliness washed over her. She didn't expect Penny to visit Noah. Walking these halls would be too painful for her anytime soon. Emma would miss their chats, which always broke up the monotony of waiting. Stopping at the door, she peeked in and prayed the outcome of the child that now occupied the bed where Anna had lain would be different.

After turning the corner at the nurse's station, she noticed Noah's door was shut. Through the blinds, she saw the head nurse with an older woman seated in the chair beside his bed. She recognized his mother from the family photograph Noah had shown her that afternoon by the river. Her snow-white hair was pulled back in a neat bun, and her expression was pensive.

Not wanting to interrupt their conversation, Emma waited in the hall. The wait tied her stomach in knots.

As the nurse left the room, Emma took a deep breath, tapped on the door, and walked in. Mrs. Anderson lifted her dark eyes and smiled. She looked weary.

Emma extended her hand. "Hello. You must be Noah's mother. I'm Emma."

Mrs. Anderson rose from her chair, brushed past her extended arm, and gave her a warm hug. "It's wonderful to meet you." She stepped back. "You're as lovely as my son said. Why he was plumb giddy when he told me about you. You must be a very special young lady."

She felt her face flush. "I don't know how to respond other than to say that's certainly nice to hear. I can return the sentiment. You've raised a mighty fine son."

"Thank you, but Noah was an easy child to raise. He always wanted to please. I'm glad he finally mustered the courage to introduce himself to you. He spoke of you every time he called home but said he couldn't drum up enough courage to sit in your section at the restaurant. Noah never gets in a hurry about anything and treads carefully when it comes to the ladies. He knows what he's looking for and isn't about to settle for anything less."

Emma motioned to the chair beside his bed. "Please, have a seat. You must be terribly tired from the long trip. Buses stop at every hole in the road." She sat across from her. "Where are you staying while in town?"

"With a good friend in Spring Lake. Her husband is a retired lieutenant colonel. They moved to Fort Bragg from Winston-Salem when our children were small, and we've always kept in touch." She nervously pressed out the wrinkles in her skirt with her short, plump fingers. "Both times I've come to visit Noah at Bragg, I've stayed with them. She's been an incredible support throughout this whole ordeal. She visits Noah regularly and informs me of his condition. I'm surprised you haven't bumped into each other."

"I wish I had. She sounds like a lovely person." She glanced over at Noah. "How's the patient today? I saw the nurse talking to you earlier, but I didn't want to interrupt. Did she have anything new to report?"

Her eyes brightened. "His vital signs are good, and they're very optimistic. He's showing more signs of awareness, and they hope to wean him from the oxygen over the next few days."

"That's great to hear. I feel good about Noah too—more so now that you're here. I can't imagine how hard it is for you to see him like this, but you'll be his best medicine."

"I certainly hope so." She rested her arm on the mattress and stroked her son's hand.

Emma stood up and moved closer to the bed. "I must say he looks better than he did right after the accident. The color has returned to his cheeks, and his eye isn't nearly as black and swollen. It's amazing how much difference a few days make." She walked over to the window, opened the blinds to let in the morning light, and returned to her seat. "He gets great care here. The doctors and nurses are very attentive. I've been impressed."

Mrs. Anderson leaned forward and patted her hand. "I'm thankful you didn't suffer any severe injuries from the accident, dear. Would it upset you too much to share the details of what happened?"

Emma turned her head and stared out the window as a lump rose in her throat. "Until now, I've tried not to think about the wreck and to only remember the good moments. But, if I were you, I'd want to know too, so I'll try."

She leaned back in her chair and shared about her beautiful afternoon on the river with Noah and the harrowing accident that followed. She assured her Noah hadn't done anything careless to cause the accident. "As a matter of fact, if he hadn't turned the wheel when he did, I'm convinced my side of the car would've taken the brunt of the impact. In my eyes, your son is a hero." She looked at him. "I can't wait to tell him so and thank him for saving my life."

His mother pulled a handkerchief from her pocket. "Thank you, child. Thanks for understanding and caring for my boy, like you have. She leaned over and hugged her. "The nurse said you're here every day. Now I know why Noah was attracted to you. You're as lovely on the inside as you are on the outside. Any young man would be blessed to have you as a friend."

A voice from the doorway startled them. "Knock, knock. I hate to interrupt, ladies, but do you mind if I come in?"

Mrs. Anderson shot from her chair, ran over, and threw her arms around their unexpected guest. "Now, lookie here. Tucker Baldwin. Aren't you a sight for sore eyes?"

"It's wonderful to see you again, Mrs. Anderson." He slipped his garrison cap into his back pocket. "I'm sorry it's under these conditions, but I'm sure Noah will come through this with flying colors." He nodded toward Emma. "You and I both know he's not about to duck out and leave this lovely young thing behind."

Emma dropped her head. "Thank you. You're kind."

"I know you're right," Mrs. Anderson said. You've got Noah pegged. "I think he may have found all he's looking for in Emma."

Emma felt the heat return to her face. Her prayer had been that Noah's mother would like her, but her praise had taken her off guard. Especially in front of Tucker. "Okay, you two. Let's talk about something else now."

Tucker laughed. "I think it's a great topic myself, but if you insist." He motioned toward the chairs. "Ladies, have a seat." He folded his arms and leaned against the wall, then crossed his ankles. "How are things in Jonesville? Is Mr. Anderson good?"

"Other than working too hard, Jesse's doing great. It's been a good season for his tobacco crop. He expects it will bring a pretty penny at the market in Winston-Salem this year."

"In this depressed economy, that's great to hear. Mr.

Anderson runs a tight ship. Until I came to your place with Noah, I knew nothing about tobacco farming—a fascinating process. Hard work. He deserves every penny it brings in."

Small talk and laughter filled the room. While Tucker and Noah's mother reminisced, Emma's thoughts drifted. Hearing of Noah's pranks as a young boy on the farm in Jonesville made her wish she'd been a part of those times too. There was so much left to know about him.

As the others talked, she studied his face. For a split second, she could have sworn she saw his eyelids flutter. Probably wishful thinking, but if she could will it, it would be so.

Please, Lord, bring Noah back to me.

Chapter Fifteen

Saturday, July 2, 1938

Emma balanced a tray of piping hot food above her head and worked her way through tables spread with red, white, and blue cloths. A young couple waited at the door to be seated while their two children swatted each other with small American flags.

"Here you go, Sam. For your lovely wife, the poinsettia tomato with chicken salad and a side of cucumbers, onions, and vinegar. And for you, the porterhouse steak, medium rare, with O'Brien potatoes and steamed broccoli." She placed a bottle of steak sauce in front of a glittery sparkler centerpiece. "Did y'all enjoy the parade?"

"We did. Fayetteville always does things up right for our Bragg boys. They deserve it, as do soldiers everywhere. I'm afraid our nation will be pulled into this war before it's over with."

"I hope you're wrong, but I couldn't agree more about the soldiers deserving it." She tapped the card in the wire holder displaying the dessert menu. "Be sure to leave room for some of this. Our chocolate torte is to die for."

"I bet." He winked at his wife. "Liz spotted the chocolate the minute we sat down."

"So, you should treat her, Sam. It is a special day, you know?" She scanned the room. "Good thing you left the parade early. We're filling up fast. People are happy to get in out of the heat." She topped off their water glasses. "Is there anything else I can get for you?"

After checking with Liz, he glanced at the table. I believe that's got it. It smells delicious."

"Wonderful. Let me know if the steak's not cooked to your liking, and I'll take care of it for you." She turned to leave, then hesitated. "And, happy anniversary."

As she started toward the kitchen, the brass bell above the door jingled, and Penny walked in. Elated, Emma zig-zagged between the tables and threw her arms around her. "Oh, my, it's good to see you come through that door. Are you here to work?"

"Not today, Em. Soon, though. I'm here for lunch." Her eyes twinkled as a playful grin spread across her face. "The Rainbow is the talk of the town, so I thought I'd drop in and see what the buzz is all about." She laughed. "Word on the street says the food's terrific and the service is over-the-top. What's your response to that?"

Emma planted one hand on her hip and gave an assenting nod. "Sounds like words you can bank on to me."

Catching a glimpse of Penny's lighter side refreshed Emma's spirit. Her friend's laughter had been buried far too long—long before Anna's illness.

"Will you eat alone today, or is someone joining you?"

"There will be two of us." The twinkle in her eyes returned. "I'm dining with Mrs. Priddy."

Emma's eyes bulged. "Mrs. Priddy? Really? How . . . wonderful." But as the words rolled off her tongue, she questioned their truthfulness.

The bell jingled again as the robust lady walked into the crowded restaurant and scanned the room. Penny was quick to wave and motioned for her to join them.

"Good afternoon, Mrs. Priddy." Emma's words caught in her throat. "Welcome to the Rainbow."

Her somber appearance gave way to a broad smile. "Thank you, Emma."

Teeth. Mrs. Priddy has teeth. She rebuked her thoughts, but it was the first time she'd seen the woman smile. "Please follow me, ladies." She led them to a booth in the far corner. "Will this table be okay?"

Penny nodded. "It's perfect."

After lifting two menus from behind the napkins, Emma laid them on the table at their places. "I'll be right back with your water."

She pulled two glasses from the shelf behind the counter and reached for the pitcher of cold water. Cutting her eyes toward the table, she watched the mismatched pair chat with one another like a couple of long-lost friends. What could have triggered this encounter? She'd give anything to be in on the conversation.

"Whoops." She jerked the pitcher away and watched as water flowed over the rim of the glass and onto the shiny Formica countertop. Grabbing a towel, she wiped up the spill and collected her thoughts before carrying the glasses to the table.

Mrs. Priddy was a mystery. There had to be an intriguing story beneath her dour demeanor. Perhaps Emma would make her the subject of her first novel—the one she'd always believed she'd write—the New York Times bestselling one.

The lunch rush was over. Most of Emma's customers had left except for a young private with his parents and Penny with Mrs. Priddy. Immersed in conversation, they seemed oblivious to everything else around them. After Emma made sure both tables had what they needed, she prepared the others for the evening dinner crowd. It was difficult for her to keep her mind on her work and off the intense conversation taking place in the corner booth.

Once the military family left, she seated herself for lunch at a table across the room from Penny. She feigned reading her book and kept an ear tuned to their exchange. To her dismay, their hushed tone made it impossible for her to follow. At one point, Mrs. Priddy dabbed her eyes with her napkin. Why this stalwart lady was in such a vulnerable state was hard to imagine. Later, Mrs. Priddy rose from the table, gave Penny a lingering hug, and walked toward Emma. Pulling a white envelope from her purse, she laid it in front of her.

Emma looked up. "What's this?"

She choked out her words. "I owe you an apology. Penny will fill you in on the details. Although there's no excuse for my rudeness, I think after you talk with her, you'll understand why I've been so distant." She leaned over and gave Emma a quick hug. "I'm sorry."

Before Emma could reply, Mrs. Priddy turned toward the door and walked away. She sat stunned, then looked at Penny and shrugged.

"Give me a few minutes to clean off the table," Penny said as she cleared the dishes. "Then, I'll come and fill you in while you finish eating."

Emma gazed at the envelope in front of her and warily slipped the notecard from within. Opening it, cash dropped to the table. Her eyes widened as she picked up the bill and nestled it to her chest while she read.

Dear Emma,

How do I even begin to apologize for my insolence over the past few months? I hope you can find it in your heart to forgive me.

I regret I've ignored the wreck and your ongoing sorrow concerning Noah's injury. I know you've had to miss a bit of work, so I've enclosed a few extra dollars. Perhaps it will help cover your bills.

Know I pray for you and Noah, and that I trust he will be okay. Let me know if I can ever do anything for you.

Sincerely,
Beatrice Priddy

The words blurred on the page as her emotions rose to the surface. She unfolded the bill—ten dollars—enough to cover a week's salary. She looked toward the door and stared, her heart pounding.

Penny slid into the seat across from her. "What's the matter?

Emma's eyes widened as she held up the bill. "What on earth is going on? I'm speechless."

Penny gasped. "Oh, Em, it's a sad story and explains so much. As hard as it was for me to lose Anna, I can take a certain amount of consolation in her death after talking with Mrs. Priddy today."

"How's that?"

"She wanted to share the details of her story with you but said it was too painful to tell it all again."

"What, Penny? Tell what?"

"I know this tragedy took place before you came to live in Fayetteville, but do you remember when the little boy drowned in the Cape Fear River?"

"Yes. It upset Mama. I remember her talking about it several times before she died. I understand they've never located his body."

"You're right." She reached across the table and laid her hand over her friend's. "Em—that little boy was Mrs. Priddy's grandchild. Only five years old. His name was Richie."

She pressed one hand to her chest. "No. That breaks my heart."

"Losing her grandchild was hard enough, but what made things even worse was Richie was in her care that day."

"How horrible." She slowly shook her head and dropped her face into her hands.

"She'd promised to take him fishing for his birthday. They were standing on a rock at the edge of the river when she turned to get something from her tackle box and heard him scream. Unable to swim herself, she watched in disbelief as he struggled in the water, then shouted to a man a few hundred yards away. By the time he got there, the little boy was gone. He never resurfaced."

Emma sat glassy-eyed. "Oh, Penny. That explains so much. I don't know how anyone manages to get through something so dreadful."

"She's lived under a ton of guilt, and her daughter no longer has anything to do with her. She's very lonely. When Anna died, she said it was difficult for her to come to the funeral, but she wanted to console me in my grief. No one understands that kind of heartache unless they've experienced the same pain."

"I'm sure."

"The bright spot in all of this is during Anna's funeral, Mrs. Priddy realized she could no longer shoulder her grief alone. Pastor Gardner's message, along with the spirit of celebration that day, opened her eyes to the reality of her condition. After all her years attending church and serving on committees, she discovered she'd never known Jesus as her Savior. For the first time, she understood salvation was not about what she could do for Jesus but about what He'd done for her—real salvation was about a relationship with Him. During the funeral, she prayed in her pew and gave her heart to Christ. She'd never been able to reconcile the idea that a loving God would allow her to lose her grandson—especially while in her care. She asked Him to help her overcome her anger and bitterness. Since then, God's shown her she had no control over Richie's death, and she had to forgive herself. After the funeral, she came to me and shared that through Anna's death, she'd found new life."

Emma blotted her cheeks with her napkin. "Oh, how wonderful. I saw her talking to you after the service and was surprised when she took the white rose from her dress and pinned it on your lapel. It was so unusual to see this stodgy lady warm and broken."

"Yes, she'd worn the rose to the funeral in memory of

Richie. After her experience, her heart was filled with so much joy, she wanted to share her gratefulness with me by giving me the rose in memory of Anna. She told me today when she pinned it on my lapel, she felt the weight of her grief lift. Since the accident, she's believed she didn't deserve to be happy or smile again. She's suffered several tragedies throughout her life, and the loss of her grandson sent her over the edge. When you came to the church, she saw much of herself in you at that age—bright-eyed and filled with hope for the future. You reminded her of the life she never had. It was hard for her to be happy for you, and she couldn't bring herself to befriend you."

Emma shook her head in disbelief. "There were so many times I was tempted to snap back when she was mean to me, but I tried to do what I knew I should instead of what I felt like doing. It shows me, we never know what causes a person to be the way they are. I'm so glad I didn't act on my emotions. It pays to be gracious." She took Penny's hand. "Thank you for sharing this with me. I'm happy for you both. I know this helps to soften the pain of losing Anna. I must admit I questioned God's love and actions myself when Anna died. I remembered the verse about all things working together for good, but I couldn't imagine how the death of one so young and innocent could work for good or bring God any glory. Now I know. Hearing this reminds me God's words are always true, and He never makes mistakes. We need to trust Him with every part of our lives—the good and the bad. Trusting has always been hard for me."

"Trusting God can sometimes be hard for all of us, Em. Today's experience has helped to strengthen us both." Penny looked at her watch. "I've got to run and pick up the boys. They begged to go home with their friend for a while after the parade." She leaned over and hugged her. "I'll see you at work on Monday."

"That makes me happy. I've missed you so much."

"Oh, and one more thing. Please help me pray for Mrs.

Priddy's relationship with her daughter and that somehow Richie's remains will be found. I want them to be able to put his body to rest and find solace in this horrible ordeal."

"I certainly will. God knows where his remains are. And if He can reveal and forgive our sin, He can uncover Richie's whereabouts and bring healing to Mrs. Priddy's family."

Emma slid the ten dollars with the note into the envelope and slipped it into her apron pocket. After clearing the dishes from the table, she walked toward the kitchen.

"Thank you, Lord. Once more, you've reminded me that with you, all things are possible. No one is beyond your reach. Today, I choose to trust you completely with my life—and Noah's."

Chapter Sixteen

Emma tossed her purse on the table by the door and pulled the scarf from her hair. "Mama T, I'm home."

"Back here in the kitchen, child."

Emma gave her a peck on the cheek, then dropped into a chair at the table where Mama T was rolling out a pie crust. After kicking off her shoes, she plopped her elbows on top of the checkered cloth and rested her chin in her hands. "Wow, what a day. I'm bushed." She peered into the blue spatterware bowl in front of her. "Yum. Peaches. Is that pie for us?"

"It sure is." Mama T brushed several sprigs of hair away from her face with the back of her hand.

Emma smiled at the flour smudge she'd left on her plump cheek—the mark of a true master chef.

"After cooking for Penny and her family over the last several days, I thought it was time for me to treat us to something nice. Sis brought me fresh peaches from Candor this week. I want to make sure I use them before they go bad."

Watching Mama T throw herself into her cooking, always calmed Emma. Her confident moves throughout the kitchen assured her the world was still on its axis, regardless of how crazy things got beyond the door of 405 Maiden Lane.

"You're late tonight."

Emma stood and pulled a glass from the cabinet, then poured milk from the bottle on the table. "I ran by to check on Noah after work." After returning to her seat, she propped her feet on the chair across from her.

"How's he doin'? Any improvement?"

"There is. Yesterday, the doctors began to wean him from the oxygen.

"Wonderful. Hearin' that makes the little bird in my heart sing."

"Yours and mine both. Did I tell you Noah's mother is in town?"

"You told me she was comin', but I didn't realize she was here. I'm glad to know she got in okay. So, you've met her?"

"I have. When I went to the hospital yesterday morning, Mrs. Anderson was in Noah's room. She's a sweet lady. Very down to earth and easy to talk to. I feel like I've known her forever."

"How long will she stay?

"She goes home next Sunday for a doctor's appointment the following week. I'm happy she's here. It'll mean the world to Noah when he wakes up."

"How about his back?"

"Whenever he's alert and stabilized, they'll schedule surgery to repair several vertebrae. His healing will take a while, but he should be okay. Good news, huh?"

"I'll say. God certainly answers prayers."

"That's not all God's done. Listen to this. Guess who came into the Rainbow for lunch today?"

"Hmm. Let me see." She looked up from her work. "Penny."

"How'd you know?"

She laughed. "I talked to her yesterday. She told me she was havin' lunch with Mrs. Priddy. Did she show up?"

"Yes. I couldn't believe my eyes. I wanted to be in the middle of their conversation so bad."

"Did Penny ever tell you why they met?"

"She did, but first, I have to tell you this. On Mrs. Priddy's way out, she came over to my table and apologized for being rude to me these past few months. Can you believe that?"

"Oh, my. That *is* big."

"You've only heard half of it. You may want to sit down for the rest."

"Goodness, child. You've really got my curiosity up now. Let me get this pie in the oven, and I'll do that. I'm ready to take the load off my feet and have a cup of hot tea anyway."

Mama T pressed the dough into the bottom of the pie plate and poured the peach mixture on top. After covering it with another crust, she pricked its surface with a fork, crimped the edges, and slid it into the hot oven. "Go ahead, Em. Start your story." She hung her apron on the pantry door and tucked several loose strands of hair back into her bun. After pulling a cup from the cabinet, she poured her tea and settled into the chair opposite Emma.

Emma shared the stories of Mrs. Priddy's salvation experience and the ten dollars. "And did you know the little boy who drowned in the river last spring was her grandson?"

"I did. The news broke the hearts of everyone at the church. I've heard her daughter and husband moved away and have nothing to do with her now. Richie was their only child."

"That's what Penny told me. Will you help us pray his body will be found, and their family will be restored?"

"Of course I will, Em. You know, the Bible says two are good, but a cord of three strands is not quickly broken. There's power in people comin' together and agreein' in prayer."

"Thank you. I knew we could count on you." They sat quietly for a moment. "Mama T, do you believe in love at first sight?"

"Sure do."

"Well, Lily says that at nineteen, I'm not old enough to pick a husband."

"A husband?" Her eyes widened as she reached for the teapot and refilled her cup. "Have you been holdin' out on me, Emma Rose?"

"No. Not really. But I have thought a lot about Noah and me. I know I haven't had many boyfriends, but there is something about my relationship with him that's different. I've never felt so comfortable with a man—like it was meant to be. You know what I'm saying?"

Mama T nodded and let Emma continue to pour out her heart.

"As I've prayed for him this week, my feelings for him have grown stronger. I can't explain why I feel this way, but I do. When I think back on how he turned the car so the brunt of the crash would be on his side, it reveals a lot to me about his character. Then, on Friday, I sat and listened to his mother and Tucker share about their experiences with him, and it made me sad."

"Sad? Why sad?"

"Because I couldn't share in those memories. I knew I wanted to know more about Noah. Does that make sense to you?"

"Yes, dear, it does." She sipped her tea as Emma sat silent.

"Mama T, you were married for sixty-three years. How long did you and Mr. Turner know each other before you knew you loved him?"

She chuckled. "Oh me, Emma. I'm not sure I can remember that far back." She checked on her pie, then walked over to the sink and took the lid off of an old sugar bowl. After lifting out a white pouch, she opened it with an air of reverence and pulled out a silver locket and a small, worn picture. Returning to her chair, she pushed her wire-rimmed glasses up on her nose and gazed at the photo before handing it to Emma.

"This is a picture of Albert and me the day we got married—July 18, 1873."

Emma stared at the yellowed image of the young couple and tried to find a hint of resemblance in the girl looking back at her. She didn't appear to be a day over thirteen.

"How old were you?"

"Albert was eighteen, and I was sixteen—sixteen and one day, mind you. My father had put his foot down about any young'un of his marryin' too early. He said I couldn't marry one day before I turned sixteen. So, we waited till one day after and went to the Justice of the Peace." She shook her head and let out a sigh, her eyes softening at the thought of it. "As if one day, either way, would make a difference. Looking back, I don't know how we made it all those years other than love and the good Lord. We were only children."

"How did you meet him?"

"Grew up in the house right beside Albert's. Of course, our houses were barely within shoutin' distance. Both our families had large cotton fields, but neighbors were neighbors then. We knew one another. Relied on one another. Sat on each other's porches after a long, hot summer day. Albert and I would play while our parents talked. He'd shoot marbles, and I'd make sand pies and feed them to my homemade rag doll. We simply grew up knowin' we were gonna marry."

Emma nodded. "Tell me the story behind the locket."

Mama T picked it up, cradled it in her palm, and read the inscription on the back: "*Now and forever. Love Al.* This was my wedding gift from him. I didn't have a present for him, but he said he didn't mind. Told me that I was all he ever wanted." She laughed. "Through the years, whenever we'd have a tiff, I'd remind him of that. Then he'd quip back under his breath with, 'So I guess I was too young to know better.' Anyway, he'd earned some money pickin' cotton and helpin' his dad around the farm. He'd been savin' it up for a while. I felt like the richest girl in the world with his locket hangin' around my neck and me on his arm."

"What a sweet story." Emma straightened in her chair and sniffed the air. "The pie."

Mama T jumped up and yanked open the oven door. "Jeepers. Caught it in the nick of time." She grabbed a couple of potholders from the counter and pulled it from the rack. "Rather brown around the edges, but it'll be fine. I like a toasty crust."

"Me too."

As she placed the pie on the cooling rack, the phone rang. Emma looked at the clock—11:15 p.m. "Who would call this late?"

Mama T lifted the receiver from the phone on the wall. "Hello. Yes, this is Florence Turner."

Emma could hear the operator's voice on the other end of the line.

"Sure. I'll hold." Mama T leaned against the pie safe while the operator made the connection. "Yes, she's here. Let me get her." She held the phone toward Emma. "It's Mrs. Anderson. She says she has something she needs to tell you."

A lump lodged in her throat. She tentatively took the receiver from Mama T's hand. "Hello, Mrs. Anderson. Is something wrong?"

"I'm sorry to call you this late, dear, but I knew you'd want to know."

Her heart raced. "Has something happened to Noah?"

"I didn't mean to scare you by calling this late, but I knew you'd want to hear the news right away. It's good, Emma. Noah's awake. He's sitting up. He's awake."

She fell against the pie safe and slid to the floor. "Oh, I can hardly believe it's happened. Our prayers have been answered. Does he know you? What's he saying? Anything?"

"Yes, he knows me, and the first thing he said after he asked what happened was, 'How's Emma?'"

Tears streamed down her face. "Oh, thank you, Jesus. How's he feeling?"

"He's groggy and says his back hurts, but otherwise seems fine. He's asleep now."

"Well, tell him I'll come by to see him first thing in the morning." She looked at Mama T and smiled. "Thank you so much for calling me. Try to get some rest, and I'll see you both in the morning."

"You too, dear. Sweet dreams."

Mama T took the receiver from her and returned it to its cradle. "Hallelujah, praise the Lord! This has been one day of miracles for you. I'm happy to hear Noah's back."

Emma sat, staring at the pattern in the linoleum. "Can you believe it? Noah's awake. He's going to be okay."

Mama T extended her hands. Emma grasped them and pulled herself up, laughing, then danced Mama T around the kitchen. When they were both out of breath, Mama T teetered and grabbed hold of the sink. "Goodness, child. This is certainly a reason to celebrate. Calls for a midnight treat, don't you think?"

Emma collapsed in the chair while Mama T pulled a couple of plates and a knife from the dish drainer. She sank the sharp blade deep into the center of the peach pie. "How big of a celebration are we havin', child?"

Chapter Seventeen

Sunday, July 3, 1938

Emma pushed open the door of Noah's dimly lit hospital room. Tiptoeing, she picked up a chair and placed it at the foot of the bed. As its legs hit the floor, Mrs. Anderson jolted in her seat.

"I'm so sorry. I tried not to wake you."

"Not a problem, child." Yawning, she tossed her blanket aside and stood to hug Emma. "I'm happy you're here."

"How'd you rest?"

"The best since I've been here."

"Makes sense. I can understand why, now that Noah's improving."

Mrs. Anderson motioned for her to have a seat and dropped back in her chair. "I didn't expect to see you until after church today." She grinned. "You playin' hooky?" Glancing over at her son, she covered her mouth to muffle her laughter.

"Sure am, and I don't feel guilty about it either." She hung her purse on the back of the chair. "I couldn't get here fast enough this morning. I want to be here when he wakes up."

Mrs. Anderson snickered. "You're a few hours late for that. The nurse woke him from a sound sleep earlier to check his vitals, but he managed to drift back off. They say he's making good progress."

"What a blessing. He's been through so much." She walked over to his bed. "The bruise on his face has healed nicely."

Noah moved one leg and moaned.

Her eyes widened. "He heard me."

Mrs. Anderson moved to the opposite side of the bed and called his name. "Noah. Someone's here to see you."

He turned his head toward her voice.

"You have company, Son." She motioned to Emma. "Stand over here."

Emma moved closer and placed her hand on his shoulder. "Good morning, Noah." After no response, she leaned in. "Hey, handsome, it's Emma Rose."

He blinked several times, then opened his eyes halfway. She'd almost forgotten how blue they were. Smiling, she patted his hand. "Noah, it's Emma."

His lips eased into a slight smile.

She turned to his mother. "I believe he knows me."

"Em. My Emma . . . Rose."

"Yes." Her heart raced. "I've waited so long to hear you say my name."

He tried to speak.

She placed her finger on his lips. "It's okay, Noah. Just listen. I have something important to say." She took both of his hands in hers. "Thank you for saving my life. You may not remember what happened after we left the river, but I'll never forget it. Your response as our car skidded across the wet pavement made all the difference. By turning the wheel so your side of the car would take the brunt of the crash, I only received a few scrapes. You're my hero, Noah, and always will be." She laid her head on his chest and wept. "I prayed this day would come. I've missed you so much."

He stroked her hair and softly uttered, "Don't cry."

She lifted her head and drank in his eyes. "Oh, Noah. I'm crying because I'm happy." She moved closer and placed her lips on his. As his formed to hers, she knew she never wanted to be without him again.

A tear slipped from his eye.

Grabbing a tissue from the nightstand, she blotted his wet cheek. "It's going to be all right, Noah. Everything's going to be fine. We're together again."

He closed his eyes and smiled.

Wednesday, July 27, 1938

Emma cleared the remaining dishes from the table and glanced at the clock on the wall—8:45 p.m., almost quitting time.

It had been more than two weeks since Noah was moved from Highsmith to Station Hospital at Fort Bragg and one week since his back surgery. She wanted to visit more often, but work made it impossible. Business at the Rainbow was bustling, and Cee couldn't afford to give her more than one day off a week. After eating lunch with her sister in Hope Mills on Sundays, she'd hop a bus to Fort Bragg and stay till nightfall. Last week, Noah had grown more impatient with the long healing process. But Mama T's coconut macaroons or a slice of her chocolate pie always brought a smile to his face. That day she'd had both.

The bell over the door jingled. "Hi, Emma. You about to call it a day?"

"Fifteen more minutes." She smiled and gave Tucker a hug as he slid into the booth she was cleaning. "Do you want a menu, Sergeant, or are you simply passing through again?"

"Passing through." He winked. "I'm on another mission."

"Wonderful. You're a good courier. Noah needs to raise your pay."

Laughing, he pulled a letter from his shirt pocket and handed it to her.

"Thank you, sir." She held up her finger. "Hold on a minute." After walking behind the counter, she slid open a drawer and pulled out a book she'd been reading on her break. Slipping an envelope from its pages, she replaced it with Noah's letter, then returned to the table and handed Tucker hers. "How was he when you left?"

"Despondent." He placed the envelope in his pocket.

"Staring at the four walls day in and day out gets the best of him. He said to tell you he's counting the minutes till he sees you on Sunday."

She frowned. "I know it's hard for him." She pushed a couple of chairs under one of the tables and centered the flower vase. "What's new with you? Still hear from your girl back home?"

"No. I guess she got tired of staring at the walls too. I hear she has a new beau."

Emma paused. "I'm sorry. You were together for a long time." She tucked the menus beside the napkins and checked the shakers. "Maybe she'll have second thoughts once she realizes what a fine fellow she let slip away."

He fiddled with his cap. "Thanks for the compliment, but I've decided to call it quits. Evidently, for her, distance *didn't* make the heart grow fonder."

She slipped her apron over her head. "So, let's both call it quits. It's been a long day."

"Want a lift home? It's on my way. Besides, you haven't seen my new wheels."

"Aha. You caved and got the car you've looked at for so long, huh?"

"Yep." He followed her to the front. "It's nothing fancy, but it gets me where I need to go."

"Sure. I'd love to see it. Give me a minute to grab my things and tell Cee I'm leaving."

When she returned, Tucker opened the front door and followed her onto the sidewalk. With a sweep of his hand, he motioned toward a shiny green and black car parked at the curb. "There she is. What do ya think?"

Emma rolled her eyes. "Nothing fancy? It looks new."

"It's new to me. It's a 1933 Chevrolet Master Coupe. Has a rumble seat to boot."

She walked the length of it. "It's beautiful. The street lights really show it off. I'm happy for you. Noah and I have felt so bad since the accident."

"As you see, Em, cars can be replaced, but there's no replacement for good friends. I'm thankful you weren't hurt, and my buddy is on the mend." He opened the passenger door. "Hop in."

She dropped into the seat and rested her head against the cushion as he slipped behind the wheel and pulled onto Hay Street. "This is really nice. Thanks for the ride. It's been a long day. I'm not sure my feet would've made it."

"My pleasure." He noted the book in her lap. "What are you reading now, Miss Bookworm?"

"The sequel to *Look Homeward, Angel*—Thomas Wolfe's *Of Time and the River.*"

"How is it?"

"Wonderful. I love Wolfe's writing. One day, I hope to visit some of the places he writes about. But for now, I'll have to live vicariously through his protagonist as she moves from North Carolina to New York. Have you ever been?"

"I haven't. The extent of my travels has been home and back again. Nothing exciting, but I hope I can say the same several months from now. With the way things are heating up in Europe with Germany, a voyage overseas may be in my near future."

She slapped his arm. "Hush. Don't say that. I can't bear the thought of it." Straightening in her seat, she turned to face him. "One of my customers plans to visit the World's Fair in New York next year. It sounds amazing. There will be exhibits highlighting 'the world of tomorrow.' I hope it lifts people's spirits out of this horrible depression. Sometimes I think things will never change. Hard times is all I've ever known."

He pulled up in front of the boarding house and turned off the engine.

"Thanks, Tucker. Please don't bother to get out. I'm sure

my feet can take me from here." She leaned over and hugged him. "Maybe I'll see you on Sunday. Tell Noah I'll be there, same time."

"Sure will. He'll be happy to hear it. And thank goodness, it'll give my ears a welcome reprieve. That boy's got it bad for you."

"I sure hope so." She laughed and stepped onto the sidewalk. "You rest well. I plan to."

After a warm bath, Emma pressed both pillows against the headboard and slid between the cool sheets. Pulling them up around her, she slipped Noah's letter from her book and eased it from the envelope. His words would be the perfect ending to her exhausting day.

Station Hospital
Fort Bragg, NC
Wednesday, July 27, 1938

  Hello Sweetheart,

   I received your card and letter a few minutes ago. You'll never know how glad I was to hear from you. I miss you so much. Tucker said he is going into town today and will pass by the Rainbow, so I thought I would write you before he leaves.

   I'm so lonesome. I laid here today and looked out the window so long I imagined you getting out of the car and coming up to see me. The sad part was I awakened to find it was all a dream. I realize your work schedule only gives you a chance to visit once a week, but I do miss you. Why? Because I love you!

The doctors say my back is healing, but it's very painful. Because of the six hypodermics, the doctors gave me after surgery, my legs are still numb. My recovery will take longer than I expected, and as I feared, I'll be forced to take early leave from the Army.

Early leave?

That wouldn't be so bad, except I know it will take me miles away from my darling Emma Rose. But I can't think about that right now. I must focus on the days I have left with you.

What? Miles away? From me? Absolutely not.

Tucker just stuck his head in the door and said he's leaving in five minutes, so I'd better wrap this up. Try your best to visit me on Sunday. I can't wait to lay my eyes on your beautiful face.

Tell Mama T hello and thank her for the chocolate pie and cookies she sent. You're blessed to have such a wonderful landlady, not to mention someone who cooks like she does.

Take care, my love, and don't get distracted by all the soldiers eating at the Rainbow. Be sure to shoo them away from my seat. Let me know if any of them make eyes at you, and when I'm well, I'll reckon with them.

Will write again tomorrow. I'll always love you,
Noah

She dropped the letter to her lap. She couldn't imagine life in Fayetteville without Noah. A lump welled in her throat. *No. This could never be. You just returned to me, Noah Anderson.*

Chapter Eighteen

The acrid smell of disinfectant threatened to steal Emma's breath as she walked toward Noah's third-floor room. Unadorned plaster walls, radiators, beadboard ceilings, and linoleum-tiled floors were bathed in shades of white as daylight spilled from the corridor's adjacent rooms. Some were occupied with soldiers reading the Sunday papers or napping, while others erupted with the laughter of young men playing board games. Military personnel dressed in starched white uniforms busied themselves at their stations as patients visited with family and friends in crowded alcoves. Emma knew Noah's transition from medical technician to patient had to be difficult. He was accustomed to giving help, not needing it.

The rhythmic, mechanical sound of a flickering light overhead greeted her as she entered the stark white room. Four empty, white-iron beds with rumpled linens hinted of the well-being of their missing occupants. Noah, dressed in striped pajamas and a blue robe, sat by the window with his back to the door and gazed into the parking lot below.

Sneaking behind him, Emma covered his eyes with her hands. "Betcha can't guess who."

Jerking, he grabbed hold of her wrists. "Hmm ... let's see. Bet I can. I'd know your voice anywhere, Ellen."

"Ellen?" Scowling, she edged around his wheelchair, hands planted firmly on her hips. "And so who is Ellen, sir?"

"Oh, pardon me. Of course—it's Emma. I must be talking

out of my head again. Probably the pain medication." He laughed, pulled her to him, and kissed her. "Aren't you a sight for sore eyes."

She placed the palm of her hand on his forehead and pushed him away. "You're a nut. At least you must feel better. It's good to hear you joke again. I've missed this playful side of you."

"I watched for you. How'd you come in?"

"I came through the side door this time. I'm learning my way around this place." She pulled up a chair, sat facing him, and held both of his hands. "So now, tell me how you're feeling."

He smiled. "Today's a good day. Not as much pain."

"Wonderful."

He squeezed her hands. "And now that you're here, I don't feel any pain at all."

"Are you insinuating I have a numbing effect on you, sir?"

"Maybe this will 'rouse your senses." She laughed and handed him a brown sack. "Something from Mama T—more pie. This time, it's lemon meringue."

"Yum! Tell her I said thanks. It'll be gone before bedtime. I'll have the aide put it in the icebox for me."

"Are you ready to break out of this room?

His face lit up as he straightened in his chair. "So ready."

"Where shall we go today? Downstairs to the sunroom or for a stroll in the courtyard?"

"Outside sounds great. I'd love some fresh air."

She helped him position his feet on the footrests and pushed him toward the doorway.

"We need to stop at the second floor on the way down. Tucker's on duty this evening and has asked us to come by. He has something he wants to show you."

"Oh? How intriguing. By all means, then, let's roll."

She wheeled him down the corridor and stopped at the nurse's station to pass off the pie before getting onto the elevator. A man in a white surgical smock held open the door for them as she rolled him inside.

"What floor, Noah?"

"Two, sir."

He pushed the button and leaned against the wall. "That's a mighty fine-looking nurse you've got there."

"I agree. This is my girl, Emma Walsh." He turned to her and winked. "Emma, this is Captain Carlisle, the surgeon who carved on my back."

"Whoa there, boy. What a way to introduce the guy who put you back together. You make me sound like a butcher."

She shook his hand and smiled at their banter. "Nice to meet you. I'd say you must've done a fine job. He seems to be getting along well."

Captain Carlisle laid his hand on Noah's shoulder. "This one will be okay, but he needs to take it slow for a while." He squinted his large brown eyes at her. "Think you can hold him down?"

"I'll do my best. But he does get mighty cantankerous at times."

He nodded. "Sounds about right."

Stepping off on the second floor, Emma followed Noah's directions down the hall to the adjoining wing. Tucker spotted them from the nurse's station and came to greet them. He patted Noah on the shoulder. "So, how's the patient today?"

"Better now that Emma's here."

"I bet so." He leaned over and gave her a hug.

She brushed her hair away from her face. "Noah said you have something you want to show me."

"That I do." He grinned at his friend. "How about it? You game?"

"Ready as I'll ever be."

Tucker pushed him out of the hallway and into an empty waiting area. After lifting the footrests on the wheelchair, he stood in front of it. "Let's see what you can do, my man."

Noah looked at Emma and grinned. Putting his hands on

the arms of his chair, he grimaced and slowly hoisted himself up.

Emma gasped, then stood wide-eyed as Tucker steadied him and backed away.

With clenched teeth and several shaky steps, Noah moved toward her.

Bouncing on her toes, she clapped. "Look at you, hon. You're walking."

Tucker followed closely with his hand at Noah's back. At his first teeter, he grabbed him and eased him into his chair

Noah flashed a broad smile at Emma and let out a deep sigh. "Not great, but it's a start, right?"

"I'd say. I had no idea the doctors would have you walking this soon. You'll be out of here in no time." She bent down and kissed his forehead.

"Okay. I can take a hint. I'll leave you two love birds alone. Some of us have work to do, ya know." Tucker shook Noah's hand. "Good going, pal. Keep it up." He turned. "It's nice seeing you again, Em. Take good care of him."

"I'll try."

After taking the elevator to the first floor, she pushed Noah to the end of the hall, where a young private opened the door to the courtyard. Stopping under a tree, she positioned his chair beside a two-tiered fountain and took a seat on the brick wall that encircled it. "This feels like a nice cool spot."

Noah inhaled deeply. "The air feels wonderful, and the best part is there's no antiseptic smell." He looked around at the other soldiers and their visitors. "I'll be glad when I can leave this place."

"I'll be happy for you too, but your recovery will mean you're closer to leaving me." She stared at her reflection in the fountain's pool. Splashing the water with her hand, she watched as the ripples distorted her image.

"I know. It's bittersweet, isn't it?"

Shaking the water from her fingers, she shifted her body to face him. "What do you think the future holds for us, Noah?"

"Nothing but the best, sweetheart. As soon as I get well and get a job, I'll come back for you."

She reached for his hand and gripped it. "Can't you stay in Fayetteville and look for a job? I can't bear the thoughts of you being over a hundred miles away."

He kissed her fingers. "My only option right now is to go home. It'll be a while before I can work again. Who'd take care of me until then? Pop says he'll dress my wound, and I know Mama will make sure I'm well fed." He brushed the hair from her eyes. "It's the only thing that makes sense right now."

"I know. But I wish there was another way."

"Me too."

They sat silently staring into the water as several military planes flew overhead. As they faded into the distance, Emma spoke up. "There is one good thing. At least you'll be out of harm's way if we get pulled into this horrible war in Europe. I am thankful for that."

He slid his finger down the bridge of her nose. "Like Mama T says, baby doll, there's always a silver lining."

She smiled, scooted up next to his chair, and looked into his eyes. "Tell me more about Jonesville. What are you looking forward to the most when you go home?"

"That's easy. Mama's cookin'."

She sighed and shook her head. "I should have known you'd think of your stomach first." She combed his hair with her fingers. "I mean, what do you do for fun at home? Say I came to see you. Where would you take me?"

"Hmm . . . now that's a great thought. There's not a lot to do in Jonesville. It's rural, mostly farmland. I'd for sure take you over to the big city of Elkin, population twenty-five hundred. It's a popular hangout for young people." He squeezed her hand. "We'd go for a stroll down by the dam at Elkin Creek, where I'd steal a kiss. Then, I'd take you to a show at the Elk Theater, where I'd steal another kiss."

She blushed and laughed.

"Afterward, we'd grab a bite at Turner's Drug Store.

They're known for their hot dogs—best in the world—and no one makes a lemon meringue pie like Rosie."

"What? Better than Mama T's?"

"Whoops. Come to think of it, Rosie takes second place. How's that?"

"Much better, but where's the part about the kiss?"

He let out a belly laugh and pinched her cheek. "Can't overload on sugar, ya know. You've got to keep your girlish figure."

"You're hopeless, Noah Anderson."

"True. Hopelessly in love." He winked. "You really think you might come to see me?"

"Maybe."

"Wow. Wouldn't I be the cat's meow strollin' the streets of Elkin with you on my arm? A sea of people would part in front of us."

"I'm so glad you're in a good mood today." She turned his chair to shield his eyes from the setting sun. "I'll have to work it all out with Cee, but I'd sure love to come. I want to meet the rest of your family—see the mountains."

"You know what, Emma Rose?" He pulled her toward him, took her face in his hands, and kissed her. "We're going to have to make that happen." As the sun dropped behind the trees, he leaned in for another kiss.

Four weeks later
Friday, August 26, 1938

"Morning, Glory!" Cee shouted from behind the cash register as Emma came through the door. "Did you enjoy your day off? I see you survived the storms."

"I did. And some storms they were." She lifted the shade

on the door and walked toward the back. "Two nights in a row but so good for the gardens. Makes for great sleeping too. I love to hear the rain on Mama T's tin roof. It reminds me of home. I was off to sleep in no time last night."

She hung her hat on a hook in the back hall and tossed her purse in the drawer before studying the daily specials on the board and picking up an armful of menus.

"Well, I'm glad somebody got some sleep." He dropped the last of the coins into the register, shut the drawer, and shook his head. "Mary Beth and I ended up with two boys in our bed and the dog under it. Jack's afraid of the thunder, and Benjamin hates the lightning. He says God shouldn't flick the lights on and off while people are trying to sleep."

She chuckled. "Oh, how funny. Sounds like something that little fella would say."

Cee picked up his apron and cap and walked toward the kitchen, tucking an occasional stray chair under the tables as he went. "Did you get Noah off okay Wednesday night?"

Thoughts of Noah waving goodbye beneath the street lamp replayed in her head. She swallowed hard. Pausing at the seat where he'd sat the day they met, she slid her hand across the table's slick, reflective surface. "It will be mighty lonely here without him." She slipped a napkin from the container and blotted her cheeks.

"I'm going to miss him too. Noah's a fine fellow. But he'll be back again soon, Em. He's not going to let a few miles stand in the way of seeing his girl."

"I sure hope you're right." After straightening the shakers, she lingered to watch a young couple walk hand in hand past the window. "Do you think absence makes the heart grow fonder, Cee?"

"If it's meant to be, Em." He put on his cap and apron. "If it's meant to be." His voice trailed as he disappeared into the kitchen, then burst back through the doors. "By the way, Penny won't be here until after lunch. I'll need you to help cover her tables. Sarah's coming in a few hours early to help out. Think you two can handle it?"

"We'll do our best, Boss." She welcomed the prospects of a busy afternoon to take her thoughts off of Noah. She lifted her apron from the coat tree, tied it around her waist, and smoothed it out with her fingers. "Is Penny okay? It's not like her to be late."

"The boys are sick this morning." Cee's eyes mirrored his concern. "Ever since Anna's death, she's been extremely protective of her brothers—panics at the slightest sniffle." He shook his head. "Can't say I blame her, though. Her aunt will come this afternoon, so she can work." He wiped down the lunch counter. "That girl's got a lot on her plate. I hope I don't lose her. She's a top-notch waitress."

"I hope we don't either. She's the best. Not sure how I'd get along without her. She's been a big help to me since I've been here, and now that Noah's gone, I need her more than ever."

Penny's situation reminded her of her own childhood. After her papa's stroke, her mama struggled to care for their family, but God had been faithful. By his grace, they'd made it through, and she trusted Penny would too.

She checked the shakers and condiments on the tables and tucked four menus behind the napkins in each booth. Returning to the one at the window, she struggled to keep her composure. Her time with Noah had been too short. Oh, what she'd give to take his order again today. *A grilled ham and cheese with a cup of white bean soup.* If not for the accident, he'd still be here. She'd never understand God's timing.

After glancing at the large clock on the wall, she walked over to the window and flipped the switch. The red neon sign flashed: OPEN!

Chapter Nineteen

Monday, August 29, 1938
Jonesville, North Carolina
Noah

Noah set the glass of milk on the nightstand, lifted the suede box from the drawer, and dropped onto the bed. After stuffing several pillows behind his back, he flipped the box lid to reveal the stationery and pen Emma had given him. It seemed longer than five days since they'd said their goodbyes. Writing her would make the time without her more bearable.

Hello Darling,

Pop and I just got back to the house from Winston-Salem. We took a trailer of leaves over to the Southern Loose Leaf Tobacco Warehouse today. I forgot how crazy that town could be during the market. Farmers going to and fro, everyone trying to sell their wares— shoe strings, razor blades, and whatever else under the sun. Street musicians making music for any amount they can get. Then there is the medicine show, the largest horse in the world, and a six-legged mule. Yes, I said a six-legged mule. I wish you could see it all. It's a circus. I simply stood back and tried to take it in.

All the men coming and going made me think of soldiers on payday. If they'd been dressed in uniforms instead of overalls, I wouldn't have known the difference. The farmers here may not dress like other people, but their faces are honest. They're hardworking and the best human beings on the planet—at least most of them. You'd like it here, Em. I know you would. I can't wait for you to come and see where you're going to live one day.

Pop got a good price for what we took, so he's feeling pretty chipper. When he pulled in the drive, I was out of the car before the wheels stopped rolling. Once inside, I asked Mama about the mail. She was a-grinnin' and asked me if I was expecting some kind of business deal to turn up. She gets a kick out of teasing me. As a matter of fact, Pop does too. They both know I've got it bad for you.

He took a swallow of milk and returned the glass to the nightstand next to Emma's picture. It wasn't her favorite. She thought it made her look plump, but he'd insisted she give it to him. The gleam in her eyes was the same flicker that was there every time she looked at him—a look he would get lost in.

Anyway, Mama walked over to the sideboard in the dining room, and lying right there on top of all the mail in Granny's old dough bowl was your letter. I knew my sweet Emma Rose wouldn't fail me. Mama wanted me to talk with her tonight and wait till tomorrow to do my corresponding, but I told her I had to answer you right away. I'm propped up on my bed reading and rereading your sweet letter.

While in Winston-Salem today, I ate lunch with my first cousin, Helen, while Pop was at the market. She's eighteen. I told her all about you. After lunch, while we were walking back to the warehouse, that little rascal started swinging on my arm. She asked me if I wished she was Emma. I tried to act nonchalant about it all. I didn't want to tell her how I really felt. I never realized I could miss any one person as much as I miss you. Do you miss me? I sure hope so.

Helen goes to Draughon's Business College. The president of the school hopes I'll go to night school there. That's if I get a job in Winston-Salem. He said to call him if I need a recommendation. I thought that was nice of him, seeing how he hasn't met me or anything. He thinks a lot of Helen, so I guess he figures if I'm her cousin, I have to be all right too.

Pop told me about a couple of job possibilities in Winston-Salem, so later in the week, I'll check them out. I can't do any heavy lifting for a while. Sometimes I wonder if I'm ever going to be well enough to go to work for us. My heart's greatest desire is to get a job and make it possible for you to be my wife.

Noah laid his head against the headboard. The day he could make Emma his wife couldn't come fast enough. He hated the thought of her waiting tables and feared the distance between them would dampen her love for him. The temptation for her to fall head-over-heels for another GI would be great.

I was glad to hear that Penny is back at work. I hope she can go to the fair with you and Tucker next month. It's not that I don't trust my best friend, but I'd feel better if she was along.

I can hear Sadie and her boyfriend downstairs on the front porch. They went to the Elk Theatre tonight in Elkin to see *Boy Meets Girl* with James Cagney and Pat O'Brien. Ronald Reagan is in it too. It's supposed to be a funny flick. Sure wish I could take you to see it. I want to be with you so bad. Hearing those two laughing downstairs makes me miss you even more. I'm not very good with words, but what it all adds up to is I love you now and forever. Please believe it, darling, because I mean it.

I guess I'll close for now. Pop needs to dress my wound tonight. My back is feeling much better, but there is still an open place that needs more time to heal. Don't worry your pretty little head about me, though. I'll be fine. Tell Tuck and Mama T, I said hello. I sure miss everyone. I'll be down soon. I promise.

Write soon. Write me every day!

I'll always love you,

Noah

Noah folded and tucked Emma's letter back in the envelope, then held it to his nose. Its sweet lavender scent triggered memories of his last evening with Emma. Her shrill squeal and the softness of her lips on his cheek after he'd bought her favorite perfume was worth far more than a few U.S. dollars. He'd buy her the moon and all of the stars in the heavens if he could. Shaking away his thoughts, he swung his feet over the edge of the bed and placed her letter and his pen in the box. Brushing his fingertips over its smooth suede surface, he whispered, "Dream of me, darling," then returned it to the nightstand.

After descending the stairs, he dropped his letter into the dough bowl and pulled the chain on the bulb in the kitchen. The door to the adjoining bedroom was shut. So as not to wake his mama, he eased a green milk-glass cup and plate from the cupboard. Next, he opened the heirloom pie safe, cut a large slice of apple pie, poured his milk, and tiptoed to the front porch. When he pushed open the screen door with his shoulder, Sadie and Vince ceased talking. They'd dated for something over a year and planned to marry after her graduation in the spring.

"Hey, lovebirds. Mind if I join you?"

"Not at all." Sadie lifted her auburn hair from her neck and let it fall around her shoulders. Then cutting her large green eyes at Vince, she elbowed him. "We're fine with it. Aren't we, Vince?"

Glaring at their intruder, Vince furrowed his brow, pushed

his wire-rimmed glasses farther up on his nose, and nodded.

Noah straightened his stance and inhaled the fresh night air. "It's certainly nice out here."

"Yes, it sure was . . . uh, is," Vince said as Sadie elbowed him a second time.

"I've missed these cool mountain evenings and the crickets' song." Noah pushed a small table to the opposite end of the porch with his foot. "Sadie, where's Pop? He said he'd dress my wound."

"He ran out to the barn. Said to tell you he'd be back to take care of that before bedtime."

Noah settled himself into one of the white rockers. "Y'all are going to have a piece of Mama's pie, aren't you? There's plenty left."

"No, thanks," said Vince. "Sadie and I stopped at Turner Drug after the show and shared a banana split. Hard to beat their ice cream."

"How was the movie? Good?" He moaned with delight as he took a large bite of pie.

"It was hilarious. You've got to go see it," said Sadie. "By the way, you'll never guess who we bumped into at Turner's."

"If I'll never guess, why don't you go ahead and tell me." He shoveled another fork piled high into his mouth. "Who was it?"

"Your old flame, Alice Jordan." She pushed the swing back and let it fly forward, her long hair blowing behind her.

"Alice?" Thoughts of their last evening together flooded his mind. "I haven't seen her since graduation. How is she?" He'd dated her most of their senior year and still remembered her painful reaction when he broke things off with her. He'd left for Fort Bragg the week after graduation and hadn't wanted either of them to be tied down while he was away.

"She's doing great. She looks like a million bucks too,

doesn't she, Vince?"

He stared into the darkness. "Yep. She sure does. Hasn't changed a bit."

Noah could feel the air fanning around him as Sadie gave the swing another push. "She was there with Margie Teasdale. You remember Margie, don't you?"

He nodded as he wiped his mouth with his napkin and swallowed another large bite. Since meeting Emma, he'd really thought very little of Alice. Emma was several years younger than both of them, but she seemed older, more mature.

"Anyway, Alice heard you were back home and asked about you. She sure seemed interested." Sadie bumped Vince's knee with hers. "Didn't she, Vince?"

He clasped his hands behind his head and held his legs straight out as the swing glided forward. "Yep. She sure did."

"You know Alice has never gotten over you. You should ask her to go see *Boy Meets Girl*. I know she wouldn't turn you down."

He dropped his fork onto his plate and scowled at his sister. "Sadie, you know my heart belongs to Emma."

She scowled back. "Now, Noah. Surely you won't sit at home day in and day out pining over some girl you'll hardly ever see. Emma lives too far away. Besides, I doubt a pretty girl like her will sit idly by on weekends waiting for you to visit once in a blue moon." She pushed the swing harder. "You live here now. It's time to get reacquainted with some of your old friends."

Heat crawled up his neck as he felt his blood start to boil. He uncrossed his legs, moved to the edge of the rocker, and swallowed what he really wanted to say with his last bite of pie. "Don't talk like that. I love Emma, and as soon as I'm well enough to work and save enough money, we're getting hitched."

"Sure. I hear you. Time will tell." She rolled her eyes. "I'll give you two months. Absence doesn't always make the heart grow fonder, you know."

He choked back his words, gathered his dishes, and stormed into the house—his chair still rocking as the screen door clapped shut behind him.

Chapter Twenty

Wednesday, May 9, 2012
Asheboro, North Carolina
Caroline

The sun rose above the rooftops as I followed Stephen down the back steps to the driveway.

Pulling the keys from his pocket, he murmured, "No telling where you'll find the newspaper this morning, Caroline—that is *if* you find it."

"Maybe today will be my lucky day." As he got in the car, I gave him a quick kiss and then walked around the house to collect the paper.

"Ouch." Molly Tuggle, our spinster neighbor, dug her morning edition out of the rose bushes, while her Yorkshire terrier raced around the garden's perimeter yapping. Molly rolled her eyes at me and shrugged. "I guess someone needs to complain. That young man's aim isn't getting any better."

I stifled the temptation to laugh. "So sorry. I know what you mean." Picking up our paper from the pavement, I waved it over my head like a victory salute and grinned. "I guess today's my day. No hiking boots needed."

She shook her head and examined the scratch on her arm. "Have a good day, Caroline. It looks like it's going to be a nice one."

"Only up from here, right?"

She swatted her paper at me and laughed before carrying Lucas down the stone path toward her house.

After hooking the screen and pushing back the door to let

in the cool morning air, I laid the paper on the island and poured myself a second cup of coffee. Inhaling its earthy aroma, I savored every sip as I read the morning headlines. The remains of a female soldier, who'd disappeared years before, had been found, and a suspect arrested. Sipping my morning brew, I thought of my own search for a Fort Bragg soldier and took a seat on the sofa.

Removing the leather box from the coffee table drawer, I slipped a yellowed letter from its contents, hoping to piece together more of Noah and Mother's courtship. With each letter, I grew fonder of Sergeant Noah Anderson, adding to my determination to leave no stone unturned.

Monday, September 5, 1938

Hello Darling,

I hope you didn't have to labor too hard on this Labor Day, but I bet you did. I'm sure the Rainbow was hoppin' with soldiers from Bragg. Have you seen Tuck or any of the fellas lately? I miss getting' together with them at the restaurant, but most of all, I miss my sweet Emma Rose. Do you miss me?

We had a large crowd at the Gentry reunion this afternoon. Mama's relatives packed the house like sardines. Funny how we're all family, but I hardly know anyone.

I could certainly relate. Mother had always enjoyed attending our family's reunions, but I never got over feeling like a stranger. Now I was sorry I hadn't made more of an effort to know my relatives.

One thing I can say, though—the Gentrys sure know how to cook. I've never seen so much food. Thankfully, the weather cooperated so we could eat under the trees. There was a nice breeze, and my little cousins had a great time playing together. I spent most of the day with my older cousin, Dan. I complimented him on his hand-tooled leather belt. Come to find out, he'd made it. His dad owns Mineral Spring Tannery over by the Yadkin River. Dan says he'll show me how to tool. I'm going to head down there next week and try my hand at it. Who knows, maybe I'll make you something. I wish I could help him out over there, but I know the work would be too much of a strain on my back.

To cut the morning chill, I took the light green afghan from the back of the couch and threw it over my legs. It was one I'd given Mother. She'd used it every day. It's strange how something so simple gives me such comfort now that she's gone.

Friday, I went in to see the manager at Sears & Roebuck in Winston-Salem. He told me it was my lucky day, and he could put me to work right away. The job wouldn't be waiting on the public, though, but working in the shipping department. When I told him I couldn't do any heavy lifting for a while, he was disappointed. Bet he wasn't half as disappointed as I was. Some luck, huh?

Then, I went over to Efird's Department Store. The manager there said he had someone leaving at the end of the month, and if his customers didn't spend all their money at the county fair, the job would probably be regular. Maybe it will work out, but I hope to have a job before then. Efird's flagship store is in Charlotte. My Uncle Guy has some business to do there tomorrow, so I'll ride with him and see if they have an opening. I would think they'd pay more in a bigger city, but of course, I'd have to move, so I'm not sure it would benefit me by the time I paid rent. Pop says if I find a job around here, he won't charge me much—only enough to help out with groceries and the electricity. The rest I could save for us, sweetheart.

Thanks to Pop, the incision from my surgery is healing. He's been a good nurse, very attentive. Hopefully, by Thanksgiving or Christmas, I'll be well enough to make the long ride to Fayetteville. Hold on, honey, I'm comin'.

By the way, I found out at the reunion that the girls up here call me conceited. They think because I've been away for three years, I feel above them. The truth is, I don't care anything about them. Even Sadie's been trying to connect me with my old high school sweetheart. But don't worry your pretty little head, I'm not interested in dating anyone but you. I love you more now than I ever have.

Rereading the last line, I wondered if Mother had been as taken with Noah as he'd been with her. If only I could ask her about their relationship. I glanced at my watch—still time for a third cup of coffee before meeting Kate to open Mother's security box. I returned to the kitchen, emptied the pot, and settled back on the couch.

Have you noticed the moon for the last three nights? I sure have. Last night, I hardly slept. After laying my head on the pillow, I watched a full moon rise above the mountain behind our house. Our land goes almost to the top. All I could do was think of how much I'd love to build a home up there one day for you and our kids. Do you think you'd like that, sweetheart, or would you miss the sand between your toes? I know with you by my side, I could be happy anywhere, but I really can't see this mountain boy living in Fayetteville. What do you think about one day living in a house here on top of the mountain?

I smiled and shook my head. Wow, Mother. How different your life would've been if you'd married Noah. I know you loved the mountains, but would you have been content to live as a mountain mama? At least with Daddy, you saw most of the states—some of the places you'd read about in books. Just think, if you'd married Noah, there would be no letters for me to read. I laughed. Come to think of it, there'd be no me.

I guess I'd better help Mama take down the tables and chairs. Almost everyone has gone home. After Dan left, I couldn't wait to come up to my room and write you. Writing makes me feel like I'm with you. I hope and pray you rest well and that you dream of me. If you don't, please think of me when you wake.
    I'll always love you,
    Noah

There it was again—*Dream of me.* Could it be a coincidence that Noah's sentiment was the same as the one on the ribbon attached to the roses at Mother's grave? The funeral home offered no clues as to the sender. Only that the roses were an anonymous gift.

It had been several days since I'd left the message for Noah's nephew Franklin to return my call. I considered calling him again but decided to give him a little more time. Perhaps he was out of town. I placed my cup in the dishwasher and prepared to meet Kate.

As I pulled into a parking space directly across the street from the bank, Kate entered the double glass doors. How was it she always managed to arrive a few moments ahead of me? I chuckled to myself. Perhaps it had something to do with birth order.

When I entered the bank, she was talking with a young teller whose dark shoulder-length hair and large round eyes reminded me of my oldest daughter, Jenna. I hugged Kate and greeted the teller. "Good morning. I'm Caroline Myers, Kate's sister."

"It's nice to meet you. I'm April Conover. Of course, the minute you walked through the doors, I knew you had to be Kate's sister."

Kate pounced. "*Older* sister."

I rolled my eyes in exasperation. "Oh me, we don't have time to go there this morning. Miss Conover, my sister seems to get younger every day."

The teller gave me a knowing look and smiled. "I understand. I also have a *younger* sister."

The tone of our conversation changed as the teller offered us her condolences. "Your mother was such a lovely lady. I always enjoyed chatting with her. She routinely came to my window, and without fail, somewhere in the course of the conversation, she'd mention her girls."

Kate and I smiled and responded in unison. "That was Mother."

We followed the stately young teller to the far corner of the bank and went through a pair of thick metal doors. My heart pounded as she unlocked the large vault inside the room. Would there be something in the drawer that would lead us closer to solving our mystery?

Kate read my apprehension and whispered, "There's probably nothing, Caroline. Don't get your hopes up."

We signed the log, and Miss Conover placed the key in the drawer lock before stepping outside the vault. As I slid the box from the drawer, we saw one tiny brown envelope inside. Kate lifted it out and shook it before offering it to me. "Would you like to do the honors?"

"No. You open it." I jumped at the chance for payback. "Since you're the oldest, that is."

She smirked and opened the metal clasp. Lifting the flap, she shook the contents into the palm of her hand. Out dropped a ring. We gasped.

I carefully picked up the modest diamond in a white gold setting as if it would somehow disintegrate when touched. "Is there anything else in the envelope?"

She pinched it open and slid out a yellowed slip of paper. Written in a beautiful familiar script were the words, *Till death do us part. Noah.*

Kate lifted her large blue eyes to mine. Her face was ashen.

Chapter Twenty-One

Saturday, September 10, 1938
Elkin, North Carolina
Noah

Noah pulled his dad's black 1929 Model A Ford onto the gravel drive of Galloway Chapel in Elkin. One of his best friends from Jonesville High School, Wade Callahan, was marrying Winnie Greenwood. He was happy for his friend but envious of Wade's long-term relationship with his fiancée. They'd known each other since the first grade and began dating the minute Winnie turned sixteen.

Wade was forever cautioning Noah to take his time with Emma and refused to believe an extended courtship wasn't necessary for an enduring marriage. Yes, he'd only known Emma a few months, but he was the ultimate romantic and believed in love at first sight. Hopefully, Wade would understand once he met her. As a matter of fact, he knew he would.

Noah parked the car in the shade of a tree and rolled up the window. The chill in the air and hint of color in the leaves suggested fall was on its way. Fall was his favorite time of year. It would soon be dove hunting season, and he looked forward to sporting a 20-gauge shotgun instead of the Bragg M1 carbine he'd carried on routine field maneuvers. Stepping from the car, he stretched out his tall frame and brushed at the wrinkles in his new green gabardine suit. He wished Emma could see him now. *Hot stuff, Em. You'd think I was hot stuff.*

This was the first suit he'd bought since before he left for Bragg. He couldn't believe the $15 price tag but needed one for job interviews and Wade's wedding, so his purchase was justified. As soon as he could save enough money, he'd return to Efirds in Winston-Salem to purchase brown and white shoes he'd seen in the men's department. Then he'd top off the look with a new tan fedora. *I'll mow 'em down for sure then, Emma Rose.*

The chapel sat perched on a hill above Elkin Creek. The soothing sound of water spilling over the dam into the clear pool below made it a popular place for families to spend the afternoon. Today, several children picnicked with their parents on the opposite bank. He waved at one of the young boys wading along the edge of the creek with his dog. Memories of cooling off here on a hot summer day with Wade and his spaniel, Trapper, made him miss the carefree days of his youth.

Strains of organ music filled the air as Noah climbed the steep hill to the chapel. He wondered how Wade was feeling. Winnie had been planning her wedding since grammar school. Though small, it would be beautiful. She did everything with class. Wade was one blessed man.

Noah took the stairs to the white clapboard church two at a time and entered the foyer right as the church bell rang three o'clock. After he was ushered to his seat, Wade and the minister entered the church. He could tell Wade was nervous by the way he clasped his hands behind his back and rocked back and forth on his heels. His dad served as his best man, and a couple of his buddies were groomsmen. Noah would have been one too if they'd known he would be discharged early, but no one saw it coming.

The church was half full. Decorated with magnolia leaves, large blossoms, and ivory-colored candles in hurricane globes, it was old South elegance. The flower girl made her way down the aisle tossing pink rose petals, followed by two bridesmaids dressed in pale pink chiffon. Noah glanced across the aisle.

Several young ladies whispered and giggled, trying to contain their excitement. A lovely blonde on the end of the row caught his eye. She turned her head, smiled, and gave him a quick wave—*Alice Jordan.* He swallowed hard and smiled back as the organist struck the chords to "Here Comes the Bride." He was grateful for the distraction.

Winnie, dressed in an off-white cotton-and-lace gown with a long train, entered the sanctuary on the arm of her father. The sheer veil covering her face didn't begin to hide her radiance. Noah turned to look at Wade. He beamed.

As the bride and her dad stepped up to the altar, the pastor asked the congregation to be seated. Although the service was beautiful, Noah's thoughts were with Emma. He wished they were the ones marrying today. If only he could find a job and buy her a ring. She'd assured him one wasn't necessary, but he wanted to do things right. After all, a girl like Emma Rose deserved the best. They didn't plan on a church wedding. Neither one of them could afford a large celebration. They planned to invite a few witnesses and say their vows before the Justice of the Peace in Fayetteville. In her last letter, she'd told him Penny would shop with her soon for a wedding dress. He couldn't wait for the day he'd see her in it and make her his wife.

When the ceremony ended, Noah waited in line to greet the bride and groom.

"Noah. Oh, Noah, wait up."

There was no mistaking Alice's syrupy voice. He masked his sentiments with a courteous smile as she latched onto his arm.

"Fancy meeting you here. It feels like forever since I've seen you." She stepped back and studied him from head to toe. "And don't you look spiffy in your swanky city suit."

He shoved his hands in his pockets. "Thank you, Alice. And you look lovely as always." Of course, she did. She was a beautiful girl. Slim and petite, her long dark hair complemented her fair skin and clear green eyes.

She blushed. "Did Sadie tell you I saw her last week at Turner's?"

He inched forward in line. "She did."

"Now there's another wedding we'll probably attend soon. I love weddings. Don't you?"

"I suppose. I haven't had a lot of time to think about it." He jingled the change in his pocket. "Been busy settling in and looking for work. If you know of a job opening anywhere, please let me know."

"I sure will."

As they entered the foyer, Noah motioned for her to move ahead of him. Wade looked at her, gave him a wink, then leaned over and whispered in his ear. "Ah-ha. Maybe I'll be attending your wedding soon, huh, bud?"

"Don't go getting any ideas. Hopefully, there will be a wedding soon, but not with this one. My heart belongs to a pretty young girl in Fayetteville, and I can't wait for you to meet her."

His eyes widened. "Ah. That's good news. But I'm not sure you're going to convince Alice that your heart belongs to another. I hear she's excited about you being home again."

"Well, you keep your mind on your pretty little wife here, my man, and let me worry about the rest of the women in town." He patted him on the back and planted a kiss on Winnie's cheek. "Congratulations, you two. You look smashing together." He winked and moved on.

Stepping onto the porch, he looked over the creek and breathed in the cool, crisp air. The only thing that could make this day more beautiful would be to have Emma by his side.

"Noah, honey."

He forced a smile as Alice greeted him at the bottom of the steps.

"A friend of mine told me about a job opening over at the general store."

He perked up. "Is that right?"

"Yes, Daphne's uncle bought the store about six months ago. You remember my friend Daphne, don't you?"

"Sure." He loosened his tie and slipped off his jacket.

"How about we ride over there? I'll be happy to introduce you to him."

He dropped his head and stared at his spit-shined shoes. "Um . . ."

"Oh, come on. You want a job, don't you? Where's your spunk?" She threaded her arm through his. "Look at you, all slicked up. This is a perfect time."

"That's mighty nice of you, but I'm sure you have something else you need to do today."

"No. Not at all. I'll run and tell my friends you're taking me home." Before he could answer, she'd turned on her heel and ran to tell several girls waiting in a car. As she spoke, they looked his way, nodded, and drove off. Alice spun around, flipped her hair over her shoulders, and sauntered back, smiling.

He winced.

Alice slid into the booth by the window at Turner Drug Store. "Noah, I'm really sorry. Who would have thought Mr. Bettendorf would be gone on a Saturday afternoon?"

Yeah. Who would have thought? "Don't worry. I'll catch up with him next week."

"I hope so. But in the meantime, the least I can do is treat you to a milkshake."

"You don't have to do that."

"I know. But I want to."

"That's mighty nice of you." His gaze bounced around the room. "This place hasn't changed much."

She twisted a strand of hair around her finger. "It's like old times here, isn't it?"

"Not really. Elkin may be the same, but I'm a different man." He pulled a napkin from its holder and wiped a water ring from the table. "You can't spend three years as an army medic and not change."

The waitress placed two menus on the table. "Thank you," said Alice, "but we know what we want." She looked at Noah. "At least I do." She pointed to a picture on the menu. "I'll have a strawberry milkshake with whipped cream and a cherry on top." She looked up. "How about you, Noah?"

"Chocolate for me, please."

"Aha. I guess *some* things remain the same."

They sat in awkward silence.

Noah fiddled with the straw in his ice water while she slipped off her sweater and placed it on the window ledge with her purse. "Oh, look, *Boy Meets Girl* is still playing over at the Elk. Have you seen it yet?"

"No. I've been rather busy since I've gotten home." He took a sip of his water.

"Well, Sadie and Vince said it's a riot. We should go see it."

He shifted in his seat and pressed out the folds in his napkin.

"Well?" she huffed. "What do you think? Wouldn't you like to see it?"

Her pained expression concerned him. He cared for her and had hoped she'd moved on since their breakup. "Alice, I've got to be honest with you. Before I left for Bragg, we discussed the fact it wasn't going to work between us." He squirmed in his seat. "A lot has changed since then. My heart belongs to someone else now."

"But, Noah, you're home." Her large eyes pled with him. "I know all about Emma Walsh, but she lives over a hundred miles away. Are you saying we can't even be friends? Enjoy a movie now and then?"

"It wouldn't be fair to her, Alice. Put yourself in her shoes. How do you think you'd feel?"

She slapped her hand on the table. "I don't have to *think*. I know. I experienced it, remember?" After yanking a napkin from the container, she blotted a tear from her cheek.

He straightened in his seat. "Well, I didn't date Emma behind your back. If you recall, we were no longer a couple."

The waitress brought their order to the table. "Let's see. Strawberry for you." She placed a large shake in front of Alice. "And chocolate for the gentleman." She stepped back. "Is there anything else I can get for the two of you?"

Alice jerked her sweater and purse from the ledge as she glared at Noah. "Yes, there certainly is. Please bring the bill." She motioned across the table. "It goes to the *gentleman.*"

Noah looked at the waitress and nodded, then took a long sip of his shake.

Chapter Twenty-Two

Tuesday, September 13, 1938
Jonesville, North Carolina
Noah

Dan was standing in the doorway of the tannery when Noah and his dad pulled into the driveway. "Take your time in town, Pop, and don't worry about pickin' me up. Dan said he'll give me a lift on his way home tonight." He slammed the door of the black Ford and tipped his straw hat as his father pulled out onto River Road toward Elkin.

After climbing the steps to the front porch of the hand-hewn log structure, he reached out and patted Dan on the back. "Good evening, my man. You look bushed. You okay?"

"Sure." His cousin raked his fingers through his salt and pepper hair. "I stepped out to get a breath of fresh air. It's been a full workday." Wiping the sweat from his brow with the back of his hand, he leaned his stocky frame against the doorpost. His muscular arms glistened in the late-afternoon sunshine. "We had to coat and spray several dozen hides for a customer to pick up on Friday. The air gets pretty pungent in there." He cocked his head toward the door. "We'll be in the back room tonight, so hopefully the fumes won't bother you none."

Noah hadn't anticipated the unpleasant odors that went with the job. He swallowed hard and second-guessed his decision to come as the stench drifted onto the porch and hung in the air. "I'll be fine. I appreciate you letting me come and try my hand at tooling."

Dan ushered him into a room filled with large wooden vats.

Soaked animal hides hung up to dry encircled its perimeter. Noah's throat tightened as warm air that smelled like a mixture of rancid meat, rotten eggs, and acrid ammonia smacked him in the face. Holding his breath was all he could do to keep his dinner from showing back up. As they stepped into the finishing room at the opposite end of the building, he exhaled. Large open windows lining two of the walls provided adequate cross-ventilation and made the air tolerable.

With two swipes of his fingers, Dan smoothed his graying handlebar mustache. "So, you'd like to try your hand at tooling a belt, huh?"

"Well, I don't know how good I'll be at it, but seeing your belt at the reunion moved me to give it a try."

"You'll do fine. It's not hard, but it does take patience." He smiled. "Got any?"

When it came to enduring the long days without Emma, no. "I can do pretty good in that area when I want to."

Dan motioned. "Walk over here." He led him to the opposite end of the room and pointed to a row of leather straps hanging by the back door. "Take a look at these and see if any of them suit your fancy."

He thumbed through the selection and picked out a tan strap that would go well with his new green suit.

"Good choice." After walking over to a large wooden workbench lined with tracing tools, lead weights, and different sized bevels and swivel knives, Dan opened a long drawer under the bench. "Let's pick out a pattern first. What do you have in mind?"

"Something similar to what you had on at the reunion would be fine. Not too flashy, but classy."

After shuffling through the patterns, his cousin selected a simple oak leaf design that suited Noah's taste and wouldn't be hard to master. "Now, let me move this box out of the way, and you can take a seat right here."

"That's a mighty nice box. Beautiful finish." He raised it to his nose and inhaled deeply. "I've always loved the smell of fine leather."

"I finished that one for a customer, but they backed out on the deal. Typical." He shook his head. "I understand, though. Living in a depression doesn't change the fact that people appreciate and want beautiful things. Problem is they can't always see their way clear to get them."

Noah ran his hand across its smooth leather surface. He thought of the suede one Emma had given him when he left Bragg. "Think you could find me a pattern to cover this lid?" He imagined her tucking his letters neatly inside, then tracing the tooled design with her fingers as thoughts of him lingered.

"Of course. Why?" He leaned back against the workbench and crossed his legs at the ankles. "You thinkin' about buying it?"

"Well, if the price is right, I might."

"How does five dollars sound to you? You can pay in installments."

He clapped his hands together. "Sounds fair to me. You've got a deal." He pulled out his handkerchief and wiped the dust from the box. "This will be a great Christmas gift for my girl. Have you got a pattern with roses in it?"

"I do." He reached into the drawer and pulled out a pattern of interlocking long-stemmed roses and handed it to him. "You were telling me about your girl at the reunion—name's Eva, right?"

"No. Emma. Emma Rose." He looked at the pattern, smiled, and handed it back to Dan. "This will be perfect."

"Sounds like it will be. Roses for Rose. You set a wedding date yet?"

"Not yet. But as soon as I find a job and make a little money, I plan on making it official. Emma says a ring's not important, but a girl like her deserves the best. No woman of mine is gonna have to do without."

"Hmm. You need a ring, huh?" Dan clicked his tongue and

pointed at him. "You're in luck. I might be able to help you out in that department too."

Noah raised his brow. "I thought you were in the leather business. Aren't diamonds outside your area of expertise?"

Dan went over to a cabinet by the window, pulled open a drawer, and took out a tiny brown envelope. "Here. Hold out your hand." He opened the clasp and turned the envelope upside down. A white gold ring with a small diamond dropped into Noah's palm. He picked up the delicate ring and whistled as the light bounced from its polished facets. "Where on earth did you get this beauty?"

"I've had it for a long time. Planned on marryin' a girl once, but before I could pop the question, she ran off with another fella." His voice trailed as he lowered his head. "I really loved her. Took me a long time to get over that one." He lifted his steel-gray eyes and stared out the window. "Never had the desire to marry anyone since. 'Bout too old now. Too set in my ways." With a jolt of his head, he looked back at him. "You interested in the ring or not?"

Noah tilted it back and forth in the light and watched a rainbow of colors spray across the ceiling. "It certainly is a pretty thing." He envisioned it reflecting in Emma's wide eyes as he slipped it on her finger. "I know she would love it." Trying to curb his excitement, he sighed and dropped it back in the envelope. "What kind of price tag you got on it?"

"Have no clue what it's worth now. It's a near-perfect diamond, but I'll sell it to you for what I've got in it—fifty bucks. I'll even give you a 20-percent family discount to boot. Sound like a deal?"

"I'll say. Sounds like one I'd be a fool to turn down, but without a job, I don't see any way I can make it happen."

"Don't worry about it. It's been sitting in the drawer for over ten years. You pay me when you can, and if you want to pop the question before it's paid for, I'll let you take it with you."

"Sure thing?"

"You bet." Dan laughed. "I'm not worried. I know where you live, cuz."

Noah slid from the stool, slapped Dan's shoulder, and shook his hand with a firm grip. "I'll invite you to the wedding, my man. May even name my first son after you."

"Whoo-hoo!" Ignoring the twinges in his back, Noah loped toward Dan's red Ford pickup truck. He grabbed hold of the open window and hopped onto the running board. "Let 'er roll."

Dan shouted over the rumble of the engine. "Get in this truck, you crazy fella. You'll be lucky if you can walk tomorrow. This buggy's not going anywhere till you get inside."

"Aw, you're no fun." He drew a long breath, tossed his straw hat onto the floorboard, and eased onto the seat. "It's good to be home. I didn't realize how much I'd missed these hills and the smoky smell of the fall night air."

"No better place to live." Dan pressed on the gas, routed the sputtering truck up the drive, and turned onto River Road toward Jonesville. "It's hard to get the mountains out of the boy, ain't it?" He plopped his fedora on his head and chuckled. "Can't imagine why anyone would want to, anyway."

"You've got that right." Noah stretched his arm out the window and resisted the wind with his palm. Dried leaves illuminated by the truck's headlights danced across the road and swirled into the air as the 1932 pickup rolled along. "Fall's my favorite time of year. Not much can beat the beauty of the mountain behind our house blazing with color, or the sound of dry leaves crunching beneath my feet. Funny how simple things end up meaning the most to you after you've been gone a while."

His cousin floored the accelerator and propelled the truck to its maximum speed down the dusty, pothole-filled road, gravel flying.

"You go, Dan." He turned in his seat and pushed the top half of his body through the window into the clear night air. Looking up at the starry sky, he yelled at the top of his lungs, "Hear this, world! Noah Anderson is marrying Emma Rose Walsh. You got that?" He collapsed into his seat, laughing hysterically, and ran his long fingers through his windswept hair.

Dan threw back his head and laughed, then let up on the gas. "Okay, sport, that's enough fun for one night. It would be my luck for someone to turn me in for driving like a crazy man."

Noah reached over and gave his shoulder a push. "Gotta be true to the Gentry character, cuz." He gathered his composure. "By the way, Pop and I are going dove hunting Saturday morning. It's been way too long. How about you coming with us?"

Dan shook his head. "Sorry, but I'm afraid I won't be able to make it."

"Aw, come on. I guarantee I'll act like I've got some sense with a twelve gauge in my hands." He reached down and picked up his hat from the floorboard.

"Wish I could, but I promised my brother I'd help him re-chink his tobacco barns and get them ready for next year's crop. Thanks for asking, though. Maybe next time." Dan adjusted his rearview mirror. "Did you enjoy the tooling tonight?"

"You bet. But I enjoyed our conversation more. Thanks again for taking the time to show me the ropes and for putting up with all my banter. I'd like to come back next Tuesday and finish my belt and maybe start on Emma's box if you'll have me."

"That'll be fine. We'll have our big order out the door by then. Does the same time work for you?"

"Should be perfect."

Dan shifted in his seat and yawned. "How's the job search comin'?"

"Slow." He shook his head and grimaced. "I've had a few good leads but nothing concrete yet. There's a possibility I could get on as a driver with Greyhound. That's been the most promising prospect so far." He crossed his legs and threw his elbow up on the window. "I left an application with the supervisor in Charlotte last week. We got along really well. I hope to see *how* well by the end of next week."

He looked over at Noah. "Well, I've got another lead for you."

He raised his brow. "For real?"

"Yep. One of my customers told me yesterday the county has an opening. They're looking for a new clerk over at the Agriculture Extension office. How good are you with numbers?"

"Pretty fair, actually." He cleared his throat, straightened himself in his seat, and threw back his shoulders. "Graduated at the top of my class." A chance to work for the county seemed too good to be true, but he'd do whatever it took to show them he was worthy of the job.

"Well, Alton said the position involves maintaining expense records for the different departments and issuing periodic reports to the commissioners. They haven't made the opening public yet. He was giving me the heads-up in case I knew of someone who might be interested." He leaned over and slapped him on the knee. "Of course, I thought of you right off, pal."

"I appreciate that. It's nice to know someone's got my back. I'm pretty desperate. Gotta get my girl up here before I lose her to a GI down at Bragg. Who wouldn't want to date a beautiful girl like Emma?" Although he knew he could trust her, Noah couldn't tolerate the thought of another fellow thinking he had even half a chance with her.

He gave his hat a twirl on the end of his finger. "Tell your friend I'm interested and that I'm a fast learner. I'm confident the pay will be as good as anything I can get around here, and, of course, I like the sound of those government benefits." He tossed his hat on his head. "Yep. Tell him I'd love to talk to him."

"I should see Alton again tomorrow. I'll let him know." Dan turned right onto Watson Mill Road and shifted gears. "He won't be the one you'll interview with, but as a county commissioner, he certainly has a lot of pull. I'll have him get in touch with you right away. He'll steer you in the right direction. His name's Alton Jordan."

"Alton Jordan?" Noah squirmed. "When did he get to be a commissioner?"

"Oh, so you know him?"

"Let's say, I've met him a time or two. I dated his daughter, Alice, before I went to Bragg."

"Wow! How perfect. That is if you left a good impression. You did, didn't you?"

"Oh, I impressed him all right. He liked me a lot at one point, but I'm not sure how he feels about me now." He scratched his head. "I broke his daughter's heart when I left for boot camp." His hope of landing the job as clerk took a nosedive as he remembered the look on Alice's face as she slammed the door. *"Good riddance, Noah Anderson. You'll rue the day you let me go."*

Dan turned the truck into the Andersons' driveway and brought it to a stop at the side door of the modest white clapboard house. "Maybe you'd better set about puttin' those pieces back together. Sounds to me like you may need to get in Alice's good graces. She's the apple of her daddy's eye. I'm certain whatever Alice wants, Alice gets." He put his hand on Noah's shoulder and looked him square in the eyes. "She could certainly tilt the table in your favor, my man."

"You know how I feel about Emma. The ring—remember? The box? Wedding bells?"

"Ah shoot, Noah. No one said you had to fall in love with the girl. It's politics, son. You do what you gotta do to get the job. That's the way I see it, anyway." He winked. "Besides, Alice is quite a looker. I can think of worse assignments. Who says Emma needs to know?"

"I couldn't do something like that behind her back. We promised we'd be honest with one another."

"Okay, be honest then. Tell her. Tell her why you're doing it. Not only does she understand you need the job so the two of you can get married, she knows it's a stretch for your parents to house you without a little bit of help with household expenses. Times are tough." He patted him on the back. "I'm sure she'll understand."

Noah shook his head, opened the door, and stepped out of the truck. "I don't know, man. I'm not convinced of it at all. Not at all."

Chapter Twenty-Three

Friday, September 16, 1938
Fayetteville, North Carolina
Emma

The screen door clapped shut behind Emma as she stepped onto the porch. Chummy neither flinched nor offered to relinquish his relaxed position on the swing.

"Bye-bye, Chummy Choo. The swing's all yours today. I'm on a mission."

The morning was already warm and humid after the previous night's storm. Maiden Lane's towering live oaks would offer her welcome shade before she reached Hay Street's business district. Pulling her long hair to one side, she put on her wide-brimmed straw hat, tied it under her chin, and stepped onto the sidewalk. Swinging her small purse by her side, she dodged an occasional puddle and even a crack or two. Her sister Lily used to warn, "Step on a crack, you'll break your mother's back." Since their mama's passing, Emma really didn't know what it would matter, but she found she couldn't stop avoiding them.

Two blocks down, she paused in front of a lavender bungalow and greeted a lady on a small wooden stool weeding her flowers. "Good morning, Mrs. Brumble."

She brushed her hair from her face and looked up from her work. "Morning, Emma. You look mighty nice. Are you off work today?"

"I am. I'm meeting a friend for lunch and a day of shopping."

"Sounds divine."

Emma peeked over the less-than-sturdy picket fence that was in dire need of a coat or two of paint. Not to mention the yard, which could use a good mowing. But as the eccentric spinster would say, *"I'm growing a meadow."*

"Your flowers still look lovely."

"Thank you. They've held up well. I watered them a lot over the summer. I thought after last night's rain, this would be a good time to do a bit of weeding."

"I suspect you're right." She opened and closed her hand in a parting wave and turned on her heel. "Pardon me, but I've got to run. I hope you have a wonderful day."

"You too, hon."

Emma's day promised to be a marvelous one—she was off to find a wedding dress. Though she and Noah had yet to set a date, the Capitol Department Store advertised a sale too good not to explore. She'd wanted Lily to join in their adventure, but in the wake of Fleishman's Labor Day sale, her office job commanded her unwavering attention.

Emma missed her mama now more than ever. She never imagined losing her would create such a void. She missed everything about her. Nights on the swing with Chummy served only to remind her of warm summer evenings spent on the porch swing with her mama. Oh, what she'd give for one more after-dinner chat, surrounded by the sweet fragrance of wisteria and the ethereal sound of the whip-poor-will. Though haunting, the lonely bird's song had always brought calmness to her soul.

Noah would have loved her mama's meals of homegrown summer squash, butter beans, and okra, served with fried cornbread, sweet tea, and the world's best chocolate meringue pie. She'd yet to eat a meal that could rival her mama's.

As she turned onto bustling Hay Street, American flags fluttered in the morning breeze, embracing a spirit of better days to come. Bargain shoppers admired window displays still decked in red, white, and blue, while others saluted the morning with cones of home-made ice cream scooped by a vendor on the corner. From a distance, Emma saw Penny on the bench in front of The Capitol, scanning the sales flyer.

"See anything you think is worth our time today?" she said as she approached.

Penny jolted, then stood and embraced her friend. "I don't know. Even the sale prices look pretty steep." She smiled and put her arm around Emma's shoulders. "But we won't know until we go in and browse. . . Mrs. Anderson."

The owner, Mr. Kalman Stein, and his son Bernard, residents of the fashionable Haymount district west of town, greeted them as they passed by the shoe department. "Good morning, Penny, Emma. You both off work today?"

Penny smiled. "We are. All day long."

"Good for you." He chuckled. "But whatever is Cee going to do with his top two Rainbow girls out at the same time?"

Bernard stepped into the aisle and flashed a sheepish grin. "You're looking mighty nice, Penny. Is there something I can assist you with?"

She stepped around him. "Thank you, Bernard, but we're only passing through. Headed upstairs to Misses Wear. Emma has a special event on the horizon."

"Wonderful. We have some excellent after-summer deals up there. Hopefully, you'll find exactly what you're looking for, Emma. Let me know if you need a snazzy pair of pumps to match. I've got plenty of bargains down here too. Maybe even something you'd take a fancy to, Penny."

"Thank you."

Emma linked her arm through Penny's and leaned in close as they ascended the stairs. "Well, well, if I didn't know better, I'd say Mr. Bernard Stein has eyes for you."

She smacked her arm. "Hush. You know Horace is my man."

"Yes, I do, but Bernard doesn't." At the top of the stairs, she threw out her arms and spun around. "Maybe you should rethink your future, Miss Watson. *This* could *all* be yours."

"Stop it," she said with a dismissive wave. "We have more important things to discuss. Keep your focus."

Penny grabbed Emma by the wrist, pulled her out of The Capitol and up Hay Street toward the corner. "Well, if you're not going to eat lunch, let's at least grab an ice cream cone. I'm starved."

"You go ahead. I don't think I can eat anything."

"Come on. Snap out of it, Em. You've got plenty of time. You'll find a dress when the time is right."

She plodded behind her friend. "I don't think my budget will ever match their prices, sale, or no sale."

"You don't know that. Now you have time to put away more money. Don't let it spoil your day." She stepped up to the portly man under the red, white, and blue umbrella. "What flavors do you have, sir?"

"Strawberry, vanilla, blueberry, chocolate, and blissful banana."

"Strawberry for me. Two scoops, please." She turned toward Emma. "How about you?"

She shrugged.

"My treat. Hurry up," she said, speaking through clenched teeth. "The kind gentleman is waiting. What will you have?"

"A small cone of blissful banana, please."

"Perfect. You could use a bit of bliss right now." Penny paid the vendor, pulled a few napkins from the metal container, and passed Emma her cone. "Come on. There's a spot over here in the shade."

Emma followed Penny to a bench under a sprawling pin oak and took a seat.

"So, how's the banana?"

"Okay."

Penny rolled her eyes. "Just okay? My strawberry is spectacular. Hits the spot on this muggy afternoon."

Emma sat with her legs crossed and jiggled her foot while she licked her cone and stared off in the distance.

Penny huffed. "Well, you're a ton of fun. Are you going to mope the day away?"

"I'm sorry. I do appreciate the cone. It is delicious, but I think I need to head home. You should finish your shopping without me. I don't want to spoil your day too."

"I know you're disappointed, Em, but things will work in your favor. You'll see. God must have something better in mind for you. Trust His timing." She lifted Emma's chin. "Will you?"

She nodded and hugged Penny. "I know you're right. I'll be fine. I need a little time alone to adjust my attitude, that's all."

"Are you sure?"

"I am."

"Okay. I'm on my way then." She stood and tossed her napkin in a nearby trash bin. "I'll see you bright and early in the morning. Cee's expecting a busy day. Don't be late."

"I'll be there with bells on. I promise."

"That's my girl." Penny blew her a kiss and hurried toward Mae's Boutique.

Emma opened her new tapestry purse, pulled out her mirror, and touched up her red lipstick. Snapping it shut, she rose and walked toward home.

Emma sped past as Mrs. Brumble pulled her mail from her mailbox.

"What? Not even a passing glance. Are you okay, dear?"

She reluctantly turned as sadness tore at her chest. "I suppose."

"Oh my. What happened to the happy-go-lucky young lady who passed my way this morning?" She moved closer. "No packages? I thought you went shopping."

"I did, and I had a nice time with my friend, but I didn't find what I went for—at least not at a price I could afford."

"I'm certainly sorry. Can I help? What is it you need?"

"You're very kind, but there's nothing you can do. I'd hoped to find my wedding dress today."

"Wedding dress? How wonderful. Flo hasn't mentioned a wedding. When's the date?"

"We've not set one, but maybe next fall."

"It sounds like you have plenty of time to find the perfect dress. Be patient. It'll happen."

"I wish I had your confidence. I'm not sure I'll ever be in a position to afford one. Even the sale prices are way above my budget."

Mrs. Brumble embraced her. "I'm sorry. You were simply glowing this morning. It hurts my heart to see your beautiful face so downcast." She placed her hand on Emma's back and nudged her toward the fence. "Please come in and join me for a spot of tea. I'd love the company."

"That sounds wonderful, but I wouldn't want to trouble you. Besides, Mama T will worry about me."

She gave her a dismissive wave. "Oh, phooey. We'll call her when we get inside. Come on. I won't take 'no' for an answer." She turned and opened the gate.

Emma rolled her eyes and shrugged, then followed the slender woman with a slight stoop up the wobbly, slate walk through knee-high grass. As she stepped inside the foyer of the faded lavender house, peace washed over her soul.

"Put your purse on the table by the door and come into the kitchen."

They passed through a lime green sitting room with a lemon-yellow sofa that appeared to have welcomed its share of weary bodies. As they entered the Wedgewood blue kitchen, the hospitable neighbor pointed to the telephone on the wall. "Go ahead and call Flo and tell her you're with me. I'll put the kettle on. Then, I want to hear all about this lucky young man of yours."

Moments later, Emma took a seat at the white, drop-leaf table beneath a window with a view of the back yard. It, too, was becoming a meadow. "Mama T sends her love, Mrs. Brumble."

"Oh, please, child. Call me, Opal. All my friends do. I'm not much on formalities."

"Of course—Opal. How nice."

Opal pulled two china cups and saucers from the cupboard and placed them on the table with a bowl of sugar cubes and tarnished silver tongs. She took out a pitcher of cream from the icebox and a dish of lemon slices with a few sprigs of fresh mint and placed them in front of Emma. After carrying a robin's egg blue teapot filled with steeping hot tea to the table, she pulled out a chair and sat. With a deep sigh, she shook out her linen napkin and placed it in her lap. "There now, tell me about your fine young man."

Later, when the cuckoo clock above the sink struck three, Emma sipped the last of her tea. "This has been wonderful. Thanks for inviting me, but I really must go. I feel so much better and have enjoyed hearing about your travels. I hope to travel one day too."

"I've led a blessed life. Been able to see a lot of places and do a lot of things that wouldn't have been possible if I'd had a family."

Rising from the table, Opal led Emma back through the sitting area. "Before you go, follow me. I have something I want to show you."

The minty, pine scent of a dried eucalyptus wreath flooded the air of an adjacent bedroom. Underneath it sat a tarnished brass bed with a sun-drenched, cathedral-window quilt covering it. In the corner of the room sat a tall, pine wardrobe with mirrored doors. Opal tugged on them, then jolted backward as it released.

Emma lunged and braced her with her hands. "Are you all right?"

"Whew. Yes, I'm fine," she said, covering her heart with her hands. "I suppose you can tell this wardrobe hasn't been opened in a while." She reached in and lifted a hanger from the rod, then faced Emma and pulled off the sheet that draped it.

Emma felt the blood drain from her cheeks as she stood frozen, then dropped on the bed. "What—? Whose—? I mean— it's gorgeous, but . . ." She shook her head as her eyes pierced Opal's. "I don't understand."

Hanging from the pink quilted hanger was an elegant, ivory satin and lace floor-length gown. Offsetting the modest square-neckline was a wrap waist with a large satin sash that tied in a loose bow on one side.

"Well. Do you like it?"

"Like it? I've never seen anything so lovely. Was it yours?"

"Yes. While on a summer holiday in my late twenties, I ran across this in a quaint little dress shop on the outskirts of London. Like most young girls, I dreamed I would one day find my handsome prince, so I bought it and hung it in this wardrobe."

"You never found him?"

"Oh, I thought I had one time, but it's a long and pretty depressing story. In hindsight, I see things turned out for the best. I wouldn't trade my life for another. God doesn't make mistakes." She gestured. "Enough about that. Come over here and stand in front of the mirror."

Emma rose and faced the wardrobe. Opal removed the dress from the hanger and stood behind her. Reaching around with both hands, she held it in front of Emma. "Looks like a perfect fit to me. Would you like to have this?"

"Have it? It's certainly more beautiful than anything I could ever dream of wearing, but I don't have anything to offer you."

"Offer me? It not for sale. It's a gift."

Emma's large hazel eyes widened. "What have I ever done to deserve such grace? I haven't enough words to thank you." She fell into Opal's arms.

"No words needed, dear. I'm thrilled you like it. God knew forty years ago, this dress would be yours. You can thank Him." Opal returned the dress to the hanger and covered it with the sheet. "Here, run on home and try it on. If it needs a tuck here or there, bring it back, and I'll alter it for you."

As they stepped out on the porch, Emma gave Opal a parting hug, held the dress closely, and bolted home. The day had promised to be a good one. She'd set out to find the perfect dress, and she did—or so it found her.

Chapter Twenty-Four

Thursday, May 10, 2012
Asheboro, North Carolina
Caroline

Opening the leather box, I pulled out the envelope Kate and I had found in the safety deposit box and shook the dainty ring into the palm of my hand.

"What a precious diamond, Mother. I wish you'd shared this with your daughters. Were you afraid you'd dishonor Daddy?" Slipping it on my right ring finger, I then pulled out Noah's note and reread it. *Till death do us part. Noah.* "What happened to that promise, Sergeant Anderson?"

Seeing Franklin Montgomery's phone number on a sticky note I'd stuck on the top of the box, I took a deep breath, picked up the phone, and punched in his number. Perhaps today I'd make a connection.

On the third ring, a raspy male voice answered. "Hello?"

I rose from my place on the couch and walked to the window. A light breeze brushed through the irises Mother had helped me transplant along the driveway after she'd sold the home place. Their purple and white heads bobbed as if to nod their approval. "Good morning. Is this Mr. Montgomery?"

"It is."

Finally. My hopes of finding answers peaked. "My name is Caroline Myers, and I live in Asheboro. I spoke with your sister Mary Ann several days ago, and she suggested I call you concerning your uncle Noah."

"My uncle?" I sensed suspicion and a hint of aggravation in his voice. "What about him?"

"I recently discovered a box of letters he wrote to my mother in 1938. He met her at the Rainbow Restaurant in Fayetteville while stationed at Fort Bragg."

"O-kay?" He whistled loudly in my ear and yelled. "Here, Jax. Come here." After a short pause, he cleared his throat and returned to our conversation. "What do you want from me?"

I paced back and forth. *I need your favor, Lord.* "I wondered if you had any information about your uncle you'd be willing to share with me. Ultimately, I hoped you might have a picture of him."

"Not got one that I know of." His voice drifted. "Jax, you'd better get back over here with that bone!" I yanked the phone from my ear as he let out another shrill whistle. A moment later, he was back, clearly aggravated. "Don't know why I'd share a picture with a stranger even if I had one. You writin' a book or somethin'?"

Oh boy. This guy's a piece of work. I walked back to the sofa and sat on the arm, groping for the right words to subdue the tension. "I can certainly understand your reservations, Mr. Montgomery, but I assure you whatever information you give me will be kept confidential."

"Well, I don't know much about my uncle, and at this point, I don't think you need to be nosing around and digging up our family tree."

I heard a dog panting in the background.

"Thatta boy, Jax. Good dog."

I waited. *Am I really playing second fiddle to a dog?*

He returned. "Ms. Myers, I suggest you let dead bones lie."

"I'm terribly sorry if I've offended you, sir. Since Mary Ann suggested I call you, I didn't think it would be an issue. I do thank you for your time."

The line went dead.

I stared at the phone. "Uh . . . and you have a nice day too, sir. Wow. Now there's a friendly guy. I hope his apple fell a long way from your tree, Noah. I can't imagine my mother settling for anyone less than a gentleman."

After dropping back onto the sofa, I lifted a stack of letters from the box and slipped one dated Wednesday, September 14, 1938, from underneath the ribbon.

Good morning, Darling,

I'm not out of bed yet, but I couldn't wait to write you and tell you about my trip to the tannery last night. Dan and I had a great time. It's been nice getting reacquainted with my cousin after all these years. He's a fine fella. But then again, all of us Gentry men are. (Just kidding, sweetie. But I sure hope you think that's true of this Gentry offspring.) I'm making a really neat belt to go with my new green suit. One more visit and I should have it finished. Then I'll start on something for you— the perfect Christmas gift.

Speaking of Christmas, I've checked the calendar, and I plan to come down sometime after Thanksgiving. That will give me enough time to finish up your gift and a bit more time to allow my back to heal. How does that sound? Talk to Cee and ask for a few days off, then tell me what days will work for you. I should be able to stay the better part of a week. You know I'll squeeze out every moment I can to be with my sweet Emma Rose.

Uncle Guy and I made the trip to Charlotte last week, and I stopped in at Efird's. The bad news is they didn't have any job openings. The good news is a clerk in the men's department told me Greyhound Bus Lines is hiring drivers. He said if I was interested, I could talk to Mr. Ingram, who's in charge of the drivers. Ingram's supervisor, Mr. Love, is the one who does all the hiring and the firing but leans heavily upon Ingram's recommendations. When Uncle Guy finished his business in town, he drove me over to the terminal to pick up an application. I had no clue I'd get to talk to

Ingram on such short notice, but it turned out I walked in at just the right time—divine providence, I'd say. Anyway, he told me that they'd be hiring five to ten drivers soon. They're gearing up for the holiday travel and want their drivers to be trained and ready to roll by the end of October. I told him I want to be in that number and that I would appreciate anything he could do for me. I think I made a good impression. He told me if I'd sit there and fill out my application, he'd make sure it went to the top of the stack.

How do you think I'm doing, darling? I hope you think I'm doing good. Good enough for you to keep holding on. We'll be together soon, sweetheart. Forever. I promise.

Well, I guess I'd better get on with my day. I imagine you are up now and about ready to go to work yourself. I know you don't like the hours or so many GIs making passes at you, but hopefully, you won't have to work there much longer. Your honesty and knowing that I can trust you are two of the many reasons I love you so much.

Sweetheart, your letter was a lifesaver. I don't know what I would have done if it hadn't been there when I came home. Write me again as soon as you find out something from Cee so I can start counting down the days till I see you. In the meantime, dream of me. I'll certainly be dreaming of you.

I'll always love you,
Noah

I slipped the letter back into the envelope and studied the diamond on my finger. The *dream of me* sentiment continued to be a mystery, and Franklin Montgomery's refusal to work with me would make my search for answers much more difficult. "I will not be deterred, Mr. Montgomery. You've underestimated the Walsh in this girl."

Later in the afternoon, I paced the floor with my tablet in one hand and the phone in the other. Four rings. "Come on, Kate, pick up."

"Hi, Caroline. What's on your mind?"

I dropped onto the sofa. "I'm so glad you're home. I've tried your phones all day. I want to know if you're busy on Saturday."

"Hmm. Tell me what you're thinking, and I'll let you know."

I shook my head. "Funny, Kate. I know you hope I want to go to that new consignment shop you told me about, but I've got something in mind that's far more interesting than that."

"No way. What's could be more exciting than finding a bargain?"

"A grave—finding a grave."

"A grave?"

"You've got it. I want to make a trip to Jonesville on Saturday and hoped you'd go with me. I'm on a mission to find Noah's grave."

"I take it you got in touch with Franklin?"

I rolled my eyes. "I got in touch with him, all right."

"Oops. That doesn't sound good."

"Let me put it this way—we can forget about Noah's namesake giving us any information."

"You're kidding me."

"Nope. I wish I was. He wasn't nearly as receptive as Mary Ann. Instead, he advised me to let dead bones lie."

"Oh, my goodness. Franklin didn't know who he was talking to. That's not something you want to say to someone who has Walsh blood coursing through their veins. He should have dangled the bone right in front of your face."

I laughed. "I know. I'm more determined now than ever to

find out about Noah. His sister's obituary said her burial would be in the family cemetery, so his grave won't be an easy one to find. I've tried to get back in touch with Mary Ann, but she hasn't returned my call. I'm afraid Franklin may have gotten to her before I did."

I could hear her flipping the pages of her day planner. "Well, it looks like my calendar is clear for Saturday. What time do you want to leave?"

"I googled Jonesville, and it looks like it will take about ninety minutes to get there. Let's say we leave around eight a.m. That will put us in before lunch and give us most of the day to scout out the area."

"Sounds good to me."

"Great. I'll pick you up at eight. See you then." I returned the phone to its dock, tucked the box of letters into the coffee table drawer, and leaned back on the sofa. "Jonesville, here we come." I chuckled as I thought of how my cousin, the family historian, would always sign her letters *disturbing the dead and irritating the living.*

"C'est la vie, Franklin. Such is life."

Chapter Twenty-Five

"Ugh!"

I hit snooze on the alarm clock and promised myself I would spring out of bed on the next ring. Well, maybe not spring. Stumble would be more like it. Once again, I'd had a hard time shutting down yesterday, and this morning I was paying for it. Rolling over, I buried my head in the covers to block out the morning light. I could hear Mr. Rise 'n Shine, putting his breakfast dishes in the dishwasher. I was positive he'd started the morning with a hard-boiled egg, cereal, milk, juice, and some sort of sweet roll or muffin. As for me, hand me a mug of coffee with cream and a peanut butter sweet-and-salty granola bar. I know it's not the healthiest breakfast, but it's my favorite way to start the day—light and easy.

Stephen tapped me on the shoulder. "Hey, Caroline. The coffee's ready. I'm on my way out. I have a 7:15 tee time with the guys."

Turning over, I shielded my eyes from the morning sun and squinted, bringing his face into focus. "'Bye, sweetheart. Have fun and stay safe, okay?"

He leaned down and kissed me on the forehead, then gave me his quintessential cautionary look. "Same goes for you. Be careful on the road—and you two stay out of trouble."

"Who, us?"

"Yes, *us*. Pair you with Kate, and it's double trouble. I don't have the money to post bail for both of you this weekend—only Kate."

As he turned to go, I shoved my foot out from under the cover and kicked him on the rear end. "Ha-ha. Funny, Mr. Until-Death-Do-Us-Part."

Once my alarm summoned me for the second time, I hit the off switch and muttered, "Okay. You win, loudmouth. I'm up."

Two hours later, Kate and I were on the road. With Jonesville plugged into my GPS, we were armed and loaded for bear. She was totin' her green smoothie, and I was packin' my large tumbler of coffee with cream and a granola bar. The forecast for the day was perfect—low seventies, light breeze, and not a cloud in the sky. I dared Mr. Franklin Montgomery to rain on our parade. Hopefully, by the end of the day, we would have unlocked the answers we were searching for.

The drive to Jonesville was pleasant. Traffic was light the entire way. We exited Interstate 77 about the time I'd expected, but then the real challenge began. Noah had never included a street name, house, or route number in the return address of his letters, only Jonesville, North Carolina. Locating the Anderson homeplace would take shrewd guesswork.

In my initial conversation with Mary Ann, she'd said the house was on Watson Mill Road and that Franklin still owned and rented it to family members. Because their mother's funeral was held at Watson Mill Baptist Church, I'd entered it into my GPS and hoped to get within shouting distance.

We found the Jonesville vicinity to be a quaint area, a step back in time—precisely the one we'd hoped to make. We could see why this Blue Ridge gateway, with its gently rolling hills, narrow winding roads, and freshly tilled farmlands, would have been so desirable to Noah. I could understand why he would prefer this tranquil setting to the hot, sandy soil of Fayetteville.

We followed the GPS's instructions down a winding road to the Main Street intersection. On the corner were two flat-roofed, red-brick buildings. One housed a small public library, and the other one, now deserted, was the former town hall. Taking a left onto South Swaim Street, we headed in the direction of Watson Mill Road.

"Kate, when we turn onto Watson Mill, help me look for a white-frame house with a mountain behind it, okay?"

She straightened herself in her seat, lifted her sunglasses, and glared at me with her large blue eyes. "Of course, Caroline. Let's see if I've got this right. We're in the foothills of the Blue Ridge Mountains, and you want me to help you scout out a white house with a mountain behind it." She rolled her eyes. "Is there a dog in the yard too? And what kind would it be? A Doberman, maybe?"

"Oh, hush, smart aleck." I shook my head. "Noah mentioned in one of his letters that his family owned most of the mountain behind his house. Other than that, and Watson Mill Baptist Church, we have no landmarks to clue us in on his home's location. Work with me here, will you?"

After driving several miles down Watson Mill, the GPS chimed in right as we saw a sign that read *Watson Mill Baptist Church. One mile ahead.*

"Okay. Help me look now. Noah's house could be any of these along here."

"Yes. But, it looks to me like all the houses are white and there's a mountain behind each one. Probably a demon behind every tree, too, don't you think?"

I swatted her on the arm. "Will you straighten up? I'm serious here, and you're cracking jokes. We haven't come this far to drop the ball now."

She held up her hands in defense. "Whoa. Settle down. I'm only kidding." She pointed. "Okay. There's the church up ahead on the right. How about pulling into the parking lot so we can get our bearings? Maybe someone will be there. We can ask them if any Andersons or Montgomerys live around here."

I pulled the car into the lot. "Look. The good Lord is smiling down on us this morning. There's a car parked under the overhang." I drove around to the side of the building and cut the ignition. "I hope whoever is here has some divine direction for us."

After leading the way to the office entrance, Kate rang the buzzer.

Within moments, a tall, slender man with a pleasant smile opened the door. "Good morning, ladies. I'm Pastor Jacobs. What can I help you with?"

After we explained why we were there, he stepped to the corner of the building and pointed up the road. "Franklin Montgomery lives about a mile that way. See that red barn up there on the left? His house is about half a mile past there. You'll come to a white house first. That's the Anderson homeplace. Next, you'll see Franklin's house. It's a long brick ranch. The two homes share a split driveway. You can't miss it."

"Sounds easy enough." I reached out my hand. "We certainly appreciate your help, Pastor Jacobs."

"I hope you all have a nice visit. They're a wonderful family. Very well thought of around these parts. They've been a big asset to this church for generations—helped found it."

I pointed to the graveyard beside the church, which had a number of old tombstones. "Are any of the Andersons buried here?"

"No. They have plots at the base of the mountain behind the homeplace. You'll see a gated dirt road that leads to a small cemetery right before you get to the house. They've buried their loved ones there since before this church was established. I buried Franklin's mom there a couple of years ago. He still struggles with her death. They were very close."

We thanked the pastor again and returned to the car. "Wow, how easy was that?" I shrugged. "Let's go take a look."

As soon as we passed the red barn, we saw the house in the distance. I turned to Kate and smirked. "Note the mountain behind the white house."

She laughed. "Okay. It's as you said."

We slowed down as we passed the gated road leading to the cemetery and then stopped at the driveway of the two houses. Both sat a good distance from the road. "Look. There it is. The house from which Noah wrote the letters to Mother over seventy years ago. It's hard to believe, isn't it?"

"It is. What a charming house in a beautiful setting. I feel like I'm in the middle of a Nicholas Sparks movie. I can hardly wait to see how this story ends."

I glanced down at Mother's diamond ring on my right hand and giggled. "I believe we know, but I understand what you're saying. There's a lot more to learn about their relationship." I pulled off the road, parked at the end of the driveway, and reached for my phone.

"What are you doing?"

"You know I can't get this close to the house without taking pictures."

But what if Franklin's at home and he sees you? He's already upset with us."

"Listen. I didn't come all this way to return home with only a memory. Would it make you feel better if we drove up to his house and asked for permission?"

"Caroline. You're not serious. He told you to let dead bones lie, remember?"

"I heard what he said, but perhaps he was having a bad day. You heard Pastor Jacobs. Franklin's well thought of around here. He's just taking his mother's death extremely hard. I can go to the door while you wait in the car."

She slumped down in the seat and crossed her arms. "Okay. I can do that."

I pulled up the long drive and parked at the end of the front walk. Taking a deep breath, I looked at Kate. "I hope your hotline to heaven is open because I need you to pray right now—hard."

"I can do that too."

I walked up the slate path lined with pink and purple thrift, stepped onto the porch, and rang the bell. The chimes set off a chorus of barking dogs. I waited. Although the dogs continued to bark, I heard no one instructing them to quiet down. I checked my watch. In one sense, I was relieved and in another, disappointed. Our search for information concerning Noah appeared to have come to an abrupt halt, and it wasn't even noon. Glancing back at Kate, I shrugged and pressed the bell again. This time the dogs' refrain came to a high-pitched crescendo. It was apparent we'd hit a dead end.

"Bummer," Kate said as I dropped into the car and laid my head against the seat. "But look on the bright side. Now you can take all the pictures you want."

"I suppose you're right, except Mary Ann did say Franklin rents the homeplace."

"There aren't any cars in the driveway. Go ahead and get your pictures, then we can drive to Elkin for lunch. I'm starved."

"Okay. I'll take my chances here, and then drive down and snap a few pictures at the gate. At least we found Noah's house. If that's our only victory, it's big—and more than we had yesterday."

Chapter Twenty-Six

Friday, September 16, 1938
Elkin, North Carolina
Noah

Noah parked his father's truck in front of the large, two-story brick colonial home in Elkin. Its pristine lawn gave no hint of the towering oaks and red and yellow maples that had begun to shed their leaves. He'd always felt out of place in this part of town, but he never tired of driving beneath the street's arched canopy of trees, especially in the fall.

He tried to imagine what it would be like to live in one of these stately homes. The families who lived in them had lifestyles vastly different from his. Most of the estates belonged to Elkin's elite—bankers, lawyers, and owners of the cotton and grist mills down by the Yadkin River.

He turned off the ignition and stared at the long walk, which led to a porch that stretched the length of the house and imposing double doors. He moistened his lips and swallowed hard. His throat was dry, and his mouth like cotton. Inhaling deeply, he toyed with the idea of restarting the engine and turning the truck back in the direction of Jonesville. Then he thought of Emma. Finding a job was crucial. With no word yet from Greyhound, his hopes waned. He'd do whatever it took to be with her.

Picking up his tan fedora, he tilted the rearview mirror and ran his fingers through his hair. After putting on his hat, he peered into worried eyes staring back at him. *Please, Lord. I need your favor. This visit could make or break me.*

Yellow and amber leaves crunched beneath his feet as he stepped out onto what looked like streets of burnished bronze. Skirting the front of the truck, he ambled onto the curb. Well-manicured boxwoods lining the walkway stood like staunch soldiers observing and surmising whether to negate or approve the guests who came to call. As he walked toward the house, he envisioned two swords at the end of the path, clanging together to form a large X forbidding access to his future.

Thunder rumbled in the distance as a chilly breeze infused with the scent of rain brushed his skin. He inhaled deeply. Stepping onto the porch, he thrust his hand toward the bell. Not wanting to allow himself an easy exit, he pressed it hard, then paced back and forth.

After no response, he rang again.

Through sheer lace curtains covering beveled panes of glass, he saw someone approaching. After Mrs. Jordan, a well-dressed lady with a stylish bob, dark eyes, and soft wrinkles, opened the door, she clapped her hand to her mouth. "Noah Anderson, aren't you a sight for sore eyes?" Rushing onto the porch, she wrapped her arms around him. "I can't begin to tell you how much we've missed you."

"I've—"

"When Alton ran into Sadie a while back, she told him all about your accident." She tilted her head. "How is your back, by the way?"

"It's quite—"

"I was so relieved when I heard you were coming home. One never knows what will happen with all the unrest overseas. Horrible. Simply horrible." Hesitating, she motioned toward the door. "Oh, listen to me running on like a crazy person and not inviting you in. Come in, son. Please come in."

He took off his fedora and stepped into the large foyer, where mixed aromas of supper lingered in the air. "Thank you, ma'am. It's nice to see you."

"Come into the parlor. It begs for company." She led him

to the formal living area and motioned toward the sofa. "Please, have a seat while I get you something cool to drink. Lemonade? Iced tea? I've got fresh mint."

"That sounds mighty nice, but I'm fine. It hasn't been long since I pushed back from Mama's table, and you know how that is."

"Do I ever. She's quite a cook. I can taste her homemade pear preserves and biscuits now. It'll soon be time for those pears to be dropping off, won't it?"

He nodded. "I picked up a basketful this morning. When I carried them inside, Mama said she guessed she had her work cut out for her tomorrow." He motioned. "You should give her a call. She'd love to hear from you."

"I'll do that. We need to catch up. Funny, she lives only a few miles down the road, and I hardly see hide nor hair of her. We all stay too busy these days. A sign of the times, I guess." She seated herself next to him on the sofa. "What brings you here tonight, young man?"

"Well, uh—I was passing through the neighborhood when I thought I'd stop in and see if Alice was around."

"I guess it's your lucky day. After supper, she went upstairs to take an early bath and read the book she picked up at the library this morning." She patted him on the knee. "You sit right there while I run and tell her you're here. She'll be thrilled to see you."

As she hurried into the foyer and ascended the stairs, her voice faded. "Oh, how I wish Alton was here. He'll hate he missed you. He got away right after supper. Had an important commissioner's meeting tonight."

Noah swallowed hard and wished he'd taken Mrs. Jordan up on her offer of something to drink. Looking around the room, he tried hard to ignore the door closing upstairs and the muffled conversation between Alice and her mother. After fluffing the pillows on the sofa, he fiddled with the band on his hat, then walked to the window. The sky was dark.

Walking the perimeter of the room, he remembered evenings spent here with Alice before leaving for Bragg. The memory of the night they broke up sent his anxiety level through the roof. Stopping at the shelves lining one wall, he examined a row of pictures situated as if someone had taken a ruler and measured the distance between each frame. In the line-up, he was surprised to see the last photograph taken of Alice and him sitting beneath a giant oak in the front yard. Picking it up, he noted their smiles. It was a happier time. Neither of them knew then how quickly their relationship would deteriorate.

He wondered what their lives would be like if he hadn't joined the army—hadn't met Emma. Perhaps he and Alice would be married. He'd have a job as a clerk in her father's bank, the First Bank of Elkin, and who knows—maybe there would even be a child on the way.

Hearing the upstairs door open and footsteps on the stairs, Noah returned the frame to the shelf and rushed to reclaim his place on the sofa.

"Alice will be down in a few minutes," Mrs. Jordan said as she stepped into the parlor. "Are you sure I can't get you something to drink?"

"On second thought, tea would be nice. I suppose the country ham I ate for supper made me thirsty."

"Certainly. I'll be right back."

Noah fell against the cushions. Maybe this wasn't such a good idea. If Dan hadn't suggested he try to get back in Alice's good graces, he might not be in this position. He nervously brushed the felt of his fedora. What would he say to Alice after their little fiasco at Turner Drug Store?

"Alice!" He jumped at the high-pitched sound of Mrs. Jordan's voice in the foyer. "Noah is waiting, honey." She entered the room and set a tray holding two glasses of tea with sprigs of fresh mint on the coffee table. "There you go, my dear. Alice will be down in a moment. I'll finish washing up the supper dishes, while you two get reacquainted."

Rising to his feet as she left, he laid his hat beside the tray and picked up a glass of tea. As the cool liquid filled his mouth, Alice entered the room. Startled by her sudden appearance, he spewed tea across the coffee table.

She burst into laughter. "Is my mother's tea that bad, Noah?"

He grabbed a linen napkin and dabbed at the puddles on the table. "Alice. I'm sorry. I didn't hear you coming."

She rushed over, picked up a napkin, and squatted beside him. "You have such a way about you, Noah Anderson. Here, let me help."

After blotting up the tea, they looked at one another, paused, and broke into hysterics. Relieved that the incident had broken the ice between them, Noah rose to his feet and helped Alice to hers.

"What brought you this way tonight, Noah? It's apparent you didn't come for Mother's tea."

He motioned for her to be seated, then took his place beside her on the sofa. "Actually, I came to apologize for my behavior last Saturday. I've thought about what you said, and there isn't any reason we can't be friends. To make up for it, I thought I'd treat you to a milkshake at Turner's this evening. You game?"

"Of course. I'll always take time for a milkshake." She patted his hand. "Give me a moment to freshen up and grab my sweater." Noah's eyes followed her as she left the room.

Leaning back, he stretched his arms across the top of the sofa. All seemed right again. He still cared for Alice and had felt bad about their argument. He was merely doing what was needed to get a job at the extension office—certainly no harm in that. Since Alice now understood they would see one another as friends, his guilt subsided.

Alton Jordan entered from the foyer. "My, oh my. Look who's here. How are you, young man?"

"I'm good." He stood and extended his hand. "It's nice to

see you, sir. Mrs. Jordan said you were at a commissioner's meeting tonight."

"I was on my way when I remembered my notebook. It has all my notes for my presentation tonight, so I rushed back to get it. I'm happy I did." He gripped Noah's shoulder and shook his hand. "It's good to have you home, son. We've missed you around here."

"Thank you. After being away, I have a new appreciation for this area and the people who make it so special."

"Your cousin Dan called to say you're interested in the county clerk position."

"Yes, sir. I am."

"Be sure to go by the office and apply as soon as you can. The position won't be made public till next week, so tell them I sent you. In the meantime, I'll put in a good word for you to the powers-that-be. I'm confident you'd make a good pick. Besides, any young man who's a friend of our Alice must be a fine one." He winked.

Noah's guilt resurfaced, but he tamped it down as quickly as it rose. "Thank you, sir. I appreciate your vote of confidence. I'll get over there first thing next week."

Alice stepped into the parlor, her sweater draped around her shoulders. "Hi, Daddy. I thought you were gone."

"I was, and I'm out the door again now, dear." He patted the binder in his hand. "Had to return for this." He walked over and gave her a quick hug. "You look like you're headed out yourself."

"I am. Noah's invited me to Turner's for a milkshake, and you know that's an offer I can't refuse."

He scratched his balding head. "Hmm. Let me guess. Strawberry with whipped cream."

"And—"

"Oh yes, how could I forget the cherry on top?"

She giggled.

He kissed her lightly on the cheek. "Grab an umbrella on

your way out. There's a storm brewin'.'"

As the door closed, Alice looked at Noah. "Nor would I pass up the opportunity to catch up with an old friend."

Recognizing her all-too-familiar gaze, he brushed aside a twinge of guilt and ushered her into the foyer. Picking up an umbrella from the Victorian hall tree, he glanced in the mirror and firmly pressed his fedora onto his head. *I'm doing this for us, Emma. You'll understand, won't you, sweetheart?*

As he reached for the doorknob, a peal of thunder cracked overhead.

Chapter Twenty-Seven

Later that evening
Jonesville, North Carolina

After shaking the rain from his fedora, Noah closed the door and turned off the porch light. He fumbled with the stiffness of the key in the lock until he remembered he was in Jonesville. Locks weren't necessary. It was one more thing he loved about his hometown, and yet, he was no longer content here—not without Emma.

He tossed his hat on the ottoman, made a beeline for the sideboard in the dining room, and shuffled through the envelopes in the dough bowl—bills, bills, and more bills. *What's up with you, Emma? Four days? I need to hear from you.*

Trying not to disturb his parents in the adjoining room, he tiptoed into the dark kitchen and grabbed a glass from the dish drainer. After filling it with tap water, he leaned against the counter and downed it in three gulps. *Ice cream always makes me thirsty.*

Rain peppered against the window panes. His dark reflection, backlit by the faint light of the desk lamp in the living room, reminded him of how empty his life was. Without Emma, he was but a reflection of himself, moving through days that were colorless and flat. It was hard to believe it had only been three weeks since he'd seen his darling Emma Rose. It felt more like a lifetime. Why hadn't he received a letter today? After all, wasn't she the one who had given him the stationery set and insisted he write?

He'd felt awkward with Alice tonight, but he knew his plan would work. She'd keep her ears tuned for job openings in the area. The clerk position at the General Store was no longer an option. Mr. Bettendorf had hired his neighbor. Alice had also mentioned overhearing her father talk about the county clerk position. When he told her he was applying for it on Monday, he'd asked for her prayers. Her reply was, "I'll go a notch higher. I'll talk to Daddy." Although he wanted her to talk to her father, her spiritual blindness saddened him. Emma may have been in a period of questioning God's activity in her life, but at least she came from a home rooted in faith. He saw first-hand one pitfall of wealth the Jordans had succumbed to—self-sufficiency. They were fine people but blinded to their greatest need.

Noah turned off the lamp in the living room and climbed the stairs. He was desperate to talk to Emma, to hear her voice, but long-distance calls were far too expensive to be an option.

After changing into his pajamas, he arranged the pillows against the oak headboard and turned the radio on the nightstand down low. He lifted the box containing her letters from the drawer, took out a sheet of paper and the pen Emma had given him and poured out his heart to the girl of his dreams.

Hello Sweetheart,

It's late, but I don't want to go to sleep without telling my darling how much I love and miss her.

Do you miss me? Evidently, not as much as I do you since I haven't gotten a letter from you in several days. I looked for one again today, and as I feared, it wasn't there. I know you're working long hours at the Rainbow, but do you think you could write me more often? You can't imagine how I feel. Every day I don't hear from you, I grow more and more insecure. I try not to believe you've lost your love for me, but then I think of every mile, every foot, every inch that separates us. I picture the fellas from Bragg going into the Rainbow and sitting in your section. They'd be insane not to notice how beautiful you are and want to date you.

Oh, darling, you must get tired of waiting, but please be patient. It will be hard to wait until the holidays to see one another, but I won't have enough money for a trip down until I find a job. Things are looking up in that area, though. I'm still waiting to hear from Greyhound, and in the meantime, another job possibility has opened up. I'm applying for a county clerk position with the agriculture extension office in Yadkinville next week. I'll need to take the state exam, but I'm not worried about it. I've got what it takes to pass it with flying colors. When I was at the tannery on Tuesday, my cousin, Dan, gave me inside information about the job. The position hasn't been made public yet, but one of his customers told him about it. If I get my application in on Monday, I should be one of the first to apply.

I've got a bit of a confession to make, though. I hope you won't get mad, but it's not in me to hide anything from you. Remember me talking about my old girlfriend, Alice Jordan? It turns out it was her father who told Dan about the opening. Mr. Jordan's a county commissioner now. He thought Dan might know of someone who would be interested in the position. Of course, Dan thought of me. When I told him Alice and I was no longer on good terms, he said, "Why Noah, you're a sap if you don't get back in with her. Her father can help you get the job. Remember, when it comes to Alice and her father, whatever Alice wants, Alice gets."

You see, sweetheart, I want you to look at what I'm about to tell you as strictly a business proposition, okay? Tonight, I took Alice to Turner Drug Store for a milkshake. I made certain she understood we'd go as friends. What I intend to do is play on her sympathies by poor-mouthing my chances with Greyhound, so she'll see how much I need the job. Hopefully, she'll put pressure on her father, and he'll do all he can to get the extension office to notice me. Mr. Jordan and I always got along good, so if he thinks Alice and I are seeing one another, he'll do everything he can to not disappoint her.

Don't worry about us being together. I know my heart. As far as Alice is concerned, you've nothing to fear. I'm just playin' a bit of politics here. As a matter of fact, I felt funny tonight and very much out of place with her. I don't know how to act around anyone besides you. I love you, and I thought of you the whole evening. I couldn't wait to get home and write you.

Darling, I wouldn't do this if I didn't feel it would speed up our coming together, so let me put it this way . . . if you don't like my plan, ask me to quit, and I will. I'm being honest with you, and I'm asking you to be honest with me—even if it hurts. Will you?

He reached over and turned up the volume on the radio.

The song playing on the radio now is "You're a Sweetheart If There Ever Was One" by Sammy Kaye. That's the most perfect title ever because you are a sweetheart if there ever was one. I'm so blessed to have you. Please, wait for me, darling, and write me soon. Okay?

And, oh yes, I ran into my cousin today. He's the Register of Deeds in Yadkinville. He said if we decide to get married up here, he wants to sell me the marriage license. It's going to happen, Emma. For me, our wedding day can't get here fast enough.

I guess I should turn in. Pop wants me to go to the market again with him tomorrow. Our tobacco crop is slimming down. I'm praying we'll get a reasonable price for this load, since it may be our last one this year. We've had a good season and have a lot to be thankful for. Dream of me, sweetheart.

    I'll always love you,

    Noah

He tucked the box in the drawer and laid his letter on the nightstand beside Emma's photos. Studying one of her in front of the waterfall, he remembered the events that altered their lives and whispered. "You are the only star in my blue heaven, Emma Rose." He turned off the lamp and slid beneath the covers. The rain had stopped, and the moon peeked through the clouds to reveal the outline of the mountain behind their house. Closing his eyes, he imagined the day he and Emma would have a home near the top, and enough children to fill every room with laughter. He couldn't conceive of living his life without her and hoped he'd never have to.

Noah woke to the ring of the telephone and the smell of bacon. He glanced at the clock—9:30. He'd told Pop he'd go to the market with him at 8:00. Throwing back the covers, he slid out of bed, then shuffled across the wooden floor to the doorway. He stopped and listened to his mama talking, and then he heard the receiver drop into its cradle.

"Mama. Where's Pop?"

"He's at the market, Son."

"Why didn't he wake me?

She came to the foot of the stairs. "He didn't have the heart to. We knew you'd gotten in late from your date last night with Alice."

"It wasn't late, and it wasn't a date. We went to Turner's

for a milkshake, and we went as friends. Simply catching up, that's all."

"Well, evidently, you have more catching up to do because that was Alice on the phone. She said she has something important to tell you and for you to call her whenever you get up."

What could possibly warrant such an early morning call? "Okay, I'll call her in a little while."

"Would you like some breakfast?"

"No, thanks. I'll grab a couple of biscuits if Pop hasn't eaten them all."

"He made sure he left you a few." She opened the front door. "I'm walking over to Thelma's to borrow some paraffin. I want to can those pears today and forgot to get wax at the store. Maybe you can help me peel the pears when I get back."

"Sure thing. I'll be down by the time you get home."

He yawned and returned to his room. Rubbing the stubble on his face, he picked up yesterday's clothes from the chair and opened his closet. *Please, Lord. Let Alice have news about the county clerk position. Let this work out for Emma and me. Please, let it be.*

Chapter Twenty-Eight

Saturday, May 12, 2012
Elkin, North Carolina
Caroline

After winding down country roads, we crossed a steel bridge that spanned the Yadkin River and connected the Jonesville community with the city of Elkin.

"Okay, navigator, help me out."

Kate scooted forward in her seat and pointed to a renovated service station. "Look, Caroline, an antique store."

"Not today, Sis. Focus. We're on a mission, remember? Antiquing will have to wait. Besides, I thought you were hungry."

"I am." She settled back in her seat. "Just noting it for future reference."

"Well, how about making note of a place to eat?"

As we turned left onto West Main, we were impressed with the city's nineteenth-century Romanesque-Revival style architecture. Several buildings along the quaint street had been restored to their original glory—a testimony to the pride Elkin citizens take in their rich history. Most of the afternoon's activity appeared to be centered around a red-brick building on the corner—Royall's Soda Shoppe.

"There you go." Kate pointed to a parking space not far from the door. "Let's grab something to eat at Royall's. It should be fun."

As we pushed open the door of the charming fifties-style restaurant, a bell jingled overhead. All eyes turned our way while two silver-haired ladies at a nearby booth appeared to make us the topic of their conversation. The rumor mill in this close-knit community had begun.

A young girl, elevenish, seated us at the front window, handed us menus and took our drink orders. From our table, covered with a red-and-white-checked vinyl cloth and topped with a fresh flower dropped in a mason jar, we held ring-side seats to small-town USA.

"Kate, look." I pointed to the top of the menu—*formerly Turner Drug Store.* "Noah wrote of this place in his letters to Mother. Isn't this exciting. Maybe he sat at this very table with his friends."

She glanced at the Elk Theater across the street. "Yes, I can see him taking in a show with his buddies and then walking over here afterward for a milkshake or a banana split, can't you?"

I pressed my hand to my heart. "Wow. What a morning. Our search has just begun, and I couldn't be happier." I rummaged through my purse and retrieved my glasses. "Stephen will be so proud of us, and he'll especially appreciate the fact he didn't have to post bail for either of us today."

Kate peered around her menu. "Shh! The day's not over."

I smirked. "Let's order. I think I'll get a couple of their 'world-famous' hotdogs along with an order of onion rings. How about you?"

"Sounds like a winner to me. Let's split the rings." She closed her menu and leaned back in her seat. "But one hotdog is all I want." Her eyes widened. "I'm saving room for their homemade peach cobbler with ice cream."

I peered over my readers. "You would. For an *older* sister, you're such a terrible influence on me."

The bell above the door jingled as Kate finished her last bite of cobbler, and I reapplied my lipstick.

"Good afternoon, Franklin. We'll have your table ready in a minute." The cashier picked up a menu and motioned to the young girl who'd taken our orders.

Observing the short man with a stocky build and graying hair, I leaned across the table. "Kate."

Looking up from her now-empty bowl, she wiped her mouth with her napkin. "What? And why are you whispering?"

"Don't look now, but the cashier addressed the man who came through the door as Franklin."

"She did?"

"Yes. Do you suppose that's Franklin Montgomery?"

She dropped her napkin onto the floor, then leaned over to pick it up while craning her neck. Straightening up, she tossed it onto her plate. "Well, age-wise, he could fit."

The young hostess escorted the man to a booth in the back corner. After seating him, she filled his water glass and slipped into the kitchen.

"I'm dying to know if that's him." Dropping my lipstick in my purse, I grabbed my wallet. "Sit here while I pay the bill and get change for the tip."

The petite, middle-aged cashier smiled as she reached for the check. "How was your meal?"

"Wonderful. This place reminds me of my youth. How long has it been here?"

"My grandparents took the building over in 1954. Before then, it was Turner Drug Store. The soda shop side of the store was a popular hangout for young people." She counted back my change. "I take it you're not from around here?"

"No. We're only in for the day." I leaned over and lowered my voice. "Maybe you could help me with something." I motioned toward the corner booth. "I heard you call the gentleman over there 'Franklin.' Would his last name be Montgomery?"

"Yes, it is. You know him?"

"My sister and I are in town researching our family. He's someone we'd like to talk to."

"Franklin's here almost every day for lunch. Same time. Same order. He's not big on conversation, but he's nice enough. You should speak with him."

"Maybe I'll do that. Thanks so much for your help."

"Certainly. And please stop in whenever you're in Elkin."

I nodded, then slid into my seat across from Kate and placed the tip on the table. "I was right. It's him. Noah's nephew."

"You're kidding me. Now what are you going to do?"

"Well, I thought *we'd* go over and talk to him."

"How about a little more you and less we? Count me out. I'll sit here. You're the one who talked with him on the phone. Besides, I wouldn't want him to feel ganged up on."

"You're probably right." I sipped my tea and took a deep breath. "Here goes. Wish me luck."

As I approached Franklin's booth, he squeezed a mound of catsup onto his plate. "Hello. Mr. Montgomery." I extended my hand. "My name is Caroline Myers."

"Carolyn who?"

"It's Caroline. Caroline Myers."

"Am I supposed to know you?"

I slowly withdrew my hand. "We spoke briefly on the phone a couple of days ago."

"We did?" He took a large bite of his hamburger and looked off into the distance. "Oh, yes, we did. I do remember that conversation. You were the one poking around in our family business."

"Yes—I mean, no, not exactly." I twirled Mother's ring on my finger. "I found a box of letters from your uncle to my mother in her trunk. I'm interested in learning more about him."

He dipped a large fry in the catsup and popped it into his mouth, oblivious to the bright-red, vinegary substance that dripped onto his shirt. "If I remember correctly, I told you we don't make a habit of doling out personal information to strangers."

A hush swept over the room. Sensing the quizzical glares

of the other diners, I wanted to run. "Yes, you did, but since my sister and I are in town, we hoped you'd change your mind and talk to us."

"Nothin' to talk about. Didn't know him. And know nothin' about him now."

"But surely you know where he's buried."

"Of course, I know. He's my uncle." He glanced down. "Oh, shoot. Now look." He pulled a napkin out of the stainless container and dabbed at the bright-red spot on his shirt.

"Would you at least tell us where his grave is? My sister and I would love to visit it while we're here."

"Not possible." He dipped the napkin in his water glass and dabbed at the now pinkish circle getting larger by the second. "Haven't got time for that. Got an appointment."

My heart raced. "I'm sure we could find it ourselves."

"I told you, it's not possible. He's buried on my property, and the gate is padlocked." Frustrated, he tossed the napkin on the table and took another bite of his hamburger. "Now, if you don't mind, I'd like to finish my lunch."

I hovered, contemplating my next move.

He looked up at me and glared. "Look." With two quick jabs in the air, he pointed to the clock on the wall behind the counter. "I've got an appointment in twenty minutes. Do you mind if I eat?"

Amid the murmurs of those at neighboring tables, I apologized and turned to leave—then pivoted. "If we came back on a day when you're not busy, would you let us in to see the grave? We'd be happy to pay you for your time."

"Good grief, you're persistent. Just leave me alone, and I'll think about it."

Pin him down, Caroline. "Will it be all right if I call you in a few days to see if we can work something out?"

He shrugged and shooed me away with his hand. "Whatever."

I sighed. "Thank you, sir. Thank you—and have a good day." My knees all but buckled as I lowered my head and walked past annoyed patrons, then collapsed in my seat across from Kate.

She slid my tea glass closer to me. "Well, that was a rather spirited conversation."

"Oh, it was spirited, all right. And I think I know which spirit."

Kate grimaced.

I gulped down the last of my tea.

"So, what now?"

I glanced out the window as a woman walked by with her dog. "He did affirm Noah was buried on his property and agreed to me calling him in a few days."

She beamed. "Well, that's progress. I'm proud of you, Sis."

I fanned my face. "Pass me my purse, and let's get out of here before I lose my 'world-famous' hotdogs."

Once outside, I leaned against the car and inhaled the cool, crisp air. Kate popped the trunk, took out the box of Noah's letters, and motioned. "Get in, I'll read while you drive."

"Deal." I started the car and turned in the direction of Interstate 77. As Kate lifted one of the letters from the box, a scrap of paper fell to the floor. Bending over, she picked it up and stared. I could see the handwriting was Mother's.

She moved her lips while reading silently.

"Well?" I struggled to keep my eyes on the road. "What does it say?"

She shot forward in her seat. "Oh, my."

"What? What is it? Read."

"*March 21, 1947 - I dreamed of Noah last night. He was going to ask me again to marry him. I was nervous with excitement. Today, it all seems so real. I want to put red roses on his grave one day, but if I can't, I hope someone will do it for me. Ever thine, E.*"

Pulling the car off the road, I jolted it to a stop. We stared into one another's eyes and sat speechless. Then we both broke the silence at once.

"We've got to get in to see Noah's grave."

Chapter Twenty-Nine

Saturday, September 17, 1938
Noah

Noah snatched two biscuits from the pan on the stove, tossed them onto his plate, and placed it on the table in front of the window. After pouring a glass of milk, he threw one leg over the chair and dropped into the seat. How he'd missed his mama's homemade biscuits. Splitting one open, he inhaled its aroma, then slathered its hot, flaky surface with homemade butter and pear preserves. Savoring his first bite, he propped the *Elkin Tribune* against the Zenith radio in front of him and flipped to the job listings. A gentle breeze brushed his face as the window's sheer white curtains moved in and out, breathing the promise of a fine autumn day.

A shrill ring pierced the morning stillness as the phone on the wall beside him screamed for attention. He lifted the receiver and pulled down on the mouthpiece. "Hello."

"Good morning, Noah. I hope you slept good."

"I did. And you?" He sensed uneasiness in Alice's voice.

"I tossed and turned all night. I couldn't wait to talk to you this morning."

"What's the matter?"

"I'd rather not discuss it over the phone. One never knows who's listening in. Would you have time today to meet me at Turner's?"

He tilted his chair against the wall and sighed. "If you need me, I'll make it."

"Thanks. I knew I could count on you."

"What time?"

"How does three sound? And today, it's my treat."

He looked up at the clock. "Three's fine. I'll see you there."

As he pulled the receiver from his ear, Alice's voice escalated. "Oh, and Noah. Please don't tell anyone you're meeting me today. Okay?"

"Sure. See you soon."

After replacing the receiver, he leaned his head against the wall and wondered what could be so urgent. He'd not heard this much fretfulness in her voice since the night they'd broken up.

Noah dropped his letter to Emma in the mailbox on the corner and pulled out his pocket watch—2:55 p.m. Lunch rush was over. Returning the timepiece to his pocket, he walked into Turner's and requested a table for two in the back. The waitress led him to a corner booth and wiped off the table. He slipped into the seat facing the door, glanced in the mirror beside him, and brushed back his tousled hair.

As he scanned the daily selections, the bell over the door jingled, and Alice walked in. Before he had time to rise, she'd made a beeline for his table and slipped into the seat opposite him. Her distressed look disturbed him. "What's wrong?"

She shook her head. "Let's order first. Then talk."

After placing their orders, she slipped off her sweater and laid it with her purse on the seat. When she looked up, tears began to flow.

"Please, Alice. Tell me what's wrong. You're scaring me." He fumbled in his pocket for his handkerchief and handed it to her.

She dabbed her cheeks and tried to regain her composure. "I'm sorry I'm such a problem."

"You're *not* a problem. Tell me why you're upset."

"I wanted to tell you last night, but I couldn't find the words. Besides, I hated to put a damper on our first evening together. You deserve better."

He squirmed. "Spill it, please."

She dropped her head and took a deep breath. "I'm pregnant."

Searching for words, he leaned forward and slid his hand across the table. She grasped it firmly. "Oh, Alice. Do your parents know?"

"No. You're the first person I've told—besides the father." She narrowed her eyes at him. "You think I'm awful, don't you?"

With no time to process her words, he had no idea what he thought. "How far along are you?"

She placed her hand on her flat belly. "The doctor said around seven weeks."

He placed his elbows on the table, folded his hands, and lamented. "You know I've gotta ask."

She nodded.

"Who's the father?"

"Tom. Tom O'Leary."

"O'Leary? The guy who works over at Elkin Manufacturing?"

She dropped her head. "Uh-huh."

"I can't believe you dated him."

Embarrassed, she lifted her eyes. "Only for a short time."

"What did he say when you told him about the baby?"

Her eyes bulged as her voice intensified. "He said if I tell anyone he's the father, he'll deny it."

Noah bristled. "What a heel." Releasing her hand, he fell against the back of his seat. "How did you ever get tangled up with that lady's man? You know his reputation."

She sank in her seat. "Please, don't be mad at me. I don't know why I did. He caught me in a weak moment, and I believed he loved me. I see now what he really cared about." She shook her head and buried her face in her hands.

"What's next?"

She lifted her eyes to his and sighed. "The first thing I've got to do is break the news to my parents. They're going to be heartbroken. Beyond that, I haven't a clue."

After the waitress brought their orders to the table, there was a long silence. Noah poured A-1 sauce on his hamburger steak, cut it into pieces, and took a bite, while Alice nibbled on a cracker, then poked at her salad with a fork.

He looked up. "Aren't you going to eat?"

"I've lost my appetite. I hoped I could eat something, but now I'm not hungry."

He took another bite of his steak. "At least try."

"Noah." She paused.

"Uh, huh?"

"Would you go with me to tell my parents?"

He dropped his fork on his plate and grimaced, envisioning Mr. Jordan's face as she broke the news. "I uh …"

"Please. I need a strong arm to lean on. They're going to be so disappointed in me."

He shook his head. "I don't know, Alice."

"Please." She bit her lower lip. "I can't face them alone."

He sat and stared at his plate, then answered. "On one condition."

Her face brightened as she straightened her shoulders. "What?"

"You'll eat your salad and promise me you'll let me pay for your lunch. You know how I hate to eat alone." He winked. "Deal?"

She smiled. "Deal."

Noah pulled up the long drive behind Alice and stopped at the end of the sidewalk leading to the Jordans' front porch.

Alice got out of her car and walked back to his truck. "You haven't changed your mind, have you?"

"I did think about it." He grinned. "But no, I'll see you through."

"I can't thank you enough. I'm sure this isn't easy for you, either."

He climbed out of his truck, placed his hand on the small of her back, and ushered her to the door. As they entered the large foyer, Mr. Jordan was in the adjacent office, pulling a folder from the wooden file cabinet in the corner. He laid it on the desk and walked toward them.

"Hi, Princess," he said as he hugged Alice. "Who's this nice-looking young fellow following you?" She grinned as her dad reached out and shook Noah's hand. "Good to see you again, son. What have you and my daughter been up to on this beautiful Saturday afternoon?"

"We grabbed a bite to eat at Turner's, Daddy. Is Mother around?"

"Yes. She's cleaning the kitchen."

She turned to Noah. "You two chat while I ask her to join us."

Mr. Jordan shrugged as she left the room, then directed his attention to Noah. "Well, my boy, are you ready to trot over to the extension office Monday morning?"

"You bet. Good Lord willin'. I appreciate your offer to put in a kind word for me, sir. I need the work."

He motioned. "Come into my office and have a seat." He walked to a large oak desk in the middle of the room and pulled out his leather chair. Noah seated himself on the sofa across from him and looked around the study at the floor-to-ceiling bookshelves. He wondered why anyone would need so many books.

"You two must have something pretty important on your minds to want to talk to Janice and me together."

Grasping for an answer, he was relieved when Alice and her mother walked into the room.

Mrs. Jordan lifted her eyebrows and hugged Noah. "To what do we owe this fine pleasure?"

"Mother, please have a seat." Alice took her place beside Noah on the couch. An awkward silence loomed as she folded her hands in her lap and looked up at him.

He nodded.

She turned to her parents. "Mother. Daddy. I won't be able to soften the impact of what I have to say, so I want to preface it with . . . I'm terribly sorry. I never set out to hurt you." After swallowing hard, she confessed. "I'm pregnant."

Mrs. Jordan gasped and dropped her face into her hands.

Her father sat stoic, his eyes darting back and forth between the two of them.

She continued. "Let me follow by saying Noah is not the baby's father. I told him at lunch and asked him to come with me for moral support." She reached for his hand. "I couldn't be more grateful that he agreed. He's a true friend."

Her father leaned forward in his chair and folded his hands on his desk. "Who *is* the father, Alice?"

She hung her head. "Tom O'Leary."

He shot from his chair. "The county commissioner's son?"

She lamented. "Yes, sir."

"For heaven's sake, Alice. That boy has always been trouble. If I'd known you were out with him, I would have put a stop to it immediately." He cut his eyes at his wife. "Janice, were you in on this?"

She glanced up and shook her head. Tears streamed down her flushed cheeks.

"No, Daddy. Mother didn't know. Tom and I only went out a few times, and we always met somewhere. I knew neither of you would approve, so I didn't tell you."

Mr. Jordan walked to the window, stood with his back to

the room, and pulled a handkerchief from his pocket. "Now what?" He blew his nose, then jerked around. "What's done is done. There's no rewinding the clock on this one," he said, stuffing his handkerchief into his pocket.

The tension in the room was palpable. Alice squirmed beside Noah as her father walked over and placed his hands on his wife's shoulders. She reached up and clung to them.

"This isn't the way we envisioned the announcement of our first grandchild." Mr. Jordan's words caught in his throat. "We'll need time to adjust—sort through the hurt and discuss how to proceed from here."

Alice ran to him. Throwing her arms around his waist, she buried her head in his chest. "Daddy, I'm so sorry I've hurt you both. Please, forgive me. I need you and Mother desperately right now."

He encircled her with his arms and kissed the top of her head. "Don't cry, Princess. We'll get through this."

Mrs. Jordan walked over and embraced them. As they stood huddled in silence, Noah sighed, relieved at the support her parents gave her.

Moments later, Mr. Jordan approached him and looked him in the eyes. "Son, I've always thought you were a special young man. Now I know it." He patted him on the back. "Thanks for coming with Alice. She'll be fine. We need time alone now."

Alice skirted up beside him. "Daddy, may I walk Noah to the door?"

"Of course."

She grabbed his hand. When they stepped onto the porch, she peered at him through glistening eyes. "How can I ever thank you for coming with me today?"

He placed his index finger on her mouth. "Shh! Thanks isn't necessary. What are friends for?" He took her face in his hands. "Now, give me a smile before I leave, so I'll know you're all right."

She giggled.

"That's my girl. Run inside now. Good will come from this, you'll see."

She rose on her toes and pecked him on the cheek. "I hope you're right." Stepping inside the door, she eased it shut, holding his gaze until the latch clicked.

Noah stepped off the porch and sighed. *How did I get into this mess? If Alice ever finds out that I entered this relationship as a means to an end, she'll be devastated.*

Chapter Thirty

Hello Sweetheart,

You'll never know how relieved I was when I returned from my interview today and found your letter on the sideboard. I've worried I wouldn't hear from you again since telling you I've renewed my friendship with Alice. Thanks for supporting me in my plan to see her and for being truthful with me. I know it's difficult for you to think of me with her, but I always want us to be honest with one another. I can assure you, she's only a friend—sort of like a sister. She's going through a difficult time right now, and she told me her father is impressed with how I've been there to encourage her. It never hurts to impress the one I need to put in a good word for me at the extension office.

The man I had my second interview with today told me Mr. Jordan gave me a glowing recommendation. I'm confident I did well on the state board, so I feel good about my chances of getting the job. We'll know more after my test results come in, so hang on, we'll be together soon. The wait will be worth it in the end.

It's good to know Cee will give you time off work when I come after Thanksgiving. We'll celebrate our Christmas early. I can't wait for you to open the gift I made for you at the tannery. I hope you love it as much as I enjoyed making it for you. I'm marking off the days on the calendar till we're together again.

Noah looked up from his writing as a soft tap came on his bedroom door.

"Noah, can I talk to you for a minute?"

"Of course, Sadie. It's unlocked." He put down his pen. "Come in."

She smiled, whisked across the room, and positioned herself on the edge of the chair by the window.

"You look nice. Did you and Vince have a good time at the show?"

"Uh-huh." Her eyes scanned the room as she fidgeted with the strap on her purse.

Her uneasiness caught him off guard. "What's playing?"

"Frank Capra's *You Can't Take It with You*."

"How was it?"

"It started off slow, but overall, it was hilarious. Jean Arthur played Alice Sycamore, a secretary at a bank who got engaged to the banker's son. You'd probably enjoy it." She scooted back in her chair. "But that's not what I came to talk to you about."

He felt his stomach knot. "What's up?"

She hesitated. "Well . . . a couple of girls were sitting in the row behind us at the theater. Evidently, the Alice in the movie triggered their conversation. One of them asked the other if she'd heard about Alice Jordan."

"Alice?" He swallowed hard and took a sip of water from his glass on the nightstand.

"When she said she hadn't, the first one told her she'd heard Alice was pregnant." She studied Noah's face. "Is that true?"

He dropped his head and sighed. "I wish I could tell you it's a wild rumor, but she's right." His stomach churned as his eyes darted to Sadie's. "And don't you dare go around saying I said so."

She grimaced. "Of course, I won't. How's Alice doing?"

"Okay. At least her parents are supportive. That helps a lot."

"Good." She cleared her throat. "I don't know how to tell you this, but there's more to the story."

He slowly shook his head and winced.

She squirmed. "I don't even want to repeat it."

He looked up. "Just say it, Sis."

"This is so hard." She shifted in the chair. "One of the girls said she'd heard the baby belonged to . . ." She dropped her head and murmured, ". . . to you."

"What?" He covered his face with his hands and dropped back, his head hitting the headboard.

"Is that true too, Noah?"

He sat up straight and looked dead in her eyes. "How absurd. I can't believe you asked me that, Sadie."

She flinched.

He threw his legs over the side of the bed, rested his arms on his knees, and wrung his hands. "Absolutely not. I haven't even been home long enough for that to be possible."

"How far along is she?"

"Going on three months." He got up, shoved his hands in his pockets, and paced back and forth, jingling his change. "I hope you turned around and told her it wasn't true." He stopped and glared at her. "You did, didn't you?"

She fixed her eyes on the oak boards beneath her feet and shook her head.

He thumped his forehead with his palm. "Oh, good grief."

"I'm sorry, Noah. I was so shaken when I heard your name. I didn't know what to say. I couldn't imagine the baby being yours, but—please forgive me. I should never have even considered the possibility."

He dropped onto the foot of the bed and stared at the door. "I'm ruined. If my own sister wonders about me, you can bet the whole town will." He shook his head. "Wow. What a mess.

If this rumor gets back to Emma, I'm cooked." He wiped the perspiration from his forehead, then stood and paced the floor again.

Sadie cringed, then blurted, "I don't know how she'd find out, but if you're worried, maybe you should tell her yourself."

"I don't know." He walked over to the nightstand and picked up his glass. Throwing his head back, he downed what was left of his water and slammed the glass onto the stand.

Sadie jumped.

Wiping his mouth with his sleeve, he spun around. "If you and Dan hadn't encouraged me to see Alice again, maybe I wouldn't be in this mess."

She sat silent, then stood and wrapped her arms around him.

He remained rigid.

She backed away. "I'm sorry I had to tell you, but I thought it would be better if you heard the news from me."

He walked to the window and stared into the darkness.

"I'm sorry. I'll leave you alone. Try not to worry about it. We know the truth, regardless of what's said."

"Yeah, sure. That's easy for you to say."

Sadie left the room and eased the door shut.

Noah gazed out the window for a long time, then fell onto the bed and stared at the ceiling. *How will I ever break this to Emma?* He picked up his letter to her and held it to his chest. *Oh, Emma Rose. How did everything get so twisted? All I wanted was for us to be together.*

Soft shadows danced on the wall as the rays of the morning sun filtered through the sheer curtains. Noah blinked, trying to bring the bulb hanging from the ceiling into focus. Still dressed in the white shirt and navy-blue pants he'd worn to his interview the day before, he sat up and glanced at the clock—6:30. As thoughts of his conversation with Sadie came crashing in, he fell back on the bed and groaned. *It wasn't a nightmare.*

Rubbing his forehead, he got up and stepped into the hall. Sadie's door was shut. She'd probably sleep late after her date with Vince last night. Hearing his parents' laughter in the kitchen saddened him. People would soon talk, and their firstborn would be in the middle of a scandal. They didn't deserve the embarrassment.

Crossing the hall to the bathroom, he looked at himself in the mirror and rubbed the stubble on his chin. Perhaps he should grow a beard. Maybe people wouldn't recognize him. After splashing cold water on his face, he reached for the towel and buried his head in it. How must Alice feel? For him, it was a false rumor. For her, a reality.

He finished up in the bathroom, then pulled a fresh pair of jeans and a flannel shirt from the closet, along with the belt he'd made at the tannery. Typically, he'd be starved by now, but the smell of sausage rising from the kitchen nauseated him. He considered going back to bed but knew it would be better to stay busy. He couldn't rein in the rumors, but he could choose to control his thoughts. He'd finish his letter to Emma after his trip into Elkin to pick up the part for Pop's tractor.

He descended the stairs and stooped to stroke the cat lying on the braided rug at the door. "Good morning, Callie. The sun feels good, doesn't it?" He entered the kitchen and nodded at his parents. "Morning."

Mr. Anderson sat reading the *Elkin Tribune* while his mother scribbled a few things on her grocery list. After pouring himself a steaming cup of coffee, he joined them at the table.

His father looked over his wire-rim glasses. "How'd you sleep?"

"Like a rock. Don't think I moved a muscle." He reached for the pitcher and added cream to his cup.

"I'm sorry I was in the barn when you got in last night."

His words dwindled as he shook his head. "Still tinkering with that blasted tractor."

"Yeah, that's what Mama said. Thought I'd run over to the Tractor Supply today and pick up the part you need."

"Sounds good to me. Thanks, Son. I forgot what it was like to have help around here. It's nice to have you home."

He smiled. "Hopefully, I'll be more helpful in a month or two. Thanks to your good doctoring, my back feels a lot better." He turned to his mother. "I can also pick up the groceries if you want."

"I'd love that. I've got enough to do around here to keep me busy. Let me jot down a couple of more items, and I'll give you my list."

His father folded the paper and pushed his chair from the table. "How'd the interview go yesterday?" He stretched out his legs and crossed his ankles.

"Swell. Mr. Lewis said Alice's father gave me a glowing recommendation. I'm sure it'll help me stand out from the rest of the applicants. He'll let me know something more after my test results come in, and he interviews a couple more people."

"Sounds promising." Mr. Anderson rose from his chair and patted Noah's shoulder as he walked to the stove. Filling his cup, he then leaned against the sink and took several sips before pouring the remainder down the drain. "It's about time I head out and see what I can accomplish this morning." He pulled his denim jacket from the hook by the door. "Thanks for picking up the alternator. Hopefully, I've diagnosed the problem, and it will do the trick."

"Glad to help. Got to earn my keep around here. At least for a few more days. Maybe I'll be able to contribute something to the expenses soon."

"If you can, that'll be good. If not, we'll do what we've gotta do. The Lord's been good to us. Got a better price at the market for this year's tobacco than I expected. Not gonna complain." He brushed back his thinning hair with his hand and put on his wide-brimmed felt hat, its faded brim frayed and smudged with oil. "Well, the day's not getting any longer. See you two later."

Noah watched through the window as his father walked to the barn with Shep and Molly, their two border collies, at his heels. Shep limped along as Molly ran circles around him. Shep had been a part of the family since Noah was ten. No better dog around. Even now, he thought he had to be in the center of the activity.

"Get yourself something to eat, Son. There are sausage biscuits under the foil on the stove."

"Thanks, Mama, but I'm not hungry."

His mother looked up from her list and peered over her glasses. "What? Not hungry? You sick?"

"A bit of a queasy stomach is all."

She stood and placed her hand on his forehead. "You don't have a fever."

"Probably something I ate yesterday. Don't worry. I'll feel better once I start moving around."

Walking over to the pantry, she jotted down another grocery item.

Noah continued to stare out the window.

"Son, I know something's bothering you. What's weighing so heavy on your mind this morning?"

He took a sip of coffee as he struggled to find the right words. "I guess now's as good a time as any."

She eased herself into the chair. "What is it?"

"It's Alice."

"Alice?" She leaned in. "Is she okay?"

"She . . . she's pregnant."

His mama clapped her hand over her mouth. "Oh, dear. Are you positive? Who told you?"

"She did."

"Oh, poor dear. She's so young. Wanted to be a teacher, so I hear. When's the baby due?"

"Sometime in March."

"Is she going to marry the baby's father?"

"Hardly. That cad said if Alice tells anyone the baby's his, he'll deny it."

She shook her head. "Oh, how sad. I wonder how the Jordans took the news. People are prone to talk, you know."

"Oh, believe me, I know."

"Why do you say it like that? Have you already heard something?"

"You might say so."

"What? Don't play games with me." She tapped her pencil on the table. "What have you heard?"

"I'm glad you're sitting down, Mama." He took a deep breath. "Sadie told me last night she overheard two girls at the theater talking about Alice, and one of them said she'd heard the baby was . . . was mine."

"Yours?" Her eyes bulged. "Did I hear you right? People think her baby is yours? Why that's not even possible. You've only been home a few weeks."

"People don't care about the facts, Mama. They only want to run with the rumor. I hate this for everyone. And you and Pop don't deserve to be pulled into this scandal. It's so unfair."

"Life's seldom fair, my boy. Of course, dealing with the whispers and stares will be difficult. But we know the truth, and that's all that matters. The truth sets us free."

"Now you sound like Sadie."

"Well, she gave you a good word. Our job is to pray for those who speak poorly about us, and we especially need to pray for sweet Alice. We all make mistakes, and not one of us is outside the realm of God's grace."

He smiled. "How did you get so wise, Mama? You always say the right things."

"Not my doin'. It's the good Lord's. Comes from staying in the Word and prayer—lots of it." She reached across the table and placed her hand on his. "You hold your head high and don't worry about what people say. You've got nothing to be ashamed of. Remember, Satan may power the ship, but God steers it. He can use it all for His purpose and glory. Eventually, the truth will come out. You'll see."

"Boy, I wish you could talk to Emma. I'm afraid when she finds out all of this, she'll never speak to me again."

"Be honest with her, Noah. Even if it means losing her love. If you're not, it will come home to bite you and destroy your relationship. How she responds to the news isn't yours to control. You do your part and trust God to do His. If you and Emma are meant to be together, you will be."

"Thanks, Mama. I've missed our talks." Standing, he bent down and kissed her on the forehead. "Hand me that list, and I'll run along. You've got work to do, and I've got a letter to finish."

He walked past the stove, then returned to snatch a biscuit from underneath the foil.

Chapter Thirty-One

I took the box from Kate as she climbed down the steps from Mother's attic.

"Whew! I should've brought my face mask. With all this dust and the pollen this spring, I'm a mess." She crooked her arm over her mouth. "Achoo!"

"Bless you." I carried the box marked "miscellaneous" to Mother's bedroom and placed it on the bed. "What do you suppose we'll find in this one? Anything of interest?"

"I'd say more of the same." She plopped down on the bed and snipped the air with her fingers like a pair of imaginary scissors. "Clippings, clippings, and more clippings. I wonder if we'll ever sort through all this stuff."

After picking up the box cutter from the nightstand, I slit open the top.

Kate peered in. "See, I told you. Do you think Mother really thought we'd read all this?"

"Hardly." I handed her a thick black scrapbook, then lifted out an old Whitman's Sampler labeled *Fayetteville Observer clippings*. "I suppose saving it passed the time and brought her comfort."

While I thumbed through the box, Kate flipped through the album and sighed. "As I thought, more clippings. Have you talked with our friend Franklin yet?"

"No. He was pretty agitated when we spoke at Royall's

Saturday. I'm giving him a few more days to cool off."

"Dollars to donuts, he doesn't let us see the grave."

"Thanks for your vote of confidence." I sat on the bed beside her. "You're probably right, but I'm trying to stay positive."

Kate leaned over, picked up a clipping that had dropped on the floor, and stuffed it back in the album. "I don't think Mother ever really got over Noah, do you?"

"Evidently not. I know she loved Daddy, but there's something unforgettable about first love, wouldn't you say?"

"I'd love to forget mine. He loved himself more than me." She shook her head. "Such a lady's man. Glad I found out before we walked the aisle."

I rolled my eyes. "Oh yes, good old Marvin—Mr. Marvin Godfrey Miller, III—alias MGM *in* living color."

Kate tipped her nose in the air, lowered her voice an octave, and dragged out her words. "God's gift to the world."

We laughed.

"I warned you about him. But, oh no, you wouldn't listen to your baby sister."

She shrugged. "I guess you have been right a few times in your life."

"Oh, wow! An acknowledgment. Where's my phone? I need to record this."

Kate rolled her eyes.

I stuffed a handful of the clippings in the box and added it to the discard pile. "I don't think there's going to be much worth keeping in this box. How are you coming with the album? Anything of interest?"

"Not really. There are a few photos taped in here. I guess we should hold onto it and go through—wait. What's this?" Kate held up a sepia-toned photograph that had slipped into the album's spine, "Maybe this is Noah?" She flipped it over and slid her glasses down from her hair.

I inched closer and peered over her shoulder as she read

mother's note. "'*My heart can hardly stand it. My dear friend is missing. Hold tightly to the cross, love. It will see you through.*' I can't make out the date. It's too faded." She read the cryptic message a second time. "Who is this? Is this Noah?"

I took the photo from her hand and looked at the handsome soldier leaning against a car. "I don't know, Kate. This venture gets more perplexing by the day."

She laid the album on the bed and put the picture on the nightstand. "We've been at this for several hours now. Let's break. I'm famished."

"Sounds like a plan to me."

Kate disappeared into the dining room while I pulled a couple of glasses from the kitchen cabinet. "What's on today's menu?"

"My homemade chicken salad croissants and chips. I threw in my neighbor's brine pickles too." Walking into the kitchen, she dropped a dead rose in the trash, then grabbed a pair of scissors from the catch-all drawer. "That rose has seen its best day. I'll be right back with another."

I pulled the food from Kate's carry-all and set the round knotty-pine, dining room table. "Oh, if this table could talk, the stories it would tell." Memories of meals around it with Mother and Dad were now bittersweet.

Returning, Kate filled a white hobnail vase with water, dropped in a fresh red rose, and placed it in the center of the table.

After blessing the food and biting into my croissant, I pulled one of Mother's journals from a stack on the sideboard. Spreading it open beside my plate, I thumbed through it. "I think this is the one we were looking at last time. As time-consuming as it is to go through all of these things, I'm certainly glad Mother kept these journals. She taped all kinds of things in here."

"Of course." She snipped the air with her fingers and laughed.

"Wait a minute." I studied the page, then passed the open journal across the table. "Look at this."

Kate scanned it. "Look at what? The postcard?"

"No, the receipt. Read it."

"Saturday, August 13, 1938. Sunnyside Floral Nursery, Fayetteville, North Carolina." She looked up at me and shrugged.

"Read on. Who's it made out to?"

Kate mouthed the words to herself as she read, then spoke them aloud. "Mr. Noah Anderson, Fort Bragg, North Carolina. Two American Beauty red rose bushes. $6.00."

"There you go."

"No way." She dropped the journal onto the table and fell against the chair back. Our eyes met and then simultaneously moved to the single red rose in the center of the table. We sat spellbound until I broke the silence.

"It all makes sense now, doesn't it?"

"It does. Mother dragged that rose bush to every house she and Daddy ever lived in."

"You don't need to tell me. Stephen dug the huge hole for it under her bedroom window when she moved here. His back was sore for a week."

Kate shook her head, picked up the vase, and sniffed the rose. "Noah has literally been under our noses all of our lives."

"Yep! Unbelievable."

Monday, May 21, 2012

A smile inched across my face as I wiped the writing surface of Mother's mahogany desk with the soft cloth. She loved nothing more than a sheet of pretty paper to connect with friends across the miles. Of course, those endearing relationships diminished in her later years, as had the fine art of letter writing with the emergence of our techie society. I brushed my fingers over the slight impressions left by her pen in the polished finish. Life without her unwavering presence was surreal.

A shrill ring pierced the morning stillness and scattered my thoughts. The caller ID read Greg Miller. *Greg Miller?* I picked up the handset. "Hello."

"Hi, Caroline. This is Mary Ann from Hickory."

"Yes. How are you? It's good to hear from you."

"I'm doing pretty well. I'll be better once all this pollen settles down. The question is—how are you?"

"I'm all right. The last couple of weeks have been difficult. After eight months, my sister and I decided it was time to sort through Mother's things."

"I can relate. Even though Mama's been gone a couple of years, I still have my days. Her death affected me more than I imagined it would. I thought her long illness had prepared me, but I guess there's no way you can prepare for losing your mother. I think I told you the last time we talked that there's still a lot of Mama's things Franklin and I need to go through. We've managed to make progress, but with me living over an hour away from Jonesville, it's been hard."

"I'm sure. At least Kate and I live close enough to run over to Mother's whenever we want."

"How perfect. I called to tell you Franklin told me he ran into you at Royall's last week."

"Yes. We were so surprised. I'm glad I finally got to meet him."

"I hope he was cordial. If not, I apologize. My brother can be hard to get along with at times, and Mama's death has exacerbated it. Since he lived next door and cared for her during her illness, he's felt the impact of her passing more than I have. The timing of it brought back a lot of hard memories for him. Six months before Mama's death, his wife died suddenly. He's had his hands full settling both estates. Going to the graves isn't something he's been able to manage emotionally since we buried Mama."

"I'm so sorry. He was a little agitated with me but had an appointment that afternoon, so I understood."

"Yes, with Mama's attorney. Franklin told me you'd like to visit Noah's grave."

"We'd love to. And since we bumped into Franklin last week, something's come up that makes it even more important for us to visit."

"Well, I think I've about talked my brother down off the ledge. He's agreed to take you to the family plot."

"Oh, Mary Ann. I can't thank you enough."

"No problem. If it was something that involved my mother, I'd want to search it out too. Franklin wants me to be there when you come, so I thought I'd call you to set up a day. I work part-time. Will a Saturday work for you?"

"Let me get my calendar." I pulled my day planner from the desk drawer in the kitchen and flipped through it. "June 16th will be fine." We settled on one o'clock.

Mary Ann said, "In the meantime, I'll get in touch with Franklin and see if the sixteenth will be good for him. If he doesn't want to go to the plots, I'll get the key from him and take you myself."

"Perfect. Kate will be thrilled. You have no idea how much this means to us."

"I think maybe I do. Oh, and one other thing. I went through more of Mama's things and found a couple of items you'll be interested in."

"Really? Care to give me a hint?"

"If it's all right with you, I'd rather not. I want it to be a surprise. I'll bring them with me when we go to the grave."

"Now you've really got my curiosity up. I can hardly wait. I've inked in Saturday, June 16th, on my calendar."

"It'll be a great day. We'll talk again soon."

As quickly as I hung up the phone, I dialed Kate's number and danced through the house. "Mother, your daughters made it happen. Noah is going to get your roses."

Chapter Thirty-Two

Thursday, October 13, 1938
Jonesville, North Carolina
Noah

Noah pulled the lawn chair underneath the pear tree in the backyard and sat down. After placing the stationery box on the table beside him, he clasped his hands behind his head. The pressure of his back against the cold metal set the chair's spring-like action into motion. His incessant rocking was an outward indicator of his mounting anxiety.

Twelve days had passed since he'd written Emma about Alice's pregnancy, and he'd yet to receive a reply. His vision of their future home on the mountain was fading as rapidly as the autumn colors that had first set the trees ablaze. Dry, brittle leaves now covered the ground, offering it their protection from the long, cold nights ahead. Would Old Man Winter also usher in a world without Emma?

He couldn't shake her tales of soldiers who continued to tease her about her loyalty to him. They did everything possible to plant seeds of doubt in her mind concerning his faithfulness to her. At least Tucker was there to encourage and reassure her of his devotion. Noah's upcoming trip to Fayetteville, the day after Thanksgiving, couldn't arrive fast enough.

He pulled the envelope containing her engagement ring from the box, shook the ring into his palm, and held it against the evening sun. Rainbows of color danced on each tiny facet. He'd made a couple of payments to Dan with his final checks from Bragg, and with the prospects of a job, the ring would soon be his. More importantly, Emma would too.

Hearing the crunch of gravel beneath the tires of a car pulling into the driveway, he dropped the ring back into the envelope and returned it to the box. The glare of the setting sun made it impossible for him to see the visitor, yet he threw up his hand and waved. The car stopped at the foot of the back steps, and the driver stepped out.

"Good evening, Noah."

He shielded his eyes. "Mr. Jordan, how are you, sir?" He walked over and shook his hand, then placed another chair under the tree across from his. Hopefully, Alice's father had come with good news concerning the job in Yadkinville. "Have a seat. What brings you here this nice evening?"

"I've been rolling a few things over in my mind. Thought I'd stop by and run them by you."

His hopes of a job announcement diminished. "Sure, but first fill me in on how Alice is. I haven't talked to her in a few days."

"She's all right. Experiencing some morning sickness, but it's to be expected." He took off his straw hat and laid it on the grass beside his chair. "How are you fairing? Alice told me about the rumor going around town." He shook his head. "A shame. Mighty sorry, son."

"Don't worry about me. You've got enough on your mind. Every now and then, I run into someone who makes a crude remark, but I keep right on walking."

"You're a better man than me. Hearing cruel comments about my daughter makes me fighting mad."

"I can certainly understand why they would."

"Alice is a good girl. Made a mistake, that's all—a big one, but a mistake just the same." He sat silent for a short time, then cleared his throat. "This whole situation is what I came to talk to you about."

Noah rocked back and forth in his chair,

"First, I want to thank you for supporting Alice as you have. Your kindness has meant a great deal to her—to all of us."

"You don't need to thank me, sir. I'm glad I can be here for her. Alice means a lot to me too."

"I can tell. Not many men would stick around and remain under the gun like you have. Young men like you are few and far between."

"I don't know about that, sir, but I appreciate the compliment."

"I suppose I should get to my point." He paused as if words eluded him. "Janice and I have talked this through. As you know, Alice is under a lot of stress." He stretched his legs and pushed back in his chair. "She's ashamed her baby doesn't have a daddy—at least not one to speak of."

Noah leaned forward and rested his elbows on his knees.

"I don't mean to put you on the spot, but Janice and I need to make some important decisions about our daughter's future."

Noah looked up at Mr. Jordan, sat back in his chair, and resumed rocking. "What do you mean?"

"We've talked about sending Alice to her aunt's in Charlotte for a while. At least there she could drive into town and not suffer ridicule like she does here. Then, after the baby's born, we could help her find a place of her own. She could get a fresh start, so to speak."

Noah's apprehension waned. "What does Alice think?"

"We haven't talked to her about it yet. Still pondering all of our options." He looked straight at Noah. "That's where you come into play, son."

He rubbed the back of his neck and swallowed hard. "Me? Really?"

"As I said, it's apparent you care for Alice." He crossed his arms. "I certainly don't want to put pressure on you, but her mother and I have wondered what your feelings are concerning her. We thought if you care about her as much as it appears you do—and if you still plan to date her—maybe you two would consider marriage."

He met Mr. Jordan's penetrating gaze and ceased rocking. "Marriage?"

"I realize this comes as quite a shock, but we figure if Alice were married, she could stay in the area."

Noah froze.

"With no job, I understand you're strapped right now, so Alice's mother and I would see you lack for nothing. At least until you land a job and can make ends meet."

His voice cracked, "I don't know what to say." He stared at his shoes, then shut his eyes as the ground started to spin.

"Don't worry. You don't need to give me an answer tonight—that wouldn't be fair. But I do hope you'll consider what I'm saying."

Noah's muscles went limp as he slid back in his chair and stared at the outline of the mountain against the night sky.

Mr. Jordan placed his hand on Noah's knee. "Sleep on it, son. Give yourself a day or two to mull things over." He picked up his hat from the ground and stood. "We'll talk again later."

Unsure if his legs would support him, Noah edged forward and slowly pushed himself to his feet. "Yeah, I definitely need time to think about this."

Mr. Jordan put his arm around Noah's shoulders as they walked toward the car. "Thank you for hearing me out. I know it's a lot to take in." At the car, he placed his hat on his head and shook Noah's hand. "Have a nice night."

He nodded. "You too."

Mr. Jordan opened the car door, then hesitated. "Oh, I do have a bit of news you might be interested in."

Noah stepped back and locked his knees. "What's that?"

"I heard through the grapevine yesterday that Mr. Lewis at the extension office has boiled the selection for the county clerk position down to two prospects—you and a business school graduate. Lewis said he really likes you. Thought you had a lot of charisma, but it was hard for him to ignore the other man's credentials." He smiled. "If you want me to, I'll pay Mr. Lewis a visit and put in another good word for you. Having a stable position with the county would certainly help a young family starting out. Would be a good stepping stone to a higher position." He winked. "You sleep on it, son." He tipped his hat, slid behind the wheel of his car, and backed down the drive.

Noah stood stoic. As he watched the car's headlights recede, every beat of his heart pulsed in his ears. With two taps of the horn, Mr. Jordan disappeared, and the last rays of light were sucked from Noah's world.

Returning to the backyard, he collapsed in his chair and rocked. As he peered into the starless sky, his thoughts drifted to Emma. Perhaps her letter would never come.

Oh, Lord, what have I done? I've made such a mess of things. Perhaps she would be better off without me.

Sunday, October 16, 1938

Noah hoisted himself into his pop's truck and rolled down the window. Watson Mill Baptist Church was within walking distance, but he planned to drive to Elkin and drop by the Jordans' home after the service. Since his mama was under the weather, his parents had stayed tucked in. Not wanting to add to their distress, he hadn't mentioned his conversation with Alice's father. Besides, he couldn't bring himself to repeat it. He knew it was crazy, but he felt if he released the words into the air, the whole outrageous scenario would come to pass.

It had been over two weeks since he'd written Emma about Alice's pregnancy, and she'd still not replied. He'd dropped another note in the mail, but not enough time had passed for her to receive it. If his parents hadn't needed the truck the following day for a doctor's visit, he'd drive past the church and head straight to Fayetteville. He could be there by nightfall.

Pulling into the church's gravel lot, he parked and waited for a young family to walk inside. The last thing he wanted was to converse with anyone. The uncertainty of what people had heard left him self-conscious and guarded. To remove any chance of exchange with others after service, he planned to duck out during the closing prayer.

He passed through the foyer and slipped onto the back pew. Mrs. Ferguson, his boyhood Sunday School teacher, smiled and handed him her hymnal, then opened another for herself. She'd retained this pew for as long as Noah could remember, always keeping a strict eye on her junior boys.

The congregation was singing the opening hymn, "Trust and Obey." Yep, he knew the words well. *"Trust and obey for there's no other way to be happy in Jesus but to trust and obey."* A dose of being happy in Jesus was exactly what he needed. Too bad he'd messed up on the obey part. He never should have thought he could use Alice to improve his chance of getting a job with the county. Now he'd have to see how he would do with the trusting part. If he confessed his wrongs to the Jordans, could he trust God with the outcome? Could God trust him?

After the offering was collected, Pastor Applegate stepped to the pulpit and opened his large Bible. "Turn in the Holy Scriptures to the second chapter of Philippians, verse three."

Noah flinched as he thought of the Bible he'd left on his nightstand. From the corner of his eye, he saw Mrs. Ferguson flip through the worn pages of her Bible and then stop. Feeling her all-too-familiar glare, he cut his eyes to meet hers.

She furrowed her brow and pursed her lips.

This time, he reckoned he deserved her scowl. He'd forgotten to pick up his Bible a lot lately.

"Let's all stand for the reading of God's Word." Everyone rose. "'Let nothing be done through strife or vainglory; but in lowliness of mind let each esteem other better than themselves.'" Pastor Applegate scanned the congregation. "May God bless the reading of His Word. Please be seated."

Noah squirmed as the words of the lone verse ricocheted through his mind. The pastor's message seemed to be directed at him. He wondered if he'd received his inspiration from the rumor mill. Noah had always thought if the sermon didn't step on his toes, the pastor wasn't earning his keep. This morning, Pastor Applegate's worth wasn't in question. His message confirmed what God had already spoken to his heart. He'd have to come clean with the Jordans. Job or no job, he could no longer live with his dishonesty.

As he walked to the truck, he asked God to forgive his foolishness and to give him the words to say—especially to Alice. More than anything, he didn't want her hurt again. She'd suffered enough rejection and didn't deserve any of it.

While driving at a snail's pace down Watson Mill Road, he rehearsed his confession out loud. The closer he got to Elkin, the lighter his heart became.

Chapter Thirty-Three

Elkin, North Carolina

Stopping in front of the Jordan's estate, Noah resisted the urge to pull away and set the parking brake. As the lump in his throat grew larger, he removed his tie and unbuttoned the collar of his starched white shirt. He wasn't sure if the sweat rolling down his back was due to the unseasonably warm day or his nerves running amok. He prayed.

After reaching for his suit coat on the passenger's seat, he pulled a linen handkerchief from its inner pocket and wiped his brow. Then, stuffing it into the pocket of his trousers, he walked down the pathway leading to the long, freshly painted porch.

The words he'd rehearsed now seemed inadequate given Pastor Applegate's reference to those of Ralph Waldo Emerson. *"What you do speaks so loud that I cannot hear what you say."* Aware no confession could reverse or alleviate the pain of his selfish actions, he prayed the Jordans would hear his heart and forgive him.

After pressing the bell, he turned to see Mr. Jordan's shiny green '37 Packard roll up the driveway. Alice's father stopped the sedan at the end of the porch and shouted. "No one's home, Noah. Come around back while I park the car."

He walked behind the house and greeted Alice's father as he slid from the car's plush interior. "It's good to see you, sir. I'm glad I didn't miss you."

"Me too, son. I just dropped Alice and her mother by Marge Whitson's house. She thought teaching them how to crochet would help Alice pass the time and look forward to the baby's birth."

"Sounds like a swell afternoon for them."

Mr. Jordan motioned for Noah to walk ahead of him toward the house. "Amid all of the rumors, it's been hard to stay focused on what matters. We don't want to forget Alice carries a precious life inside of her—a baby whose arrival should be anticipated, not dreaded. It's nice to see Janice and Alice getting excited about the baby. Crocheting blankets and booties has been great therapy for them."

He turned the key in the lock and pushed open the door to the mudroom. After hanging his hat on the hall tree, he ushered Noah into the kitchen. "How about a glass of cold water?"

Finding it difficult to swallow, Noah was grateful for the offer. "Sounds perfect." He paced the floor and jingled the keys and change in his pockets as Mr. Jordan grabbed a couple of glasses from the cupboard and pulled a pitcher from the icebox. "Has Alice decided on names for the baby, yet?"

"She has several in mind but hasn't settled on any of them." He poured two glasses of cold water and handed one to Noah. "There's still time." He led Noah to the study and gestured toward the sofa.

Sitting where he did the night Alice broke the news of the baby to her parents, Noah downed a few swallows of water and placed his glass on the end table. Mr. Jordan sat in one of the large wing-back chairs opposite him.

"Since you've had time to think about our conversation, I assume you've arrived at a decision. Correct?"

"Yes, sir, I've given my answer a lot of thought and prayer." He reached for his glass and took another sip. "As much as I appreciate your confidence in my ability to be a good husband for Alice, and father for your grandchild, I can't in good conscience take on those roles."

Mr. Jordan shook his head and cast his eyes to the floor. "I'm sorry to hear that, son. Care to share your thoughts?"

"I certainly don't want to disappoint you or cause more heartache for your family, but I'd do just that if I married your daughter. Although I care a great deal for Alice, I'm not in love with her, sir."

"Your feelings could grow into love, don't you think?"

"No. I'm certain they wouldn't. You see, I fell in love with a girl in Fayetteville a few months ago. I plan to visit her after Thanksgiving and ask her to marry me."

Mr. Jordan sat stunned. Then, clearing his throat, he searched Noah's eyes. "If you're so in love with this girl, why are you courting my daughter?"

Noah squirmed. "There are a couple of reasons. I can't say they're good ones, but they have been my thinking. The first time I bumped into Alice after coming home from Bragg, I told her I was in love with someone else. Although heartbroken, she insisted we should remain friends and continue to do things together. At first, I refused, but later I contacted her and told her she was right. There wasn't any reason we couldn't see each other as friends."

Mr. Jordan rose from his chair, walked over to the fireplace, and wound the clock on the mantle. "What caused your change of heart? Didn't you think continuing to see Alice would give her hope your friendship would evolve into something more?"

"Yes, sir, I understood there was that possibility, but I was willing to take the risk, because—" He cleared his throat. "Because I had a motive."

He spun around. "A motive? What kind of motive?"

"I'm not proud of it, sir. Actually, I'm ashamed." He gulped. "I'd hoped if I courted Alice, and you grew to like me, you'd put in a good word for me at the extension office."

Mr. Jordan's face reddened. "You what?" He kicked at a small piece of wood on the hearth, then lifted his steely gaze. "You mean, you used my daughter to better your chance of getting the job with the county?"

Noah dropped his head and choked out his words. "Yes. That's what I said, sir."

Mr. Jordan shoved his hands in his pockets, walked over to

the window, and stared outside. "How could you? What kind of person toys with the emotions of someone so vulnerable?" He whipped around. "You had me fooled, boy. And to think, I was ready to take you in as one of my own."

"I couldn't be sorrier, sir. That's why I've told you this. I can't live with the deception any longer. I never meant to hurt Alice, you, or Mrs. Jordan, but I realize now that's exactly what I've done. Forgive me. I was only thinking of myself and my future."

"You're right. I hardly know what to say." He walked over to his desk, sat on the edge of it, and folded his arms. "I'm disappointed in you, Noah." He hesitated. "There are a couple of things I need for you to understand. One, I don't want Alice to ever hear about our conversations of Thursday and today. Got that?"

"Yes, sir, I do."

"And two, I don't want you to say anything to her about the callous way you've used her. She's too fragile, and nothing good can come from it. What I do expect you to do is tell her in no uncertain terms about your love for this girl in Fayetteville and your plans to marry her. I don't want Alice to have any false expectations of a future with you. We'll move her to Charlotte soon to stay with her aunt, so that should eliminate any future opportunities for contact."

Noah's chest tightened. "I understand. When would you like me to tell her, sir? Should I come to your house?"

"Yes. I'll arrange a time and get back with you. As for now, I need you to leave." He walked toward the foyer. "I'll show you to the door."

Noah followed him onto the porch and extended his hand.

Mr. Jordan declined.

"Thank you for hearing me out, sir. I'll wait for your call. And again, I'm sorry." He walked down the steps.

"Oh, and Noah."

He turned. "Yes, sir."

"Just so you're aware . . . there will be no further good

words put in for you at the extension office. You're on your own."

He nodded. "I understand."

As he walked to the car, he passed through boxwoods, which stood like staunch soldiers observing, surmising, and approving his departure.

Behind him, he heard the front door slam—slam on him and his future.

Monday, October 17, 1938

Noah stepped out onto the porch of the tannery and shook Dan's hand. "Thanks for your help with this. I think it turned out nice, even if I did make it myself." He looked down at the leather box and rubbed his fingers across the tooled roses on the lid. "Emma will love it." He threw his scarf around his neck and wrapped his coat tighter. Fall's chill had come to the foothills of North Carolina. "And thanks for your patience with me on the payments for the ring. I promise I won't leave you hanging."

"Don't mention it, my man. Not worried at all. It wasn't doin' me any good locked away in the drawer. Nice that we've kept it in the family."

Noah looked up at the clear night sky and walked to the truck. *At least, I hope Emma likes my gift. If she ever sees it, that is.* Hopefully, there'd be a letter from her in the dough bowl tonight. His awkward exchange with Mr. Jordan yesterday had left him licking his wounds. Words from her would serve as a healing balm.

When he arrived home, he flipped off the porch light, tossed his jacket onto the chair in the front room, and placed the leather box on the table. "Hi, Mama. I figured you'd be in bed by now."

"I couldn't sleep. Been feeling rather puny today, so I thought I'd stretch out on the couch and read a chapter or two in my book. Try to get my mind off of myself. Reading usually makes me drowsy."

"What's the matter? Do you need to go see the doc again?"

"No. Probably something I ate. I took a dose of apple cider vinegar earlier, which should take care of it."

"O-k-ay, but if you need me to take you to see Dr. Marion tomorrow, I will."

"Thanks, Son. I should be fine."

Noah made a beeline for the sideboard in the dining room.

His mother laid her book across her lap, then said in a singsong voice, "I think you're going to be happy."

He picked the light-pink envelope out of the bowl and inhaled its fragrance. "Oh, man, I thought this would never come." He clutched it to his chest, returned to the parlor, and sat on the edge of the chair. "Now that it's here, I'm almost afraid to open it."

"Don't be. I've got good news for you."

"Really?"

"Melvin brought the mail to the door today. He was sorry you weren't here." She put her feet on the floor, leaned back against her bed pillow, and yawned. "Said he owed you an apology."

"An apology?"

"He found Emma's letter behind one of the large mail bins when he went in to work this morning. Said according to the postmark, he must've dropped it over a week ago as he loaded his basket for his route. Thought he'd hand deliver it instead of putting it in the box. He knew it would be important to you."

Noah looked at the date and sighed. "He's right. And all this time, I thought she was mad at me about Alice." He tore open the seal. "Of course, she might be, but at least now, I'll have a chance to respond." He stood, then picked up his jacket and the leather box from the table.

"What've you got there, Son? Emma's box?"

"Yep, but I'll have to show it to you later."

She laughed and slid her feet into her slippers. "I understand. Well, I hope everything's okay. If not, I trust you'll both work things out. Love has a way of doing that, ya know." She tucked her pillow under her arm and shuffled toward the bedroom.

Noah took the stairs two at a time. "I hope you're right."

Chapter Thirty-Four

After reading Emma's letter, Noah uncapped his fountain pen and dipped it into the depths of his heart.

Monday, October 17, 1938

My Darling Emma,

What must you be thinking? Please know I just received the letter you wrote more than two weeks ago. The mailman brought it to the door today, apologizing profusely. It seems he accidentally dropped it behind a mail bin and didn't find it until this morning. I hope you'll understand. When I didn't receive an answer to my last letter telling you about Alice's pregnancy, you can't imagine all that went through my head. In your letter today, you said you couldn't go along with me seeing her any longer, and I want you to know you won't have to. I spoke with her father today and will talk to Alice and end our relationship soon—this week, hopefully. Breaking things off with her may ruin my chance for the clerk position at the extension office, but I've learned I must trust God with my future. If it's meant to be, it will be.

I've not heard from Mr. Love yet about the bus driver position with Greyhound, but hopefully, it's still a possibility.

And while I'm talking about the future, you said you were counting the days till we see one another. I am too. You're right, the days go by too slowly.

I'm glad you had a good time with Tucker and Penny at the county fair last weekend. I'm sure it did your heart good to see Penny enjoy herself again. Oh, how I wish I could have been on top of the Ferris wheel with you. It would've been the perfect place for me to steal a kiss. Soon, baby, very soon. You owe me bunches of them.

Thanks for giving me the news about the fellas at the base. I'm glad my pals haven't forgotten me. If they want to see me when I come, I'm not sure they'll be able to coax me away from my sweet Emma Rose. We'll see how everything falls into place. You and I have lots of lost ground to cover. Tell Mama T I appreciate her offer of a room, but Tucker has already arranged for me to stay in guest housing at the base.

I hate to cut this letter short, but I'm on the verge of needing toothpicks to keep my eyes open. I've had a hard weekend and have a job interview bright and early in the morning at Chatham Manufacturing Company in Elkin. I promise I'll write tomorrow night to let you know how things went.

Please write me. I watch daily for a letter from you. They lift my spirits more than you realize. I hope you're dreaming of me.

I'll always love you,
Noah

He propped his letter against Emma's picture on the nightstand and shut the window. Briskly rubbing the chill from his arms, he yanked the chain on the hanging bulb and climbed into bed. Pulling the covers around his shoulders, he gazed into the October sky and watched the quarter moon rise above the mountain. As he envisioned his future home with Emma, his eyelids grew heavy. He closed them and prayed Emma Rose would wait for him. Thanksgiving seemed a lifetime away.

Sunday, October 23, 1938

Noah stood as Alice entered the parlor. She was as beautiful as ever with only a hint of a protruding belly beneath her chestnut-brown sweater and plaid skirt. Few would suspect a new life was budding within her.

"Hi, Noah. What a nice surprise." She stood on her toes and planted a kiss on his cheek.

The scent of her perfume ushered in memories of their evenings together in this very room. It was déjà vu—another conversation sure to break her heart and sound the death knell to their friendship.

"What brings you here? Daddy told me you had something important to discuss with me."

"I do. But first, tell me how you're feeling?"

"Better. I'm almost in my second trimester. Not as nauseated, and I have a lot more energy."

"That's good to hear. I've been worried about you."

She laid her hand on top of his and gazed into his eyes. "Thank you. Your thoughtfulness is one of the things I love most about you."

He looked down and grimaced. The black residue beneath his fingernails—a telltale sign of stubborn tractor grease—was a reminder of the obstinate nature of his heart. He'd rehearsed his confession for days, but now as he tried to speak, intelligible sounds failed to emerge from his parted lips.

Alice lifted his chin. "Look at me. What's wrong? You're scaring me."

Her bewildered expression intensified his regret concerning the impending fallout. He cleared his throat and blurted,

"There's no easy way to say this, so I'll spit it out—I'm still in love with Emma."

He plowed through the next few sentences, hoping the flood of words would push away the response he feared. "You'd hoped if we spent time together, my feelings for Emma would change. You were right. They did. I love her now more than ever. They say absence makes the heart grow fonder, and I've found it to be true."

Fear flooded her eyes—ones that moments before had reflected an air of hopefulness.

"I do care about you, Alice. If I didn't, I'd go on letting you think we had a future together. But I can't pretend any longer."

Her shoulders shook as she buried her face in her hands.

Focusing on the steady swing of the large pendulum in the grandfather clock, Noah cringed, then nearly choked on the rush of words that tumbled from his lips. "After Thanksgiving, I'll ask Emma to marry me."

Amid her muffled sobs, he fumbled for words to comfort her.

She collapsed on his chest and wrapped her arms around his waist. "No, Noah. Please don't leave me again. Not now." She lifted her head and stared into his eyes—her face merely inches from his. "What will I do without you? You've been my rock."

After brushing her hair from her eyes, he pulled away. "I'm sorry, Alice. I never meant to hurt you." He slipped her arms from around his waist. "I should go. Putting off the inevitable will only make this harder." He stood and offered her his hand.

She looked into his face. Squaring her shoulders, she smoothed out her skirt, then rose and linked her arm through his. "May I at least walk you to the door?"

"Of course. I want you to."

After stepping out onto the porch, Noah kissed her lightly on the cheek. "You're a great girl, Alice. I wish nothing but the best for you and the baby."

"Thank you. Hearing those words means a lot." She let go of his arm and placed her hands on her small belly. "Maybe one day, I'll get to introduce the two of you."

"I'm sure you will."

He gave her a soft, sympathetic smile, then hugged her before descending the steps. After climbing into the truck, he turned around in the Jordans' driveway and looked up. Alice watched from the porch. She raised her arm high above her head and waved.

He tooted the horn and sighed.

One month later
Friday, November 25, 1938

Noah hugged his father's broad frame. A lifetime of work in the tobacco fields had kept him in good physical condition. "Thanks for the lift and extra cash, Pop. Hopefully, I'll be able to pay you back soon."

"I know you'll pay me, Son. Put it out of your mind for now and concentrate on having a good visit with Emma." Jesse Anderson draped one arm around Noah's shoulders as they walked toward the platform. "And don't worry about your mama. I'll keep a close watch on her."

"I know she's in good hands. My back is testimony to your healing touch."

He smiled. "Hop on board before you get left behind. It would be a shame to leave your future Mrs. waiting at the station."

"No chance." Noah tipped his hat, picked up his bag, and climbed the steps of the 1:40 Greyhound from Winston-Salem to Fayetteville. Edging his way down the aisle of the crowded bus, he looked for an empty seat.

"You can sit up here, sir." The driver bent over and removed a stack of newspapers from the front seat. "I'm sorry. I forgot I'd left these here."

Noah moved toward the front. "Thank you. Looks like your forgetfulness worked in my favor." He tossed his bag on the overhead rack and took his place in the seat behind the driver. "Last one on, first one off, and a bird's eye view of the road ahead. Can't beat it."

He slipped the round-trip ticket in his billfold and placed his coat and sack dinner in the neighboring seat. The bus was scheduled to arrive in Fayetteville at 8:40 p.m. Emma would be waiting at the station with Tucker. It was hard to believe it had been less than three months since he'd left Fort Bragg. So much had happened since, it seemed like a lifetime ago.

Noah settled in his seat and carefully studied the driver's every move. "How long have you driven for Greyhound?"

He straightened and looked in the rearview mirror. "Twelve years this coming February."

"Twelve. That's a long time. You must like it."

"It's a good steady job, which is important when you've got two growing boys."

"I imagine so. Where you from?"

"Headed home now—Fayetteville. Ready to call it quits for a few days. We were short a driver over the holidays, so I had to pull extra hours. I missed Thanksgiving dinner with my family. It's one of the sacrifices of life on the road. But it doesn't happen often. How about you? You from Winston-Salem?"

Noah shook his head. "Jonesville. I was stationed at Fort Bragg for three years. Left in August. This trip is the first time I've been back to see my girl."

"Terrific. What do you do now?"

Noah leaned forward in his seat. "I've looked for a job ever since I left Bragg, but next week I'll begin training as a driver for Greyhound."

His eyes widened. "Sure 'nuff?"

"Yep. That's the reason for all the questions. I've watched you maneuver this baby. Was it hard for you to get the hang of it?"

"Not as hard as you might think. Greyhound has good instructors. You'll do fine." The driver glanced at him again. "Where will your home base be?"

"Charlotte. I'm eager to get started. Want to marry my girl soon."

"Congratulations. Does she work?"

"Yeah. She's a waitress at the Rainbow Restaurant on Hay Street. We met there."

"The Rainbow? My wife has a cousin who's a waitress there."

"No kidding. What's her name?"

"Fran. Fran Matthews.

"Whaddya know? Fran's a great lady. It's a small world."

"Who's your girl?"

"Emma Walsh."

"I've heard Fran mention her. Of course, we always sit in Fran's section, but I'd probably know her face. "Pardon me." The driver cleared his throat and raised his voice. "Next stop, Kernersville. We'll arrive in five minutes. If you want to get off to stretch your legs, use the restroom or grab a snack, we'll be there fifteen minutes."

Noah looked at his pocket watch, then leaned back in his seat. Grabbing a few winks before dinner would make the time seem to pass faster.

Chapter Thirty-Five

Same evening
Fayetteville, North Carolina
Emma

Emma took a deep breath and shifted in her seat to face Tucker. "After Lily's Thanksgiving spread yesterday, I swore I'd never eat again, but you see how long that lasted. I appreciate the dinner, Tucker. You've done too much. Driving me to the station would have been enough."

"Think nothing of it. Can't have you waiting in the dark on an empty stomach. And, before you pile on the accolades, coming to the station isn't much of a sacrifice. I'm anxious to see the old boy myself."

After pulling into the Greyhound parking lot, Tucker slipped the key from the ignition and walked around to open Emma's door. "We're thirty minutes early, but maybe the bus will be on time."

She laughed. "That's wishful thinking. Since when are buses on time?" A blast of frigid air took her breath and caused her eyes to water as she stepped from the car. She pulled her gray cape closer to her body and adjusted her red wool hat as the first few flakes of snow started to fall.

The bells on the fresh evergreen wreath jingled as Tucker opened the terminal's large oak door. Placing his hand on her back, he pointed toward seats on the opposite side of the room. "Why don't you sit over near the radiator while I check to see if the bus is on time?"

Emma took a seat beside a tall, slender cedar tree in the corner and slipped off her gloves. Topped with a silver star, it leaned to one side. Despite its sparse decorations and several burned-out colored lights, it added a spot of warmth to the station's stark décor. Underneath were a couple of wrapped packages and a small wooden nativity. The tiny baby Jesus, surrounded by shepherds and wise men, brought a smile to her face.

Tucker walked over to the radiator and briskly rubbed his hands together. "Looks like we're in luck. The clerk said Noah's bus will pull in as scheduled."

She placed her hand over her mouth and audibly inhaled. "Oh, me. It's a Thanksgiving miracle."

He shook his head. "You're something else, Miss Walsh." Sitting beside her, he shed his hat and scarf and laid them on the adjoining seat. "I'm surprised the station isn't more crowded. I guess most people are still enjoying the holiday with their families."

Emma fidgeted with her gloves.

"You nervous?"

"A little, but mostly excited." She tucked a wisp of hair under her hat. "You?"

"Yeah. It will be great to see my old friend again."

She turned in her seat to face him. "What's your plan for Christmas this year? You headed home?"

"If all goes well. I haven't seen my family since spring, and I have a new nephew I want to meet. He's four months old now. What about you?"

"Hopefully, I'll have the day off. I plan to spend it with Lily and our cousins from Florida. Cee's keeping the Rainbow open—plans to serve turkey and dressing with all of the trimmings for those who don't have a place to go. Cee Wellons may be small in stature, but he has a heart bigger than most."

"I'm glad you told me. If I don't get home, maybe I'll stop in."

"I pray neither of us will have to spend Christmas day at the Rainbow." She repeatedly checked the large Coca-Cola clock over the door. The closer the hour hand came to Noah's scheduled arrival, the slower it seemed to move.

The intercom crackled overhead. "Attention. The 8:40 bus from Sanford to Greenville is pulling into Gate B. Gather your belongings and have your tickets ready. Before boarding, please allow all passengers to disembark. Have a great trip, and thanks for choosing Greyhound."

Emma grabbed Tucker's arm and shook it. "He's here. He's finally here."

"Yep. Looks like lover boy made it to the station on time." Picking up his hat and scarf, he stood and offered her his arm. "Shall we?"

Others exited the terminal in front of them. As the bus pulled to a stop, and the driver set the airbrake, the moments seemed to stretch into forever. Then, the doors flew open, and Noah exited first, his feet soaring above the bottom two steps. Cutting through the crowd, he dropped his duffel bag and lifted her off her feet. He kissed her—slowly, then lowered her to the ground and looked into her eyes. Stroking his fingers along the side of her face, he whispered, "Man, I've missed you."

Holding tightly to his waist, she gazed at him. "I can't believe you're here. I thought this day would never come."

Leaning down, he kissed her again, then pulled her to his side and turned to Tucker. "Who's this dapper-looking gentleman following you around?"

"You mean you've already forgotten me, pal?" Tucker gave his friend a hug and a swift pat on the back. "Civilian life must agree with you. You're lookin' great."

"I'm settling in. Living at home is quite an adjustment after being away for so long. But my back is healing, and I'm about to become a productive member of society again."

Tucker picked up Noah's bag and motioned toward the car. "Thought we were going to get some snow, but now it looks like maybe not."

"I thought so too. We came through quite a few flurries on the way down."

Emma laced her fingers through Noah's, her eyes fixed on him as they walked.

He opened the door for her as Tucker threw his bag into the trunk. "Here you go, madam." After she slipped to the middle of the seat, he slid in after her, and Tucker took his place behind the wheel. "Hey, this is one nice vehicle, sport. You shouldn't have any trouble picking up dames in this beauty."

Tucker shook his head. "Nope. Not interested in another relationship. Too soon." He started the car and pulled onto Person Street. "Okay. Where to? Y'all hungry?"

Noah placed his hat in his lap. "Always."

"Not me," Emma said, holding her stomach. "I'll settle for a cup of hot chocolate, but you guys make yourselves happy."

"Then I'll decide," Tucker said. "The café it is—best hot chocolate with plenty of marshmallows. I could use a cup myself on this bitter night. Does the Central Café sound good to you, Noah?"

"I'm not hard to please. Any place with you two is perfect." He placed his arm around Emma and pulled her closer. "It's been way too long, and we have a lot to catch up on."

The café bustled with activity as movie-goers greeted one another. *Scrooge* had just let out at the theater down the street, and the Christmas spirit filled the air. Strains of "A Winter Wonderland" drifted through the room from the Wurlitzer jukebox in the corner.

After choosing a booth, Noah hung their coats on the coat rack and took a seat beside Emma. Tucker slid in opposite them. Noah whipped out a menu from behind the napkins. "Man, I'm famished. I didn't realize how hungry I was. Anyone else going to have something to eat besides me?"

Tucker looked at Emma. She shook her head. "It looks like you eat alone, pal. Emma and I ate before we picked you up."

"Ah-ha." He cut his eyes at her. "Should I be worried?"

She slapped him on the leg and laughed. "Check out the menu."

"Where did y'all eat?"

"We grabbed a sandwich and fries at Horne's."

Noah decided on a hamburger steak with grilled potatoes

and steamed broccoli, while Emma and Tucker ordered the hot chocolate with extra marshmallows.

When the cocoa arrived, she inhaled the aroma and took a sip of the hot, creamy liquid. "Mmm. Now that hits the spot." After a bit of small talk, she shifted her body toward Noah. Encircling her hands and locking her fingers around the warm mug, she asked the question she'd been eager to have an answer to all night. "I'm all ears. Tell us the exciting news you teased me with in your letter. I'm dying to know."

A puzzled expression swept across his face. "News? What news?"

"Don't pull that on me, Mr. Anderson. You know exactly what I'm talking about."

Throwing his head back, he laughed. "Oh, yes. That news." He shoveled in another bite of steak and wiped his mouth with his napkin. "Let's see, where do I begin?" He locked his eyes on the Tiffany lamp above his head and drummed his fingers on the table.

Tucker looked at Emma, rolled his eyes, and looked back at Noah. "Enough with the suspense, Sherlock. Just say it."

"You both know I've worked hard to find a job."

Emma lurched forward and grabbed his arm. "Oh, Noah. You got the clerk's position."

He shook his head and grimaced. "No. As I thought, that fell by the wayside after my talk with Mr. Jordan."

She sighed. "What is it then?"

"Mr. Love called from Charlotte and offered me a driver position with Greyhound."

Emma flung her arms around his neck and kissed him several times on the cheek. "How exciting. My man in uniform is back."

"Yep. I'm exchanging the green for the gray. And to top it all off, the pay is ten dollars more a month than the clerk position." He pointed upward. "Simply goes to show how faithful God is. When you do what's right, He honors it."

Tucker extended his arm across the table and shook his hand. "Congratulations, Noah. When do you start?"

"I drive down on Monday to take care of all the paperwork, and then on Tuesday, I leave for ten days of training in West Virginia."

Emma's jaw dropped, and her eyes widened. "Monday? I thought you were staying in Fayetteville till Wednesday."

"Well, that was the plan, but I can't pass this up, sweetheart. You understand, don't you?" He smoothed her hair and tucked it behind her ear. "This is what we've hoped for."

She folded her arms and huffed. "I know. I'm happy for you. Really, I am. Just disappointed that we only have one day to catch up."

"We have more than a day. My bus doesn't leave till three on Sunday. We'll make the most of the time we have, baby doll."

Tucker dropped another marshmallow in his cup. "Charlotte. That's quite a city. Largest in the state."

"I know. I'm excited. Of course, Mama hates to see her baby boy leave the nest again. She's afraid big city life will ruin me." He guffawed. "I told her that if I could survive a barracks full of forty GI's and not be corrupted, I could survive any place."

Tucker laughed. "You've got that right."

Emma sat silent and toyed with the marshmallows in her cup.

Noah drew her close. "What's the matter?"

She looked off and shrugged. "Nothing."

"Don't pull that on me. I know you better than that." He took her hand in his. "What's the frown for?"

She shook her head. "It's silly. I hate to bring it up."

"Bring what up, Em?"

She lifted her eyes to his, took a deep breath, and then spoke. "Alice."

He lifted his hands, palms up. "Alice? What's she got to do with anything?"

"Didn't you say she'd moved to Charlotte to live with her aunt?"

"Oh, goodness. I've not given it one thought. Walking around a city of a hundred thousand people isn't like strolling through Fayetteville, you know. My chances of bumping into Alice will be slim to none."

She smiled and looped her arm through his, then laid her head on his shoulder. "I know. You're right. I told you it was silly."

"Even if I did see her, my dear, you'd have nothing to worry about." He kissed the top of her head. "She doesn't hold a candle to you."

"Okay, you two lovebirds." Tucker downed the last of his cocoa and dropped his napkin on the table. "We need to finish up here, so Noah and I can get back to the base. You can pick up on this lovey-dovey stuff in the morning."

"Sounds like a plan to me." Noah's eyes gleamed as he scooped the last bite of potatoes into his mouth. "Almost finished here, Sergeant. You sure you trust me with your wheels again tomorrow? I've not got the best driving record, you know."

He looked at Emma. "Those wheels aren't what I'm concerned about."

Emma blushed. "You two are hopeless. Let's go before I rethink my plans for tomorrow. Mama T's probably pacing the floor right now, knowing I'm out with you two hoodlums."

Noah reached for the receipt as Tucker snatched it up. "I've got this one, my friend. You leave a tip."

"That I can do. Thanks, pal." He placed some change on the table, helped Emma with her coat, and ushered her onto the sidewalk.

"Oh look, Noah. It's snowing again."

As the mellow sounds of Russ Morgan crooning, "I Want You for Christmas," spilled into the street, he pulled her close and kissed her.

Chapter Thirty-Six

Saturday, November 26, 1938
Emma

Emma studied Noah as he sat behind the wheel of Tucker's car and all but pinched herself. The blue-and-green-plaid wool scarf neatly tucked inside the neck of his overcoat and the tan fedora cocked at an angle on his head made him look more mature than she'd remembered. Embarrassed when he caught her staring, she looked away.

He chuckled. "Why are you sitting way over there, Em? I don't bite." He patted the seat beside him.

Blushing, she scooted closer and laid her head on his shoulder. "I can't believe you're here."

"Me neither. It's incredible."

The warmth of his body next to hers affirmed she wasn't dreaming—her prince had finally come. "Where are you taking me?"

"Not telling."

She turned and pointed toward the back seat. "I suppose you're going to be hush-hush about what's in the paper sack, too, aren't you?"

"How'd you guess?"

She smirked. "You're just full of surprises today." She glanced up at the sky. "At least, the sun is out. After last night's flurries, I was afraid we'd be stuck inside all weekend."

He laced his fingers through hers. "I'd have no problem being stuck anywhere with you."

Feeling the heat rising in her cheeks, she dismissed his

comment. "How do you feel about your job with Greyhound? Excited?"

He nodded. "And nervous. I hope I'm able to maneuver such a huge contraption. Big responsibility having all of those lives in my hands. But I'm determined to make it work." He glanced over at her and smiled. "Hopefully, by next fall, I'll have enough money set aside for us to become Mr. and Mrs."

"Mmm." She snuggled closer. "I stash away all I can too, but it's not as much as I'd hoped."

"It'll happen, Emma Rose. We've got to keep the faith." He turned onto State Road 401.

"Are you taking me where I think you are?"

"And where would that be?" A smile crept across his face as he stared at the road ahead. "I'm not a mind-reader, you know."

She rolled her eyes. "To the river—are we going to the river?"

"Let's see." He drummed his fingers on the steering wheel. "Maybe."

"We *are* going there. I know we are."

"Aren't you the inquisitive one." He placed his hand over hers and squeezed it. "Yes, we're going to the river. So sit back, take in the scenery, and quit asking so many questions. Let a fella surprise you, okay?"

She pulled one of the wool blankets from the back seat and threw it over her lap. "I'm glad you thought to bring these. We'll need them by the water."

"Hopefully, the weather will continue to cooperate. The almanac says mid-fifties and sunny. If we sit in the sun, we should be fine." He put his arm around her shoulders and drew her closer. "Besides, we've got our love to keep us warm."

Clearing his throat, he waved his hand in the air and in a loud baritone voice belted out a melody. *"We've got our love to keep us warm."*

Her eyes widened. "Why, Noah, I didn't realize you could

sing." She combed the fringe on the blanket with her fingers.

"There's lots about me you don't know, baby doll—all good, of course." He winked and continued his song.

It was true. There was so much more to learn about this man who'd stolen her heart. She gathered the blanket under her chin and chimed in. *"What do I care how much it may storm."*

Harmonizing, they brought the last line to a lengthy crescendo. *"We've got our love to keep us warm."*

Laughing, he pulled the car over on the side of the road and cut the engine.

She leaned forward and scanned the area. Brown pine needles covered the ground fronting a hedge of shrubbery and trees.

"Look familiar?"

"Does it ever. It's bittersweet, actually."

He cupped her chin in his hand and turned her face toward his. "I'll never forget our time here. When we sat by the river last summer, and I looked into your eyes, I knew you were the one for me."

She lowered her head as heat returned to her cheeks.

"Things didn't end well for us that afternoon, but I don't want the wreck to be our final memory and overshadow the beauty of our time here." He kissed the tip of her nose. "It's chilly. Are you tough enough for a walk to the water?"

"Absolutely. Try and stop me."

"Hang on to your blanket then. Let's go." Noah snatched the other one along with the paper sack from the back seat and stepped out of the car. Emma slid past the steering column behind him.

After walking several yards, she stopped and blocked him with her arm. "Shh!"

"What?"

"Listen." Her heart quickened. "The river."

"Ah, yes. Sounds like it's calling our names." He grabbed her hand. "Come on. This day's a-wastin'."

She wrapped her coat tighter and hugged the blanket as

Noah led the way. She felt safe with him. It had been a long time since she'd had a man to watch over her. Her Papa had tried.

A master carpenter and hard-working farmer, he'd built their first home, grew his own grapes, and ran a thriving storefront. Then the government swept in to build Camp Bragg and took everything for a pittance. He was a broken man. By the time they forced them to leave their home, he'd had a massive stroke. She was thirteen when he died and much too young to know what it felt like to give *all* for your country.

When they reached a bank of trees, Noah pulled aside low-hanging branches for her to step through. She inhaled the crisp air and drank in the surrounding beauty. "I'd almost forgotten how peaceful this place is."

"Let's move to the rocks. I believe I see one with our names on it." He gazed into her eyes. "Remember?"

She smiled. "How could I forget?"

He steadied her as they inched along the bank. "You wait while I go first." Holding the blanket and bag in one hand, he moved sideways down the incline, steadying himself with his other hand. As he reached a rocky ledge near the bottom, he took a short leap and laid his things on the ground. "Okay, crouch and take it slow. When you get to the ledge, I'll grab you."

She edged her way down the embankment. Noah took hold of her waist with his strong hands and swept her to the ground. "Light as a feather, you are." He pulled her into his embrace and kissed her. "I've dreamed of this minute since the day I left."

"Me too. I wish it would last forever."

He placed his finger over her mouth. "There you go. Running ahead again, Em. Enjoy the moment."

"You're right. I will." Clinging to his hand, she led him toward a sunlit boulder—the one with the river birch tree springing from it. "Look, Noah. You can still see them." She ran her fingers over their initials, crudely carved into the bark.

"Always and forever, they will be—like you and me," he quipped.

She rolled her eyes and laughed. "So you not only sing, you're a poet too, huh?"

He set the bag on the ground and spread out one of the blankets. Emma scooted next to the warm rock, pulled her knees to her chest, and tucked her coat tightly around her legs. Throwing the other blanket over his shoulders, he sat beside her and wrapped it around them both. "There. Snug as two bugs in a rug."

"Perfect." She laid her head on his shoulder and closed her eyes. "Mmm. The sun feels heavenly."

Noah picked up a few pebbles and cast them into the river one by one. Each splashed and made an ever-widening ripple as it inched its way to the shore. He threw another. "See that, Emma Rose?"

"Uh, huh."

"It didn't make a big splash, but it changed the surface of the water until it rippled to the shore. That's the way I want my life to be. There might not be a book written about me, but I hope my short time here will have a lasting impact on the world around me."

She scooted closer and kissed him on the cheek. "You're a good man, Noah. I have no doubt it will. You've certainly made an impression on me."

He reached over and picked up the sack. "I know you're dying to see what's in here, and I can't wait any longer to show you."

She took the bag from him and drew it to her chest. "I can't imagine what it could be."

"Go ahead. Open it."

Peeking in, she pulled out a present wrapped in tissue paper. She placed the square package on the rock in front of her and peeled back the layers to reveal the hand-tooled leather box.

As her eyes darted to his, she tilted her head. "Oh, Noah, how beautiful." She rubbed her hand over its textured surface. "And roses. Is this the secret project you worked on at the tannery with Dan?"

He flashed a toothy grin. "It is."

She pulled it to her chest, leaned over, and kissed him. "I love it. Thank you. I'll cherish it always."

"There's more." He nodded toward the box. "Take a look inside."

She lifted the hinged lid and peered in. "What's this?"

His eyes danced as he shrugged.

With a puzzled look, she slipped a black-velvet pouch from the box. Pulling one end of the gold cord, she loosened the mouth of the bag and shook its content into the palm of her hand. As the sun caught the facets of the diamond set in white gold, she gasped and lifted her eyes to Noah's.

"I hope that look is one of approval." He took the ring from her hand, stood, and then dropped to one knee in front of her.

She covered her mouth with her hand.

"Emma, from our first meeting at the Rainbow, I knew I wanted you to be my wife. But I never dreamed that a beautiful girl like you would look at an average Joe like me. We've only known one another a few short months, but I couldn't be more certain. Throughout our time apart, I've discovered I don't want to live another day without you by my side. I promise I will remain faithful to you now and always. I love you, Emma Rose Walsh. Will you marry me?"

Her heart raced. She placed one hand on his cheek and drank in his eyes. Then with halting words, she said, "I'd consider it an honor to be Mrs. Noah Franklin Anderson." Kissing him lightly on the lips, she whispered. "Yes. I'd love to be your wife."

He reached for her left hand and slipped the sparkling circle of gold on her ring finger, then pulled her close. As his lips covered hers, the roar of the falls behind them melted into the distance.

"You're back." Mama T glanced up from the cross-stitch dresser scarf she'd worked on since fall. "Did you have a good day?"

"It was fabulous." Emma pulled off her hat and gloves and threw her coat over the sofa. Dropping onto the couch, she glanced at Chummy curled up on the warm marble hearth and burrowed herself in the throw pillows. "Chummy's got the right idea. I'm chilled to the bone." The aging cat cocked one ear in her direction and peered through narrow green slits before shutting them again.

"Where did you two end up? I was hopin' you'd get in before sundown."

"We spent the afternoon by the river, then grabbed dinner at the Rainbow. Noah wanted to say hello to Cee before he leaves tomorrow. Besides, we had something we wanted to show him."

She peered over her wire-rim glasses. "Yeah?"

Emma jumped up from her place and held her left hand under the light of the brass candelabra floor lamp beside Mama T's chair.

She placed her needlework in her lap and pushed her glasses up on her nose. "Oh, my goodness, child!" Her hand flew to her chest. "Be still my heart."

Emma laughed. "It's gorgeous, isn't it?"

Mama T took her hand in hers, pulled it closer to her face, and squinted. "Why, I think it's absolutely divine." Leaning in, she squeezed her. "When's the big day?"

"Hopefully, sometime next fall. Noah starts as a driver with Greyhound on Tuesday. Maybe in a year, he'll have enough money put back for us to marry."

As she reclaimed her place on the sofa, Chummy dived in

her lap and nestled his head in her arm. Mama T sat and blankly stared into the crackling fire.

"Is something wrong, Mama T?"

She shook her head. "No. I'm happy for you, dear. Slipped into feelin' a little sorry for myself, that's all." She glanced over at her. "Things won't be the same around here without you."

"It's a bittersweet time, isn't it? I'll hate leaving you too. It makes me sad to think about it."

"Now, don't you go worryin' your pretty little head about me. An engagement is supposed to be a happy time. Besides, I realize you've always wanted to see the world."

She laughed. "Jonesville and Charlotte are a far cry from the world, but I suppose it's a start. Maybe I'll get to ride with Noah on a few of his long-distance runs."

Mama T resumed her cross-stitch, while Emma rubbed Chummy's silky coat and watched firelight dance in the facets of her ring. Life as Mrs. Noah Franklin Anderson would be amazing.

Chapter Thirty-Seven

Sunday, March 5, 1939
Atlanta, Georgia
Noah

Noah dropped his duffel bag onto the floor beside the mahogany desk in the lobby of the exclusive Hotel Winecoff and dropped his Greyhound cap on top. After draping his jacket over the back of the wingback chair, he took a seat. According to the sunburst wall clock above the check-in desk, he had an hour before he'd need to be at the station a few blocks away. He slipped a sheet of letterhead stationery and a pen from the wooden tray in front of him.

Hello Sweetheart,

Did you think I was never going to write? I'm sorry. I haven't had a chance until now. Mama's been in and out of the hospital. Her heart is getting weaker by the day. Between running back and forth to Winston to visit her, and my job, I hardly have time to catch my breath. It was after ten last night when I arrived in Atlanta, and by the time I checked into the hotel and got ready for bed, I was bushed. It was a long ride down two-hundred and eighty-eight miles, but my back faired pretty well, and I had lots of time to think of you.

Atlanta is a pretty town. I wish I could scout around some, but it's too short of a trip. Maybe after you become Mrs. Anderson, I can bring you with me, and we can explore the area together. The Winecoff is one of the tallest buildings in the city. Of course, I couldn't afford to stay here, but I stopped in this morning and took the elevator to the rooftop, fifteen floors up. Too bad I didn't know to go up last night. It would have been some sight.

How's my girl getting along? I wonder if she loves me as much as she used to. Do you?

Darling, I love you more and more each day and want to see you so bad. You know I would come if I could, but business is too pushing. I've been able to stash quite a bit of my paychecks aside each month. I'll soon be in a position to make life easier for you. No more waitressing for my girl. Has that rock on your beautiful hand kept the fellas at bay? I hope so. I can't stand the thoughts of anyone makin' eyes at my baby.

I need to run and grab a bite to eat before I head to the station, but I wanted to take a minute to write and remind you of how much I love you. I'm sending you a book of matches from the Winecoff. You should have quite a collection by now. Enough to keep the home fires burning, I pray.

I'll write more tonight when I get back to Charlotte. I hope your day goes well. Tell Cee and all the Rainbow girls "hello." Dream of me.

I'll always love you.
Noah

The art deco Greyhound bus terminal on Cain Street bustled with activity. Noah stashed his duffel bag in the belly of the shiny thirty-seven-passenger motor coach and grabbed a piping hot cup of coffee. After receiving his detailed assignment, he systematically went through his checklist. He noted his return route would consist of stops in Stone Mountain, Athens, Augusta, Aiken, Columbia, and Rock Hill before arriving in Charlotte at 6:20 p.m. He considered himself one of the lucky ones. He'd soon sit behind the wheel of the industry's flagship—the new diesel-engine, air-conditioned 743 Super Coach.

Although his run was routine, by the time he pulled the streamlined bus into the Rock Hill station, his back felt the strain of the arduous two-day journey. Thankful for a thirty-minute layover, he made his way to the employee lounge and stretched out on the sofa. After twenty minutes, he grabbed a Coke at the lunch counter and walked to the platform. When the announcement came over the intercom for passengers to board at Gate B for Charlotte, Noah put on his cap and pulled a hole puncher from the leather sheath on his belt. A line of passengers quickly formed as he took his place at the door of the motorcoach. He boarded all previous passengers first so they could claim their original seats and then punched the tickets of the new travelers.

As the last passenger in line handed him her ticket, he checked the destination and glanced up. "I hope you enjoy . . ." His words drifted, and his hands froze as he looked into the petite passenger's large green eyes.

"Hello, Noah."

Words formed neither on his lips nor in his mind.

"Are you going to punch my ticket, or will you make your old girlfriend hop the next bus to Charlotte?"

He stuttered as he grasped for words.

"You do have a seat for me, don't you?"

He punched her ticket and forced a smile. "Of course I do, Alice." Heat wafted from his collar as he took hold of her elbow and helped her into the coach. "Watch your step." His words ricocheted through his mind. *Watch your step—Noah.* He turned and scanned the platform as the intercom bellowed overhead,

"Last call for Charlotte. Boarding at Gate B."

When he was confident all of his passengers were aboard, he climbed the steps and sank behind the wheel. Looking into the rearview mirror, he saw Alice had found a place several rows behind the driver. Swallowing hard, he closed the doors and bellowed.

"Ladies and gentlemen, my name is Noah, and on behalf of Greyhound, we're happy to have you aboard. You're traveling in our new 743 Super Coach, so you should find your trip to be cool and comfortable. For those of you who have transfer tickets, we'll arrive in Charlotte on time, so sit back, relax, and enjoy the ride." He released the brake, checked his side mirrors, and edged the large silver and blue bus away from the platform.

Once on the main road, he settled back in his seat and let out a long sigh. Glancing in the rearview mirror, his eyes were met by those of Alice. He quickly averted his to the road but sensed hers remained glued to the mirror. He'd noticed she didn't appear pregnant and did the math in his head. It had only been six months since that day in Turner's when she'd told him she was expecting. He turned his thoughts toward Emma with only an occasional glance in the mirror. Each time, he met Alice's unbroken stare.

After pulling into Charlotte's terminal, the baggage handler pulled the luggage from underneath, while Noah helped the passengers from the bus. Alice was the last to descend the steps.

"Thanks for the ride. It was nice seeing you again."

"Same here," he said as she turned to locate her suitcase.

After making sure the last passenger was on the platform, he wiped his brow with his handkerchief and loosened his tie. The temperature seemed unusually warm for March. He picked up his bag and walked toward the terminal.

"Is this seat taken?"

Noah looked up from his dinner at the terminal's lunch counter. Alice stood beside him. "No. Doesn't appear so."

She set her suitcase on the floor and eyed his cap on the stool. "Can a lady sit down?"

"Oh, sorry. Of course." He snatched his cap and placed it on top of his duffel bag on the opposite side.

Alice swiveled herself toward the counter, her knees brushing against his leg. "I've always been attracted to a man in uniform."

He swallowed the large bite in his mouth, reached for the salt shaker, and showered his food with salt.

"Don't you think it's rather odd our paths have crossed again? It must be fate." She took a sip of the water the waitress had placed in front of her. "Divine intervention, wouldn't you say?"

He dropped the shaker back into the metal rack. "Not sure I'd go so far as to say that."

The waitress pulled out a menu and offered it to Alice.

"No, thank you," she said. "Water's fine." She swiveled toward him, crossed her legs, and fingered the embroidered patch on his sleeve. "When did you start driving for Greyhound?"

"First week of December. I trained for two weeks in Charleston, West Virginia, before taking my exams. Passed with flying colors."

"I'm not surprised. I always knew you could do anything you set your mind to."

"Thanks." The uncomfortable silence that followed magnified the scraping sounds of his fork on the plate.

Alice used his spoon to fish out a piece of the ice from her glass and dropped it into her mouth. "You still seeing Emma?"

"Yeah. We're engaged now."

"Oh, you are?" She pulled a napkin from the dispenser and wiped a ring of water from the counter. "When's the big day?"

"We're hoping for this fall. Both of us are putting away part of our paychecks each month." He sopped up steak gravy with his dinner roll, popped it into his mouth, and pulled another from the wire basket in front of him. "How are things with you?"

"Well . . ." She placed her hands on her slender hips. "I've been working hard to get my figure back. Did you notice?"

"I did. Hard to miss." He took another sip of Coke. "You look really nice."

"One hundred sit-ups a day. It's wretched, but the effort's paying off, wouldn't you say?"

"It sure looks like it."

Her joyful demeanor faded as sadness filled her eyes. "I guess you heard . . ." Her words caught in her throat. "I lost the baby." She looked away as she fished for another cube of ice.

"Oh, Alice—I'm sorry. I hadn't heard. I was puzzled when I saw you, though. When?"

"Not long after I came to Charlotte, but by then, I'd grown to like it here and decided to stay on with my aunt rather than face the questioning stares back home. Aunt Sophie loves having the company, and I need a place to stay until I get my feet on the ground again. It works great for both of us."

"I'm sorry to hear about the baby. I can't imagine . . . but I'm happy things are working out for you. What were you doing in Rock Hill?"

"Checking out Winthrop College. My cousin is in the teacher's training there. She invited me to spend the weekend with her in the dorm and look over the campus."

"You considering studying there too?"

"Yes. I've decided I want to be an elementary school teacher. I love children. Daddy said if I liked the school, I could enroll this fall."

"Sounds swell."

"I'm excited about a fresh start. There is one problem with the school, though."

"What?"

"No men. It's an all-girls school, you know?"

"Yes, I'd heard. But I hear it's one of the best schools in the nation for women. I'm happy for you."

"Well, I figure if I'm going to be an old maid, I'd better have a way to provide for myself."

"Oh, Alice. No chance of you being an old maid. You'll meet the right man in time."

"Maybe." She paused and looked into his eyes. "Thought I already had. Guess I was mistaken though, huh?"

He dropped his head, took the last bite of his meal, and pushed his plate away. "I've always been convinced whenever you meet the right person, both parties know it without a doubt."

"Is that the way it happened with you and Emma?"

"Pretty much."

"She's a lucky girl."

"Luck has no part in finding a soulmate. When you find the perfect one, it *is* divine intervention."

"I hope so. As I said, I love kids and want a whole house full. How about you? Do you and Emma want children?"

"Yep. At least two. We'll see. Can hardly afford to take care of ourselves right now, but things are looking up for us. Sounds like they are for you, too."

"I think they are." She swiveled around in her seat. "Well, I guess I'd better see if my aunt's arrived yet. It's been great catching up with you. It's good to know I have another friend in town."

He stood as she rose. Her perfume stirred hidden emotions within him as she leaned in to hug him and then picked up her suitcase. "You think we could get together again for a bite to eat sometime soon?"

He was silent.

"As friends . . . of course."

He smiled. "Sure—as friends."

"Swell. My aunt's in the phone book—Mrs. S. A. Markham. If you have any problems, ring the operator and ask for Dot. She'll know who you're talking about."

He nodded. His eyes followed her as she walked through the station. It was hard to ignore the familiar sway of her hips. Sighing, he put on his cap and dug through his duffel bag for his car keys.

Divine intervention? Probably not, but . . .

Chapter Thirty-Eight

Wednesday, March 15, 1939
Emma

Emma slipped the envelope into the pages of her book and motioned for Tucker from the corner booth. As he walked to the table, she thought of what a blessing he was. He'd certainly stood by his promise to look after her in Noah's absence. He'd been her rock on more than one occasion, the male influence and confidante she'd never had.

He leaned over and kissed the top of her head before sliding into the seat opposite her. "Hi, beautiful. How was your day?"

"Routine. But I'll take it." She slipped off her apron, laid it on the seat beside her, and snickered. "I forgot I still had this on." She passed him a menu. "Penny's brewing a fresh pot of coffee. Care for something to eat?"

"No. Coffee's perfect." He slipped the menu behind the shakers. "Don't like going to bed on a full stomach."

"Me neither." She waved and flashed a courteous smile at the couple in the booth across from them as they stood to leave. Then she returned her attention to Tucker. "Was your day good?"

"Routine—but I'll take it." He laughed, then looked at her as if trying to read her thoughts. "So . . . is all this routineness about to change? You seemed upset when you called."

She fought to find the right words.

"What is it, Em?" He reached for her hand, then jerked it back as Penny placed two stoneware mugs of hot black coffee in front of them.

"Hi, Tuck. It's good to see you. You ordering tonight?"

"Coffee's all. Emma and I are just catching up."

She nodded. "Good. I'm glad you're here. She could use a strong arm right now."

He lifted his arm and flexed his muscle. "It's all hers."

They laughed.

"You're too much, Tucker Baldwin." Penny looked over at her friend. "If anyone can make you smile, this guy can." She turned to leave. "Take your time and holler if you need anything. Coffee's on the house tonight."

"Wonderful. Thanks." He pulled napkins from the container and passed them to Emma. "What's gotten you so upset?"

She whipped the envelope from her book and slid it across the table.

He glanced at the return address and furrowed his brow before sliding the pages from the well-worn envelope.

Emma sipped her coffee and studied him as he silently read Noah's letter telling her he'd bumped into Alice on his route.

He shook his head. "Oh, Emma. I'm sorry. I see why you're concerned." He carefully folded the pages and tucked them back inside the envelope. "Long-distance communication is hard." He rolled his eyes. "Take it from a fella who knows."

"What do you think?" She blotted her eyes. "Should I be worried?

He hesitated before speaking. "Probably not. You know how much Noah loves you. Alice is there for him like I'm here for you tonight. Try not to make too much out of it." He reached for the container of sugar and poured some into his coffee. "You should call him."

Her eyes widened. "Noah wouldn't want to hear what I have to say. I'm too steamed."

"You've got to communicate, Em."

"Looks like he just did. He knows how I feel about Alice, yet he keeps throwing her in my face. I know he's not pursuing her, but he's a male, and she makes no bones about her availability. I'm sorry she lost her baby, but she shouldn't use her misfortune to play on Noah's sympathy."

Tucker slid the envelope back across the table. "You've got to trust him."

She picked up the letter and flapped it in the air. "But he keeps putting himself in harm's way."

"He's a soldier. He knows how to dodge the bullets. Unfounded jealousy will destroy you both."

"I know. Sometimes, I wish he wouldn't be so honest. I don't need to hear about every move Alice makes toward him. He's so afraid I'll think he's hiding something from me."

"Try to put Alice out of your mind. With Noah's driving schedule, he won't be in town much anyway."

"You're right." She straightened in her seat and slapped her hand on the table. "But if he doesn't stop, I'll tell him a few things he doesn't want to hear."

"Oh?" He folded his arms on the table in front of him and leaned in. "And what would they be?"

She tilted her nose in the air. "There's a new artist in town—Mr. Andrew Brown. He's here for breakfast most mornings and always makes it a point to sit in my section."

"And?" He grimaced.

"Quit looking at me that way. He's too old for me."

"How old?"

She shrugged. "I don't know. Maybe ten years or so."

"Why's he in town?"

"He's here on an assignment, drawing ads for the *Fayetteville Observer*. Before he came to the states, he drew for newspapers in Canada."

"Canada?"

"Uh-huh. He lived with his twin brother in Toronto for several years." Her eyes brightened. "He's from Dundee."

"Dundee—as in Scotland?"

"Yes. I've never had a friend from another country. He's fascinating and has a charming brogue."

"So he's a travelin' man, huh?" He shook his head and lowered his voice. "You'd better be careful, Em. He bears watching."

She laughed and thrust out her hand. "Do you see this ring, Mr. Baldwin? I'm spoken for. I know how to dodge Cupid's arrows."

"Uh, yeah—and, no, Noah doesn't need to hear about this."

Friday, March 17, 1939

Emma brushed the hair out of her eyes and placed a stack of dirty dishes in the bin by the kitchen.

"So they've got you back here this morning, do they, lassie?"

Although she'd grown accustomed to the brogue, it never ceased to make her heart race. She turned to see the distinguished-looking Scotsman with the twinkle in his eye. "Good morning. A happy St. Paddy's Day to ya." She laughed as she wiped off the counter.

His eyes widened. "Not bad. Not bad at all. You must have Irish blood coursing through those veins." He unbuttoned his plaid sport coat and laid his fedora on the stool beside him.

"A wee bit." She placed a roll of silverware and a glass of water in front of him. "What can I get for you this morning, Andrew? Fran is off today, so Cee asked me to cover for her."

"First things first. All my friends call me Drew, and I've come in here long enough now to consider you a friend."

"Drew? What a great name for an artist."

"I come from a long line of artists on my father's side. Whenever his friends tried to shorten my name to Andy, he insisted they call me Drew."

She gave an affirmative nod. "I like it. Drew, it is." She

slipped her order pad from her pocket. "Will it be your usual this morning?"

"Almost. But add one more egg over easy and a couple more strips of bacon."

"Oh, my. Somebody must've missed dinner last night." She placed a pitcher of cream in front of him and poured his coffee.

"Who, me?" He chuckled. "Not a chance. Got to fill up. I have an early-afternoon appointment, so no lunch for me today." He examined the jars of preserves. "I see you don't have mint jelly yet."

She shrugged. "I've done all I can. I've mentioned it to Cee. He said when you start eating his grits, he'll think about getting your mint jelly."

"Ha. Playing hardball, that guy." He pulled a jar from the metal rack. "Strawberry, it'll be then." He poured cream into his cup and stirred his coffee, clanking the spoon against its sides.

"Your order will be out shortly, Andrew." She pushed open the swinging doors, then glanced back. "I mean, Drew." She smiled and disappeared into the kitchen.

Ten minutes later, she placed the platter in front of him. "Three eggs over easy, toast, extra bacon and hold the grits. Sound right?"

He folded the newspaper and put it on the counter. "Looks good to me. Only one problem."

She studied the plate. "Oh?"

"Yes. You."

"Me?"

His clear blue eyes met hers. "I hate to eat alone."

She laughed nervously. "I'm convinced Cee would frown upon that."

"You're probably right. But how about you?" He picked up the catsup bottle and dotted his eggs with the thick red sauce. "Would you frown upon it too?"

She was silent.

"I hear those wheels turning." He grinned as he replaced the cap on the bottle and wiped his fingers with his napkin.

"Don't think I haven't noticed that rock on your hand. Who's the lucky lad?"

"Noah Anderson. He lives in Jonesville. I met him while he was stationed here at Fort Bragg."

"When's the big day?"

"We've not set one, but hopefully sometime this fall. He's a new driver with Greyhound,"

"A driver for Greyhound, huh?" He shook his head. "You know a traveling man bears watching, don't you?"

She smirked. "So I've been told. Are you making a prediction or talking from personal experience?"

"Hmm. Could be a wee bit of both." His eyes danced with amusement. "What's to do around here on the weekends for fun?"

She propped her elbow on her arm at her waist and placed her chin in her hand. With a pensive stare, she tapped her index finger on her pursed lips. "Hmm. Let me see. Take orders, bus tables, scrape plates, wipe counters, roll silver, dump coffee grounds…"

"Whoa." He held up both hands and drew back. "I can't take all the excitement. Sounds to me like you could use a little diversion."

"Diversion doesn't pay the bills. And if I don't stop talking, I'll have plenty of diversion as I go door-to-door in search of a new job." She pulled a plastic tub from beneath the counter. "Can I get you anything else this morning?"

"No. I'm good. Thanks, lass. I hope you have a good day."

"You too, and thanks for your business." She smiled and placed the check beside his plate.

Emma's morning was busy. She hardly had time to breathe, much less notice Drew's departure. To her surprise, the sight of his vacant stool disappointed her. She slipped the tip in her pocket and cleared his dishes from the counter. Picking up a napkin, she started to crumple it, then noted doodling. He'd drawn a caricature of a waitress flung back in a chair—shoes off, hair mussed, arms dangling at her sides with a tray of dishes scattered at her feet. In black ink above her head, he'd scrawled, *Eat, drink, and be merry. All work and no play makes Emma a dull girl.*

She smiled as she wadded it up and tossed it into the large plastic tub of dishes. After wiping off the counter, she set the tub in a bin at the kitchen door. Turning to walk away, she stopped, reached into the bin, and pulled out the napkin. She placed it on the counter and smoothed out the wrinkles with her hand. After carefully folding it, she slipped it into her apron pocket.

A voice spilled from the kitchen. "Order up, Em."

Chapter Thirty-Nine

Thursday, March 30, 1939
Emma

Emma reclined on the sofa with Chummy curled at her feet and poured her heart into her journal.

Mama T looked up from her embroidery and peered over her glasses. "You look mighty intense over there. Your pen's traveling across those pages so fast, I can almost smell the smoke."

She laughed. "Maybe so. I have things I want to write down while they're fresh in my mind. How's your project coming?"

"Slow, but I'm not in any hurry. Thought I might donate several handkerchiefs to the church's bereavement ministry. Mrs. Priddy's heading it up this year. God's using her to touch people who've lost loved ones. Amazing how much her life has changed since she let go of all her bitterness and guilt."

"I agree. She's such a pleasure to be around now and a great example of how it's never too late to change. God can use us regardless of our age or past. I keep praying they'll find her grandson's body, and her family will find it in their hearts to forgive her. The division must only add to their sorrow."

"There's been somewhat of a breakthrough with her daughter, so keep prayin'. God's working, and He always completes what He begins." She laid her hoop on the table beside her chair and slipped her glasses on top of her head. "Would you care for a cup of hot cocoa? Made a pot fresh this morning."

"No, thanks. I'm still full from dinner."

Mama T slipped on her bedroom shoes and rose from her chair while Chummy bounced from the sofa and wound his way through her legs. "I think I'll heat up a cup for myself and settle in for the night. Got a few more chapters to read in my book. It's so good, I hate to turn the last page." She placed her hands on the small of her back and shuffled toward the kitchen. Chum led the way. "Oh, me. I guess I've been sittin' too long." She stopped at the doorway. "I thought you said Tucker was droppin' by this evening."

"He is. He'll be here whenever his shift is over at the hospital. It might be as late as nine."

"Are things good with him?"

"Yes, he's fine. We've got catching up to do, that's all."

Mama T walked toward the stove. "Tell him I'm sorry I missed him. And don't stay up too late, missy. Workday tomorrow."

"I won't. Sleep well."

"You too, child."

Emma laid her journal on the coffee table, kicked off her shoes, and stretched out on the sofa.

"Anybody home?"

Emma threw back the afghan and ran toward the door as Tucker peered around it.

"I'm sorry to let myself in, but I worried when no one answered my knocks, and I didn't want to ring the bell this late."

"I'm sorry. I must've dozed off." She waved him over. "By all means, come in." After hugging him, she reclaimed her place on the sofa, tucked her legs under her, and patted the cushion. "Here, have a seat. How was work?"

"Hectic." He settled next to her and leaned against the

armrest. "We had an emergency as I was leaving. Thought I'd have to stay longer, but everything worked out quicker than we thought. I hope I'm not too late."

She looked at her watch. "Not at all. It's only nine-thirty. You know I'm a night owl. Mama T and Chummy went on to bed. She wanted to finish her book. Said to give you her love."

"Tell her the same." He leaned over and patted her hand. "The question is . . . how was your day? I'm guessing you've heard from Noah."

She shook her head. "Not a word. It's been a couple of weeks. His letters have gotten farther and farther apart, and this has been the longest stretch. I've tried not to be overly suspicious since he told me he bumped into Alice in Charlotte. I believed him when he said he couldn't write as much due to his mother's illness and his frequent runs to Atlanta, but today—today—well, this explains a lot." She handed him an envelope.

"I thought you said you hadn't heard from him?"

She pursed her mouth and squinted. "You heard right. I haven't."

Tucker looked baffled and took the letter from her. "No return address. Who's it from?"

"Now, who would you think?" She motioned with two quick swats of her hand. "Go ahead. Open it."

He inhaled deeply. "From the fragrance, I'd say a female wrote it." He slipped it out of the envelope and glanced at the salutation. "Sincerely, Alice." He looked up at Emma. "Alice Jordan?"

"Yep. Darling Alice." She nodded and fought to keep her composure as Tucker read the letter aloud.

Friday, March 24, 1939

Dear Emma,

It's hard to believe I've not met you because I feel like I've known you a while. Noah always speaks highly of you, so it breaks my heart to have to write you these words. Noah's been saying he's going to drop you a note but keeps putting it off. He doesn't want to hurt you. I felt it was unfair to not tell you the truth as soon as possible, so I've taken it upon myself to write. I don't know of any other way to say this other than to put it out there—Noah and I have fallen back in love. Please don't be upset with him. He really does care for you, but our love runs deep and has for a long time. You are a beautiful girl, and I'm sure you have guys falling all over themselves to date you. I wish for you love like Noah and I share. Every girl deserves such. Hopefully, one day, when the dust settles, and the emotions aren't running so high, we can all get together as friends. Take care and best wishes from us both for your future.

Sincerely,
Alice

Emma sobbed as Tucker read the last few words. He slid over and pulled her close. She buried her head in his chest.

"Oh, Em. I'm sorry. After experiencing my break-up last year, I know how much this hurts."

She sniffled. "I can't believe Noah didn't have the common decency to tell me himself."

Tucker stroked her hair and shook his head. "This is unbelievable." He paused and stared across the room. "So much so, perhaps we *shouldn't* believe it. I think I know my friend. He's a better man than this."

She pulled away and looked deep in his eyes. "I want to believe you, but if it's not true, why hasn't Noah written me?"

"I don't know, Em, but I'll find out, and if it is . . ." He clenched his teeth and raised his fist. "I'll give him a piece of my mind."

Emma straightened her back. "Don't you dare. I will not give Mr. Noah Anderson the privilege of knowing how much he's hurt me." She jumped up and paced back and forth in front of the fireplace. "Nor will I be a girl like Alice who grovels after a man." She placed her hands on her hips and sashayed toward the window. "I have far too much pride." She looked at her reflection in the dark glass and fluffed her hair. "As darling Alice said, there are lots more fish in the sea. I have plenty of men coming into the Rainbow who want to date me. Now, at least I'm free to take them up on their offers."

"Emma, stop. You should write him. Tell him about the letter. Give him a chance to explain."

She plopped down on the couch and sobbed, then lifted her head and peered at Tucker through squinted eyes. "You really think I should?"

"I do."

"Okay. I'll write him tomorrow." Her eyes cut into Tucker's. "But not one word from you. Do you hear me, Tucker Baldwin? Not one word."

"Believe me. I hear you. I won't do anything outside of your wishes." He scooted next to her and took her hand in his. "I can't bear to see you hurt like this. I'm here for you, Em." He squeezed her hand, then noted her ring finger. "Your diamond? Did you send it back to Noah?"

"Are you kidding me? Not on your life. If he wants his ring back, he can face me like a man and ask for it. Until then, I've stashed it away for safekeeping."

He wrapped his arm around her. She stiffened at first, then leaned into him and laid her head on his shoulder. "I'm sorry for yelling at you. You don't deserve my wrath. You're such a wonderful friend."

"Not a problem. I'm a soldier, remember. We're trained to dodge bullets. If it makes you feel better, you can let them fly all you want." He lifted her chin. "You can call on me anytime, and I'll come as soon as I can. Do you need me to stay awhile?"

"No. I'll be all right."

He glared at her.

"Really, I will," she said with a half-hearted smile. "We've both got work tomorrow, so we should call it a night. I can't thank you enough for coming. It helped to vent my emotions. I had to tell someone, and I wasn't ready to worry Mama T with it. I hope I didn't wake her up. She thinks so much of Noah. This news will break her heart."

"Glad I could be here." He hugged her, then reached for her hand as he rose from the couch and pulled her to her feet. "I'll call you tomorrow to see how you are. In the meantime, you get that letter written, you hear?"

"I hear." She walked Tucker to the door and locked it behind him. Peeking through the sheer curtain, she watched his car pull out of sight before she flipped off the light, returned to the couch, and picked up her journal.

> *Dear Li'l Book,*
>
> *Tucker is such a good friend. What would I do without him? I pray all he said tonight is true, but it doesn't seem like it could be. What do you think? How will I move on if he's wrong? If Noah really has fallen back in love with Alice, will I hurt like this forever? Life without Noah seems unbearable. I didn't realize how much I loved him until now. His absence leaves a gaping hole in my heart. I'm wondering . . . can we ever really know someone? I'm not sure—not sure I can trust anyone again. If not for you, li'l book, Mama T, Tucker, and my Jesus, where would I be?*
>
> *Ever thine,*
> *E.*

Chapter Forty

Saturday, May 6, 1939
Emma

As the newsreel rolled, the usher escorted Emma down the aisle of the Princess Theatre. Stopping midway, he spoke to a young couple on the end of the row. They stood and allowed her to pass through.

"Pardon me," she said as she followed the beam of the usher's light and took a seat in the middle of the otherwise empty row. Sam Goldwyn's *Wuthering Heights* was a movie she'd looked forward to ever since she'd heard Emily Bronte's novel would become a feature-length film. She'd read the book twice and believed the casting of the Shakespearean stage actor, Laurence Olivier, was a perfect choice for the role of Heathcliff.

Although she and Noah had talked about seeing the movie together, she wasn't willing to let their relationship's likely demise ruin what she'd looked forward to for so long. He'd caused enough strife in her life. It had been five weeks since she'd written him, and still no word. Perhaps, it *was* time to move on. She'd refuse to grovel. Although her tears were less frequent now, there were still days they'd spill out at the most inappropriate times. At least if she cried in the darkened theatre, people might attribute the deluge to Catherine and Heathcliff's stormy relationship.

Settling into her seat, she reached into her purse and pulled out one of Mama T's embroidered handkerchiefs—*just in case.* She'd always loved this large stucco building that sat next door to the Rainbow. It housed one of only two mirror screens in the state, and its plush opera chairs had always served her well after a hectic day on her feet. Today was no different. In her grief, they offered her a soft place to fall.

Her stomach rumbled as the buttery smell of popcorn wafted through the theater lobby. But after stopping by the Rainbow to pick up her paycheck, popcorn would have to wait. She wasn't about to forego one minute of this long-awaited experience.

She sat through the first half of the movie, blotting her tears. When the house lights rose for intermission, she dug in her pocketbook for change and noticed the folded paper Penny had handed her. Flashing a telltale grin, her friend had pulled it from her pocket, saying, "Oh, by the way, a customer asked me to pass this along to you."

Opening the first fold of the heavy paper, she noted a cartoon drawing of a slender waitress crying over a pile of broken dishes. Scribbled above the sketch were the words, *I can help you pick up the pieces.* She unfolded it further.

"You don't need to read it, lassie, I'll tell you what it says."

Emma's breath caught in her throat. The brogue was unmistakable. She looked up at Drew standing in her row, holding a large bag of popcorn and two sodas. "Care to lighten my load? And if you don't make me wait too long, I'll share my popcorn with you."

She laughed. "Drew. What a surprise." She smiled and took the Coke from his hand. "Thank you so much. You read my mind." She glanced down at the drawing. "In more ways than one, actually."

He motioned toward the seat beside her. "May I?"

"Of course." She moved her sweater to the opposite side. "By all means, take a load off your feet." She tossed her hair over her shoulders. "What a coincidence. I wouldn't have taken you for a *Wuthering Heights* kind of guy."

"And you'd be right. I much prefer westerns. I'd planned to see John Wayne in *Stagecoach* over at the Carolina but changed my mind." A playful grin broke across his face.

"What's the grin about?"

"I should confess. I was in the Rainbow earlier and overheard you tell Penny you were coming here. I've been sitting several rows behind you."

"Aren't you the sly one." She took a long sip of her soda. "Oh my, that tastes good."

"With all those tears, I'm surprised you're not dehydrated."

Emma slapped him on the arm. "Shame on you for spying on me, mister. I'm not sure how I feel about that." She laughed. "The Coke is nice, though." Taking another sip, she gazed up at him through her lashes.

"Try not to worry your pretty little head about it, lass." He handed her a napkin and held out the popcorn. "Here, help me eat this."

"Oh, yum. I've been hungering for this ever since I walked in." She dug her hand into the bag and placed a pile of popcorn onto her napkin.

Drew tossed a few kernels into his mouth. "What do you think of the movie so far?"

"I love it. Emily Bronte's one of my favorite authors. Of course, Heathcliff is a cad." She paused, then mumbled under her breath. "But then aren't all men?"

"What?" He leaned to the far side of his chair. "Did I hear you correctly? I'm not sure how I feel about that."

She smirked and took another handful of popcorn from the bag. "Try not to worry your handsome little head about it, laddie."

"Okay. You win. I guess I deserved that."

They laughed, then sat in awkward silence. The lights flickered to signal the moviegoers back to their seats.

Drew took a sip of his soda, then brushed salt from his gabardine dress pants with a napkin. "Would you like me to tell you what the note says?"

She was happy the lights were dim so he couldn't see her blush. "If you want."

"I wrote to tell you how sorry I am. Penny told me what happened. It's not easy to lose someone we love. But I must be completely honest with you."

Wary of the words to come, she swallowed hard.

"If you don't hear from Noah, I'm counting on his loss being my gain."

She was silent.

"Will you let me help you pick up the pieces?"

The lights went out as the velvet curtains slid open to reveal Catherine and Heathcliff's faces filling the screen. She looked up at Drew's silhouetted profile, placed her hand on his arm, and whispered, "I think I'd like it very much."

Monday, May 8, 1939

Emma glanced at her watch, tied the crisp white apron around her waist, and picked up the tray of freshly filled shakers. As she pushed the swinging door to the dining room with her shoulder, it met with stiff resistance. "Oh."

Cee laughed from the opposite side, then stepped out of the way as she pushed through.

"I'm so sorry, Cee. Did I hit you?"

"Nope. Caught it with my hand." He swept his arm toward the dining room. "Be my guest, madam. Far be it from me to stand in the way of a hard-working woman."

Emma blew out a long breath and set the tray on one of the tables. "Whew. Close call. Sweeping salt and broken glass off the floor wasn't on my list of things to do this morning."

He chuckled. "Still swooning over Heathcliff, are you?"

"Funny, Cee."

"How was the movie Saturday night? Was it all you hoped it would be?"

"I guess you could say so." She placed the shakers on the

tables as she talked. "But there was a surprise twist."

"You serious? They changed the storyline?"

She threw her head back and laughed. "No. It ran pretty true to the book. The twist came in the middle—Drew showed up." She turned toward her boss. "Actually, he bought me a soda and shared his popcorn with me."

"No kidding? Now isn't he the cat's meow."

"He *is* quite the charmer."

"So, how did things end?"

"With the movie or Drew?"

He rolled his eyes. "Drew, of course."

She gave him an assenting nod and stopped what she was doing. "I'd say the evening went rather well. He's asked me out for Saturday." She thrust out her hand. "Don't worry. I checked the schedule. I work the lunch shift."

"Sounds good. I hope things work out for you. You deserve it." He walked behind the register and pulled a starched cap from the drawer. "Still haven't heard from Noah?"

"Not a word."

"Maybe you'll hear something this week."

Emma huffed. "I don't want to talk about Noah anymore, Mr. Wellons. If he hasn't gotten in touch with me by now, he's not interested. He needn't think I'll chase him down—like one woman I know." She slammed the shakers on the table. "He knew how I felt about Alice and still continued to inform me every time she gave him a passing glance. I'm convinced he wanted to see some green-eyed jealousy in me. Well, I don't play games with people's hearts and don't need to be with someone—"

Cee's arms shot in the air. "I surrender. Mary Beth tells me all the time I should keep this large Greek nose where it belongs." He wiped off the lunch counter. "So, where's Prince Charming taking you?"

A grin spread across her face. "The Prince Charles Hotel. Where else?" Her eyes danced with excitement as she raised her nose in the air. "We . . . will be feasting . . . in the *grand* dining room."

"Whoa. Classy."

"Since Drew's staying at the hotel while in town, he gets a nice break on his room and meals." She slid a few misplaced chairs under the tables. "I've always wondered how it would feel to have dinner there."

He pointed to the clock and strolled toward the kitchen. "Time to slide your thoughts back down to the Rainbow, missy. We've got a few people of our own to feed."

She lifted the shade on the door. The sun had begun to peek over the buildings on Hay Street. She breathed in. A new day dawned.

Chapter Forty-One

Saturday, May 13, 1939

Emma slipped into her best dress and freshened her makeup before walking from the Rainbow to the Prince Charles Hotel. With moments to spare, she'd pause along the way to peek in shop windows and admire the latest spring arrivals. Mae's Boutique always had eye-catching displays. She'd hoped for something new to wear tonight, but her floral silk-chiffon dress with cape sleeves would have to do. At least it would be new to Drew, and it did flatter her figure.

As she approached the doorman at the seven-story, Colonial Revival-style hotel, he nodded. "Good evening, miss. Welcome to the Prince Charles—the most magnificent place in town."

"Thank you. I tend to agree with you. I look forward to a nice dinner here this evening."

"First time?"

"It is."

"Ah. You're in for a treat. Chef Martin has Beef Wellington on the menu. Melt in your mouth. You should try it." He looked around. "You meeting someone?"

"Yes. He should be inside."

He smiled. "Lucky guy."

"Lucky gal too," she said as she walked into the mosaic-tiled foyer and ascended several steps to the lobby. Her eyes grew large as she admired the enormous crystal waterfall chandelier hanging from an ornate plaster medallion in the center of the expansive room. Gracing the interior and supporting the tray ceiling were four massive columns. Two split staircases led to the mezzanine, where a gentleman dressed in a double-breasted tuxedo and bowtie tickled the ivories of a grand piano. The clerks at the check-in desk looked frenzied, while bellmen stood at each column, waiting to assist incoming guests with their luggage. Others lounged on tufted blue-velvet sofas and club chairs while chatting with friends.

Emma stood spellbound and wondered about the lives of so many seemingly well-to-do people amid such a depressed economy. What were their stories? If only she knew.

"Oh, dear!" She jumped as someone from behind covered her eyes with their hands.

"Guess who?"

"The only Scotsman I know," she said, laughing.

Drew dropped his hands to her shoulders and turned her around. "Hi, beautiful. Enjoying the sights?"

"I am." She gave him a playful push. "But how dare you scare me, Mr. Brown. And you shouldn't think you'll ever fool anyone in the South with your accent."

"Accent?" He chuckled. "You might have a point, my lass." He brushed a strand of hair away from her cheek. "Have you been here long?"

"Long enough to be slain with the beauty of this place." She whirled around with outstretched arms. "Look at this. What a treat. Thanks for inviting me."

"My pleasure. I'm happy you're here. Are you hungry?"

"Quite. And after speaking with the doorman, I won't need to see a menu. The Beef Wellington sounds to-die-for."

He extended his arm toward the dining room. "Shall we?"

She nodded. "Yes, we shall." Emma followed the hostess to a table in front of one of the three floor-to-ceiling palladium windows. Drew seated her, then took his place across the table. While the hostess poured their water, Emma glanced out at Hay Street. "This is perfect. I feel like a princess this evening."

"As you should. You fill the bill."

She blushed.

"No better place for a princess to eat than at the Prince Charles."

Soon the waiter brought a basket of hot bread and took their dinner orders. After passing the bread to Emma, Drew buttered a roll for himself and bit in. "How was your day?"

"Hectic, but good. I'm happy Cee's business is growing. He and his family work hard. They deserve it." She took a bite of her bread and followed it with a sip of water. "I love working with Penny. For me, meeting her has been the best part of it all. I couldn't have found a better friend if I'd tried."

"She *is* one sweet lady." He wiped his mouth with his napkin and returned it to his lap.

"How was your workday?"

"Busy. Several deadlines all fell at once, but I managed to pull everything together. The *Observer's* managing editor said he's gotten lots of nice feedback about my ads. Customers are happy, and that's always good to hear."

"Sounds like job security to me."

"I hope so. Especially since I now have more than one good reason to stay in town." He winked.

Emma fidgeted with her hair, repeatedly winding a strand around her finger. "Now you're embarrassing me." She stared out the window and tried to comprehend her good fortune. After the painful events of the past few months, she'd wondered how she'd ever move forward again. Meeting Drew had been a lifesaver. Whenever she'd feel overwhelmed by her circumstances, he'd walk into the Rainbow and buoy her spirits. And then, of course, there was Tucker, always her safe place to fall.

"A penny for your thoughts."

She shifted in her chair. "I'm sorry. I didn't mean to drift away. I was thinking of how at peace I feel. Happy. I haven't felt like this in a while."

The waiter came with their food and refilled their water

glasses. Emma had ordered the Beef Wellington, and Drew had chosen lamb chops with steamed vegetables. She tasted the beef. "Yum. The doorman had it right. Melts in your mouth. How's your lamb?"

"Excellent."

She grinned. "And I noticed they have your mint jelly."

"As they should. A proper Scot doesn't eat lamb without it."

"You're too much." She took another bite of her meal. "So, I've gotta know."

Drew looked up. "Gotta know what?"

"Have you bumped into Charlotte yet?"

"Who?"

"Charlotte?"

"No. I can't say I have." He looked from side to side, leaned forward, and whispered, "Who's Charlotte?"

She feigned surprise. "No one's told you?"

"Told me what?"

"The hotel is haunted."

"Oh my. I've heard nary a word about it," he said with a playful grin. "Should I be scared?"

"Hmm." She shrugged. "Maybe so."

His eyes twinkled as he leaned back in his chair and crossed his arms. "So tell me about this, Charlotte? Is she pretty?"

"How would I know, silly. She's a ghost."

Drew's blue eyes widened. "A ghost, huh? Intriguing. Carry on."

"Rumor has it, not long after the hotel opened, a young lady named Charlotte married her childhood sweetheart in the grand roof-top ballroom. Later that evening, she opened the door to their seventh-floor honeymoon suite and found her new husband in bed with one of her bridesmaids."

"Oops. No way to start a marriage . . . or end one, I might add."

"Charlotte was so shocked and humiliated by it all, she jumped to her death from the rooftop garden."

"How tragic."

Emma lowered her voice and leaned forward. "Now, it's told many nights when the clock strikes twelve, Charlotte's spirit rides the elevator to the ballroom. The doors open, but no one gets off."

"Seriously? That's quite a tale."

"Housekeepers have stated the ghost has been known to play tricks with room locks, and seventh-floor guests have reported hearing someone in high heels walk across the ballroom floor above them."

"Hush. I'm in Room 703." He laughed. "If I have nightmares, I may have to camp out with you and Mama T tonight."

After a slice of dark chocolate cake, generous enough for the two of them, and two cups of coffee, Emma glanced at her watch. The evening had flown. She'd sat captivated by Drew's stories of his teen years in Scotland and the high-sea tales of his sea-captain father. But most of all, she'd loved how their conversation would frequently erupt into laughter—laughter that had evaded her for weeks.

She pushed her dessert plate to the side and sipped the last of her coffee. "This has been wonderful, Drew. Thank you for treating me so royally, but I must go. Church tomorrow. And besides, Mama T will be worried about me."

He slipped his hand across the table and laid it on top of hers. "Thank you for joining me. I've enjoyed tonight. The best time I've had since arriving in Fayetteville. How about I walk you home?"

"You're kind, but it's not necessary. I'll be fine. It's only a few blocks, and the street is well lit."

"I'm not asking because I think it's necessary. I'm asking because I don't want our evening to end."

She smiled. "In that case, I'd love the company."

Drew slid her chair away from the table and ushered her to the lobby. "Before we go, I want to show you something."

She wrinkled her brow. "O-kay."

"No need to worry. You're going to love it." He took her by the hand and led her to the elevator. The operator nodded and rose from his stool. "Good evening."

"Evening, Carl. How was your day?"

"It had its ups and downs."

Emma tilted her head back and laughed.

"I was born to go up and down," he chuckled. "I've learned to ride with it." He closed the brass gate. "You going to seven, Mr. Brown?"

"Not this time, sir. To the top, please."

Emma's heart skipped a beat. "The roof? The grand ball— where are you taking me?"

"Don't worry, lassie. You'll see."

As Carl pulled on the brass lever, the car rumbled upward. Emma watched the large black numbers painted on the doors of each floor sail past the gate, and then a large letter B slid into view. The elevator jolted to a stop. With a few slight adjustments of the lever, Carl worked to position the car parallel to the floor. He bumped it up and then down again. Opening the brass gate, he pulled open the large wooden door. Drew handed him some change, then led Emma down the dimly lit hall, past the ballroom.

"Drew, this is spooky. There's no one up here."

"Relax. We're fine. Almost there." At the end of the hall, he opened a door leading to a narrow passageway. Emma's chest tightened as he guided her up several steps. Pausing at the top, he turned. "This is it. Are you ready?"

A chill ran through her. "I'm not sure."

He turned the knob and pushed open the door.

Cool air brushed her warm skin.

"Come on. You've got to see this."

Emma stepped onto the flat roof, admired the well-manicured garden, and looked out over Fayetteville. Under a waxing crescent moon, the soft city lights glittered like stars that had dropped to the earth and scattered trails of stardust in their wake. She pressed her hand to her chest. "I'm speechless."

"I told you you'd like it."

"Like it? I love it." She walked to the brick wall, peered over, and inhaled the sweet fragrance of the flowering redbud trees lining Hay Street below. "What a magical evening." She felt the warmth of Drew's body against her back as he slipped his arms around her waist.

"One fit for a princess. I couldn't ask for anything more than to share this with you." He kissed her hair, then turned her around to meet his gaze. "Hi, beautiful. Enjoying the sights?"

"I am," she whispered, then pulled back and thumped his chest with her fist. "But how dare you scare me, Mr. Brown."

He leaned in until their foreheads touched. "Still afraid?"

"Hardly."

At the beating of his heart against her chest, her knees weakened, and she melted in his embrace. Then, as their lips met, the world fell away.

Chapter Forty-Two

Three and a half months later
Friday, September 1, 1939

Emma huffed and stared out the window. "Now you sound like my sister."

Tucker sat silent as he turned the car off of Maiden Lane and onto Ray Street.

"I'm old enough to know my mind, even if no one believes me—no one except Penny, that is . . . and Mama T." Her voice softened as she fumbled with the new teal blue hat in her lap. "Please. Can't you at least be happy for me?"

His face remained stoic as he kept his eyes on the road ahead. "It's hard for me to be happy, Em, when I think you're making a huge mistake."

"But you don't know. At least give me the benefit of the doubt. I'm happy, and it hurts me to think you can't be happy for me. You and Penny are my best friends, and she's excited."

"I told you. I think you're making a mistake. What kind of friend would I be if I didn't speak up?"

"Okay. I know it's because you care." She slid next to him and laid her head on his shoulder. "I don't want to argue. You mean too much. Let's not discuss this anymore."

"Sounds like a swell idea to me." They drove the next few miles in silence. After pulling into the parking lot on Franklin Street, he cut the engine and turned to face her. "I remember the three of us coming here when you were seeing Noah. We certainly had some good times together."

She straightened his tie beneath his rust-colored V-neck

sweater. "This won't be the last of them. Not for you and me anyway. You'll see. For now, I've got to move on. Put the past behind me. Change the scenery. Start a new chapter in my life."

"I know. And I don't want to keep you from your dreams, but I didn't expect you to move at breakneck speed. We're different that way, I guess. I take my time and think through things before I act." He searched her eyes. "Maybe to my detriment."

"I've got something for you." She opened her purse and pulled out a small package and handed it to him.

A slight smile softened his worried expression. "Really?"

"Go ahead. Open it."

He carefully tore the wrapping paper from the box and lifted the lid. His eyes widened as he took out a silver pocket cross. "Oh, Em."

"Flip it over."

He read, "A friend loveth at all times—Proverbs 17:17." Pulling her close, he kissed the top of her head. "Thank you. I'll carry this with me wherever I go." He dug into his pocket, slid out a tiny box, and held it in front of her face.

She tilted her head and smiled. "And what's that?"

"I suppose you'll have to open it to find out."

"You really shouldn't have," she said, tearing into the paper and pulling off the lid. Turning the box over, she shook out a smaller black velvet one and opened the hinged lid. She sighed, then fingered a silver cross necklace, and lifted her eyes toward Tucker's.

"Go ahead." He beamed. "Turn it over."

"Proverbs 17:17? Oh, Tucker. Really?" She threw her arms around him and buried her face in his chest.

He rubbed her back. "I'm sorry, Em. There wasn't room to inscribe the whole verse. I didn't realize it would upset you so."

She pounded her fist on his shoulder and laughed. "You silly creature. You know why I'm crying." She handed him the necklace and turned her back to him. "Here. Help me put it on."

The light touch of his fingers as he slipped the delicate chain around her neck sent a shiver up her spine. She waited for him to hook it. "Is something wrong?"

"My fingers are too big for this tiny clasp, but I'll get it." He patted her shoulder. "There. Done."

Turning to face him, she let her hair fall to her shoulders and fingered the delicate cross. "How does it look?"

"Perfect."

She reached for the rearview mirror and angled it downward. "It's beautiful. I'll wear it always."

He turned her face toward his and lifted her chin. "Promise."

She smiled. "Promise."

He kissed her on the nose and pulled her to his chest. Wondering if he'd say more, her eyes rested on the second hand of the large depot clock. As it seamlessly swept away each moment and ushered in the next, she wished life would transition as effortlessly. Instead, the painful push and pull of emotions always seemed to tag along.

Her thoughts were interrupted by the forlorn sound of a whistle in the distance.

"It sounds like your ride is on time, Em. Got your ticket ready?"

"Uh-huh." Straightening in the seat, she fluffed her hair and put on her hat while Tucker pulled her bags from the trunk. Then grabbing her train case, she stepped out onto the gravel parking lot and walked with him to the platform.

The conductor bellowed. "All aboard for Washington, DC."

Tucker's eyes darted to hers. "I guess this is it."

Her words caught in her throat. "I suppose so."

"I'll pray you make your connection to Chicago."

"Please do."

After the porter checked her ticket and labeled her bags, he nodded. "You can board now, miss."

She turned and fell into Tucker's embrace, tears sliding down her cheeks.

"I'm going to miss you, Em. Be sure to write and let us know you're okay."

Pulling away, she flicked tears from her cheeks and squared her shoulders. "I will. I'll send Penny a telegram as soon as I get to Chicago." She swallowed hard. "And whenever I'm settled in my room, I'll write you a long letter. Promise."

He tilted her face to his and kissed her lightly on the cheek. "I'll be waiting."

After taking the porter's hand, she ascended the steps to the vestibule, then turned and waved.

Tucker blew her a kiss and hollered above the rumble of the engine. "Tell Drew he's a lucky man, and he'd better take good care of my girl."

She nodded and entered the coach.

Shuffling back to the car, he kicked one rock and then another before his thoughts were intercepted by the shrill cry of a young boy waving a newspaper high above his head. "Extra! Extra! Read all about it! Germany invades Poland!"

Chapter Forty-Three

Monday, May 28, 2012
Elkin, North Carolina
Caroline

I followed Kate past the large white flag with the green embroidered "Open" and entered the refurbished red-brick building on Bridge Street. An eightyish woman with silver hair pulled into a topknot sat behind the oak counter near the entrance. Looking up from her book, she smiled, while a Yorkshire terrier, curled on an ottoman beside her, opened one eye as if to resent the intrusion.

"Welcome to Elkin's *Then and Now*, ladies."

Kate and I thanked her, then let out audible sighs as we inhaled the earthy coffee aroma.

"Smells divine, doesn't it?" The frail lady rose from her seat and pointed to a square table in the corner by the large picture window. "Help yourself. There are homemade cookies there too. One of our consignees makes them for us every holiday. They won't last long, so you'd better grab a few while you can."

"You've made me an offer I can't refuse." I turned to Kate. "How about you?" We walked over to the table covered with a red, white, and blue-checked cloth.

"Where are you young ladies from?"

While I delighted in being called young, Kate blurted, "The zoo," and laughed. "We're from Asheboro—the geographic center of the state, and the home of the North Carolina zoo."

"Yes. I've passed through there. Hear it's a mighty fine town."

"You should visit." I picked up a napkin and helped myself to the cookies while Kate poured two coffees. "I'm Caroline Myers, and this is my sister, Kate Gordon."

"It's nice to meet you both." She extended her hand. "I'm Coralee Duggins. You can call me Cora." She nodded toward the small dog with a patriotic bow in her hair. "And this is my sweetie pie, Dollie." The Yorkie lifted her head and cocked her ear. "She's thirteen now. Almost blind." Cora leaned against the large glass display case that housed trinkets and heirloom jewelry. "How'd you find our shop?"

"Mmm." I moaned as a bite of the freshly made macadamia nut cookie delighted my taste buds. "We passed by here the first of the month but didn't have time to stop. Kate rang my phone first thing this morning with the wild notion of spending the day in Elkin antiquing. Since my husband's fishing this weekend, it seemed like a nice Memorial Day trade-off to me."

"Make yourselves at home, and if I can help in any way, holler. Most of the booths are offering Memorial Day specials, plus we have a room of sale items in the back. Lots of nice bargains in there too."

Kate rubbed her hand over the pressed back of a golden-oak rocker. "Oh, I'm all for a bargain. Thanks for the tip."

Cora reclaimed her seat behind the counter and returned to her book as we devoured our cookies, sipped our coffee, and made our way down one of the aisles.

"Kate, do you want to start in the bargain room?"

She shook her head. "Absolutely not. I've got to sneak up on a good deal. One always needs to leave the carrot dangling for a while. Let's check out a few of the other booths first."

After spending the better part of an hour pilfering through a considerable number of things and finding nothing we couldn't live without, we entered the bargain room in the rear of the store. We'd no sooner stepped over the threshold than Kate made a beeline for a child's Boston rocker in the corner of the room.

"Look, Caroline." She gave it a push. A small music box chimed the notes of a lullaby. "Remember the one Mother and Daddy gave me for my second birthday that played 'Rock-a-Bye Baby?' It was similar to this. I thought about it the other day and wished I had it for Emalie. She's the right age for one now."

"I think you should get it for her birthday."

She bent down, turned over the tag, and examined the chair. "It's reduced—$95. Reasonable enough, and it does seem to be in good shape." She dusted it off with her hands, then brushed them together several times before wiping them on her pants. "A couple of spindles are loose, but Emmy's daddy can fix those." She stood up and planted her hands on her hips. "Can't you see her rocking her baby dolls in this?"

"I can. Emalie will love it." I picked up a hobnail vase, looked at the price on the bottom, and returned it to the shelf. "Go ahead and buy it, Grannie."

"Ahem." She rolled her eyes at me. "You need to stop that, Caroline. You know Emmy calls me Mimi."

"Oh, yes. So she does." I chuckled.

Kate rocked the chair a few more times and smiled at the melody. "I'm going to get it. Laura will be thrilled."

She carried the rocker to the front of the store, while I followed close behind.

Dollie lapped water from her bowl while Cora put out more cookies. "Lookie there. You did find something." She wadded up a white sack and threw it in a trashcan underneath the table.

"I certainly did." As Kate set the rocker on the floor, a few notes of a lullaby chimed before the chair settled to a stop. "My granddaughter will love this. She'll be two next month."

"Lovely." Cora reached down, took the tag off the chair, and walked behind the counter. She pulled a pencil from a milk-glass vase beside the register and wet the tip of it with her tongue. After writing the receipt, she handed it to Kate. "That'll be $101.65."

Kate pulled out her checkbook and slipped a pen from the vase.

"I'm so happy to see this rocker go to a good home." Cora heaved a sigh. "It's from my friend's estate."

"Wonderful." Kate stammered. "I mean, um. . . . I'm sorry about your friend, but it's awesome you know the chair's history."

She smiled and waved it off. "Think nothing of it. I knew what you meant."

Kate handed her check to Cora, who slipped it underneath the tray in the register.

"What can you tell us about the rocker?"

"Goodness. Where do I start?" She closed the drawer. "My friend, Sadie, died a couple of years ago, and her children are selling things from her estate. The rocker belonged to her daughter."

Kate and I locked eyes.

"Sadie?" I leaned against the counter. "Would you mean Sadie Montgomery? An Anderson before she married?"

"Why, yes. Did you know Sadie?"

"No. But I've talked to her daughter on the phone, and we recently met Sadie's son, Franklin."

"I declare. This is a small world, isn't it?"

I nodded. "And it gets smaller every day. If you don't mind, please tell us about your friend."

She chuckled. "I'm not sure you have time, or if I can even remember back that far."

"Believe me. We have time." I leaned against the counter as Kate sank into the rocker near the coffee pot.

"Sadie and I knew each other since grade school. She came from a mighty fine family—the Andersons. I couldn't have had a finer friend." She walked from behind the counter and took a seat in one of two matching wing-back chairs. Dollie jumped into her lap and rested her head on the chair's arm. "Sadie never met a stranger and would do anything for you. She moved her mother in and took care of her during her final days. She had two brothers, Harold and Noah."

Kate and I stared at one another, not believing our ears.

"Both died long before she did. Harold died as a child. Diphtheria." She stared out the window and grimaced. "Tragic about Noah too."

I needed to hear. "Please, tell us."

"Sadie and I were in our late teens. She was engaged to be married to a fine young man named Vincent. A little odd, but very nice. Smart. He turned out to be a wonderful provider and father. They were married sixty-plus years. He died first." She paused. "Oh, me. There I go chasin' rabbits. Anyway, I was fixin' to go to work one mornin', when Sadie called me just a squallin'. She was sobbing so bad, I could hardly understand what she was sayin.' Said her brother, Noah, had been killed."

"Killed?" Kate and I blurted in unison. As my knees weakened, I took a seat in the wing-back chair beside Cora.

She smoothed Dollie's hair. "Yeah. Happened in the wee hours of the mornin'. He sure was a good-lookin' young man. Several years older than me. I'd had a crush on him for a while—ever since I saw him in his Army uniform on the day he left for Fort Bragg. It like to have killed me when I heard he was gone."

She squeezed her eyes shut and shook her head. "It was a horrible crash. He'd been out of the Army a while and had started drivin' for Greyhound. Had just gotten back to Charlotte after a long run. Been to Atlanta, I think, and was headed home in his car."

She smiled and stared straight ahead as if watching the story play out on a movie reel. "Boy, was he proud of his car—a Cashmere brown '32 Ford V8. I can see him now behind the wheel. He drove up from Charlotte one day and took Sadie and me for a ride." Her face lit up as she straightened herself in her chair. "We all three sat in the front, and I got to scoot in next to him. When he backed out of the drive, he stretched his arm across the top of the seat behind me. Why I thought I'd die happy right then and there. Man, he smelled good."

The light in her eyes faded as sadness blanketed her face. "The accident report said he ran a stop sign and slammed into the passenger side of a pick-up truck. The elderly man driving the truck was bruised up pretty bad, but Noah died at the scene."

She shook her head. "Sad. He was only twenty-three." She rubbed Dollie's head. "There were no skid marks on the road, so they think he fell asleep at the wheel." She pulled a tissue from her pocket and blew her nose. "Whew. I haven't thought about this in years. Can't believe I'm gettin' so emotional after all this time."

Kate and I sat with tears rolling down our cheeks. She grabbed several napkins from the table and passed some to me.

A middle-aged couple entered the store and smiled.

"Excuse me." Cora gently eased Dollie to the floor. "I'm sorry, ladies, but these fine people are here to pick up furniture. I must see to them." She dried her cheeks with the back of her hand. "I didn't mean to upset you with my story."

"No problem," I said. "We were more than pleased to listen."

Kate nodded.

Cora extended her hand. "I do hope you'll both stop in again soon."

"We'd love to." I rose and hugged her while Kate picked up the rocker. "And if you're ever down our way, please look us up."

"Sounds delightful." She walked over to assist her customers as we stepped outside.

My legs were like gelatin. I popped the key fob for Kate to put the rocker in the trunk while I collapsed behind the wheel. Seconds later, she slid in and laid her head against the seat. We sat and stared at one another. We had no words.

Chapter Forty-Four

Saturday, June 16, 2012
Jonesville, North Carolina
Caroline

After pulling up at Franklin's house, I cut the ignition and looked at Kate. The sweet fragrance of the dozen red roses she held in her lap filled the car. "How do you feel?"

Her eyes danced. "Excited. How about you?"

"The same—and nervous." I checked my watch. "We're a few minutes early, but hopefully Mary Ann and Franklin will be ready to take us to the grave." I glanced toward the brick, ranch-style house. Noah's homeplace sat just beyond it. An upstairs window was open, and a soft breeze moved the sheer white curtains within. After weeks of promising starts and unexpected stops, it was hard to believe this day was here—and Mother was not.

Kate straightened in her seat. "We couldn't have asked for a more beautiful day—cloudless Carolina-blue skies and a slight breeze. Perfect, huh?"

I nodded, then exited the car. After walking the long slate path to the door, I rang the bell, which set off a chorus of barking dogs. After no answer, I rang again—as if the uproar wouldn't be enough to announce our arrival. Looking toward Kate, I shrugged, then tried a final time. With each ring, the barking and intermittent howling escalated. Shaking my head, I returned to the car and fell behind the wheel. "How strange. I talked to Mary Ann two days ago."

"Maybe they're at the gravesite. Let's head down to the

entrance."

"You're probably right."

After driving several hundred yards down the road, I stopped in front of the gate. We could see it was padlocked. "I should have gotten Mary Ann's cell phone number, but it never occurred to me they wouldn't be here."

Kate leaned over and inhaled the roses. "Now what?"

I looked at my watch—1:08 p.m. "We'll wait a few more minutes, and if they don't show, we'll go to Elkin, grab a bite to eat, and come back later."

"Sounds like a plan to me. My breakfast bar deserted me a long time ago."

I settled back in my seat and flipped on K-LOVE. Kate closed her eyes and hummed along. Ten minutes later, I took a pad of sticky notes from the console, jotted down my number, and wrote Mary Ann and Franklin to tell them our plan. After driving to their house, I managed to place the note on the door without triggering a canine encore, then returned to the car. "I hope everything's all right. This baffles me."

We traveled toward Elkin in silence. As we crossed the Yadkin River, the sudden ringing of my phone startled us. "Hurry. Get it," I said, slinging my pocketbook toward Kate.

She dug through the large shoulder bag and huffed. "How do you ever find anything in here?" Locating my phone, she answered. Then looked at me and smiled. "Hello, Mary Ann."

I exhaled. *Thank you, Jesus.*

"This is Caroline's sister, Kate. Is everything okay?"

I mouthed, *"Hit speaker."*

She set it so I could hear Mary Ann's reply. "Yes, Kate, everything is fine. I'm sorry we missed you. Franklin and I went to a restaurant for lunch, and when we came out, he noticed I had a flat tire. It took him a while to change it. I could have kicked myself for leaving Caroline's cell number at the house, but we're here now. Are you still in the area?"

I chimed in. "Mary Ann, I thought the same thing about not

getting your number. But all is good, and we're relieved you're both fine. We're in Elkin. We'll grab something to eat at a drive-thru and head your way."

"Perfect. When you get here, pull down to the cemetery. We'll have the gate open for you. And again, I'm sorry."

"No problem. Not your fault. We'll see you in a few."

Kate breathed a long sigh, held the phone high above my pocketbook, and dropped it in. "Thank God. We may actually see Noah's grave today."

I laughed. "I have a feeling we will. After seventy-plus years, Noah's about to get his roses."

We pulled through the gate and drove down the long gravel road leading to the Anderson family cemetery. I rolled down our windows and breathed in the fresh air.

Kate sat straight up. "Look at how beautiful this place is."

Large oaks lined both sides of the drive, offering relief from the mid-afternoon sun, while a cool spring breeze ushered in the sweet smell of honeysuckle. As we approached a clearing, we had an open view of the mountain behind Noah's homeplace. The one he could see from his bedroom. The one on which he'd hoped to build a house and rear a family with his sweet Emma Rose.

I looked at Kate and knew her thoughts mirrored mine. Rounding a bend in the road, we saw a car parked beside a black wrought iron fence surrounding several tombstones. When we approached the entrance, Franklin tossed a handful of weeds over the border and brushed his hands on his overalls. Mary Ann held hers high above her head and waved. As I pulled the car to a stop, she ran to meet us.

"Hi. I'm Mary Ann." She hugged me. "It's good to finally have a face to put with your voice." She pulled away and laughed. "I'm sorry. I guess you can tell I'm a hugger? I hope you don't mind."

"Not at all. After our phone conversations, I feel like I know you." I took hold of Kate's elbow as she came around the car with the roses. "This is my sister, Kate."

"It's nice to meet you." She smiled, then bent over to smell the roses. "How gorgeous."

Slipping off his work gloves, Franklin came through the gate and shook our hands.

"It's good to see you again, Franklin. Thanks for letting us come today."

"We're happy you're here." He rubbed the back of his neck and looked down. "I'm sorry I was rude to you earlier. I won't try to make excuses. I was wrong."

"Think nothing of it. We certainly understand. Grief has ways of causing us to do strange and unexpected things. We're sorry for your losses. Losing a loved one is hard, but losing two back to back ..." I shook my head. "I can't imagine."

His face brightened. "Thanks for understanding." He gestured toward the graves. "Come on over. I've worked mighty hard this week to clean things up for you. My not coming for several months took a real toll on this place. I have you ladies to thank for lighting a match under me. It's a real load off of me now that it's done."

I surveyed the area. "It couldn't be a lovelier setting—so peaceful. How many family members are buried here?"

Mary Ann walked in front of the tombstones on the left side of the cemetery and pointed out the plots. "This first stone is Franklin's wife, and next to her is a place for him. Then we have additional space for family members who might need it." She turned and faced the stones to the right of us. "Over here are our parents' graves, and beside our mother are her parents." She walked on. "And next to them, by the rose bush, are their two sons, Harold, who died of diphtheria as a child, and then Noah."

A large bush laden with red roses filled the corner of the plot. "What a beautiful bush. I've never seen one with so many roses."

"It definitely showed out this year. Mama said our Uncle Noah helped his parents put up the fence and plant the bush. He loved roses. He bought the bush in Fayetteville and gave it to our granny when he returned from Fort Bragg."

Kate and I looked at one another and smiled. Like me, she knew it was the sister bush to the one that sat beneath our mother's bedroom window. I walked over to Noah's headstone and brushed my hand over the inscription.

NOAH FRANKLIN ANDERSON
Born April 28, 1916
Died March 27, 1939
"Gone Too Soon"

We wept as Kate laid the bouquet on the ground in front of it. "These roses are for you, Sergeant Anderson. They're from your sweet Emma Rose. You held a forever place in her heart . . . as you now do in ours. Sweet dreams."

Wiping our eyes, we stood and faced Mary Ann and Franklin. "Thank you both for allowing us to honor their memory this way. It means more than you know."

Nodding, Mary Ann fought to compose herself before speaking. "Franklin and I will leave you two alone. Please spend as much time here as you want today. When you leave, call and let us know so one of us can come and lock the gate."

I placed my hand on her arm. "There is one more thing. We've wondered how long it was before Mother learned of Noah's death. Do you know?"

"I recently ran across one of Mama's journals. An entry revealed that several months after the accident, Noah's friend, Tucker, dropped in from Fort Bragg to surprise him. He was devastated to learn of Noah's death. Mama apologized for not getting in touch with him. Our granny was in the hospital at the time, and when she was told her son had been killed, her failing heart couldn't take it. Our grandpa was so distraught, Mama carried the full weight of planning the burial. She had a private double funeral for them a few days later. Saddest thing ever. Tucker assured our mama he'd let Emma know."

"How tragic." My words caught in my throat. "We're so sorry. Thank you for telling us. It answers a lot of our questions."

Franklin moved toward the fence. "Before we go, we have something for you." He picked up a brown grocery sack and handed it to his sister.

Mary Ann's eyes widened as a grin spread across her face. "I've had a hard time keeping this a secret. I told you earlier I hadn't gone through all of Mama's things yet. When we knew you were coming, I went into the attic and dug through her boxes to see if there was anything that would be of interest to you. There was. Several things, actually."

Kate and I stood spellbound as Mary Ann reached into the sack, pulled out a large manila envelope, and handed it to me. I slowly opened the clasp and slipped out an 8x10 tinted photograph. I held it up for Kate to see. "Is this Noah?"

"Yes. He's a nice-looking young man, isn't he?" She beamed. "I can see why your mother was attracted to him."

"Is this ours to keep?"

"Absolutely. I had a copy made from the original. But that's not all." She reached into the sack again, lifted out an oblong box, and passed it to Kate.

Kate cut her eyes toward me, then slowly opened the hinged lid. We gasped. Inside was a beautiful tortoiseshell fountain pen, and beneath it, a faded picture of our mother.

Remembering the letter Noah had written thanking mother for the pen, I picked it up and rotated it between my fingers. Knowing he'd placed our mother's precious gift to him in the box, along with her photograph, was more than I could take in.

Franklin moved closer. "There's one more thing."

My insides quivered as I clasped the pen to my chest. "I'm not sure my heart can stand it."

He slipped his hand into the front pocket of his bib overalls and pulled out a long, yellowed envelope. "This letter was found in the wreckage the night Noah was killed. Looks like he'd written it to your mother and never had a chance to mail it."

My hand shook as I reached for it. We'd grown to love Noah. To have his last words to our mother in my hands was surreal. I wasn't ready to say goodbye, and I knew Kate wasn't either.

Mary Ann's fingertips brushed my arm. "We'll leave you alone now."

We hugged them. "We haven't enough words. Today has meant more to us than you'll ever know."

"Savor your time here. We'll talk again soon."

Kate and I walked over to Noah's grave and sat down on the cool grass. I carefully slipped the letter from its envelope and looked at my sister. "Ready?"

She nodded.

I read.

Sunday, March 26, 1939

Hello Darling,

How are you? Thanks for asking about Mama. She has a few good days but continues to grow weaker. It's hard to watch, but she's always had a strong faith, and her spirits are good. She's not only taught me how to live, she's now teaching me how to die.

I'm sorry it's taken me so long to write. Please don't think poorly of me. There are only twelve hours between shifts, and I sleep most of those so I'll be fresh for the road the next day. Know that even when you don't hear from me, you're in my thoughts night and day. Greyhound has me running to Georgia a lot. As a matter of fact, I'm in the break room in Atlanta now. I'll leave out for Charlotte in about an hour, so I probably won't get this letter mailed until I get home. I admit my schedule is exhausting, but at least I get paid well, and our nest egg is growing. Soon you'll be my wife, and I'll have you to come home to. What do you think of that, "Mrs. Anderson?"

Sweetheart, I need to clear something up that has come to my attention and quite frankly has made me spitting mad. Since I saw Alice on my bus several weeks ago, I've done everything within my power to shake her without hurting her feelings. But now I can assure you I've put my foot down with her once and for all. I saw her before I left for Atlanta, and something she said made me suspect she'd written you. I pressed her hard until she confessed every last word of it—at least I hope she did. By the time you get this, I'm sure you will have read her lies. I pray you'll see through them. She's stooped to a new low this time. I hope you know me well enough by now to realize I'd never betray you. You are and always will be the only girl for me.

I wanted to surprise you, but given Alice's shenanigans, I need to tell you I'm coming to Fayetteville Easter weekend. I'll be down on Friday, the seventh. That's one of the reasons I've worked so many hours. It's all so I can see you, baby doll. Please believe me.

It's about time for me to board my passengers, so I've got to run. Hold on till I get there, darling. Only eleven more days. In the meantime—dream of me!

I'll always love you,
Noah

Chapter Forty-Five

One week later
Saturday, June 23, 2012
Hope Mills, North Carolina
Caroline

Kate folded her arms across her chest and grimaced. "Caroline, the next time you come to my door with one of your hair-brained ideas, remind me to slam it in your face and pull the shades."

"Quit your whining. You know you love it. Admit it—your life would be pretty boring without me."

"Hmm. I prefer to think of it as peaceful, maybe even sane. If I'd known all you had in mind when you said you wanted to come to Hope Mills and put roses on Mother's grave, I'd have borrowed a pair of Franklin's bib overalls. They'd look rather stunning with my new consignment find, don't you think?" She turned around, arms outstretched. "An original Ann Taylor voile blouse. Six bucks. Pretty good, huh?"

I stood with my hands on my hips and rolled my eyes. "Come on, diva. Muscle up and grab hold of the other side of this tub. Things could be worse. At least Stephen had the nursery clip it back and ball the roots."

She grabbed the other side of the large metal washtub. "Why we couldn't bring a nice bouquet of roses like we did for Noah's grave instead of Mother's entire rose bush is beyond me."

"Just help me hoist this out, will you?"

We slid the tub to the back of Stephen's pickup, then dropped it to the ground.

"Ah!" Kate flinched and grabbed her hip.

"What now?"

She straightened slowly. "Caroline Myers, I'm going to send you my chiropractic bill."

"Oh, good grief. Consider it payback for all of the times you claimed I was the oldest. Hurry up. Let's get this done." I bent down and took hold of the tub handle. "Lift your side, and let's see if we can carry it over to Mother's headstone."

"You've gotta be kidding me. I'm not sure I can carry myself over there."

I straightened and leaned against the truck bed. "Well, it's either that, or you can help me heave it back into this truck. Take your pick."

She shook her head, grunted, and grabbed the handle.

"Okay. When I count three, move." I dug my shoes into the sand, hoping to anchor my feet to the ground. "Okay, here goes. One. Two. Three. Lift it."

"Ugh!" we said in unison before shuffling across the sand toward the corner of Mother's headstone.

"Okay. Set it down."

It dropped to the earth like a ton of bricks. Kate propped up against the side of the stone, while I plopped to the ground.

"Thank goodness," she said. "I can't believe I did that."

"I? Are you kidding me? How about less I and a little more *we.*"

She rolled her eyes. "You know what I mean."

I stood and brushed the sand from the seat of my jeans. "Now the fun begins. Get the shovel from the truck while I mark out a spot. And how about grabbing two bottles of water from the cooler while you're over there?"

I sized up the base and walked in a circle, drawing a line in the sand with my foot. I then stood in the middle of it. "Hey, Kate, how does it look from there? Do you think this is a good spot for the bush?"

Turning, she surveyed the lot. "Looks fine to me." She walked over and handed me the shovel, then placed our water bottles on top of Mother's stone. She looked down. "Oops. I'd better move this before it gets broken." She picked up a glass vase from the base of the marker. In it was a single dead rose. "I wonder who brought this."

I shrugged. "I don't know, but the flower has seen better days."

She set it beside the water bottles. "We'll toss it when we go."

"Now for the dirty work." I placed my foot on the base of the shovel. "Sit over there on the bench and rest your back. I'll need you after I dig the hole. At least this sandy soil will make for easy digging."

After hollowing out a large area, I threw down the shovel, wiped the sweat from my brow with the back of my sleeve, and grabbed my water. I downed half of it before motioning for Kate. "All right, diva. Get off your phone and come over and help me."

She slipped her cell phone into her pocket. "What do you need me to do?"

"Stand beside the bush, so I can see if this hole is going to be deep enough." Eyeballing it, it looked like the root ball came an inch or so below her knees. "Great. Now step into the hole for me."

Her mouth fell open. "You *are* kidding me, right?"

"No. I'm not kidding you."

"I've got on my new shoes, Caroline."

"Good grief, Kate. I dug the hole, the least you can do is step in there for me."

"All right. All right." She grabbed my hand to balance herself, then glared at me. "But don't even think about asking me to lie down in here."

I laughed. "Hmm. Don't give me any ideas."

Kate smacked my arm. "Oh, stop it."

I steadied her as she stepped into the hole. The top of it came right above her knees. "Yay! I think it's going to work." I offered her my hand. "Here, climb out."

Afterward, Kate helped me turn the tub on its side and pull out the bush. Then we tugged it over to the edge of the hole and dropped it in.

"Viola!" I clapped. "We did it."

Kate stopped to catch her breath and then picked up the shovel. "Now, you sit on the bench while I finish up. I can at least fill in and push the dirt around it."

I patted her on the back. "Thanks. You're a good sister. I'm beat." Turning, I took my water and the vase from Mother's headstone. "I'll put this in the truck, so we don't forget to toss it."

After throwing the dead rose in a wooded area, I noticed a small tag attached to the red bow tied at the neck of the vase. Squinting, I read the faded ink. I blinked and read it a second time, then whipped around. "Kate!"

She looked up from tamping down the sand around the bush with her foot. "What's wrong?"

I waved her over. "Come here. You've got to see this."

She dropped the shovel and ran. "What? What is it?"

I lifted the tag. "Read this."

She squinted. "I can barely make it out. Does it say—*I always loved you?*"

"Uh-huh. That's how I see it."

She looked puzzled. "I don't understand."

"That makes two of us."

I placed the vase on the floor behind my seat. "Come on. Let's get our things and head out of here. I'm tired, hungry, and ready to find a cool place to sit."

"Me too. Let's stop in at the Rainbow and grab a bite. We may not be back for a while."

"Excellent idea."

As we walked over to collect our things, a white sedan

pulled through the gate and slowly edged its way down the narrow road, which snaked through the cemetery. Putting the tub and the shovel in the truck, I slammed the tailgate shut and brushed my hands on my jeans. The car pulled to a stop in front of Mother's plot. I lifted my brow at Kate. She shrugged, and we walked back to the grave. The painted logo on the car door—a green tree and sun with rays breaking from it—read *Cumberland County Hospice.*

We stood transfixed as a middle-aged lady in printed scrubs waved, exited the driver's side of the car, and opened the passenger's door. We waited as she leaned in and spoke with someone inside. Seconds later, an elderly gentleman grabbed hold of the top of the door, pulled himself up, and stepped out. The attendant steadied him with her hand as he leaned on his cane and paused to square his shoulders. Lifting his eyes to ours, he slowly raised a knotted hand to a worn ball cap sporting an emblem. He tipped it and smiled. In his other hand, he held a single red rose.

We gasped in unison.

Smiling, the lady closed the door and guided the gentleman by the arm. With faltering steps, he moved closer. At the brick border surrounding the plot, the attendant looked at the frail man and said with a soft voice, "Watch your step, sir." Stepping over the bricks, he paused to steady himself, then lifted his time-chiseled, weather-beaten face. The emblem on his ball cap read—Fort Bragg.

As his hazy brown eyes met mine, my knees weakened. I looked at Kate, who stood spellbound as if watching a movie roll out before her. After brushing the remaining sand from my palms, I extended my hand toward the stooped gentleman in front of me.

"Hello, I'm Caroline Myers, and this is my sister, Kate Gordon."

He nodded at Kate and wrapped his large, misshapen hand around mine and then hers. "A pleasure to meet you," he said with a faltering, gravelly voice. "I'm Tucker Baldwin. You know Emma too?"

A broad smile crinkled the laugh lines around his dark eyes, offering me a glimpse of the young man who'd once been a devoted friend to our mother. Struck by his genuine candor, I felt an immediate tie to his endearing nature and stifled a chuckle. "Yes, sir. Kate and I both knew her. We're her daughters."

His eyes darted to those of the aide, still clinging to his arm. "Claire, did you arrange this?"

She grinned. "No, sir. I think someone higher up orchestrated this one."

He slapped his thigh. "Well, whadda'ya know. Emma's girls. Who would've thought it?"

I nodded and laughed. "You're right, sir. Who would've thought it?"

He held up the rose. "I don't see my vase, so I guess I should give this to you, dear ladies."

Kate spoke. "Oh, yes—the vase. We found it when we came to plant the bush. We were afraid it would get broken." She spun on her heel. "I'll run and get it from the truck."

His sweet gesture moved me. "Kate and I live quite a distance, so it's nice to know you drop by to pay your respects now and then."

"Yes, ma'am. It's my pleasure. Emma was a special lady."

Kate returned with the vase, poured bottled water into it, and held it out to Tucker.

He dropped in the rose. "Number forty."

I'm certain my eyes bulged as much if not more than Kate's. "Forty? You mean as in the fortieth rose?"

He sidestepped to stay upright, then steadied himself with his cane. Claire motioned to a bench nearby. "Mr. B, let's continue your conversation over in the shade."

He straightened his shoulders and repositioned his feet. "Swell idea." Then, taking off his cap, he extended his arm and dipped his head. "Shall we, ladies?"

Kate set the rose on Mother's headstone. "Absolutely.

We'd love nothing more."

We followed as Claire led Tucker to the wrought iron bench. Breathing heavily, he slowly turned and lowered his shaky frame to the seat, then patted the place beside him. "Please, one of you join me here."

I gestured for Kate to sit down.

Tucker curled his knotted fingers around the front edge of the bench, stiffened his arms, and stretched his torso. His chest rose and fell with each breath. "Always worse . . . on days like today," he said, sucking in the warm, moist air.

"Mr. Bald— "

He held up his hand and shook his head. "No. No. Please. Call me, Tucker."

"Of course—Tucker, you said this was your fortieth rose?"

He propped his hands on the cane clasped between his knees and gazed into the branches of the towering long-leaf pines. "Yes. Claire brings me every week. We're usually here on Mondays, but I guess as God would have it, that's the day of my doctor's appointment, so we came today."

Kate's blue eyes widened. "You've come every Monday since last September?"

"Yes." He motioned toward Claire. "Thanks to this kind lady."

She smiled. "My pleasure, Mr. B."

"Em and I lost touch years ago, but I still thought about her a lot. Always wondered where she was. What she was doing. I liked to believe her light was still shining out there somewhere. When I saw her obituary in the paper, it broke my heart." His voice cracked "To think Emma is gone—" Shaking his head, he pulled a handkerchief from his pocket and wiped his eyes. "I wasn't well enough to attend the funeral, so I sent flowers. Roses. Red ones. Lots of them."

Kate's eyes met mine as we grappled to process his words.

"Tucker. Did you send a blanket of red roses?"

He grinned. "I did. Knew they were her favorite."

I looked into his glistening eyes. "But . . . there was a

message on the ribbon?"

"Ah, yes." He nodded and leaned against the bench. "I had the florist add it for my good friend, Noah. The two of us—we were like brothers." He looked amused. "He sure loved that girl. When he was in the hospital, I'd deliver his letters to Emma at the Rainbow. "Dream of Me" was always written on the flap." He took a deep breath and wiped the sweat from his brow.

Claire moved closer. "Mr. B, we ought to go. I don't want you to get overheated."

"You're probably right." He looked at me. "You should both come by the house next week so we can talk more."

I shook his hand. "Thank you. That sounds like an offer we can't refuse. Kate and I found Noah's letters to our mother in her trunk, and we've wanted to know more about him."

Claire handed me her card. "Call my cell, and we'll set up a day."

Kate placed her hand on Tucker's shoulder and looked into his eyes. "Mother would be so touched by your kindness. Thank you for coming every week to honor her memory."

"It's the least I can do. I loved her too. Should have told her how much. Had my chance the night she gave me this." He shoved one hand into his pocket, then pulled it out and opened his palm. The sun's rays glinted from the edge of a shiny object—a silver cross. He gestured toward me. "I've noticed you're wearing the necklace I gave to Emma."

Overcome with emotion, I raised a trembling hand to my chest and fingered the delicate cross. "She wore it every day."

A wry smile twisted his lips and brought a twinkle to his eyes. "As she promised."

He leaned on his cane and pushed himself up from the bench. "Yeah. I waited far too long to express the depths of my love for Emma. Let too many opportunities slip through my fingers."

He shook his head.

"No more. Not enough time for that—not enough time."

A Note from the Author

"Your very lives are a letter that anyone can read by just looking at you. Christ himself wrote it—not with ink, but with God's living Spirit; not chiseled into stone, but carved into human lives—and we publish it." (2 Corinthians 3:3 MSG).

Hello, Dear Readers,

Thank you for journeying with me through the pages of *For the Love of Emma*. I hope you've enjoyed this work of my heart based on letters found in my mother's trunk shortly after her death in 2011. Upon reading the seventy-nine letters penned by my mother's first love in the late thirties, my sister and I realized the seeds of a fascinating book begged to be unearthed. Years after Noah wrote these letters to our mother, she placed a note inside the box. Her sentiment, found in chapter twenty-eight, took root in my heart and served as the springboard for this book and our quest to find Noah's grave. So you don't have to go back and search for it, here it is again. *"March 21, 1947- I dreamed of Noah last night. He was going to ask me to marry him again. I was nervous with excitement. Today, it all seems so real. I want to put red roses on his grave one day, but if I can't, I hope someone will do it for me."*

For the most part, Emma and Noah's story is a work of fiction based on factual, sentimental glimpses into the heart of this young soldier and the girl he pledged to marry. Although many of the words within the letters are Noah's, none were ever too sacred to sidestep the creative stroke of my pen. *Spoiler Alert—If you've not read the novel, you may want to stop reading here, so you don't spoil your journey through.*

The place and circumstances surrounding Noah and Emma's meeting are factual. I kept Noah's name but changed my mother's. She grew up in Hope Mills and worked as a waitress in Fayetteville, North Carolina, at the still popular Rainbow Restaurant. Noah, from Jonesville, North Carolina, was a soldier at neighboring Fort Bragg. As revealed in the letters, he was smitten with my mother, Rainbow Girl # 9, and planned to marry her.

Noah's friend, Tucker, is introduced in the first letter. From another note found among my mother's things, I learned he was from Kentucky. At the risk of disappointing you, I must confess—Tucker's love for Emma is a product of my imagination. I know. I agree it's a bummer. I grew to love him as much as you probably did. Our world needs more Tuckers, and I'll continue to cheer for men like him to win the hearts of young ladies everywhere.

In Chapter Forty-Two, Tucker and Emma's gifts to one another bore identical Scriptures. Some readers may find this occurrence hard to believe and difficult to accept. Personally, I've experienced times similar to this and describe them as God's divine providence. Although moments like these are rare, they are possible, especially among those who are exceptionally close. Maybe you've experienced a similar move of God in your life. If so, you know how edifying moments like these can be— definite faith builders.

Penny, a Tennessee miss whose Southern drawl continues to resonate in my ears, worked with my mother as a waitress at the Rainbow. Her husband was a soldier at Fort Bragg. Even though Mother and Penny's paths grew apart, their love for one another never diminished. Despite the miles, our families became lifelong friends and visited on occasion. Today, I remain connected with Penny's son, Phil, on social media.

And then there is Alice—the girl we loved to hate. I had little information on her, but according to our sweet Noah, his relationship with this pretty blonde was strictly "politics." He used Alice and her commissioner father to acquire a position with the county, which he did get. Proof that a young man in love will at times do desperate things to be with the one he loves, and yet, it always comes at a cost. Noah soon left his job to take one as a driver for Greyhound Bus Lines. Other circumstances surrounding Alice and her relationship with Noah are fictional.

Mama T's character morphed in my heart. I suppose she is a combination of mama figures I've met throughout the years. She stole my affection. I hope she did yours.

Drew's character, an artist from Dundee, is fashioned after my father and will play a more prominent role in *Emma's Quest*—the second book in the "Dream Beyond Tomorrow" series.

The contemporary characters, Caroline and Kate, are based on my relationship with my sister, April. I tagged her with our grandmother's middle name, Kate. My middle name is, in fact, Caroline.

Many of my secondary characters' first names are connected to people our family has known throughout the years. Lillian, my mother's sister, makes a cameo appearance as a switchboard operator at Highsmith Hospital in Fayetteville, a role she filled for much of her adult life.

Crafting *For the Love of Emma* has been a fantastic adventure. Through research, I had the pleasure of meeting Noah's nephew, Steve, and his wife, Shirley, of Jonesville. They were gracious when my sister and I showed up on their doorstep on what would have been Noah's 99th birthday. Neither thought they had a photo of Noah. Still, after a quick trip to the storage building, Shirley returned with his framed photograph, and Steve retrieved Noah's garrison cap. Our trip on that beautiful April day to the foothills of our great state and seeing the home from which Noah penned the letters to our mother was more than we could have hoped for.

I'm grateful that in the winter season of my life, God called me to do a new thing—write. His desire soon became mine, and with the help of selfless authors willing to share all they knew, I developed the skills I needed to make God's vision for my life a reality. I never set out to write a novel, so the book you hold in your hands is proof we are never too old to dream beyond tomorrow. God fashions our days and alters the course of our lives for His purpose and in ways far grander than we dare to dream.

After growing up in a creative environment, it seemed natural for me to follow in the footsteps of my father. This gifted professional artist had more talent in his little finger than I have in my entire body. My mother was an avid reader and a wordsmith. Early on, a few of her poems were published, but she never pursued writing as a career. After spending most of my life as a professional visual artist, I now feel I'm living my mother's dream as a writer.

I'm an incurable rainbow chaser, and writing a novel isn't the first rainbow I've chased. I'm profoundly grateful to my husband, Michael, who's veered off the highway on more than one occasion so I could capture their essence in photographs.

Norman Vincent Peale once said, "Shoot for the moon. Even if you miss, you'll land among the stars." I love this quote. It's the way I feel about life. I'd rather err on the side of hope than spend my time in a colorless day seeing nothing beyond a palette smudged with shades of gray.

Born to chase rainbows? Absolutely. In Matthew 19:26, God gives us His divine permission to do just that. "With man, this is impossible, but with God, all things are possible." Won't you join me in my quest? Even if rainbows aren't within our grasp, perhaps we'll land beyond them in a mountain of rainbow dust. Wouldn't that be fun?

Again, thanks for journeying with me through these pages. As you revisit Noah and Emma's story, I encourage you to unleash your imagination and follow your heart. After all, isn't giving ourselves freedom to dream beyond the reality of our tomorrows, the beauty of fiction?

If you enjoyed this book, please consider leaving a review on Amazon, Goodreads, ChristianBook.com, and your social media accounts. A book review is the greatest gift you can give an author.

And please, stay in touch. You may contact me via social media or through my website at www.starrayers.org. I'd also consider it an honor if you'd subscribe for newsletter updates on my next release by leaving your email address in the subscription link of my website.

In the meantime, Dream Beyond Tomorrow and keep chasing rainbows! It's embedded in your DNA.

Starr Ayers

The Rainbow Restaurant where Emma worked

Noah

Discussion Questions

1. Letter writing has become a lost art. Do you write letters? Is there a way in which writing cards or letters could become a ministry for you? Have you been ministered to by receiving a card or letter?

2. Caroline and Kate discovered letters in their mother's trunk from her first love and set out to learn more about him. Have you ever had someone close to you pass away and leave you with unanswered questions? If so, how did it impact your life? Did you, as the sisters in the book, leave no stone unturned to find the answers you needed? Did you uncover anything significant or life-changing in the process?

3. The romance between Noah and Emma developed quickly. Do you believe in love at first sight? If so, why? What are some significant differences in relationships today as compared to those of our parents' generation? Do you see these as positive or negative changes?

4. How did you feel about Emma's relationship with Tucker and Noah's involvement with Alice while dating each other? Do you believe men and women can have meaningful, platonic relationships while dating or married to someone else? Have you or someone you've known ever experienced this? How did it turn out? What would be your advice to someone considering a relationship such as this?

5. Emma didn't understand why Mrs. Priddy disliked her. How did Emma choose to handle the situation? Have you had a similar experience with someone only to find out there had been a deep hurt in that person's life that influenced their behavior toward you? Have your actions toward someone ever been misunderstood? How did it make you feel? Was the misunderstanding ever resolved? How?

6. At Anna's funeral, Mrs. Priddy experienced an eye-opening revelation. What was it? Have you had a similar experience? What were your thoughts concerning salvation growing up? If you attend a church, does it emphasize acts of service above a person's relationship with Christ? How do you think the two relate?

7. What did you think of Noah's strategy to involve Alice so that he could acquire a job as a clerk in the agricultural extension office? Has anyone ever befriended you to elevate themselves or their position? How long did it take for you to learn of their deceptive motives? How did you work through your feelings of betrayal?

8. Do you think Emma ever forgave Alice for her deception concerning her relationship with Noah? How important is it to forgive those who wrong us even if they never say, "I'm sorry?" Have you ever had to forgive someone without their apology? How did you extend forgiveness, and how did it make a difference in your life?

9. What was your impression of Tucker? Do you think he was right to let Emma go without revealing his true feelings? If she had known how much he loved her, do you think it would have changed her decision to leave for Chicago? Is there someone in your life you need to express your love to? If so, do it today.

10. In Chapter Forty-Two, Tucker and Emma's gifts to one another bore identical Scriptures. Do you think moments like this can occur in the lives of believers—especially with those who are exceptionally close? If so, have you experienced a similar move of God in your life?

11. What stood out to you most about the book? Would you recommend it to a friend? If so, please consider sharing it on your social media sites and/or writing an Amazon or Goodreads review. A review is one of the greatest gifts you can give an author.

Now a sneak peek at book two

From the "Dream Beyond Tomorrow" Series
Coming April 1, 2022

Emma's Quest

Chapter One

Saturday, June 30, 2012
Hope Mills, North Carolina

I followed Kate up the concrete steps of the modest frame house, which sat within a stone's throw of Camden Road. Looping one arm through my sister's, I inhaled deeply, then released it. "Are you ready for what we might hear today?"

She shrugged. "Ready as ever, Caroline."

Spotting the doorbell coated with multiple layers of cracked and peeling paint, I noted above it the black and yellow caution sign—OXYGEN. NO SMOKING—and pressed the button. Gusts of warm air peppered our backs as traffic on the extensively traveled Hope Mills thoroughfare whizzed past.

Kate said above the roar. "I didn't hear it ring, did you?"

I tried once more before knocking on the faded, olive-green door. This time, we heard the slow shuffle of feet approaching. As someone fumbled with the latch, I nervously scrubbed at the powdery white residue left from the bell on my fingertip. *What else would we learn about Mother?* The door cracked open, its security chain still in place.

"Who is it?"

"It's Caroline Myers and Kate Gordon, Mr. Baldwin."

"Who?"

I raised my voice. "Caroline Myers and Kate Gordon—Emma Walsh's daughters. You said we could stop by this afternoon and chat."

"Well, whaddya know." The chain fell away from the latch and bounced against the door frame. "Oh, yes. Yes, of course. Emma's girls." He swung the door open and motioned with his cane. "Do come in. You'll have to forgive me, ladies. A fella's brain doesn't recollect as fast this side of ninety."

I laughed and stepped inside. "Don't worry. We can totally relate. One doesn't on this side of sixty, either."

Kate pushed my shoulder. "Ahem. A little less *we* there, please."

I blinked as my eyes struggled to adjust to the darkened hallway. "It was kind of you to invite us, Mr. Baldwin."

"Of course." He peered over his wire-rimmed glasses. "But, we're gonna settle something right here and now."

My breath caught in my throat as I attempted to read his stern expression. "What's that?"

"I do remember *some* things, ya know."

Kate shot me a baffled look.

A smile crept across his weathered face. "Gotcha," he said as he threw back his head and laughed. "We decided at your mama's grave that y'all would call me Tucker. Remember?"

Kate and I both sighed with relief. "Ah, yes. We sure did—Tucker."

He raised his cane and gestured toward the end of the hall. "Let's go to the den, where my nurse has me set up."

We walked down the pine-paneled hallway toward a sparsely furnished room adjacent to the kitchen. Separating the two spaces was a small dining area with sliding glass doors that opened onto a concrete patio surrounded by overgrown shrubs. Filtering through the screen door and into the cozy sitting room was the soft tinkling of glass wind chimes caught by the warm afternoon breeze.

"Please have a seat . . . over there." Tucker labored to catch his breath as he pointed to an Early American patterned sofa against the wall. "Claire stepped out to run a few errands." His chest rose and fell with each breath. "You remember Claire from the cemetery, don't you?"

Kate nodded.

"Yes, of course. Very pleasant," I said.

Tucker steadied himself in front of an over-stuffed, burgundy velour recliner and then dropped down. "Whew. Pardon me a moment."

"That's quite all right. Take your time," Kate said.

He propped his cane against a small pine drop-leaf table stacked with newspapers and magazines. A thick, large-print Bible lay open on top of them. Beside the table, on top of a chrome stool with a red vinyl top, sat an oscillating fan. On the opposite side of his chair was a black metal TV tray with a couple of crossword puzzle books, a few pens, and a large plastic *Cumberland County Hospice* cup. He picked it up and took a couple of long sips through the straw. Then with the hand holding his cup, he motioned toward the kitchen. "You ladies help yourself. There should be soda and bottled water in the fridge."

We both politely declined his kind offer.

Directly across the room was a red-brick fireplace, its hearth and mantle crowded with framed photographs. On the wall between it and the sliding glass doors hung a large sunburst clock and several framed certificates and medals.

Tucker coughed and cleared his throat. "Let's see now. Refresh my memory. You're both from Asheville, aren't you?"

"No, sir. We're from Asheboro—the geographic center of the state, home of the North Carolina State Zoo."

He nodded his head. "Oh, yes. That's right. Great zoo, I hear. If I were younger, I'd make a trip over there. Guess my traveling days are behind me. It's all I can do to walk from one room to the other now."

"We're sorry. It's nice you have Claire to help you."

"Yes. Don't know what I'd do without her. Been widowed twenty-two years. My son is an accountant in San Diego, and my daughter and her family live in Charleston. She's an RN. Works part-time in a doctor's office. She's coming next month to spend a couple of weeks with me while Claire's on vacation."

"Wonderful. Maybe we'll get to meet her."

"Hope so." Tucker shifted in his chair and dug into his pocket. "Caroline, I've noticed you're wearing Emma's cross."

I fingered the delicate silver necklace. "Yes. You told us it was a gift from you."

"You heard right. Gave it to Emma the same day she gave me this." He held out his hand.

I stood and lifted the silver cross from his palm, then returned to the couch so Kate could see it too. Flipping it over, I read, "A friend loveth at all times—Proverbs 17:17. Why it matches the Scripture reference on my necklace." I stood and handed the cross back to him.

"Yep. Funny how it happened." He stared at the shiny object in his hand and rubbed it with his thumb. "I think of that night often. Your mother and I sat in the car at the depot while we waited for her train. She gave me the pocket cross first. I was surprised when I saw the Scripture. She had no clue I was about to give her the necklace." He looked up at us, tears threatening to spill from his eyes. "I guess it shows we were true soul mates. It was hard to let her go." He chuckled. "Not that I had much say in it. Emma Rose did what she set her mind to do."

I rolled my eyes and laughed along with Kate.

He sat in deep thought before speaking again. "Foremost, I wanted her to be happy. Sometimes I wonder if things would've been different if I'd told her that night how I really felt. For a moment there in the car, I thought I would, but she was so giddy about meeting Drew and seeing the big city of Chicago, I couldn't bring myself to stand in her way." He slipped the cross back in his pocket. "I learned a long time ago you can't live with regret. I guess we all ask *what if* at times, but *if onlys*— they're deal-breakers. Can't live there. Gotta learn to let go."

He laid his head back against the chair and locked his eyes on the ceiling fan's slow rotation. "When I put your mama on the train, I didn't know things would take the turn they did, but I can't say I was disappointed."

Chapter Two

Saturday, September 2, 1939

Emma combed the colorful skeins of embroidery thread with her fingers while rolling hills, neatly cultivated farms, and picturesque towns streaked past the train's window. The speed with which each scene appeared and then swiftly slid from view couldn't rival the rush of images that flashed through her mind or the flood of tears that threatened to spill from her eyes.

It wasn't that Mama T, her elderly landlady, disliked Andrew Brown, fittingly called Drew. He was charming. A modest soul, unlike so many blessed with similar artistic abilities. In fact, his distinguished good looks, Scottish brogue, and quick wit won over everyone who met him.

Although Mama T had tried her best to conceal her apprehension, the angst that cloaked her face was easy for Emma to read. Her plans to move to Chicago to be closer to a man twelve years her senior and one she'd only known for a little more than six months had shaken Mama T to her core. Nevertheless, the kind woman respected her wishes. "It's your footpath to tread, baby doll. Just make sure you're followin' the good Lord's leadin'."

Leaving Fayetteville had been gut-wrenching. Although Emma had resided less than two years in the two-story, yellow clapboard house on Maiden Lane, she'd developed a deep affection for Mama T. From the minute she'd spotted the floor-to-ceiling bookshelves lining the parlor's walls, she knew she'd found a kindred spirit in Florence Turner. A gentle Southern woman, widowed after sixty-three years of marriage with no children of her own, she'd all but adopted Emma and insisted from the outset that she call her Mama T.

Although Emma lamented that she'd broken her dear Mama T's heart, she believed it imperative to follow her own.

"Ticket, miss?"

Emma, startled by the sudden appearance of the conductor, dropped her embroidery hoop and scrambled to catch it as it tumbled to the floor. The portly gentleman, a sixtyish man with a monocle perched on his cheek that made one eye appear more substantial than the other, handed it to her. "Sorry I frightened you, young lady."

"It's okay," she said with a dismissive wave. "Think nothing of it."

Reaching over to the seat beside her, she slipped her ticket from between the pages of Somerset Maugham's *The Moon and Sixpence* and handed it to him.

He punched it, then returned the stub. "Got someone meeting you at the station this evening?"

"I do."

"That's good. The sun will be pretty much set by the time we pull in. Good idea for a pretty young lady like you to have someone to accompany you." He moved along, restlessly clicking his punch.

Emma double-checked her arrival time, slipped the stub into the buttoned compartment of her purse, and returned to her needlework. Piercing the cream-colored linen with her needle, she meticulously followed the faint flower pattern with a periwinkle blue chain stitch. The down-and-up, in-and-out rhythm of her handiwork quickly kept tempo with the clickety-clack of the train's wheels rolling over the iron rails.

Mama T had been impressed with how fast Emma had caught on to the craft, but she'd learned by observing during their frequent late-night chats. She pictured Mama T bent in her chair, peering through wire-rimmed spectacles, stitching handkerchiefs for First Baptist's bereavement ministry. Of course, the secret to her hour-upon-hour tenacity was her attempt to not disturb Chummy. He'd often lie sprawled across her feet, his paws and whiskers twitching as he dreamed of field mice scampering toward the barn.

"Sir." Emma waved her hand in the air as the conductor edged his way back through the aisle. "Do you think the train will arrive on time this evening?"

He pulled a gold timepiece from his vest pocket, then squinted as he figured in his head. "Shouldn't be a problem. Appears we're right on schedule." He lifted his hat and brushed his hand over what was left of his silvery-white hair. "Ready to get there, are you?"

"I am. It's been a long trip."

"Yup." He plopped his cap back on his head. "I've been riding these rails so long now I forget how tiring the distance can be for someone who's not used to it." He nodded toward a neatly arranged stack of books and magazines by her side, topped with a pile of brightly colored skeins of embroidery thread. "I see you came prepared with plenty to keep you busy. Smart."

Emma chuckled to herself. She'd never been one to sit idle.

"You coming back this way soon?"

Her thoughts raced to Lily, Mama T, the Rainbow girls, and—her hand went to the silver cross around her neck. "Yes. I hope to make it back before too long."

"Well, enjoy the rest of your trip. At least you'll have these two seats to yourself. Stretch out if you need to."

She smiled. "Thank you. I might do that."

Emma picked up a dog-eared envelope from the stack of books and pressed it to her chest before examining the surface. The pen-and-ink drawing of the Hotel Monterey in the upper left-hand corner looked like something Drew would sketch. She squinted to make out the faint postmark—Janesville, Wis., July 29, 1939, 3:30 p.m. After studying the image of the six-story art deco building with its impressive corner tower and parapets, she imagined a warm summer breeze catching the American flag at its peak. Counting the windows, she wondered which one Drew had sat in front of while penning her cherished letter.

> Hello, Peaches,
>
> This is the first time I've ever written anything like this, so you'll have to excuse me if it's not perfect. What I'm trying to say is—will you marry me? I love you and need you. I know you won't be getting much of a bargain, but I'll try very hard to make you happy. So, sweet, write and tell me your answer, then we'll go on from there. It can't be soon enough for me. I'm sure we could be very happy together—so dear, don't keep me in suspense.
>
> I hope you love me enough to say yes. I know I'm not much good at this sort of thing, but I'm trying my best.
>
> Waiting for your answer with my fingers crossed.
> All my love,
> Drew

Emma sighed, propped her elbow on the armrest, and dropped her chin in her hand. She sat mesmerized by the late-summer sun making its descent. As it dipped behind the trees lining the horizon, the fleeting colors of dusk melted into vibrant streaks of pink and orange against the deepening indigo sky.

Emma could still sense the warmth of Drew's parting embrace—the lingering scent of his favored Old Spice—and feel the remaining moistness of his soft kiss. She'd thought her heart would snap when tears welled in his crystal-blue eyes, and he whispered, "See you soon, Peaches." It had taken every ounce of resolve she could muster to suppress her tears—but only until the train exited the station. Only until she could no longer see his impassioned over-the-head wave.

Why must love hurt so?

"Chicago!"

The conductor stopped at Emma's seat. "Almost there, miss. Be sure you have all of your belongings. I'd hate for you to leave something behind." He tipped his hat and bellowed again as he hurried toward the front of the train.

Not a chance. She'd left a huge part of her heart behind once—never again. This time, she would follow it. Things would be different. She'd make certain—she'd cling tighter, cry louder, pray harder, and fight longer for the man she loved.

As the train pulled into the depot, Emma gathered her things and tucked them into the souvenir tote bag Drew had sent from Chicago's Grand Central Station. The forlorn blast of the train's whistle accompanied by the hissing of brakes brought the rusty wheels of the B&O *Capitol Limited* to a screeching halt. While well-dressed businessmen, excited children, and women with fretting babies jockeyed for positions in the aisle, Emma flipped open her leather train case and glanced in the mirror. She grimaced, then fluffed her long, dark tresses and gave each cheek a pinch before snapping the lid shut.

Straightening in her seat, she searched the congested platform. It wasn't easy to differentiate one gentleman from the other. Most wore business suits topped with seasonable overcoats and fashionable fedoras. After studying their faces with no sign of Drew, a horde of "what ifs" descended like a suffocating cloud. What if he never came? What if she'd made a mistake? What if the small amount of money she'd saved wouldn't cover a ticket home? But as quickly as the notion flooded in, she evicted it from her mind. It was nonsense. She was here—Drew would be too.

She stood and claimed her place in the aisle behind twin boys who jabbed and shoved one another toward the exit while their mother struggled with a distraught baby. Stepping into the vestibule, a blast of Chicago's brisk fall air sent a chill up her spine. The conductor reached for her hand. "Watch your step, miss."

"Thank you, sir," she said as her feet touched the wooden platform. Releasing his hand, she stepped to one side and scanned the crowd. Terror nipped at her heart. Zigzagging her way through outbound passengers, her eyes darted from one face to another. She paused as the baggage handler crossed in front of her pushing his cart to the station. Then—she spotted him.

"Drew!" She signaled with a spirited wave. Running, she called his name again. "I'm over—" As the distinguished-looking gentleman took off his fedora and turned to face her, her heart fell. Her legs grew weak. How could she have been so mistaken?

The gentleman ran to meet a young lady, lifted her from the ground, and spun her around. Then, lowering her to the platform, he pulled her close and kissed her, before escorting her into the terminal.

Emma followed them inside. After sending Penny a telegram from the Western Union desk, she motioned for a porter. He carried her suitcases outside to a wooden bench beneath a gaslight. She tipped him, then seated herself and scanned the platform. The B&O had pulled away and was nearly out of sight. All was quiet but for the pounding of her heart.

Lily, Mama T, her friends, they'd all cautioned her to take her time, to follow her head and "the good Lord's leadin'" above her impetuous heart. Tucker, especially, had warned her of traveling men. Perhaps he was right. Maybe she'd misread

Drew. Had her quest to heal her heartbreak and her desire to see places beyond North Carolina's Sandhills caused her to dismiss warning bells and ignore good common sense? Hundreds of miles now separated her from all that was familiar and the people she loved.

She was here, but where—where was Drew?

CPSIA information can be obtained
at www.ICGtesting.com
Printed in the USA
LVHW040456121220
674003LV00001B/31